a certain age

"If there's anything Tama Janowitz knows about, it's the sheer savagery of our most chic and ultra-sophisticated social arrangements." —*The New York Times Book Review*

"Janowitz has penned a brutal update of Edith Wharton's *The House of Mirth*, accurately analyzing the social codes and economic hierarchy that functions in the New York she knows, as Wharton did a century ago." —*Detour*

"Tama still has her knack for homing in on our worst fears and behavior, and initially, you feel like you can't relate to Florence. Then you realize you only hope you can't relate." —*Jane*

"A scathing satire. . . . Janowitz takes a shredder to New York City's crème de la crème."—*Philadelphia City Paper*

"[Florence's] steady descent down the social ladder she so desperately wants to climb is the stuff of black humor." —*Manhattan File*

"Janowitz's writing comes out of a tradition of comic American misanthropy that can be traced back to Twain, passing along the way through such intervening figures as Dreiser, Nathanael West, and the author of whom she is most reminiscent, Ring Lardner." —*New York Newsday*

"A sharp-tongued and funny writer." —*Chicago Tribune*

TAMA JANOWITZ

a certain age

Tama Janowitz is the author of *Slaves of New York*, *A Cannibal in Manhattan*, *American Dad*, *The Male Cross-Dresser Support Group*, and *By the Shores of Gitchee Gumee*. Her writing has appeared in numerous periodicals, including *The New Yorker*, *Paris Review*, *Harper's*, *Vogue*, and *Elle*. She was an Alfred Hodder Fellow in the Humanities at Princeton and the recipient of two NEA grants in fiction, as well as a New York State Council of the Arts Award in fiction. She lives in Brooklyn, New York, with her husband and child.

a certain age

a certain age

tama janowitz

a novel

ANCHOR BOOKS   *A DIVISION OF RANDOM HOUSE, INC.*   NEW YORK

FIRST ANCHOR BOOKS EDITION, JULY 2000

The Library of Congress has cataloged the Doubleday edition as follows:
Janowitz, Tama.
A Certain Age: a novel / Tama Janowitz.
p. cm. I. Title.
PS3560.A535C47 1999
813'.54 — dc21 98-48965
CIP

Anchor ISBN: 0-385-49611-7

Author photograph © Marion Ettlinger

www.anchorbooks.com

Printed in the United States of America
10 9 8 7 6 5 4 3 2 1

For
James Ivory
Ismail Merchant,
Ruth and Cyrus Jhabvala

"Bad deeds are terrible and I hate them, and do not want to commit any. I made mistakes before because I did not understand God. I felt him but did not understand what everyone was doing."

—THE DIARY OF VASLAV NIJINSKY

part one

I

She had an urge to tap his head with a spoon. It might wake him out of his trance. She could visualize the yellowish brains trickling over his glasses frames, such mild yolk—and the other passengers on the jitney to the Hamptons would no doubt quickly whip croissants out of their weekend luggage and come to dip the corners in the soft stuff, hoping to taste so much money.

"Florence . . . !" Charlie said. "How are . . . you?"

She grabbed the seat next to his.

"I would normally . . . drive," he said.

"You usually drive to the Hamptons on the weekend?" Florence asked.

He nodded. "Only my car is in the garage."

"Being fixed," Florence said. Maybe having so much money had made him sluggish, softened his brain, like the last Emperor of China. He seemed to be cocooned in something. He seemed swaddled, a great distance away, though she was right beside him. The traffic chugged forward and died to a halt. The air was gray and thick with exhaust. Here there were no trees, only old factories and warehouses, like rusted shipwrecks jutting from cement. If there was already so much traffic, it would be midnight before the bus got to the Hamptons.

"Not . . . exactly," Charlie said. "You see, a few . . . weeks ago, I left it . . . parked in front of that new restaurant, Derek and Trevor's . . ."

"And somebody . . . hit it?" Whatever he had was catching. She was speaking slowly too.

"No . . . it's a convertible, you see, and the roof was closed. When I got into the car, I thought, Something stinks, and next to me, on the passenger's seat, some idiot had thrown a fish head."

"Why would they do such a thing?"

"I can only assume . . . because I parked in front of someone's yard, and I know there have been a lot of local complaints in Bridgehampton that Derek and Trevor opened a restaurant there. I threw the fish head onto the sidewalk. Well, it was so warm and sunny I opened the roof . . . and this is sort of . . . complicated . . . however . . . a few days later I noticed . . . there was a terrible smell . . . and I cleaned out the car . . . but the smell didn't go away. And after another week I tried to clean it again. I put the roof up . . . because I was going into the city and—"

"Weird," Florence said. "And you really don't think it was some girl or something?"

He either didn't like her question or, having begun, couldn't stop before he had finished his story. "And when I put up the roof . . . I found wedged down in the back part where the roof goes when it's open . . . there was another fish head . . . and by now it was crawling with maggots. And the company can't get the smell out . . . they've replaced the seats, and had it cleaned, but they can't seem to get rid of the smell."

"Ugh. How creepy!" She gave his hand a squeeze. It was soft and rubbery, and next to her hand, with its long graceful fingers, his looked like a child's. This seemed somewhat sad, the reverse of one of those children who age prematurely. "You're sure it wasn't someone who knew you?"

"Oh, God, I don't know," he said. "This weekend I'm just going to go out and buy another car." Then, changing the subject, he said brightly, "Hey! A friend of mine just gave me a picture he took of me—a portrait. He's a well-known fashion photographer."

"I'd love to see," she said.

"Yes?" He was cute when he smiled. His whole face cracked open, as if sealed under the layers of skin was a trapped baby allowed out only on special occasions. "The picture's kind of artistic, if you know what I mean—I'm naked." He pronounced both "artistic" and "naked" as if they came with quotation marks around them.

He opened a manila envelope and handed the photograph to her. In the picture he was seated nude on a stool, looking as if he might topple off, balanced only by his two skinny legs, spread far apart, feet clinging to the rungs. On his face was an expression of such supreme self-pride that Florence knew it could only be related to the appendage dangling between his legs. The bus was heavily air-conditioned. She reached for a sweater and put it on while she thought of what to say.

"It's awfully hard to see in this light," she said. She was shocked, which she supposed was the point. He seemed so prissy, then to start flashing naked pictures of himself. Maybe it was a little test, to see how she would respond. She fumbled in her pocketbook for the remains of a Swiss dark chocolate nut bar she had been nibbling throughout the day. "Very nice!" The words came out slightly patronizingly, but he didn't seem to notice.

"I thought . . . he did a good job. My friend is very talented, as a photographer . . . I don't know what I'll do with it, though. Frame it, I guess, and hang it in the bedroom." He turned to her and whispered in a confidential voice, "You were right . . . I think it was this girl I was going out with who put the fish heads in my car. She knew I had just gotten a brand-new SAAB convertible."

"She must have been heartbroken," Florence said. "That you broke up with her—and that was all she could think of doing, to get revenge. But it wasn't funny! It wasn't very nice!"

"No . . ." said Charlie thoughtfully. "You know, I don't think I've ever really spent much time talking to you. This is great, that we're getting a chance to talk."

"I think so too," she said, giving his arm, padded beneath a robin's-egg-blue cotton sweater, a quick stroke. Though she appeared aloof, she was an oddly affectionate person—it was as if touch was the only way she could reassure herself that anyone else existed. The cool blond looks were blended in a boyishly jock physicality, more California than New York.

The bus held forty or fifty passengers and was completely full. The travelers, with their pinched, ferocious expressions and their too brightly glittering eyes, projected an aura of paranoia mixed with anxiety that permeated the bus. The hostess, a surly overweight young woman in her mid-twenties, stumped up and down the aisle delivering plastic bottles of mineral water and cups; she was probably a local from Long Island, hired for the season. She had the sour expression of a camp counselor devoting herself to a summer's worth of sadistic activities. And yet Florence always felt calmer heading east. The Western migration had not been the right journey for her mother, nor for her. All her life she had felt rootless. But her mother, after marrying, had gotten trapped, preserved in the amber sun of Southern California. She had always encouraged Florence to go back East, to marry rich, to return to spawn like a reintroduced salmon. And though her mother was no longer alive, she had managed, somehow, to imprint this on Florence—or perhaps it went deeper, imprinted on her strands of DNA like a celestial map carved on an ancient Aztec necklace.

"Would you like to do something?" Charlie said. "Tomorrow night, maybe?"

She was slightly surprised, but did not want to hurt his feelings by pausing too long. "Of course!" she said. "Great. I'll have to check with Natalie, though."

"How old is Charlie Twigall?"

"He's fifty, about. Maybe forty-eight."

"Fifty!" Florence said. "I can't believe he's . . . that old. He has a certain timeless quality."

"Never ages," said Natalie de Jongh, at whose house she was a guest for the weekend. "It's unbelievable. I've known him since he was at least forty and he hasn't changed at all." Natalie was forty-two. "Of course, he's lost his hair. Women go crazy for him; from what I hear he's incredibly well-built. When he had his hair he was known as Charlie Mane. Even now, though, all he has to do is come into a room and women practically leave their husbands for him."

"He asked me out on a date," Florence said. "For tomorrow night. I said I'd check with you."

"I'm afraid not," said Natalie. "I'm having a big dinner party tomorrow night. I told you. It's all arranged. You know how carefully I plan these things. You don't mind, do you?"

"Oh, that's fine," Florence said. "I told him I'd check with you. It's no problem. I'll just tell him you already had something planned. I'm not even interested in him. It's just that—I felt sorry for him."

Natalie looked her up and down. "You felt sorry for Charlie!"

"He's like a little old egg!"

"Like an egg!" said Natalie. "Oh, God, wait until I tell him. You thought he was like an egg."

"Natalie," said Florence. "Please don't tell him. You have to swear. Promise me you're not going to tell him I thought he was like an egg. I love eggs! Sweet, speckly eggs. Do you promise?"

"You'll be staying on the third floor," said Natalie. "I'm afraid there's nobody to carry your bag at the moment. John's at the golf course. The housekeeper's hurt her back. She's cooking dinner, in the kitchen. I said you'd be happy to help her when you've gotten settled. You don't mind, do you?"

"No, not at all."

"Good," said Natalie. "Because my aromatherapist is coming in ten minutes. She gives me a massage too. You should try it sometime, Florence. You'd love it."

"Is it expensive?"

"No, she's very reasonable. Only two hundred a session. Do you want her to do you tonight, if she's free?"

"Maybe some other time," said Florence.

"Up to you. Anyway, I've put you in the little bedroom. I thought you'd be more comfortable. Go to the third floor, turn right and then left, and it's the second room on the right. There's kind of a lot of junk around—I've been storing things there while I had the other two top-floor bedrooms redone—but you don't care, do you?"

"Oh, not at all, Natalie," Florence said. "I'm just glad to be here."

Natalie had told her the second room on the right, but Florence must have made a wrong turn: when she opened the door weaponry from an expensive vacuum cleaner crashed down, smashing her across the foot. There was a single bed, but its surface was covered with boxes marked COLLEGE PAPERS and WINTER CLOTHING. It must be wonderful to have such a large storage space, Florence thought, going to the window and opening it. The ocean wasn't visible, but by way of compensation a field of potato plants undulated like waves, stopping at a sand-colored strip of highway. Across the road was another house, similar to Natalie's, as large as an ocean liner, only completely square, with tiny windows the size of portholes. A tangy fertilizer scent tingled her nose and, eyes watering, she rummaged for a tissue. She had to battle the doorknob for a few minutes before she could escape: it had been installed backward, or upside down, or something. She almost panicked, and when she finally got out she realized the lock was on the wrong side, in the hall. She had been in the storage closet; what was obviously her bedroom was on the other side of the hall.

She went back down and found Natalie in the kitchen by the gleaming industrial-sized stove. "It's so nice out here," she said.

Natalie turned and for a second looked as if she had never seen Florence in her life and was trying to remember where the burglar alarm switch was located. "I was just making some tea for my aromatherapist," Natalie finally said. "She likes to drink this special herbal tea that's very hard to find. I managed to locate the only box in Manhattan and had John bring it out. It's ridiculously expensive. I can't imagine what's in it. The label is written in Tibetan, or something."

"I don't know why you're apologizing for the room you put me in!" said Florence. "It's just beautiful! That dark blue wallpaper with the white design—is it hand-painted?"

"That's not your room," said Natalie. "You didn't mess up the bed or anything, did you? It's all made up for some guests I have coming next week. I told you, the *second* bedroom down the hall."

"Oh, gosh," said Florence. "I'm sorry! I went in there, but I thought it was the broom closet. Don't worry—I can easily move my things." She should have known Natalie would stick her in the closet. It was just like her. Natalie wanted to be generous, she thought of herself as generous, and then she panicked, thinking she was being taken advantage of, or that she was being liked for the wrong reasons.

"I would have had you stay in the blue guest room, but Ana-María's hurt her back. I can't ask her to change the sheets, all the way upstairs. You don't mind, do you?"

"No, no," said Florence. "Really, it's all right. Of course, I can make the bed up myself." She meant she was happy to change the sheets in the blue bedroom, but Natalie misunderstood.

"Oh, would you?" she said. "Actually, I think I forgot to make up that bed. The sheets are in the closet in the second-floor hall. I doubt you'll need a blanket. And the sink and the toilet—you can use the one down here, next to the kitchen. I'm afraid the toilet may overflow if you use the bathroom connected to the blue bedroom. But if you want to take a shower, the outdoor shower is just next to the swimming pool—behind the bamboo screen."

"Perfect," said Florence, going back upstairs to move her things.

It took a little while to tidy the room and make up the bed, though some of the boxes were incredibly heavy. But she managed to stack them around the edges of the room so that at least there was enough floor space to get in and out with a bit more ease. There were plenty of sheets and towels in the linen closet, though she could not find a pillow or blanket anywhere. When she was finished her head was throbbing slightly and she lay down on the bed for a minute. It was only her second visit to Natalie's house; she had forgotten how exhausting it was and how little she liked being a guest. Something banged into the wall over her head. A lone fly, raisin-dark and overweight, seemed to be drunk or merely giddy. It flew slowly this way and that, trapped and sleek.

She looked at her watch: only six o'clock. There was still time for a walk on the beach, and even a quick dip. She changed into her bathing suit, a modest two-piece red-checked affair, and covered up with a floral beach robe. Natalie had told her to use the bathroom off the kitchen, but when she started to go into it, a woman came out of a room—Florence glimpsed a double bed and a crucifixion on the wall behind her—and gave her such a sharp stare she was sure she was once again doing something wrong. "Are you Ana-María?" she asked.

The woman, though short and plump, had the regal stare of ancient Inca nobility and an oddly shaped head, as if the top half had been flattened in a vise. "My bathroom," she said.

"Oh, gosh, I'm so sorry," Florence said.

"Me, Ana-María, sí. You use that toilet." She pointed to the changing room alongside the swimming pool, visible beyond the French doors and the patio.

On the far side of the pool, hunched in a peculiar position, as if a leg had been broken, a tiny gold creature sat chattering to herself.

"Hello!" said Florence.

The creature waved at Florence to go away. Then she switched positions and Florence saw she was speaking on a cellular phone while doing some kind of yoga or stretching exercises.

The toilet in the cabana had no toilet paper. "Woo, woo, woo!" the person screamed when Florence emerged, and made a dash in her direction like a hummingbird who had dipped her beak into a vial of crystal methamphetamine. "Sorry, I was on the phone before! I'm Mica Geller, Natalie's aromatherapist. I do massage too. Natalie says you might want to get a massage when she's done? See how you like this." She put something under her nose, some powder in a little vial. Florence nervously took a step back, but not before she had caught a strong whiff of artificial citrus and, behind it, something mentholated and something else, like the Sterno flames beneath a fondue pot. "Isn't that fabulous?"

"Mmm."

"I just came up with that one. We might want to work on you with it. Infusion of lemon grass, orange-blossom oil, tisane of tea-tree and eucalyptus leaves, and a few other things—this one is entirely botanic, designed for someone who doesn't necessarily want to get in touch with their spiritual side, but who needs to. I hope that doesn't offend you. Don't take it personally, I talk this way to everyone. Anyway, let's take a look at you." Before Florence could stop her, Mica had stepped forward and stripped Florence of her floral robe. "You're gorgeous!" Mica said. "You know that, don't you?" Florence didn't respond. "You know that you're gorgeous, don't you?" Mica repeated insistently.

"I'm okay," Florence said.

"You're more than okay!" said Mica. "Say it."

"I was just going for a walk," Florence muttered.

"But you don't want to say it? You can't say to me, 'Mica, I am one gorgeous creature!' "

"I'm not sure I—"

"Long blond hair, a little snubby nose—let me see your teeth." When Florence didn't move, Mica leaned forward and pushed back her lips. "Who did your teeth?"

"Nobody."

"Oh, my. They are beautiful. Has anybody ever told you, you look like you should be a movie star?"

Florence looked at her suspiciously. "Sure."

"No, I mean it! I'm serious!"

She couldn't help but feel pleased—it was nice to be admired, appreciated, like a horse led out to the auction block. If only men could be half so understanding! They looked at her with admiring glances, but so dumbly, so lacking in any awareness of the fine points. They might as well have been toddlers, jabbing fingers at Jell-O and apricot soufflé with equal fervor, unable to perceive the difference in quality. Mica walked in a circle around Florence standing in her swimsuit. "Not bad." She seemed determined to insinuate herself into Florence's existence, a remora nibbling on a shark's skin. Florence was almost ready to agree to Mica's terms. "You might want to do a little work on those thighs and the abs." She gave Florence a gentle punch in the stomach. "Hold in that stomach, girl! Stand up straight!"

"What are you doing?" said Natalie. She was lying naked face-down on a gurney that had been set up in the living room. Her buttocks were like two pancakes left behind on a plate until evening. The room reeked of something rotting and sweet.

"I was coming to look for you!" Florence said. "I thought I'd just go for a walk and a dip to clear my head. God, your butt is flat, Natalie." She meant it as a compliment, but Natalie reared her head suspiciously. "I mean, you're lucky. What's that smell?"

"Lavender and bergamot," Natalie said. "I have to lie here for fifteen more minutes. Did you see where Mica went? I'm getting a headache. She always says the aroma therapy is working when I get a headache."

"She was on the patio," said Florence. "Shall I tell her to come back in?"

"This stuff stinks!" Natalie sat up suddenly, covering herself with a white towel. She had been lying on a bed of what appeared to be rabbit turds.

"What—what were you lying on?"

"Stones. They're scented and heated. The heat releases the perfume."

"It smells delicious."

"Do you think? It's supposed to be really good for you. Each of her clients has their own scent-formula, depending on what their system needs. It might be time for Mica to make me a new formula, though. I think I've worked through whatever I was going through before."

"Is anything going on tonight?"

"Not unless you have some kind of plan of your own! I thought this evening we'd keep things simple. I figured you'd be tired from the city, and John won't be back from the golf course until it gets dark—so it will just be the three of us and leftovers."

"That sounds fine," said Florence.

"But I wish you wouldn't go out for a walk. I thought you were going to help Ana-María in the kitchen."

"I thought just a quick dip—"

"It'll take you a half hour to walk to the beach, you won't get back until eight. We're having eighty people tomorrow night; Ana-María's hurt her back and I promised she'd have help." Natalie's expression softened. Florence thought she looked nervous. If she allowed her grip to relax on those around her for even a moment, the entire universe—like one of those bars of brittle candy—might crack. "I was thinking—you said Charlie was staying at his mother's for the weekend—I might invite him to the party, if he's free."

2

"Hello dere!" Natalie's husband, John, deposited his golf clubs by the door. He was a tall man with many fine features; yet it troubled Florence that when she tried to picture him not a single image came to mind, apart from the fact that his eyes, behind thick-lensed glasses, always reminded her of a frog's. No matter what expression was on his face, his eyes were cold and amphibian. There was a sort of scrubbed, boyish quality to him; it was the look of a man who had never quite gotten over the highlights of his prep school years.

"Hi, John!" Florence said, carefully tying her bathrobe around her waist as he crossed the room to embrace her.

Then he kissed Natalie, sitting on the edge of the gurney. "How was the golf?"

"Not bad!" John said. "How have you been, Florence? It looks like you girls are having a good time. What's happening here? You're all having massages?"

"Would you mind, Florence, if Mica does John instead of you? I know she's only got time for one more before her next appointment." Since she had done Florence a favor—inviting an eligible bachelor—Florence now had to be punished. It was actually something of a relief. There was something really weird about letting a complete stranger—and one of the same sex—fondle her naked body, gradually battering it into submission. Basically, it was paying someone to molest the body while the mind lay chuckling to itself at its revenge on the entity in which it was trapped.

"I don't want to take Florence's massage from her, Nats," said John sternly.

"Oh no, that's fine, really," said Florence. "I wasn't planning to have one anyway."

"You sure?" said John.

"Mmm," Florence said. "I was actually just going up to change so I can help Ana-María for tomorrow night. It's going to be a big crowd!" Her voice sounded stiff, artificial, but John had that effect on her—he always looked slightly smirky.

"Is that right?" said John, following her up the stairs. "I'm going to have a quick shower first. Get some of this golf dirt off me. Then I'll have to have *another* shower to get the massage oil off! But what the hay. So, how are you doing, Flo?"

"I don't know, John. You know, I'm working at Quayle's."

"Quayle's, Quayle's—"

"The auction house."

"Now, I don't think I know that one."

"Well, it's not Sotheby's or Christie's. Believe me. I wanted to go to Sotheby's or Christie's, but they told me to come back when I had more experience. Which I didn't understand, because a lot of people start off there without any experience. But, whatever. For all I know, their fathers are paying money to get them a job there."

"You might be right. I never really thought about it. Listen, I'm going to run up and take a quick shower—anything you need?"

She was slightly embarrassed. "Oh no. I'm fine, thanks."

For what felt like hours she chopped onions into very precise chips, according to Ana-María's direction. Ana-María sat with her feet in an electric footbath, filled with soapy water, from time to time getting up to stump across the floor and chitter at Florence like an angry chipmunk. Florence had seen Natalie berate Ana-María so harshly she didn't know why or how the woman could keep working for her. Now it seemed Ana-María was going to dump her rage on Florence. She was about to faint with hunger when Ana-María took a big bowl of salad out of the refrigerator and carried it into the other room, returning shortly for several bottles of dressing.

John came into the kitchen. "Did you have dinner, Florence?" he asked.

"I'm starving," she said.

"Come and join me in some salad, if you like. I just came in to get a beer. What would you like to drink?"

"A beer sounds good. What's Natalie going to have?"

"She's gone up to bed. She's got a headache, from that aroma business. I think she's on one of her vegetable fasts. Is it going to be enough for you, just a salad?"

"Oh no, that'll be great!" Florence said, handing the knife to Ana-María, who gave her a disgusted glare.

It was actually quite a nice salad, though a little tired around the edges—probably it had been fresher the day before. There were red and green lettuce, dark green spinach leaves, pockets of crumbly bacon, shredded cheese, various seeds, minute thumbnail-sized tomatoes, sliced hard-boiled egg, yellow and purple pepper rings, sweet onion and corn. "So good!" she said enthusiastically, shaking some honey mustard dressing onto her plate. There was nothing she liked more than a salad. It was the only food that seemed clean, that and fresh fruit. John ate grimly, as if he were not able to taste the food, a preoccupied expression on his face. Abruptly she pushed the bacon to one side.

"How was the golf?" she asked after quite a long silence.

"Not bad! Ninety-two, which for me is about average."

"That sounds very good," she said hesitantly, since she didn't have a clue.

"Do you golf, Florence?"

"I'm afraid not. That was the one lesson my mother didn't think of sending me to. I had tennis, ballet, I had piano, I can't even remember what else, but she had predetermined ideas about what girls were supposed to learn." She didn't add that in any event her lessons had mostly ended when she was ten and her father had died—and ten was too young for any instruction to have made much of an impact on her skills or abilities. "I believe my grandfather was quite an avid golfer, though, when he was young."

"You don't think of taking it up?"

"Gosh, I would love to!" she said. "Maybe I could come with you sometime, just to watch and pick up a few pointers. Or you could recommend an instructor, if you were too busy." She saw herself on the golf course, in pink golf shoes and shorts, her muscular calves exposed, blond hair pulled back in a ponytail, legs bent just right as she swung. There were plenty of men on the golf course. She should have thought of it years ago.

"Why not! I'm thinking of playing a round tomorrow, but if I'm free in the afternoon, I'll take you out on the course—we'll rent you some clubs and see how you like it!" John looked down at his plate, embarrassed at his effusiveness. "So what were you telling me earlier? You're going to move over to Sotheby's?"

"I don't know. I'm not sure it would be any improvement. Anyway, they don't pay anything, although Quayle's pays even less. I mean, it's not that I'm in it for the money—if I was, I wouldn't have gone to an auction house, you know? I've always been more interested in . . . opportunity. So, since I had some money from when my mother died, I figured I could afford to take an apprenticeship type of position—you know, learn the business. But I don't know what happened. I mean, I bought an apartment, and anyway, it's so expensive to live in the city, and I think I'm down to my last twenty-five."

"Quarter million?" said John. "No, that's not much, but if you can leave it alone for a few years, there're some good investments—"

"No, no, it's only twenty-five thousand. I mean, that's about the same as my annual salary at Quayle's, which isn't enough to live on. And I was sort of hoping—"

"You want some financial advice? Invest it."

"But in what? I need money, a decent amount to live on!" The words blurted out shrilly. He looked slightly miffed at her outburst. She tried to change her tone. "Honestly, John, how much could I make if I was willing to take a risk?"

"If it's all you've got, I don't know why you'd risk it. I mean, if you had quite a bit, I could take the money and, I don't know, double it in a year."

She was almost panting at the thought. If he could double it in a year, then in two years she would have a hundred thousand, and so on. "I know you don't ordinarily handle sums that small."

"All right, I'm thinking. Let me see what I can do. My company doesn't handle accounts of less than a quarter million . . . Well, all right. Here's something you might want to think about. A new restaurant that's starting up. It's a very good friend of mine—he's had nothing but success. You've heard of Belfast Shipyards? East Prussia? The Liberal Party? You can't get a table in those places—all three of them are Derek's. I've done very well—I was actually one of his first friends to put money into the first place."

"How much does it cost to get in? What's the return?"

"Put it this way: I doubled my money the first six months. It has slowed a bit since then, but almost five years later he's still paying close to thirty-three percent. Of course, I'm getting more since I was one of the first to have faith in him. And I know that shares in this new place are seventy-five grand apiece. However, if it appeals to you, why don't I talk to him and see if he'd let you take a third of a share for twenty-five thousand. And I'd like to be able to help you out."

"Oh, it sounds fabulous! I mean, yes, definitely I'd be interested. Thanks, John—I don't want to inconvenience you, but it would be so wonderful!"

"Why don't you give me a call in New York next week and we can set something up. We'll have lunch. Come on." He pushed his chair back from the table. "We'll go outside and have a drink. I've got a wet bar over by the pool, and some decent port. I have to go out there to smoke my cigars—Natalie can't stand the smell. Is it going to bother you?"

"Not at all."

"Good, good. For all I know, maybe you'd like one yourself."

"Not tonight, thanks."

She followed him out and sat on a damp plastic chaise while he went into the cabana to get their drinks. He had turned on the underwater pool lights, which made the water a surreal, unnatural shade of blue, and the smell of chlorine was so strong she could almost chew it. She thought it was the way money should taste, chopped into a salad of green bills in large denominations.

"Can I ask you a question?" John said, coming up behind her in the darkness. "Did you ever think of getting married?"

"I haven't met the right person, I guess!" she said. She couldn't help but feel slightly irritated. "You know what it's like in New York. Most of the guys are gay, and the straight men that come here are the most ambitious—they don't want to get married, they just like to date some model to show her off to other men."

"In my office everybody is married, or I'd make one of them marry you. Not that I would have to force any of them. What about a roommate?"

"I can't," Florence said. "I don't know. I mean, I'm too old."

"You're not too old. How old are you?"

"Thirty-two."

"You're kidding . . . Let me think what I can do," John said. "How's your room, by the way?"

"Fine!" said Florence. "It's not going to get too cold tonight, is it? Natalie said I shouldn't need a blanket."

"I don't know. It can get kind of chilly at night. I'll find a blanket and bring it up to you, if you like. What room are you in?"

"I'm in the little single room. But I'm sure I'll be all right."

"What little single room?"

"It's the small room, there's a twin bed?"

"I thought that was the storage room!" said John indignantly. "Why are you in that room? Take one of the big rooms with a bathroom!"

"Oh no, I'm fine, really," she said. "I think Natalie has other guests who are going to be using the other rooms."

"Up to you," said John, pushing back his chair. "Listen, don't accuse me of sexism. I know I'm walking on sticky territory here"—he laughed uproariously while Florence silently watched, a smile fixed weakly to her face—"but you're still an attractive young woman, and if I were you, I would seriously look around for a marriage prospect. I realize things aren't supposed to be like this anymore. I mean, your job at Quayle's—that's a very nice job for a young woman to have—but it's not something you can really look to as a career. Did you look on it as a career? I don't get that sense with you. People must come in there—the previews and so forth— who would be very glad to meet you."

"I know!" Florence said. "It's just that . . . well, I'm very shy, and, I don't know, nobody ever seems to want to speak to me—"

"I don't see you as being shy, Florence, whatever you say." Again he began to bellow with laughter, which sounded more similar to the bellowing of an elk than to anything human. "If people aren't coming to you, it's probably that they're frightened of you. You can look quite imposing, you know. You'll have to go to them." The truth was that her superiors, hungry and suspicious as coyotes, watched her as if she were a vole. Quayle's was not to be looked upon as a marriage service. It had been tried before. In any event, the only men who came in to buy from the jewelry sales were there to buy presents for wives, girlfriends or fiancées. Or gay men acquiring for their shops.

When she didn't respond John tugged at his hair, examining a few strands in the palm of his hand. "I'm going to catch the sports on the TV downstairs in the game room before I go up. Do you want to join me?"

"No, I think I'll just sit out here for a few minutes."

"Help yourself if you want another drink—and let me know if you want me to find you that blanket."

"Thanks, John."

She was aware that there was someone else in the room with her. Natalie was right; she hadn't needed a blanket. With only one window there was no cross-ventilation, and now, at three or four in the morning, the air outside had gone perfectly still. She could hear the low roaring of waves in the distance. Whoever was in the room coughed softly but did not move, as if aware that one false step might cause a variety of appliances and objects to come crashing down. "Who is it?" she said.

"Ssshhh!" the figure said. "Don't turn on the light. I just came to make sure you were all right. It's me."

"John?" Florence said. "What are you doing here?"

He stumbled across the room in her direction, managing not to trip over anything, and sat on the edge of the bed. She was about to sit up and ask him to leave when he flattened himself on top of her, so forcefully she could barely speak. "What are you doing?" she repeated. "John, this isn't right. Get out! What about Natalie?" She wriggled away. Nevertheless, he pulled down her pajama bottoms and hooked his fingers into her as if hoisting a fish by its gills.

"Don't worry," he said, slinging his other forearm onto her chest to hold her in place. "Natalie doesn't care; we haven't slept together in years. She doesn't mind at all. We're getting divorced soon. Please, Florence, you've got to help me. I'm going to die if I have to go on like this. I've had a crush on you for years. It was when I first met you and you smiled. It was so . . . guileless, so open. You never see a genuine smile like that, not in New York. You have no idea how terrible things have been for me." He covered her face with kisses while simultaneously his fingers went about their grim, forceful inspection. "Please, Florence, please," he said, covering her mouth with the pillow. He seemed so frantic, so desperate, that she couldn't help but feel sorry for him; in the dark, in a strange bedroom, none of it seemed especially real. It was peculiar that Natalie had never mentioned this impending divorce, but perhaps she didn't feel much like talking about it, which was understandable. No wonder she seemed so harsh. At the same time, a wave of sympathy for him came over Florence; he was desperate, desperate, spinning wildly on a shimmery line of despair. These people only seemed to have everything. Underneath was nothing, an elaborately frosted cardboard box.

"Poor John," she murmured, stroking his hair. He was wearing an expensive, strong-smelling cologne, which simultaneously repelled and lured her. The odor must have appealed to some instinctive olfactory sense, the way an otherwise intelligent, sensitive lapdog might be thrown into a feral frenzy on being shown the rotten corpse of a rabbit or taken to the country and introduced to a pile of aged cow manure for the first time. A small part of her wondered what she was doing, but none of it seemed real. This had nothing to do with her. Or at most she was discharging the duties of a nurse, one who cared in a catholic sense for all her patients, but none in particular. "Poor John," she repeated, a phrase he seemed to like.

3

It couldn't have been much later than seven A.M., but she wasn't certain—there was no bedside clock and she didn't wear a wristwatch. She had been up for hours, lying in bed, her head aching, trying to muster the strength to use the toilet downstairs. Finally she gave up and went next door. To her horror, the blue-tinted water in the toilet bowl did not vanish when she flushed but slowly rose higher and higher. She searched frantically for the plunger. Moments before the water should have reached the top and begun to spill onto the floor, to her relief, it stopped.

She waited a bit; though the water didn't go down, it didn't seem to rise either. Perhaps it would drain, slowly, of its own accord. Finally she put on her bathing suit, grabbed a Madras windbreaker and went downstairs, where she made a cup of tea in the empty kitchen and headed to the beach. The washed-up detritus—friable cuttle, the amorphous glistening silicon blobs of jellyfish, green-black rubbery strands of seaweed—made her think of the contents of her own head, arbitrary and disconnected, more similar to protozoan shapes than to words.

"Florence!" She turned around. Darryl Lever was scuttling toward her, dressed in an old-fashioned-style bathing suit, like a circus strong man. "Wait up, Florence!"

There was no getting around it: it didn't matter how much time went by, whenever she saw him she felt like smacking him. It wasn't that he wasn't attractive—he was, so much so that she had once too eagerly slept with him. His hair was dark and curly, his blue eyes thickly fringed with black lashes—he might have been a Greek kouros. Except that his expression instantly changed from one of archaic repose to that of a baby who had had its nipple yanked unexpectedly from its mouth—and he seemed to blame her. It wasn't her fault that he had no money, or worse: that he had no interest in it. He was cute, he was a good lay, by now he should have met somebody else and gotten over her. But he was obviously pleased to see her; maybe this time he would forget to sulk.

He reached up to gently wipe some sand from her face. His small hands, nails buffed and polished, were soft to the touch, as if he moisturized them nightly in cream. His touch made her feel shivery—but what was the use? One simply had to be objective about such things and disconnect the body from the mind.

The fog was rolling in up the beach, cold and not particularly refreshing: perhaps there was so much garbage in the ocean that the fog was a mere methane or organic by-product from the damp foam cups, used condoms and chicken bones that had congealed together in a natural island of man-made artifacts.

"Hey, Darryl, what have you been up to?" She had known him

since she came to New York, but it had been years since their brief affair.

"I'm here for the weekend, even though this place makes me sick." He suddenly began to cough. She wondered if it was catching.

"Maybe we better go back," she said, looking ahead at the diminished view of the beach, a curving sliver of toast-brown that wound into a cloud of fishy-gray mist. She clutched her arms around her chest.

"Why?" he said. "Are you cold? Do you want me to go get a warmer jacket for you? A sweater?" She shook her head. "It's okay, I don't mind—I could use the exercise." She shook her head adamantly. "Come on, it's not cold out. Walk a little farther. I want to hear all about what *you've* been up to."

"I'm not up to anything!" she said.

"Really? I was just over at the house having coffee with Natalie. She told me you were down here."

"Oh?"

"She also told me she's fixing you up with Charlie Twigall. She called him first thing this morning and invited him to her dinner party. You don't actually like him? He's an idiot. His mother's desperate to get him married off—to the right girl, of course. That means somebody rich, Florence! Rich, from the right background, who will do what she says just like Charlie! Have you ever met his mother? Believe me, you're in for a real treat there!" He was in despair. She had never known him to be jealous before; he couldn't possibly still think there was any hope of her having a relationship with him. "You don't think he's an idiot?"

"He showed me his self-portrait on the bus. He was naked." She knew this would drive Darryl into a frenzy of contempt, particularly if she didn't sound disgusted.

"Jeez! The guy carries around a naked self-portrait of himself to show to women? How pathetic!"

"I think he just got it or something. He's very well-endowed."

"What a jerk!" He kept looking up at her pleadingly, trying to get her to agree. Again he started to cough, this time so strenuously he practically doubled over.

"What's wrong with you? You should see a doctor."

"Just some sand in my throat. Sorry."

She sighed. "How's work?"

"I have to tell you: This city, it really gets to me. You just see how easily it could happen. I had a family come in yesterday—you know, Fridays I do a clinic at St. Theresa's. This woman was a single mother, two kids. She worked for the phone company. Her husband—boyfriend—whatever—had been abusive. She finally escaped from him, but not before he almost emptied their bank account. So she was living in Flushing; the apartment building caught on fire, everything was a dead loss, and they couldn't live there anymore. For a while they stayed with friends, but that didn't work out. The last of her savings was spent in a few nights in a hotel. So she took the kids and went to a shelter. The first night she got stabbed. So they slept in the park. But she didn't have any place to leave the kids during the day. After a week she hadn't had a shower, she smelled, she didn't have anything to wear to work, nowhere to leave the kids—she got fired. Now she has no savings, no job, she's homeless. You see how easily it can happen, the whole bottom drops out. I mean, a lot of these people, they're not too bright. But others, they're just as smart as you or me. I mean, it could happen to either one of us, you know, if circumstances were slightly different."

"That's awful. But I don't think it could happen to me. I mean, I'm too determined."

"Yeah, I know. You think I'm crazy, you think, why am I working for nothing when I could be a big Wall Street lawyer, huh?"

"I don't know." She shrugged. "I mean, at least I see that the disease of the twentieth century is wanting to be rich. Rich and powerful. You don't get real power as a woman—you still get it by being married to a powerful man. Before, as a woman, you didn't even have that option. You were supposed to be grateful just for being married off before you got to be a spinster. And once you were married off, if your husband didn't beat you, if you didn't die in childbirth, you were supposed to be satisfied. At least I'm honest enough to see the world for what it is and know what it is I'm going after. Since the disease is here, and it's here to stay, why pretend that what I want is so dishonorable or distasteful?" Darryl looked sour. Once there had been a taboo against mentioning cancer, or menstrual cycles. "Why are you in a bad mood? You should be grateful that I'm being honest with you." She didn't add that she was being honest with him because she wasn't interested.

"Why shouldn't I be in a bad mood? You're no friend to me. Maybe it's true what I'm doing isn't helping anything, but at least I'm trying! You're just like all the other women in New York, wanting to grab whatever material possessions you can! I'm supposed to feel good that you claim to be more honest? It's hopeless—who wants to go on existing in a world composed of people who don't exist?"

"You're saying I don't exist?"

"You're trying not to exist. You might have had a chance of becoming a real human being, but you've devoted yourself to being shallow, superficial and unreal."

Furious, she walked quickly away, looking back only once over her shoulder. She could see him, skinny and slim-hipped, trudging along the top of the beach, already a quarter mile behind. From this distance he looked so boyish he might have been fourteen years old, pale skin, flat stomach—somehow cockily adolescent. Why didn't he do something about it, work out, grow up? He reminded her of one of those overbred, neurasthenic dogs, a greyhound or a saluki, nibbling at its paws and staring nervously into the distance, when what she wanted was a golden retriever or even a German shepherd.

"Wait up, Florence! I just want to know one thing?" By some quirk of nature—the fog or the wind—his voice carried so clearly it might have been whispered in her ear.

"What?"

"Why do you want to be a nonperson? You ever see *Invasion of the Body Snatchers? The Stepford Wives?* Why do you want to join the living dead?"

She pretended she hadn't heard him. Spare me, she thought to herself. Shaking her head, she walked faster down the shore; then, throwing off her windbreaker, she turned and walked straight into the sea. It was freezing cold, and in an explosion of salt and sand, the waves slapped her so ferociously that she was able to swim only a few strokes before getting knocked down.

She was about to go to the outdoor shower to rinse off when she realized she didn't have any towels and headed inside. John, Natalie and their daughter, Claudia, a rather plain child of about eight with a complexion of flour-and-water dough, were seated at the kitchen table in front of the remains of breakfast. "Hello dere!" John shouted. His voice rang falsely in her ears. She tried not to look him in the eyes. "Did you have your breakfast already?"

She sat down. "Not really," she said, looking at the two cold pieces of toast, one of which was burnt.

"Help yourself," Natalie said, pushing the toast in her direction. "Claudia, go get her a knife and a plate."

The child did not move. "That's okay," Florence said. "Just pass me any old knife, I can just butter it on a napkin. I didn't even know you were here, Claudia! Where have you been? I thought you were away at camp."

"She was at tennis camp," Natalie said. "She just got back a couple of days ago. You didn't do very well, though, did you? Guess where she was seeded?" Florence shook her head. "They seed the kids, you know. At the end of two weeks she was ranked last! Ten thousand dollars, and at the end of two weeks she was worse than when she started!"

"Next summer can I go to horseback riding camp instead?"

"I told you, Claudia, I'm not talking about it until January! You're going to have to do something about your grades! The rest of the summer you're going to stay here and study with a tutor."

She turned to Florence. "She's not very smart, and if she were going to be drop-dead gorgeous, she could get away with it, but that's obviously not something we can count on either."

Florence, shocked, looked at John, thinking he would put a stop to Natalie's criticism, but he was reading the sports section of the *Times*. It occurred to her that Natalie's random maliciousness was her attempt at toughening up those around her. She was like a drill sergeant at boot camp: by knocking down the plebes, she would make them fierce and ready for battle. Unfortunately, it wasn't a technique that would work on everybody. Claudia had crumpled—Florence could see she was not going to blossom but would eventually emerge clipped and root-bound like a bonsai tree, hunched and wizened. "And what have you been doing since you got back from camp?" Florence said.

"She's been staying with Jessica Walker—you know, Steve Walker's daughter," Natalie said.

"She's my best friend," Claudia said.

"Steve flew the girls back from camp by private plane," Natalie said. "That Jessica is just amazing. When you see her you can't believe she's the same age as Claudia. She's so poised; I think she's going to be very special."

"Jessica has *three* horses," Claudia said.

"That must be nice," Florence said. "So you got to ride them for a couple of days?"

"The instructor rides Popper: he's dangerous. Jessica rode Comanche: he's a chestnut nine-year-old half-Arab gelding with white socks and a blaze. I had to ride Earwig: he's not fast, he's elderly, but he's very nice. Jessica's going to sell him. I wouldn't want him, though. I'd like my own."

"Why wouldn't you want him?"

"The color," Claudia said.

"What color is he?"

"Flea-bitten."

"That's not a color!" John said. Florence waited for him to commence his animal-like chortling. Apparently he could laugh only at something he himself had said. He stared briefly at Florence with a glazed expression of smug contentment, like a man who had just acquired a red-figure Greek vase at auction for below estimate. She averted her eyes.

"Daddy!" said Claudia. "It is too. I told you before, 'flea-bitten' means a white horse with red flecks!"

"Are you sure it doesn't mean the horse has fleas?"

"No, Daddy! You're silly!"

"Your own father? Silly? What kind of thing is that to say!"

It was the sort of jovial male-to-female teasing that fathers used in interacting with their daughters. One could not imagine a mother playing a game with her daughter in this fashion. The child was pleased with the flirtation. That her father could be so daffy! Perhaps it was useful training for adult life: like a chimp teaching its offspring to crack a nut, John was teaching Claudia that men were dumb but must be cajoled—coyly—into understanding truth. She had a sudden memory of herself at Claudia's age, feeling that her father must love her far more than her mother—how could her mother not appreciate him? But now she understood no grown-up woman could ever adore a man in that same blind way.

Claudia was ready to continue her wifely parody, but John had lost interest. "I know what I forgot to mention, Nats," he said. "I bumped into Lisa Harrison last week at Joe's cocktail party. She's been seeing Lesley Crouse again."

Natalie put down the paper. "She's been going out with him for years, off and on. She always complained about him."

"All the women he's ever gone out with complained about him. His dick is too big. He hurts them," John said. "Anyway—I don't think I'm supposed to repeat this—she's pregnant."

"Oh, how great!" Florence said. "She must be thrilled. I guess this means I don't have to give up hope yet." But she felt more jealously than pleasure. How come she was only thirty-two and hadn't found anyone, nor had a baby, while someone so much older was able to do so?

"She must be forty-two at least," said Natalie. "She shouldn't go around talking about it—what if she miscarries?"

"She says she wants the baby, but there's no way she's going to marry Lesley," John said. There was a pause.

"I think that's great!" Florence repeated. By plastering the walls with enough platitudes, with enough pleasant-sounding responses, she could conceal her real thoughts. Or perhaps it was simply that the flickering rage in the room could be smothered by niceties. Really, why should she have cared one way or the other? Since they seemed to think their own child was invisible—or didn't exist—her own presence must be far less real.

Natalie glared at her. "I think that's terrible. If she's going to have a baby, she should get married. How terrible, to bring a child into this world with the stigma of illegitimacy. It just wears away at the quality of life. And by the way, sweetie"—she turned to John—"Lesley Crouse doesn't hurt women because his dick is so big. He hurts women because he likes to."

"Oh," said John. "Well. That's something of a relief, I suppose. I must have met at least six of Lesley's old girlfriends who said he hurt them. I always thought it meant his dick was too big." He laughed uproariously and looked at his watch. "I've got to go. I'm meeting Ted Sterns at Mauptauguet."

"Claudia, stop picking your nose," Natalie said. "It's disgusting. Do you have pinworm again?"

"No."

"I bet you got it at that fancy camp. I'm going to call the director. Don't they tell you to wash your hands? Why do you think I'm always telling you that? You know I can't be with you every second of your existence! . . . What time will you be back from golfing, John?"

"Around seven, I expect. What time are people coming this evening?"

"Eight, I suppose."

John rose to leave, though it was evident—at least psychologically—that he had vanished some time ago. "Bye, girls! See you all later!"

After a pause Florence started to clear the table. "I'm getting a glass of water. Does anybody want anything?"

"Did you lose some weight?" Natalie said.

"I don't think so," Florence said.

Natalie gave her a piercing stare, like a raptor seizing a rabbit. "I bet you lost five pounds. What are you now, a hundred and eight?" Within thirty seconds Natalie had evaluated her and correctly judged her weight. "Five six? Or Five seven?"

"Five eight," Florence muttered.

Natalie snorted. "I don't think so. *I'm* five seven; you're shorter than me." That wasn't true, Florence thought indignantly, though she refrained from saying anything. Natalie was taller than she only because she wore high heels all the time. The only reason Natalie had anything to do with her was because their mothers had been friends—and probably Natalie liked having an acquaintance who was so obviously inferior to her in terms of wealth, position, financial status and so forth. "You look good, but I think you were better five pounds heavier. Your face is a little gaunt. Although when you were heavier, you had kind of a little tummy. Claudia, you should try and get Florence's figure when you grow up. With your luck you'll end up with my little tits and your father's big hips. Oh, I have some news for you! Charlie Twigall is coming to dinner this evening!"

"I think you mentioned it," Florence said.

"Well, I knew he had asked you out for tonight, and he said 'Yes' right away, so he sounds like he might be interested. If I were you, Florence, I'd grab him right away. I know you don't think he's attractive—"

"No, I think he's attractive, in a kind of different way—"

"But there's not that much else out there on the market and you're not exactly virginal material. Basically, he's your last chance! If I were in your position, I'd play my cards right and go for him. He's very, very conservative; you should put your hair up and try not to wear much makeup. I think he's bringing his mother! Anyway, I'm off—I've got stuff to do all day in Bridge-hampton. I don't know what time I'll be back."

"Can I go to the beach, Mommy?" Claudia said. The kid was plain, there was no getting around that. Probably that was part of the reason why Natalie had never warmed to her own child. Florence couldn't imagine acting so cold if she had a child. At least John and Natalie were rich enough to get Claudia plastic surgery—the works—later on. Then she would look just like her mother.

"I don't want you going to the beach, Claudia!" Natalie said. "Can't you stick around for one day! Stay by the pool. Ask Florence to keep an eye on you while you're out there. Besides, you can't go anywhere. Your tutor's coming at three. Florence, you'll watch Claudia, won't you? I think there's stuff in the fridge if you want to fix lunch."

"Sure!" said Florence.

"She's really not too bright," Natalie reiterated to Florence with a certain pride as she went out. It seemed to Florence that Natalie had been seared clean of human insecurities, feelings, weaknesses, emotions. She was like an artificial flame, blunt, cold and ferocious. She got what she wanted; no one would dare cross a tiger. She got what she wanted; that was the main thing. And—at least from Florence's point of view—she seemed to have to pay no price. Goddess of vengeance: Kali. Though all goddesses were goddesses of vengeance when it came right down to it, Florence thought, as Natalie called from the front door, "Clean up and do the dishes when you're done in there!"

4

"You're not drinking water from the tap, are you?" said Claudia.
Florence looked at her glass. "Yes. Why?"

"You're not supposed to drink the tap water out here!" Claudia
said with a frightened grimace. "It's got those things in it."

"What's going to happen to me?"

Claudia shrugged.

"What subject does your tutor teach you?" Florence asked
Claudia after a pause.

"I don't know," said the child grimly, spooning vast quantities of cherry jam onto the remaining half-slice of whole-grain toast. "Different things. Math. I don't like math. We grew some radishes. Something ate them, though, before they were big enough to eat."

"That must have been disappointing." Florence scrambled for an appropriate remark.

Unable to speak, Claudia nodded. A little dark pink goo blurted from the corner of her mouth. "Is there any toast left?" she said when she had swallowed.

Florence shrugged. "I don't know. You want me to go see?"

"That's okay." Claudia pulled the jar of jam toward her. "I just like the jelly part anyway. I don't need the bread." She removed a spoonful and began to pick the cherries from the mucilage. "I hate her."

"Who?"

"My mother. I hate her."

"Oh, Claudia, I'm sure you don't hate your mother," Florence said. "You just get mad at her sometimes." She wished she hadn't spewed this platitude. But what else was she supposed to say? Claudia was right, Natalie was awful, but how was she going to get through her whole life if she saw things so clearly and said them out loud? Anyway, she didn't know what to say to a child. She couldn't remember what it was like, except for a certain vague feeling of powerlessness—but that had never gone away. "You know, I saw a program, it was about these African hunting dogs. Or maybe they were hyenas—anyway, they live in packs. And it's one of the females, not the male, who's dominant. So everybody has to obey her. And all the other females have to give her their puppies. Nobody gets to keep a puppy except for the dominant female. And if the others don't obey her, she beats them up. But it—ah—it's for their own good." Somehow the story hadn't come out exactly right.

"I hate her."

"What are your plans until your tutor comes?" Florence said uncomfortably.

"Nothing. Watch TV, I guess."

"It's such a beautiful day!" Florence said. "Don't you want to swim in the pool? Your swimming pool is so beautiful!"

Claudia sat lumpishly. "Nobody to play with."

"I was thinking of going back to the beach. You want to come?"

"My mother said I can't go to the beach."

"I'm sure she meant by yourself. I can watch you."

This seemed to cheer Claudia up. "Really?" she said. "Okay! I'll go get ready."

Florence lay in the sun by the pool, trying not to think about the night before. Perhaps it hadn't happened. The lives of these people seemed so unreal; nothing here was any more serious than the action unfolding in a film. It was only a matter of time before she, too, joined their ranks, abandoning feelings—anguish, despair, hope, caring, understanding—thoughts, wishes, dreams, ideals. She had so few of those things already. The world inhabited by Natalie and John had no more depth than a picture in a glossy magazine. Their days passed like the pages of a book. So what if the end of struggle meant the end of human suffering? What she wanted was to be the character in a poem she had once read, in which the heroine

> . . . *should have sprung from Cardin's*
> *at twenty, molded in bisque, draped in chiffon, her eyes*
> *glazed with perfection,*
> *her eyelids on gold hinges*
> *swinging open and shut*
> *at intervals marked by the sun.*

Wasn't that the only dream for women at the end of the twentieth century, even for those who claimed to want other things? At least she was honest enough to admit it.

It was already warm. She decided she didn't need a towel. The outdoor shower was behind a bamboo gate, a cubicle built into the wall, and there was only one tap; the water ran hot for a few minutes before turning cold, and she jumped out quickly, still unable to obliterate her queasy feeling. At least the sticky, oily salt was off her now, and the sensation that she had been powdered with potato fertilizer. The sour scent, crematorium-acrid, blew across the nearby fields.

Claudia came out onto the patio, carrying a huge bag, an umbrella, dressed in a bright pink polka-dot cotton hat with ruffles that tied under her chin and a long-sleeved blue-and-white-striped cotton robe that gave her the appearance of a miniature resident of a nineteenth-century workhouse. She seemed barely able to carry the bag. "I'll take that," Florence said.

"Do you need suntan lotion?" Claudia asked.

"I don't know."

"Here." Claudia handed her a huge pink plastic bottle. The stuff smelled like bubble gum and coconut. "You should put it on. I never tan. Mother has basal-cell carcinoma. That's from lying in the sun too long."

"Is it serious?"

Claudia shrugged. "I told her, there's no ozone layer, she shouldn't lie in the sun! She has to put on medicine that makes the cancers turn brown. She smokes cigarettes, sometimes, too. If I find them, I throw them in the toilet."

"It must be difficult for her to have a child who's constantly trying to turn her in. She's lucky you're not a Communist. Or a revolutionary in Central America."

"What?"

"Nothing," Florence said. They trudged in silence back across the potato field.

"This stuff they put on the field, it really stinks," Claudia said, dragging the umbrella in the sand. "It goes into the drinking water and you get cancer."

"Cancer?"

"Last week they had to close the hospital because of some kind of thing that made everybody sick."

"What kind of thing?"

"I don't know. Some little whirly thing, in the water, that you couldn't see, and in the hospital it moved into the ventilation or something and they had to shut it down because they couldn't . . . get it sterilized."

"Are you sure you know what you're talking about?" Florence stumbled. Her shoe flipped into the air. "Damn!" she said from the ground. "I almost broke my ankle."

"Here's your sandal," Claudia said, holding up the red patent leather shoe. "It's broken."

"Oh no, and those were my favorite sandals. My only Guccis, and they don't make them anymore." She grabbed it from Claudia. The heel of the shoe had twisted at a right angle in a way she knew couldn't be fixed. When she got up she stepped straight onto something sharp that gave her a puncture wound at least a half inch into her sole. "Ow!" she said. "Prickers! This just isn't my day."

They hobbled through the field. "By next year, my dad says, this will all be gone. They're going to build houses." The child was out of breath, sweaty, and stood transfixed, as if she already had sunstroke.

"Do you want me to carry the umbrella?" Florence said, though her foot hurt.

"Okay." She passed the umbrella to Florence. The metal handle was sticky to the touch.

"I think you got cherry jam on this umbrella," Florence said. "You know, your mother is one of my only friends."

"You're kidding!" said Claudia. "Poor you!"

"If you're single in New York, a single woman, I mean, nobody wants anything to do with you. If you're a single man, that's something different—everyone wants an extra single man at their dinner parties: married women like a man to flirt with, and to introduce to their single women friends, and men like an extra man around to play squash with, or golf."

Claudia looked up at her with earnest disbelief, though Florence didn't have a clue as to how much of what she was saying made sense to a kid. They spread the blanket at the back of the beach, where strands of coarse grass sprouted from gray sand. The beach was private, except for residents, and was nearly empty, even on a July Saturday.

Claudia collected pearly jingle shells and smooth blue bits of clam shells—her "wampum"—and brought them back to their blanket for inspection before venturing off again. Florence liked her. Maybe it was only because Claudia appeared to like her, but there was something nice about being looked up to by someone so guileless. She could see nothing but trouble ahead for such a child. Who knew what she would do to punish Natalie when she got a bit older? Her options were infinite: she might become a Simone Weil, anorexic, working in a factory, attempting to reach personal sainthood. Or like that young woman sentenced to life in prison for revolutionary activities in Peru. It was hard to think of Natalie being chastised by such behavior, however. Promiscuity, drug addiction, adolescent pregnancy and out-of-wedlock child-birth—all of these had been meted out by so many others trying to teach their parents a lesson, there was no shock value left.

She must have fallen asleep. When she woke with the irritat-ing sensation of being harassed by flies, Claudia was gone. She looked up and down the beach, but there was no sign. Suddenly panic hit. Earlier in the day the waves had been very strong. There was no way Claudia could swim without getting pulled out to sea. She ran down to the water. A man was walking up the beach with a dalmatian, which frolicked in a goofy, cartoonish manner. She ran over to him. "A kid—a little girl!" she said.

The man pointed beyond the breaking waves. "What's that?" he said. Florence saw Claudia's pink-spotted hat.

"Oh no!" Florence said. "That's her! She must have gotten washed out!"

"I was wondering what that was," the man said. As they watched, the pink spots went under and did not emerge. The man handed her the dog's leash and ran into the water. The dalmatian jumped up and down, barking excitedly. After a few minutes he swam back, pulling Claudia under one arm. Her hat was plastered to her head but still tied under her chin. Her eyes were closed. He put her on the sand, and she threw up all over herself just as a wave crested around her knees and slithered back out in a gurgle of white sudsy foam.

"Are you all right?" Florence bent over her. More vomit, ruby-colored, trickled down the corner of her mouth.

"She's throwing up blood!" the man said.

"No, no, she just ate a lot of cherry jam," Florence said. "How long was she under? Was she under long? How did you find her underwater?"

"She was sinking—but in the same place," the man said. He looked up and down the beach. "I think you better get her to a doctor."

"Oh, God," Florence said. "I can't believe this is happening. Are you all right, Claudia?" Claudia lay on the sand, her puffy face chalky, the wet hat a limp petal. She seemed so little, and her bumble-bee-striped swimming suit made her look like a pathetic, drowned insect. She didn't respond. "What am I going to do?"

"Do you have a car?" She shook her head. "You hang on to the dog. I'll carry her."

The man slung Claudia over his shoulder and they set off to the parking area a half mile down the beach. There were six or seven cars in the lot, and two bicycles, but the only people were sitting some distance farther away. He placed Claudia near the railroad tie that stopped cars from driving onto the beach. "Are you all right?" He shook Claudia gently by the shoulders, but her eyes stayed closed, as if covered with wax. Two men in their twenties, gleaming and expensive behind glittering sunglasses, pulled up in an open-topped Range Rover. Florence ran over to the driver as he was getting out. "Excuse me—what's your name?"

"Eric."

"Eric, this little girl—she almost just drowned—I don't have a car—could you please take us to the hospital?"

The man who had rescued Claudia began to carry her toward the car. The two men in the Range Rover looked at each other. "Oh, Christ," the driver said. "Look, Mark, you might as well grab our stuff and set up, and I'll take them to the hospital and come back afterward."

The one called Mark grabbed a couple of leather shopping bags from the back and headed onto the beach. Florence jumped into his seat and the man put Claudia on her lap.

The traffic was unbelievable. Bumper-to-bumper in both directions along the two-lane road. The cars, all luxury models—Mercedes, Jaguars, Corvettes, Cadillacs, Ferraris—were as nervous and restless as race horses at the starting gate. But snout-to-tail, snorting, glossy, primed with high octane, they could only creep along at twenty miles an hour. She thought she was going to scream with rage and fear. Surely there were some rules for what she could do in this situation, but her mind was blank. When she pulled up Claudia's eyelids, only the whites were visible. All she could do was repeat, over and over to Eric, what had occurred, as if by reciting it the episode would move into the past. But it was apparent that Eric—having heard the story once—was no longer listening, only shaping it in his own head for dinner-party conversation later on.

At last they reached the entrance to Southfork Hospital's emergency room. Before the vehicle had stopped she had opened the door and—barefooted—was hopping out, with Claudia half-dragging in her arms. "Hey! Hey!" she began to call. "I need help!"

The doors were shut. An ominous yellow band of fluorescent tape sealed the emergency room, and when she began to try to get into the hospital from the main entrance, Eric appeared and grabbed her arm. "I just remembered, they closed the hospital last week to do some kind of major cleaning or something," he said. "Come on, we'll just have to go to River Beach—there's a hospital there."

A sharp rock gouged into her foot, right in the spot where she had already gotten the puncture wound. "Ow, ow, ow. Eric, can you grab her legs, I think I'm dragging her feet on the ground. I don't know what to do. Do you have a car phone? We can call the police for an escort." They were almost back at the Range Rover. She supposed she should be grateful that Eric hadn't just driven away after dropping her off; then she'd really be stuck.

"Mark's got the phone. Why don't we put her in the backseat? At least she'll be lying down."

With Claudia in the backseat, Florence had a chance to look at her feet. They were absolutely sliced open and filthy, as if she had been dancing on broken plates and knives. Gingerly she tried to brush off the dirt until she realized Eric was looking at her with disgust out of the corner of his eye. Just then Claudia began to wake up. She made a strange, almost inhuman gargle.

"Oh, Claudia!" Florence leaned over the backseat and stroked Claudia's face. "Are you all right? Can you hear me? Just hang on and we'll be at the doctor's in a minute." Claudia's nose was bubbling. It was repellent, such thick, gooey stuff. Florence didn't have a tissue. It took all her strength to wipe Claudia's nose with her fingers.

Claudia moaned again and was sick on herself and the back-seat. Eric was shaking his head. "There should be a towel, some-place."

She was about to lean back to try to find one, but they had pulled up at the River Beach Hospital's emergency room. She raced in, shouting for assistance. Two men appeared and took Claudia from the vehicle.

"I've got to run, Eric!" she said. "Thanks for all your help!"

He had opened up the back of the car and was searching for a towel. "Good luck! Hope everything works out."

"She seems okay, but I think we'll keep her overnight for observation," the doctor said. They had somehow managed to track down Natalie on her cellular phone. "We're going to give her some intravenous antibiotics, she's ingested some fluid, but basically she's a very lucky girl."

She stayed with Claudia at the hospital until late afternoon, when Natalie finally arrived, and waited outside so Natalie could be alone with her.

"What was she doing at the beach!" Natalie said as they drove back in Natalie's silver BMW. "I told her not to go to the beach. I swear, she does these things to get attention—she waits until the day I'm having all these people for dinner, just to drive me crazy! I get home, there's a note from her tutor saying she wasn't home, I had to pay him thirty dollars just for showing up—"

"It was my fault!" Florence said, beginning to cry.

"I'm in the middle of aerobics class, the telephone starts ringing in my backpack—I run over, trying to find it, *so* humiliating, having the hospital call. I said, 'You might as well keep her for a week if you're going to keep her overnight. I'll be back in the city all week anyway; at least I won't have to worry about her ending up in the hospital again if she's already *in* the hospital.' "

"I thought it was okay for me to take her to the beach, just that you didn't want her going there alone, and I fell asleep—I didn't think she'd go in without me!" Florence said.

They didn't speak for the rest of the trip.

She went upstairs to change. There were slivers of honey and amber in her hair, so subtle as to appear natural except to the rest of Manhattan's female population—a process that set her back five hours and three hundred dollars every month. Most of her income went for maintenance on herself. Her nails and toenails were manicured and polished in the palest silver-pink, her legs waxed, as were eyebrows and facial hair. This was another hundred and fifty a month; in addition, her membership at the gym (not a very nice one, to be sure, but not the worst either) was three hundred and fifty. Then there was the expense of clothes.

She tugged on a skin-tight pair of gray trousers, Capri-length, with slits up the calves. These had come from Henri Bendel and had been expensive—at least by her standards—nearly four hundred dollars. The cotton ribbed T-shirt was from the Gap, only twenty-nine ninety-five, and probably she didn't need it, but she wanted to have something new to wear to Natalie's party. The pants, however, she had definitely needed. They were sexy yet modest: at least they didn't reveal too much skin; she didn't need or want to have hostile glances from the other women.

The shoes were flat navy-blue satin slippers. They had been *extremely* expensive, and she could see they weren't going to last much longer—the satin was beginning to fray—but she had loved them, so she had simply worn them out. Perhaps if she bought three or four pairs at once, the next time they would last longer; she could switch from one pair to the other. The outfit, including the undergarments (and regarding these items Florence could not bear to skimp; she could not feel good about herself unless her brassiere and underpants matched and were of good-quality silk and lace) in total cost about seven hundred dollars. And yet it was a modest ensemble. None of these were designer clothes, and the trousers had been reduced from five hundred dollars down to three ninety—a real saving, she had thought at the time, for pants she would be able to wear well into autumn, though now she wasn't quite so fond of them as she had been at first.

Her annual income from Quayle's was twenty-six thousand dollars, before taxes. Nobody except Quayle's directors received anything resembling a decent salary. Her position was educational, a job intended for rich girls waiting to get married, or career women with enough money to sustain them or an ability to live cheaply until they obtained a curatorial or academic position outside the city. Between the three-thousand-dollar mortgage and maintenance and her other monthly expenditures—which generally came close to fifteen hundred dollars—she spent, after taxes, more than twice what she earned. Luckily, until now she had had the money left to her by her mother. Now that was almost entirely depleted. But what else could she have done? There didn't seem to be any way to spend less money.

She thought of changing into a pair of silver sandals with low heels, which she had also brought along, but then she remembered Charlie wasn't much taller than she. He seemed so old-fashioned in his outlook that, at least for the time being, she wanted to give him the advantage of thinking he was the same height, if not taller.

She put on a little makeup; she didn't really need any, she liked to keep it simple, but this was a dinner party after all. She stroked some cocoa-colored powder on her eyelids (a Japanese brand, in a beautiful sleek black case with a tiny sponge applicator, thirty-seven dollars), applied a very pale lipstick with a faint hint of silver-pink (twenty-three dollars, from a fashionable little boutique in Greenwich Village, the only place where it was sold) and some powder (twenty-seven dollars, from an Upper East Side salon that did facial treatments and where she bought all of her skin-care products).

Finally she gave up and went down. John was standing at the bottom of the stairs, freshly showered, his hair wet and sleeked back, a martini glass in hand. "Oh, John!" she said. "Is there any more news? Is she all right?"

"Yeah, yeah. Nat finally got me at the golf course and I just stopped over at the hospital on my way home. She's fine. I don't know why they even want to keep her overnight—they say there's a chance she could get pneumonia if she got water in her lungs, but I think they're nervous we'll sue them later on if she gets sick."

"I feel so terrible. I fell asleep for a minute—I don't know what could have happened—she knew not to go in swimming without me. I think maybe she was just playing at the water's edge and a wave . . ."

"Don't worry about it," he said. "Nothing happened; it could have been worse." He leered slightly. "You're looking good, Florence!"

"Oh, gee." She was slightly sheepish. "Thanks, John." She tried to keep her tone of voice businesslike, or sisterly. "Is there anything I can do to help?"

"What I'd like to do is move some of that stuff in your room so you can be more comfortable. I still don't have a clue why Natalie put you there. Come up with me for a minute so I don't take your things out by mistake." He headed up the stairs.

"No, no," she said. "Really, it's fine. I pushed the things that were on the bed into the corner—I'm only here for one more night—honestly, it's—"

He continued up. On the landing she stopped, reluctant to follow him farther. She thought of turning and going back down, but he called from the third-floor hall. "Florence, this suitcase on the floor—is it yours?"

"Which one?" she said.

"I'd better show you. I'm going to put these things into the attic. I was meaning to do it for a while anyway."

She stood in the hall. "The brown leather-and-linen overnight bag is mine—"

He grabbed her wrist and gave her a quick yank into the room. In what appeared to be one motion, like some kind of karate move, still clutching her wrist with his left hand, he kicked the door shut behind her back, let go of her wrist, pulled up her shirt and tugged the cups of her brassiere down below her breasts, so that they stood out in the kind of frame between her shirt and the bottom of her bra. "Oh, God," she said. "No, no." In some way her protests seemed to incite him even more. Though his desire seemed to have no more significance than a sudden desire for French fries, she couldn't deny she was aroused too. It had taken her so long to get dressed for the party, she hated the way he was coming at her, determined to undo the work. How could she go downstairs afterward, flushed, with an aura of consummation, and expect to be desirable to a man offering real possibilities? She struggled to pull up her brassiere cups, but his mouth was firmly fixed on her left nipple like a lamprey; the more she tugged at her brassiere and tried to pull down her shirt, the more excited he seemed to become.

Finally she managed to get the mouth off her nipple by clamping his nostrils between two fingers. Eventually he would have to come up for air. "John, John, I want to go to the party!" she said. It wasn't exactly what she had intended to say, it was probably giving him the wrong idea, but if she let him do anything now, she knew the whole evening would be spoiled—not that it wasn't already, but she would look even more disheveled, violated. It was so horrible, the whole thing was such a mess.

His tongue, which had been fibrillating wildly, seemed to be dying in his mouth as his oxygen supply diminished. She kept her fingers firmly clamped on his nose. Finally, baffled, he stepped back to inhale through his mouth and she bolted, yanking open the door behind her, stepping into the hall, slamming it shut and trying to get her bra up and her shirt back down all at the same time. There was a button on the doorknob and she pressed it—it seemed odd to have a lock on the outside, probably it didn't work, but it might slow him down for a minute.

She walked quickly down the hall and downstairs, trying to wipe the incident off her face. Perhaps he and Natalie really were getting divorced—no doubt they were—but how could he behave like that? It was so hateful, so disgusting. She should say something to Natalie, but there was nothing she *could* say . . . no doubt if this was how he was acting with her, he was carrying on with innumerable women. Still, it was none of her business, really; it wasn't her position to tell Natalie that John was screwing around—it was hard to believe, in any event, that Natalie didn't know. Women, wives, had a way of knowing such things; if they didn't want to deal with it, it was their own solution to the problem.

5

Twenty or thirty people had already arrived. Everyone projected a bleak aura of frantic, nervous despair, as if they were not going to let the fact that they were in the country and not the city have any effect. "Florence! Florence!" She turned to find Neil Pirsig headed in her direction. There was no one she wished to see less. He was contemptible, the way he managed to appear whenever an artist died and take over, skimming the cream off the estate. He was so puffed up with his own importance—his life story, from street-gang member to Yale Law School, had been sold to the movies—

and he obviously thought all women were desperate for him. He always acted as if Florence wanted to marry him. His amused smile whenever she talked to him provided him with some kind of fix. Yet, she had to admit, there was something about him she found attractive. "Hi, Florence. Still single?" He held up his fingers, crossed, as if warding off a vampire. "Don't start looking at me with those hungry eyes! I'm still not prepared to ask you out on a date."

"Excuse me for just a second, Neil," she said coldly. She walked across the living room and out to the patio, smiling weakly, though no one was looking at her.

"Have you seen John?" Natalie approached her at the bar. An attractive blond kid, hired for the evening as a bartender, was busy making a drink. There was a silver tub of cigarettes on the edge of the table and Florence picked one up and lit it, for something to do.

"I saw him a while ago," she said. "Oh, gosh, Natalie, I just feel so terrible about what happened."

"Don't worry about it," Natalie said. "Florence, have you met Mike Grunlop?" She gestured to a short, barrel-chested man standing nearby who resembled a Roman senator. "Mike's a famous painter—you've probably noticed a lot of his works around the house. We've been collecting him for years. We were one of your first collectors, weren't we, Mike? And his wife, Peony, is a photographer. I'm sure you've seen her things in *Life* magazine; she just did a whole thing on dying gorillas in the Cameroons. Now she's off to Lima to shoot dogs. What kind of dogs is Peony going to shoot, Mike?"

Mike muttered something in a sullen voice, practically advertising his contempt for anyone who was a "collector." Probably he felt it was an astute move, politically, to accept Natalie's invitation, but at the same time he wanted to make it publicly clear that he was superior to her.

"What did you say?" Natalie looked distracted.

"Peruvian Inca orchid dog," Mike mumbled.

"That's just wild! Are you going to go with her, Mike? Excuse

me a minute." Natalie's small darting eyes glared furiously past
Florence as she looked around the room to see who had already
arrived.

As soon as she had moved away, Mike snatched his drink and
also wandered off—it was a well-known fact he was interested
only in Asian women. His paintings were imitation Chinese calligraphy, black scrawls on gray or white. His reviews always pointed
out how simple, pure and powerful his scratches were. The can-
vases went for almost half a million. Peony made Florence think of
a crumpled flower whose petals had been plucked—probably because Mike had spent their entire marriage tormenting her by
sleeping with other women.

For a minute Florence stood by the door, looking in. The
crowd was growing, the hideous details of the room becoming
progressively hidden. Natalie had decorated it in the era of chintz,
some seven or so years earlier: the overstuffed furniture was covered with cabbage roses, every end table was heaped with china
pug-dogs or wooden English lap desks. The works by Mike
Grunlop (there were only two or three, from what Florence remembered) were all upstairs—they had escalated in value only recently.

Over the fireplace hung a portrait of a pop star, an Andy
Warhol silk screen—Natalie's father had acquired it back in the
late seventies. Nearby were a series of nineteenth-century oil
paintings of dogs and opposite these what might have been a bad
painting by Sargent of an Indian couple, the man in a pink turban,
the woman in a red-and-yellow sari, but which, on closer inspection, proved to be a recent painting by another New York artist
whose summer place was nearby.

The house was virtually identical to any one of several hundred others, both in architecture and furnishings, a Levittown of
the wealthy. Built by a quite successful young architect in 1982,
the size and shape of several barns or, more accurately, an air-
plane hangar—not completely austere, with half-moon-shaped
windows and several silolike appendages to soften the modern
appearance—and it was set squarely in the middle of three ex-

tremely expensive acres on the correct side of the highway, that narrow strip of road that fronted the ocean rather than the bay.

The landscaping, including the area around the swimming pool and tennis court, had been done by a popular local landscape-gardening firm—to look at a tree was to look at anywhere between six and ten thousand dollars, to examine a plant was to examine one to two hundred. Perhaps each blade of grass was worth a dollar. There was an underground sprinkler system, and year-round gardeners, locals sent out from the same firm, uprooted impatiens—those tiny, pink, screaming petals lining the drive in late summer—and replaced them with chrysanthemums, bulgy and yellow. Diseased trees, or limbs fallen in a storm, were immediately removed; a dead or sickly plant would be replaced with one more currently in style. This year bright flowers must have been viewed as contemptible—Florence had not known that an entire bank of bedding plants could be filled with such grayish, sage-colored frowzy things. Had the land not been so carefully maintained but been allowed to return to its natural state, it would have been nothing but scruffy pines and grasses. Nowadays there were strict zoning laws against such things.

A man on the far side of the room was looking at her with a disgusted expression. It took her several seconds to realize he was offended by her cigarette smoke. It was supposed to be a party; if he didn't like the smoke, surely he could go outside. What gave such an eggy little creature the right to glare at her, as if no decent woman would light up. She was about to blow smoke in his direction when she realized it was Charlie Twigall and quickly crushed out the cigarette. She tried to distract him, turning her scowl into a smile—it was, however, perhaps just a split second too late; he had seen her contempt.

He peered over at her, wanting to talk to her yet—somehow—to avoid her at the same time. Her peculiar little eyes—narrow gray-blue slits, vaguely alien, perhaps from some ancestor raped by a Mongolian invader, a souvenir flung down across generations and the only feature preventing her from resembling a perfect, bland American doll—were half closed. Her blond hair, the color of dirty honey, hung down in messy chunks. And with the back of one graceful hand she reached up to rub her nose, a short, perfect little nose like that of a Persian kitten which had been punched in the face. She tried to make herself seductive; still, he didn't approach.

Now the only way she could compensate was to bludgeon her way eagerly across the room and act overexcited, as if she had been hoping to find him from the start. "Thank goodness!" She grabbed his forearm. "I was hoping I'd see you! I don't know anyone here! What's happening? What have you been doing all day?"

"Hi . . . Florence," he said.

It was hard not to rush him. Yet after a pause she suggested he have a drink. "I'm having white wine," she said.

"Oh . . . no thank you," he said. "I . . . don't drink."

"I usually just have a glass of wine," she said quickly. "At a party, or dinner. So what have you been up to?"

"I spent the day . . . trying to get them . . . to fix my car," he said.

"And they still haven't fixed it yet?" She spoke in a tone of shocked disbelief.

"It's in a . . . garage . . . the dealership . . . out here. It still . . . smells. They said . . . it was fixed . . . but when I went to the SAAB dealership . . . I said, 'I can still . . . detect an odor.' And the salesman . . . the man who sold it to me . . . initially . . . got in. And he said, 'I don't smell . . . anything.' I said, 'You must have an olfactory . . . problem.' "

She laughed appreciatively. "An olfactory problem! That's very good! And what did he say?"

In bliss at her laughter, Charlie averted his eyes from her gaze and stared dreamily at her breasts, as if the breasts had been pleasantly responsive rather than her. "I was extremely . . . angry . . . and I asked if he wouldn't mind . . . sitting in the car. After a few minutes . . . of sitting in the car . . . he said that they would try . . . again." How old had Natalie said he was? In his fifties? "Meanwhile . . . I ordered a new Lotus . . . but it's on . . . back order for the summer."

"A Lotus! Great!" She wondered just how many others had been down this path before her, looking at him attentively, trying to find some common ground of interest, trying to convince themselves a sexual magnetism or chemistry was possible. If he had been willing to date plain and undemanding women—a high school math teacher, for example, or a veterinary technician—a life for him with another might have been possible. But as far as she knew he wanted only the flashiest, the most glamorous—fashion models, young movie stars—and these women didn't need his money and didn't want his personality.

He was looking at her as if he could tell what she was thinking. Perhaps, like a draft horse that could read minds, break into a trot with just a thought from its rider, he was not as slow-witted as he appeared. "So how are you getting around?" she asked nervously. "Did they give you a good replacement?"

"A what?"

"A replacement while they fix yours."

His face crinkled with disappointment. "Might they . . . have done that?"

"Gosh, I don't know!" she said. "I suppose . . . maybe if you asked."

"I didn't think . . . to ask."

"Well, they should have offered."

"I took Mother's . . . car and driver . . . for the evening. Mother . . . gave up driving. She says . . . there's too much traffic these days."

"That's true!"

"When she first started . . . coming here . . . as a girl . . . it wasn't at all . . . fashionable. And it was . . . the country. In those days . . . it took five hours . . . to get to Southampton."

"Five hours!"

"The roads . . . were single-lane . . . or something. Now

. . . it takes almost that long . . . because of the traffic." She laughed merrily. He looked up at her almost suspiciously, as if she might be making fun of him, but then he studied her eager, guileless face and relaxed, pleased with himself. "Do you want to . . . sit outside? It's so . . . nice out, and it might be . . . easier to talk."

"Oh, I would love to! I'll just grab one last glass of wine on the way out."

They sat at one of the little tables for what seemed an interminable length of time, beneath a striped canvas umbrella decorated with hundreds of twinkling lights. "Did anybody see John?" Natalie said, sailing feverishly past.

A waiter circulated announcing that dinner was being served. The line at the buffet already coiled out through the dining room toward the pool. Charlie stood protectively behind her. He was very attentive. This was a good sign, she thought, if she could keep thinking of questions and acting interested in his responses. The man ahead of her turned around. "This line is moving incredibly slowly," he said in an Italian accent. "But I do not mind if it gives me a chance to talk to you."

"Oh yes?" she said nervously. Charlie, who was the same height as she, was already beginning to scowl and jostled her forward slightly, like a bulldog using his stout chest to bully an owner's leg into submission.

"I am Raffaello di Castignolli," the man said, looking down at her with a bemused smile.

"Florence Collins," she muttered. "And this is Charlie Twigall."

"How do you do?" Raffaello said. He was incredibly handsome, in an artificial way, as if a magazine page for men's cologne had been pumped into life by the exhaust pipe of a vacuum cleaner. His black hair was sleeked back, his navy suit was sharp-shouldered and expensive, he gazed at her with the expression of a man accustomed to assessing sports cars. The only thing that wasn't quite right was the suit, a little too flashy-Italian, a bit on the gangster side—too much for the Hamptons, midsummer. "I could not help noticing you when you were coming down the stairs," Raffaello said. "It was very amusing, how you pulled yourself together only as you reached the bottom of the flight. You have, as they say, an inside persona and an outside person you show to the world. For one moment, I am thinking, your inside persona is let accidentally slip. But for me, I could tell something had happened even before I caught a glimpse of your face."

She smiled weakly. He was expressing interest in her, she supposed. But to be evaluated—summed up—was to also let her know that he was in the superior position, and she the inferior. He was too handsome, too alien in his Europeanness; it made her nervous and he knew it.

"Here's a plate, Florence." Charlie reached around and handed her a plate from the top of the stack as they got to the head of the line.

"I helped make some of the food, last night!" Florence said. A waiter stood behind the table, carving a flank of tuna steak, dried and charred on the outside, bright pink and raw inside. After carving, he plonked each slice on top of a dollop of mashed potatoes and then drizzled some kind of pink sauce over it. For a moment Florence was mesmerized—the whole thing was so hideous.

"May I help you to some of this pasta?" said Raffaello. The pasta was a huge bowl of mushy-looking curly noodles embedded with chunks of tomatoes and congealed lumps of spinach glistening with oil. He spooned some onto her plate, and as he did so he leaned into her, pressing against her from behind. Through his thin trousers she could feel his erection.

She stepped away and gave him a flattered look of disbelief. "You—you're outrageous!"

"And you are just my type. Except for your provincialism—it is so American to pretend to be shocked. Tell me, which is the food you have prepared? I will take that, specially." He certainly had some kind of S and M routine worked out—it was like getting petted and slapped almost at the same time. "Some kind of Brazilian dish," she said. "I was chopping the onions."

"You must be very good at chopping onions."

She felt witless in the presence of such cynical smirkiness. "I think there's tripe in it."

"Not a popular dish, here in America!" he said. "However, for myself, I love what you call organ meat. I am very English, in that respect. You like tripe? Or kidneys? And the sweetbreads—that is my favorite."

"Are you friends of Natalie's? Or John?"

"Oh, of both," he said, helping himself to some dry slabs of white turkey meat. "And you?" He made it clear that her question was banal. Next to the turkey was the dish that she had participated in preparing—a heaving mountain of black beans, from which gray things resembling human digits protruded at various angles.

There were a few other dishes on the table: some bright green peapods, all positioned in exactly the same direction; a salad of orange segments, onion slices and lettuce leaves; and something that might have been a rice pilaf—she was uncertain. There was something that might have been beef or lamb stew, and a platter of chicken legs in a yellow-and-cream-colored sauce. As usual with these buffet dinners, nothing seemed to quite go with anything else; it was almost as if you had to create food in stranger and more peculiar concoctions than had previously been thought of, so that a meal had become the food equivalent of "The Emperor's New Clothes," with people smacking their lips and commenting "How delicious!" over a plate full of garbage.

She had only a few more minutes to decide whether to sit with Raffaello, abandoning Charlie, or wait until Charlie had finished serving himself and act as if it were only natural for the two of them to sit together. Two hundred million dollars! How her life would be changed! In one split second she had mentally purchased an apartment—penthouse duplex, terrace, fifteen rooms—and furnished it: Biedermeier, French club chairs, Mies van der Rohe. The closets were full of clothes, the maid was dusting, admiring friends had arrived, she was debating whether to fly the Concorde—when she quickly realized there was no use in such fantasies: if she indulged in them, she would never get to live them. She stopped the thought as if it were an insect under the edge of her fingernail. "Tell me, what field are you in?" she asked Raffaello.

"Oh, I am in the wine business," he said, retreating into his predatory eye routine once again. The wine business. Did that mean he owned a vineyard in Italy? Or worked in a liquor store? With her luck, it was probably the latter. If only she had the courage to be blunt and ask. But it had seemed rude enough to ask him what he did. His eyes were an intense blue, outlined in black. "And you?" he inquired. "What is your field?" His tone made it perfectly obvious he knew that whatever she did was of no importance whatsoever.

"I work at Quayle's. You know—the auction house?"

He snorted. "Yes, of course. In which department?"

"I'm in jewelry."

"You're kidding!"

She couldn't tell if he was being sarcastic. "No. Why would that be so shocking?" Before she knew it he had picked up two sets of silver wrapped in napkins, gesturing that one was for her, and Florence followed him outside to one of the little café tables, ignoring Charlie, who was still hovering wistfully nearby. She was spreading her blue-and-white-plaid napkin over her lap when Natalie emerged from the house and, looking across the patio, steamed toward her.

"What do you think you're up to?"

"What?" Florence said.

"The only reason I was ever friends with you is because our mothers were friends; my mother's always asking how you're doing, did I help you find a boyfriend. In less than twenty-four hours—as my guest—you've screwed my husband and almost drowned my daughter."

Florence looked around the patio, panic-stricken, but none of the other guests were looking in her direction.

"I don't know what you're talking about, Natalie, really. I said I was sorry about the accident with Claudia." The others dining on the patio ceased talking. Three waiters had gathered by the pool bar, motionless, straining to hear. Florence turned and went back inside.

"I think you know what I'm talking about." Natalie was not giving up; she had followed her into the house. "John's not without blame, but you're a total slut; you didn't have to come on to him. And you lock him in your bedroom just before I have a party? Is that supposed to be funny? I don't even want you on my property. I think maybe you should leave."

A droplet of liquid fell onto Natalie's forehead and rolled down her nose. Oblivious, she brushed it away and did not seem to notice when a second appeared. Surreptitiously Florence looked up. The water was coming through the ceiling. A bubble of plaster, like the blister on a burn, bulged ominously, tender and swollen. Another drop of water plashed down.

6

The third-floor carpeting was squishy underfoot. She packed and came down the back stairs into the kitchen; hopefully, she would avoid running into Natalie—or anybody else. Perhaps there would be a train schedule or the jitney timetable. Through the kitchen window she saw Charlie in the side garden. He was staring in a somewhat slow-witted, doltish way at a dish-shaped pink flower the size of a dinner plate. Both were illuminated in the glare from the building's security lamps. She put down her suitcases and went out the door. "Oh, Charlie!" she said. She tried to drape her arms around him, but he stepped back, so she knew he had already heard. "This is so awful! I didn't sleep with Natalie's husband—and I never meant for anything to happen to Claudia. Please say you believe me."

"Ah . . ." he said, half turning but not looking at her. "I'm just waiting for my driver. I told him to be back around now." She looked at her watch. To her surprise, it was after eleven.

"What am I going to do?" she said. "I don't think the trains or the jitney back to Manhattan run this late, do they?"

"Oh, are you . . . going back to the city?" he asked. "Well, if I don't see you again, have a great . . . trip." He still avoided her gaze and looked nervously through the French doors that led to the dining room, as if he might be under the observation of someone indoors.

"I don't know what to do," she muttered.

"I don't think there are any trains this late," he said, as if he were just now receiving her question through a telephone on the other side of the world.

"What a pretty flower!" she said desperately. It was hideous, the flat pinkness of it, with a wibbly-looking phallus in the center.

"My favorite." He brightened slightly and cupped the bloom in both hands. "Malva." There was the sound of car wheels on the gravel behind them, and both turned as a dark maroon Jaguar pulled up in the drive. "Well, there's my car. I never stay out late when I'm in the country."

"Would you be able to give me a lift to the station?"

"What are you going to do there?" he said. "You'd be better off waiting until morning." She followed him down the drive. "Oh, there you are. Tibor!" he called as a pimpled boy in his twenties got out of his car. "Mother's driver. Tibor!" He waved. The boy came over to the hedge. He was not unattractive, with large brown eyes and lashes, high cheekbones and broad shoulders, quite a nice slim body—but cheap-looking thin blond hair, brushed back and blow-dried, and a ghastly gray-and-red-patterned acrylic suit jacket that might have been made in Turkey or Rumania, of the sort worn only by Eastern Europeans and Pakistanis. He looked at

Florence, his eyes traveling up and down her tight outfit, and grinned nervously, almost involuntarily. "I'll just be a moment, Tibor," Charlie said. "I have to say good-bye to the host and hostess."

"Excuse me," Tibor said to her as if he were supposed to be inspecting her and had been interrupted.

"Where's he from?" she asked brightly, trying to think of anything to stall Charlie. If she could get him to chat . . . she might suggest they go for a drink, and over drinks ask if he could put her up for the night. Surely his house had a guest bedroom, a cottage, even a couch would do.

"Russia," said Charlie. He began walking back to the house. There was a grin on his face that seemed to say he was delighted to be getting even with her for sitting with Raffaello at dinner, for thinking uncomplimentary thoughts about him. He had everything going for him. He was a man, he was rich, plenty of women swooned over him. He might marry and begin a family at sixty, if he chose. Or seventy. Florence had been around too long. At thirty-two, without a good background (anyway, an ordinary background, *ordinary*, pet rather than show quality), without money of her own, having slept with a few too many men—who was going to want her? She was like an overripe banana marred by brown spots, diminished in value. "Good to see you, Florence!"

So she was dismissed. She would be damned if she'd beg him again for a lift to the station. She supposed she could sneak back into the house and call a taxi service to pick her up. The first morning train probably came in at six-thirty or seven. She would simply spend the night sitting on her bag in some train station or shelter. At least it was safe out here, in this ghetto of rich people. Then she realized she didn't even have to go back in to call a taxi. It was true the station was probably five miles away, but what else did she have to do but walk? It would take up some time and might help to calm her down. She hoisted her suitcase onto her shoulder and set off down the gravel drive. "Florence! Florence, wait!" a voice called to her from the front door; she didn't turn around. Whoever it was ran after her, the pebbles rustling dully underfoot. "What are you doing?" It was Darryl Lever. He tugged on her arm and took the suitcase in hand.

"I'm walking to the train station." She tried to yank her bag from him.

"I'll give you a lift. But I don't think there's another train until morning."

"I don't care. I'll wait."

"You want me to drive you back to the city?"

She almost collapsed with gratitude. "Would you?"

"Sure."

"Oh, God. Thank you. Everything's been so awful. Everything's been just horrible."

"You wait here. I'll go get my car. We have to swing by my house so I can pick up my things, if that's okay."

"I don't care. I just want to go home."

It was after eleven. For the first time all weekend the traffic had diminished; they spent the next twenty minutes in silence. His car was a big old Cadillac convertible, rusted to bits; it must have been fifteen or twenty years old—the smell of old gasoline fumes rose through the floor and dashboard. "I'll just run in and grab my stuff," Darryl said at last, turning down a driveway. "Do you want to come in?"

"I'll wait."

The trees along the private road were illuminated by old-fashioned streetlamps. The house was so splendid Florence thought for a minute it was some old hotel or country club—what was Darryl doing here? It had probably been built around the turn of the century: dark wooden shingles, a porch that extended across the entire facade. It was three stories high, with turrets and cupolas, and across the circular drive and parking lot, there was an old carriage house converted into a garage and caretaker's or chauffeur's quarters. He circled the car around to the front and hopped out. "I'll only be a minute," he said. "I'm not going to come back this weekend. Everyone's probably already gone to sleep, so I want to leave a note."

She sat in the car. She could hear the sea, quite close by, probably just on the other side of the house. It was the real thing, the real summer beach cottage for rich people, and it made her realize just how poor an imitation Natalie's house was: no matter how much money had been spent, nothing seemed quite right, as if aliens from another planet had constructed a human habitation based on photographs. She was about to go in and find out where Darryl had disappeared to when he emerged with a suitcase and several paper bags. "Sorry about that," he said. "My . . . uh, they were still awake, and kind of upset that I was going. They were expecting me to stay at least through tomorrow."

"Who lives here? Friends?"

"You might say."

She was surprised he knew anybody as wealthy as people who would own a house like this. They sped in silence back toward the city. She was relieved he didn't mind being quiet. She turned toward him, watching him in the flickering lights off the highway. He drove quite badly and she was grateful there was so little traffic; he had a way of pressing the gas pedal with a jumpy motion and then releasing it, so that the car jerked forward and then slowed.

"So tell me, what happened?"

"The hostess threw me out," Florence said. "She threw a big scene, and accused me of sleeping with her husband."

"Of what?"

"Screwing her husband."

"You slept with John?" He sounded sickened.

"He attacked me. I pushed him away, but he told Natalie I seduced him."

"That's terrible! These are terrible people, Florence. You should never have gone to stay with them."

"Mmm."

"God, if I had known, I wouldn't have gone to her party. I'll never have anything more to do with them."

"That's nice of you."

"I've never liked them anyway. I just went because I knew you were going to be there . . . So maybe now you are liking to come for a drink, and I will show you how are Russian peoples?"

"How are Russian peoples?"

"Just as bad." He gave her a grin.

They went to a noisy club under the subway tracks somewhere in Queens. It was an area she had never been to, full of shops with signs in Cyrillic, almost like visiting another country, dirty and yellowish and sour. The club was crowded, but the man at the door obviously knew Darryl, who held her hand and pushed through the crowd. They joined a large table of people—he shouted out their names to her, she shook her head with a dismayed smile. A bottle of half-frozen vodka was placed in front of them; he poured them each a shot and passed the bottle down around the table. A little orchestra played Russian music, hokey but charming, on a small stage while a revolving disco light spun on the ceiling.

She had the sensation she was on a ship, probably a sinking ship, but nevertheless everyone seemed determined to have a good time. Or perhaps that was why it was so much fun. At the far end of a table a red-haired woman, in her forties, sat weeping into her drink; no one else paid any attention. Next to her was a large man with a red face, who gave the illusion of having a large walrus mustache, no doubt some ancestral trait that haunted his face. He put his arm around her shoulder and pulled her to him. "Why are you looking so sad?"

"I'm not!"

"What?" the man haunted by the mustache shouted, spewing flecks of spittle. His small blue eyes almost popped out of his head. "You are not treating my friend badly?"

"Who?"

"My friend Darryl. He is a good person. You, I think, are not such a good person."

She was irritated. "What makes you think you can make a snap judgment? You don't know anything about me."

"I look." He seemed pleased to have provoked her. She wouldn't give him the satisfaction. Everything in the magazines and TV, said to be considered attractive, to get a good job, to find the right man, one should have one's nails done, keep up with the latest hairstyles, buy the latest silkening shampoos, dye one's hair gilt and bronze. Shoes should be polished, never down-at-heels. The right outfits were necessary for every occasion. Then, when a slim measure of perfection had been achieved, there was always some guy to look at her with a sneer and judge her a phony.

"Perhaps not. I'm just a typical American girl. Think whatever you want to. You will anyway." She sipped her vodka.

"No, no! Wodka must be drunk like this!" The red-faced man drank the whole jiggerful in one gulp, then gestured for her to do the same.

She couldn't figure what Darryl was doing with these people. He seemed to speak fluent Russian—that was a surprise, but not a shock. He was brilliant, he could have done anything, but instead he wasted his brains on useless projects, people, places; he had no desire to get ahead. The air almost crackled with Russian energy, vitality, despair, but she could muster no interest in this group. In some way it reflected badly on her—on Darryl—devoting an evening to people who weren't right socially. That was the way things worked here: unimportance was a qualifiable entity that could rub off on you, like a skin fungus. Associate too long with the wrong types and she would join their ranks.

If she got slightly drunk she wouldn't have to think about the humiliation of the past two days. What could she have done? John had basically raped her, sort of—at least she had done her best to cover up the whole thing. If she had told Natalie that her husband had broken into her room, Natalie still would have blamed her.

She drank the vodka in one gulp; it was like swallowing a mouthful of frozen gasoline. For a moment she was transported to some Antarctic plain, a howling whiteness where she crouched, alone, in an improbable igloo made of blocks of clear ice. When she came out the other side, the man sitting next to her, whose name she had been unable to comprehend, refilled her glass and held it to her lips. What was going to become of her? At least tonight she could have a vacation from the real world. Darryl was looking across the table at her with a worried expression. "Are you all right?" He gestured toward the ruddy-faced man and addressed him sharply in Russian.

"I'm fine!" Florence said. She took the glass from the man's hand and drank it. "I want to sit next to you," she announced to Darryl.

"What?"

"I want to sit next to you! You're too far away, on the other side of the table. I can't hear you." He looked down, embarrassed yet pleased, and fiddled with some crumbs next to one of the great puffy slabs of bread that had been left untouched on a stainless-steel salver. Then he came around to her side and switched places with the man next to her. Seated now across the table, the man began to bellow in Russian the words to the music, and those sitting beside him joined in. "Nikolai is a curator at the Tretyakov Museum," Darryl shouted in her ear.

"Yes?" she said.

He nodded. "Tell me, have you been to Russia?"

She shook her head. "You seem to know something about the art scene."

"No, but Nikolai is my best friend, and so I know a little. How's your job?"

"They don't pay me anything! If they don't give me a raise or I find a rich man to marry, I'm going to do something desperate!"

"You're just kidding, right? Oh, God, Florence—take a look around you! The reason I brought you here . . . was to show you these people, my friends. *They* don't have any money! But they're out here having a good time, happy to be together, happy just to be alive—these are real people!"

She looked around. The red-haired woman, holding a glass of vodka, was sitting in the corner singing in Russian to the music, tears streaming down her face. Her cheeks were red and rosy like those of some barmaid in *The Brothers Karamazov*. Two men were arguing passionately at a nearby table. One had a little beard and round glasses like Lenin's; the other, the beatific expression of Prince Myshkin. "If these people are real," she said, "then I don't want any part of reality."

"How can you say that?" Darryl leaned forward. "These people—my friends—they're like me. Once you're their friend, they're completely loyal. Like me. And you won't find that in New York City. Nobody even knows how to be a friend, let alone has any idea of what loyalty and friendship mean. I'm your friend, Florence."

She was drunk, she thought, and so was he. She was sorry she was so cynical, but the conversation didn't seem to make any sense. The only thing she knew was that abruptly, spontaneously, Darryl had become very attractive; perhaps it was his previously unannounced belief in the goodness of people and the world, or perhaps the idea that she had, at last, one true friend.

They began to kiss as if they were two birds, wild macaws high in some tree, and his arms were wings she could crouch beneath. Abruptly Darryl began to cough and he pulled away, gasping. "Give me some water." He finally managed to speak. "I don't know what's wrong with me. I guess I should go see somebody."

"Not tonight what?"

"What?"

"A minute ago you said, 'Not tonight.' "

"I don't remember." He looked puzzled, distracted. Now that he had pushed her away, she flung herself on him, pawing his hair and kissing the rim of his ear.

7

He got her back to Manhattan around four A.M. A Sunday morning in July, the West Side appeared shut down and there was a yellowish cast to the light, as if it had been abandoned due to some environmental disaster. There was no traffic; pulling over, he got out and went around to her side of the car, opening her door. "Why don't you come up with me?" she said, clutching him.

"No, no, I can't," he said.

"Why? What's wrong with you?" she said. Her voice was slurry. "Are you gay?"

"No, I'm not gay," he said. "Come on, Florence, are you telling me you don't remember?" She had fallen over his shoulder, a limp, clinging zoo animal nuzzling his neck. "Will you be okay? To go up in the elevator?"

The front door was locked; the doorman must have been dozing inside and it took a few minutes of pressing the buzzer before he got up. In the meantime, she kept wrapping herself around Darryl; each time he detached or pried off her arms and legs, she would manage to fasten on to him again.

"Please don't make me go home alone."

"It would be taking advantage of you, in your present condition." He kissed the side of her cheek.

"In what present condition? You think I'm drunk? I might be a little drunk, but I remember what a great screw you were."

His face crumpled. "Is that what you think happened? That's all it was for you? I was a good screw?" He looked so hurt she had to say something.

"No, just kidding," she assured him. "I just thought you might want to come up with me—even for a drink, or something."

He was still somewhat suspicious. "I don't want to go home with you and have you tell me tomorrow that the only reason was because you didn't want to be alone. You must know by now I don't feel casual about you. I'm not that type of guy." The doorman had staggered over and was unbolting the front locks on the glass door. "I'll call you tomorrow. You free tomorrow evening?"

"You want to see me again?" Florence said. "Or are you just saying that to get rid of me?"

"No, I want to see you again!" He was mildly irritated yet at the same time almost swooning with delight; he had waited for years for this.

"Okay, but tomorrow night we'll go to where I want to go. No more Russian . . . vodka factories."

"You do the choosing."

The doorman was looking out at them sleepily. Mustering what little dignity she could, she turned and went in. "I hope you have a wonderful evening," she said exaggeratedly. "Drive safely!"

There wasn't a single message on the answering machine. If she hadn't gone away, she would have sat in the dark apartment without speaking to a soul. For half an hour she paced back and forth, picking up old magazines and catalogs, only to realize she had read them all before. The words wiggled around the page. There was no central air-conditioning in the building and the two rooms were hot and stuffy. She turned on the unit in her bedroom window. Then she remembered something. She went to the kitchenette and opened the freezer: half a quart of chocolate–chocolate chip ice cream. She grabbed a spoon and got into bed. When she plunged her spoon methodically into the hardened mass, like a miner picking at chunks of coal, her mouth filled with the darkly bittersweet coolness. She ate blindly, unable to stop herself, no different from a butterfly repetitively plunging its proboscis, or a leopard tearing at a carcass. Such animal bliss! If only life could be lived in this state of pure being.

Then she felt sick, not physically but mentally. The ice cream was gone. She studied the back label over and over. There were more than four hundred calories in a cup. She must have consumed nearly three cups. Twelve hundred calories of pure fat. It had taken so little time to consume; the delicious taste had already vanished. But the calories would remain.

For a long time she couldn't fall asleep. Her bed was spinning. It was as if, having had a respite from thinking, her mind was going to punish her by working overtime. How could she have slept with John? But maybe they really were getting divorced: he would marry her, there would be gossip for a time, but it would all pass and she would be a member of that world inhabited by the right sort of people, the only world there was to inhabit in New York.

What contempt people would have for her if they could hear

her thoughts. Women—modern women—were not supposed to think this way; they were supposed to be tough, interested in their careers, cultural events. In the world she inhabited, a woman should think of mountain climbing, snowboarding, playing pool or volleyball. Romance was girlie stuff; being honest about wanting money and acceptance through marriage was contemptible. But meanwhile, of course, all those women who were on white-water rafting trips, or fly-fishing and surfing, were just trying to prove they weren't like the others—they were one of the guys. And what was the point of that, except to please men?

The stale glow from the night light by the bathroom door illuminated the blue-and-white-striped curtains blowing in front of the air conditioner, back and forth, back and forth, slapping restlessly like small boats on waves.

When she woke it was after one in the afternoon. She was freezing cold; the bedclothes were almost entirely on the floor and the air-conditioning unit blasted icy, damp air on her head. She put on her pink chenille dressing gown and staggered into the kitchen. Even in the living room it was cold. She put the kettle on the gas stove for tea and opened the window. A sickly pigeon that had been resting on the window ledge flew off in a violent flap of wings, leaving behind a puddle of greenish goo. It was cold outside too. Overnight the temperature had dropped, as if it were a fall day, with a crisp wind and bright blue sky.

She realized she was starving. She put an English muffin, left in a bag on the counter, slightly dried and curled around the edges, into the toaster. No butter in the refrigerator, just a bit of hardened Camembert cheese, mostly rind. She got out a knife. Her head felt as if it had been sand-papered on the inside. In the front hall the message light on the answering machine was blinking. There was a message from Max Coho—she knew him from Quayle's; he was often in there doing research or covering various auctions—leaving his phone number. "Call me, sweetie." He wrote for an antiques magazine, but it was a well-known fact he supplied gossip to the tabloids. There were two hang-ups, and the last from Darryl, saying he would be out all day but would come by to pick her up at seven.

She didn't have a clue how she was going to get out of seeing him. She supposed she could just not be there when he arrived; if she wanted to be polite, she could leave a message with the doorman. There was no way she wanted to see him again. She remembered pouring vodka down his throat at that club while holding his nose, and then trying to kiss him, to the general applause of a number of others at their table. Then something else came back to her—dancing with that fat red-faced man and leaving him to try to haul Darryl over to dance with her. When he wouldn't she sat on his lap and . . . then what?

She stumbled down the hall in search of some aspirin. The tea kettle was screaming as if it were being mutilated. In a way, she supposed, it was—its underside was being burned. The mirror was old and blistered, and the fixture above it had frosted glass dusty with bugs, making her face look even more greenish.

The phone rang. She scurried to answer it before the machine picked up. The place still smelled faintly of cat, faintly fishy. Some previous occupant of the place must have had one, or perhaps from next door oily yellow urine oozed in through the walls. At various times she had scrubbed everything in the room, but the odor lingered, the smell of sour rage. "Hallo, Florence." A man's voice, Italian accent. "Do you remember me?"

"Oh, gosh." It was that man from dinner last night, which already seemed like an event that had taken place several years before. "Is it, uh . . . Tony?" She lied deliberately; why should he arrogantly assume she would remember him and instantly know who he was?

"No."

"Oh, I'm sorry! Of course, Salvatore, how are you?"

To her satisfaction, she could tell he was irritated. "It's Raffaello di Castignolli. You have disappeared so suddenly last evening, I thought you have gone out or to sleep, and when I called the house today they said you had gone back to the city."

"Yes," she said. "I had a little emergency."

"Mm. I am hearing all about this emergency."

"How did you get my phone number?"

"That is my secret. So. I am still out here, in the Hamptons, but will be back tonight, and thought perhaps you will join me for a late supper."

"Oh, that would be wonderful! What time?"

"Well, that is the problem. I do not know how the traffic will be. What I am proposing, I will give you a call when I get in and we can make a plan."

She drank her tea and ate her muffin with melted cheese. It was like eating a delicious bit of rusted metal; the edges of the hard muffin cut into her mouth. How she loved foods that caused pain. Perhaps she was a food masochist, she thought. If there was something fiery, with hot peppers, or something with sharp edges, it was her dream meal. It was a way of proving she was alive, to have tears running down her cheeks without emotional anguish, to self-inflict pain that was primarily pleasure.

There was a huge stack of mail on her desk—unpaid bills, letters from the executor of her mother's estate in California. Apparently everything had been settled and she was to expect nothing more. She was pinched by a sudden twinge of remorse. She missed her mother. How dissatisfied she had been by her when she was alive. Her mother had been so paralyzed by her fears, by what people would say. There had been no sense of adventure for her, only terror. Her life had been spent in trying out the latest recipes and in trying to do the right thing. If her mother had, even once, for a second, understood how unimportant it all was, that the only way to live life was to go out and grab what you wanted!

Other envelopes contained various requests for money—an

animal shelter, public television, a home for drug-addicted teens—or to buy tickets for what must have been every benefit being held in New York through the fall: the Cinderella Diabetes Foundation, the Princess Helena of Albania Foundation, the Make a Dream Come True Foundation. But she ignored these and instead looked over an article in a decorating magazine about bathrooms in the homes of twelve wealthy people around the world. One appeared to have been designed to resemble a milking station on a high-tech dairy farm. Another was like a fallout shelter in the event of nuclear disaster. One, in a château, used ancient terracotta tiles. The photo caption explained that these tiles were available for twelve dollars each from a small French company that still manufactured them by hand.

She opened a glossy magazine—ostensibly related to current events, but really featuring only gossip—whose cover was always devoted to a movie star. This month's cover showed a mutt-faced actress in bright red lipstick, posing pretentiously, above a caption that read, "*The* mesmerizing beauty of **Ibis**." Disgusted, Florence skimmed the article. Ibis, twenty-three, came from an incredible family: her mother, an English aristocrat and well-known beauty, had once been married to an English pop star before marrying Ibis's father, an ornithology professor at Oxford. Ibis had been a brilliant actress since age fifteen. The other children in the family were named Shrike, Pheasant, Mädchen, Vireo and Warbler. Oh, in such cool bliss did the family live, roaming the grounds of their four-thousand-acre estate and their private Caribbean island, climbing Mount Everest, discovering a new species of sparrow, performing their own concertos to one another. And Ibis, the beautiful Ibis, now getting seven million dollars a film, and the reporter who had written the piece so clearly in love that he was unable to say one bad word. Ibis was beautiful (except that no matter how hard Florence stared, she still had the crunched-up face of a turkey); Ibis was comfortable with selecting the most perfect wine from any wine list. Exquisite conversation poured from Ibis's lips: she had already been married to a Nepalese prince and was about to marry a handsome French movie star of art films who had recently crossed over into the big time of action-adventure pictures. In his free time he produced and directed Feydeau farce.

By the time she finished reading the article, if Florence had seen Ibis on the street, she would have strangled her quite happily. She stuck her head out the window, half hoping Ibis would walk by and she could assist in sending her on to her next incarnation (Ibis believed in reincarnation and had studied in a Tibetan lamasery, the only woman accepted by all five hundred monks).

It was like a disease, to read these things and be filled with such spite and venom—or perhaps it was more similar to an addiction. But if it was a disease, or an addiction, she had never heard anyone else talk about it or mention how she could obtain a cure.

It was still cool out, at least that was how it felt from up here on the thirteenth floor. She showered and quickly changed into a pink cashmere-and-silk T-shirt, a black miniskirt and a pair of black suede boots that came up to her knees. Normally on a Sunday she would have put on a different outfit and gone to the gym or for a run around the reservoir. But her head hurt too much for that. She headed down Madison, walking, for her, quite slowly. The only people around were those who came into Manhattan for the day as tourists, loud, badly dressed, lugging shopping bags filled with the same items they could have bought out on Long Island or in New Jersey but which obviously held more cachet if purchased here; or residents who were too poor to go away for the weekend, who didn't own or rent a country house or hadn't been invited as guests. The parks and piers were crowded with nearly naked men and women, wearing the tiniest bathing suits imaginable, sitting in the dirt and on the dried-up grass that stank of dog urine. It always struck Florence as odd. When she was a child her mother made her change from shorts to a skirt or long pants if they went into town. It seemed lewd, provocative and unsanitary to display oneself in such a fashion.

Obviously summer was not what it once had been. There had

been a few years when she was a child during which she and her mother would visit her grandparents in Maine; they lived on a little island where during the summer the sunny days numbered only a few and in the winter, if they went up over Christmas, never came at all. Nevertheless, she had loved it there: the icy water of the little bay, the walk up the cliff through the pine trees, the osprey fishing for dinner for its young in the nest at the top of the tallest tree. She would go out to pick nearly rotten raspberries from a glade where they had spread and gone wild over the years. Her grandmother would make a pie, laden with seeds; over the brilliant fuchsia slices they poured thick cream. Her grandparents had lived on nothing their whole lives: slivers of pie, *The Saturday Evening Post* and *Yankee* magazine, volunteer-fire-department pancake suppers, the seasons changing from silver-gray to ash-blue. And they were seemingly content. But such contentment, once an element like water or air, no longer existed on the planet. Perhaps the supply had been used up or burned away when the hole in the ozone layer developed. Her grandfather had a heart attack; her grandmother, cancer. Her mother had to sell the place, for a nominal sum. With her mother's generation the grains of dissatisfaction had been planted, an invasive species that grew in Florence like kudzu. By high school she realized that no matter what women filled their lives with, there was still no status for them apart from whomever—whatever—they married.

She cut through the park. The sound of tribal drums thumped through the Bethesda Fountain plaza. A dirty man lugged a huge sack of grain, feeding the birds. He was known as the Birdman—rumor had it that he lived in a mansion and had spent his fortune feeding the pigeons and fighting tickets in court. Feeding the birds was illegal. They were disgusting things anyway, witless sacks constructed only to defecate and reproduce.

Men kept turning to stare at her; some stopped jogging, one fell off his bicycle, a tiny Latin hunchback followed her all the way past Strawberry Fields. She kept thinking that if she walked faster she wouldn't have to think. She came out of the park on the West Side and began walking toward the river. When she turned a corner a gust of wind, scented with pot roast and cabbage, blew down West End Avenue—the smell of dark apartments in which tiny old-fashioned clocks chimed the hours—and she was overcome with nostalgia for something she had never experienced.

8

She jumped into a taxi and went back over to Fifth Avenue. She started to walk home, but when she passed an expensive department store, she went in without even thinking what she was doing. The whole place had been built in cement, with imitation Japanese architectural elements; every floor had only two or three items. She went over to a glass display case of sunglasses. "May I see those, please?" she asked the salesclerk, pointing. She definitely needed sunglasses; she hadn't been able to find her old ones in months, and the other pairs she had weren't flattering or were out of style. She liked these so much she decided to get a couple of extra pairs. "At least when I lose a pair I won't have to feel so bad, since I'll still have the others," she said out loud, picking out the same style in tortoiseshell, black, and dark navy with royal blue splotches. "Can I put them on my card, please?"

She supposed she should have inquired as to the price first: they were two hundred and eighty dollars apiece. But she would be damned if now that the salesperson was ringing them up, she would make an idiot of herself and tell her to undo the charge. Besides, it wasn't all that much money; she would rather have three really good pairs of sunglasses that she could wear for years, and that would average out to be inexpensive, than to buy something she didn't like and would never use. As the salesperson was putting each pair into a fancy stainless-steel case and wrapping it in tissue, she heard someone calling her name. "Florence?"

It was Allison Thomas, with a stroller and moony-faced baby. "Allison? What are you doing in town on a Sunday in July?"

"Oh, Archie's taking us on a canal boat through France for three weeks. We're leaving tonight. It's the only vacation he could think of that his parents might enjoy. So I came back from the country on Friday to get ready. What are you doing?"

"I was staying with Natalie and John—you know them, the de Jonghs?"

"Sure."

"I had a big fight with Natalie. She threw me out."

"You're kidding." Allison had always resembled a B starlet. Now, she looked at Florence inquisitively. "Do you want to go and get a coffee?"

"Okay," Florence said.

"What about if we just went down to the basement? You know, they've opened that Japanese teahouse downstairs."

"Did you finish your shopping?"

"I was looking for a new bathing suit. But I didn't see any I liked. What did you get?" Florence pointed to the sunglasses in the display cabinet. "Oh, those are nice. Maybe I should get a pair. Do you think those would look good on me?"

"Try them on." Allison could buy whatever she wanted without thinking twice. "I think you should try on those round ones. They would go with the shape of your face better."

Allison put them on. "Do you think? I don't know."

"I like them. I think the blue glass is a nice color for you."

"What about these? Do you think they would look good on Archie?"

She could barely remember what Allison's husband looked like. "Is it the kind of thing he would wear?"

"I don't know. He's always telling me to buy him things when I shop, but then he never ends up wearing it. Actually, I think he only likes Ray•Bans, this one particular style." Allison handed the glasses back to the salesclerk. "Oh, forget it." She bent over the red-headed infant. "Plum-bun, we're going to go down and have some cake and cookies now, if you behave yourself."

"Where are your other kids?" Florence held open the elevator door.

"The nanny took them to the circus. Thank God she's coming on the trip. Archie's sister is coming with her two kids, one of them is bringing a friend, that's six kids all together under the age of nine; I begged Sara to bring her own nanny, but she said her nanny was going on vacation—I know it's just her way of getting a free nanny out of the situation."

"How many will be on this boat?"

"The six kids, Archie and I, Sara and her husband, Archie and Sara's parents, the nanny—how many is that?—and then the crew of the boat, which also has a chef and a couple of people from the tour company. Supposedly this trip is really fabulous. They do everything for you—the boat just goes along up the canals, very slowly—and if you want to get out and bicycle, they arrange bikes for you, and a picnic lunch; or if you want to go sightseeing, they take you by van and you meet up with the boat later in the day farther down the canal. It was the only kind of vacation thing Archie could think of that all the different generations would enjoy. It is expensive, but not all that much—I think we figured it at about five hundred dollars per person per day for the three weeks, plus the first-class airfare, but that includes everything."

The Japanese teahouse was in a glass structure in a kind of underground center atrium. Florence felt as if she were in an aquarium: a sheet of running water formed a fountain along one wall, the tiny tables were coral-colored wood and black-and-purple lacquer. The waitresses were all Japanese, dressed in shroud-like Japanese designer outfits. They managed to appear like superior entities despite their lowly status as waitresses. She supposed it was cultural; they must feel superior simply by virtue of being Japanese—things could always be worse, at least they were not loud, oversized, pasty-faced Caucasians, reeking of milk and meat. A couple of menus were delivered to their table; Allison, who had clumsily parked the stroller alongside, knelt to show one of them to the infant. "Look!" She pointed to a picture. "Doesn't this cake look nice? Pink and green! Or would you rather have bean-curd ice cream in the shape of a bunny rabbit, Plumbun?" The child's bright blue eyes widened slightly—his or her red hair stuck straight up like a Kewpie doll's—but it said nothing.

"How old is . . . he?"

"George's two and a half," Allison said, sitting down on the tiny pink three-legged stool that passed as seating. "He still hasn't spoken a word and his hair has never grown—he was born with it—but the psychologists at his school say he's incredibly bright. So it's just a wait-and-see, at this point. Einstein didn't speak a word until he was five years old. Isn't that right, Plummy?"

"And how old are your other two now?"

"May is seven, Thomasina is five."

Allison was a couple of years younger than she, about thirty. For a brief period they had been friends—they went out at night trying to pick up men, they went to the races at Saratoga Springs and stayed with friends of Allison's. In her early twenties Allison worked for a downtown newspaper, but she was living with a much older wealthy man who owned an Upper East Side restaurant. She wore thrift-store motorcycle jackets and her hair chopped off in spikes. Then she met Archie: he made her move in with her parents. Almost overnight she traded in her goofy glasses for contact lenses, grew her hair into a respectable chin-length and married Archie in a quiet ceremony—"for the immediate family only, Florence, I'm sorry, but that's Archie!" She had the first baby at twenty-three. And their friendship, for all intents and purposes, was over. When they were both single they could go out hunting for men, a pair of cheetahs; without this pursuit there was nothing to keep them together.

Arch was twenty years older than Allison and managed a hugely successful mutual fund. Florence couldn't understand it. It was true that Allison came from a very good family, but why had Archie selected someone not a part of his world and then made her conform to it? He had basically forbidden Allison to see her again; in fact, Allison had to drop all her old friends—everyone she associated with now had to be selected or vetted by Arch. It seemed that Archie had decided, somewhere along the line, that when he reached a certain age he would find a zany girl from a good background and marry her. And Allison must not have been quite so unusual as she wanted people to believe or she wouldn't have let herself be molded quite so quickly.

Yet why hadn't Archie wanted *her*? She remembered she had screwed him a couple of times before he moved on to Allison. She could have been living Allison's existence, happily married—or at least married and established, never needing to worry about money again—if Archie had chosen her over Allison. He had seemed so dry and deadly at the time; he reminded her of an insect casing. Now, nearly ten years later, she would have taken financial security and social respectability even if dry-and-deadly came buttered alongside.

"Look, Pup-cake, isn't the cake pretty?"

The waitress had delivered a quivering mound of artificially colored cake—or perhaps it was some kind of pudding carved to resemble a sand castle with turrets. Florence had ordered a sea-weed-and-carrot-flavored shake; a shred of kelp spumed out the top of the glass. "How about you?" Allison said. "How have you been? Seeing any guys? Why did Natalie kick you out?"

"She's crazy!" Florence said. "I don't know if she's paranoid—or going through menopause—she's a lot older than us, you know—"

"Oh, Crumb-ka! You're getting the cake all over your new outfit, you haven't even worn it once!" Allison daubed frantically at George's blue-striped shirt, a miniature version of the outfit worn by sailors from Marseilles in the twenties. "Oh, God, there's even cake on the hat!" The hat did not quite go with the outfit: it was a little red felt crown, with shiny orbs.

She felt desperate; if only Allison would pay attention to her. Once they had been so close. She was certain Allison knew plenty of guys to introduce her to; someone from a slightly different circle who would be viewing her for the first time, to whom she would still appear fresh. "The truth is, John sort of . . . broke into my room the first night and practically raped me. He told me they were getting divorced."

Allison looked up brightly. "You're kidding!" She began popping bits of George's gelatin into her mouth. "Getting divorced? I didn't hear anything about this. Why didn't you just tell him to get lost, Toots?"

"I don't know," Florence said grimly. "I suppose I felt sorry for him. It all seemed so unreal. I mean, I couldn't believe they would treat a guest like this. She basically locked me up in the storage room and then let her husband break in and screw me. Plus, he told me he was in love with me. And the worst part is, he promised to invest some money for me."

Allison looked delighted. It would be something she could tell Arch about on the plane, Florence thought, wishing she hadn't said anything. At least they would be out of town for three weeks. Maybe by that time she would have forgotten all about it and not repeat the story back in New York. "How awful!" Allison said. "Of course, John's always basically screwed around, but I thought Natalie read him the riot act. There's no way he would ever leave

Natalie. It's all her money, you know, and she would get every-thing."

"Is it her money? I thought it was his?"

"No."

"Allison, don't you know any guys for me? There must be somebody Archie works with who's single and eligible."

"Oh, gosh, I'll have to think." Allison's mouth dropped open, indicating such a task was hopeless. She had always had a reces-sive chin, Florence thought bitterly, tempted to suggest she look into plastic surgery. "Let me think about it. I'll ask Archie." Al-lison rose, leaving the table a disaster of goo and crumbs. "Do you have enough cash, Florence? I should probably get going and I don't see the waitress anywhere in sight. Archie'll kill me if I'm not all packed. He gets so nervous before a flight." She wheeled the stroller toward the elevator door, then stopped and turned around. "Are you going to Kathy's baby shower?"

"Who?"

"Katherine—Katherine Monckton. It's the night after we get back—her baby's due a couple of days later."

"I didn't even know she was pregnant! Who's the father?"

"Remember that guy she used to go out with, when we were all friends? She got back together with him. She says she doesn't want to marry him, though—I guess she doesn't want to have to end up paying alimony. Anyway, I can't believe you weren't invited. I'm speaking to Victoria before I leave; she's giving the party. I'll make sure she invites you."

She wasn't sure if Allison's attitude was one of *noblesse oblige* or if she was just being paranoid. With a regal wave Allison turned away and pushed her carriage into the waiting elevator. And re-flected back at Florence on the mirrored walls were a thousand Allisons, with her thousand chattering faces; a thousand Plum-buns, sullen in their thousand strollers; a thousand shopping bags, each matte black, pale gray tissue spilling out the top, reflecting a million dollars.

———

The drinks and cakes came to thirty-two dollars. She put it on her credit card. On her way out she passed Allison, with the baby stroller occupying the whole aisle, alongside one of the cosmetic counters—all the lipsticks and shadows came in ornate rococo cases shaped like shells, studded with semiprecious stones. Allison smiled weakly over at her and quickly averted her eyes back to the contents of the counter. The rituals of greeting in Manhattan were peculiar. It was entirely possible—had Allison not been leaving town—that the following evening they might have seen each other in a restaurant or at a cocktail party and acted as if they had never met before. Or, conversely, extended shrill cries of joy and profusely kissed and hugged. Such interaction was based on mood, location, whom one or the other was with and degree of despair. Things did not work this way just with Allison but with everyone. But, remarkably, the decision to kiss effusively, or act cold and disinterested, was somehow always arrived at mutually, even if the two parties involved were virtual strangers. And the fact that they were virtual strangers or genuine old friends had no bearing on the type of interaction.

She went up to the men's department and spent seven hundred dollars on a black cashmere crew-neck sweater, three hundred fifty dollars; two black T-shirts, fifty dollars each; a matelot shirt like the one worn by Allison's child, seventy dollars; and a pair of brown linen–silk-blend trousers with pleats and cuffs, on sale for two hundred. The items were all quite large. She wasn't entirely sure what she was doing. She somehow pictured herself with Raffaello, walking along a beach—Oregon? Amalfi?—the soft black sweater tied around his neck while the wind blew.

9

"I can't accept this," Darryl said, but he looked delighted. Didn't he understand it was given out of guilt, as a means of getting rid of him? It was no different than in the old days, when a man gave a woman a piece of jewelry or a fur to signify the end of an affair.

"If you're going to devote your life to doing ridiculous good deeds, at least you can look like a successful good-deed doer," she said. She felt angry. She hadn't really intended to give the things to Darryl. Why had she bought them? She knew as soon as she got home it would be insane to give them to the Italian; it would only frighten him. She should have put them in her drawer until Christmas, when hopefully they would be having a real relationship. But getting a present for him now would only jinx things. "Also, Darryl, you should do something about your hair."

"What's wrong with my hair?" She was beginning to suspect her present had misfired. He ran his fingers over his head, brooding, but obviously willing to make changes, thinking it was going to get her into bed.

"Quit blow-drying it. And get a decent haircut."

He looked sulky, but he changed into the clothes she had bought and came out of the bathroom modeling sheepishly.

"Oh, you look good," she said. "A different person." He resembled a dark, skinny cherub now, an artist or maybe a businessman in film, his waist emphasized by the pleated pants and the tucked-in black T-shirt. It was true the items were several sizes too large, but for some reason he didn't look ridiculous. "You need a belt. And don't get some cheap belt either."

He ran his hands over the black sweater held in his outstretched hands. "I don't know. Why did you do this, Florence? Was it expensive?"

"It's cashmere!" she said indignantly. He began to neatly fold the crummy clothes he had been wearing and put them into the department-store bag. "Oh, God. Just throw that stuff away! It's hideous," she said.

"I mean, I could return the stuff and use the money to get a fax machine for my office. Or give the money to someone to take their kids out of the city and go to the country for a few days." But she could tell he didn't mean it; he looked uncomfortable in the outfit but also mischievous—the clothes represented some attachment to her.

He put the bag down on the table and crossed the room. She thought he was going to kiss her on the cheek, but his mouth was aimed for hers. "Come on, let's go," she said, pushing him away. "I'm not in the mood. It was just a present. I can't stay out long. We'll just go for a drink."

Sunday night, the Oceanic Café was nearly empty. She sat down at the bar and gestured to Darryl to do the same. "Hi, Dave," she said to the bartender. "How's it going?"

"Everybody's still on Long Island," he said. "What are you drinking?"

"I'm not sure," she said. "A glass of white wine, I guess."

"Nothing for me," Darryl said.

"Nothing?"

"Okay, I'll have a beer." Why did he have to be so quick to try to please her? It was like having a really dumb Labrador retriever when what she wanted was a rogue Afghan hound, blond, long-legged, scampish and wild.

"What kind?" Dave chanted a long list of the various beers available. Darryl looked nervous.

"How long did you say you were in this country?" Florence asked.

"Always so many decisions," Darryl said. "By the time I am hearing what there is, I have forgotten what I wanted." She didn't find the fake Russian accent amusing. Under the bright track lights she saw that the space between his eyes, just above his nose, was wrinkled and furrowed like a frightened baby chimp, and she wondered what she was doing with him. He made no effort to ask her any questions, just sat staring at her with the expression of a woozy deer.

"So has it been this quiet all summer?" she asked Dave as he handed them the drinks.

"During the week it's unbelievable," he said. "Weekends, it's been like this. Wait till around ten o'clock, though, you'd be surprised how many come in for dinner when they get back."

The café catered to a slightly older, more upscale clientele than many of the other restaurants along the avenue nearby, all of which seemed to be packed with hordes of recent college graduates newly arrived in Manhattan to make it on Wall Street. Just then Max Coho came in. He was with a rather oversized girl.

She waved him hello. "Florence!" he said, coming over to the bar and kissing her. "How are you! Can we sit here with you, or is this some kind of romantic date?"

"Sit down, sit down," she said, pointing to the barstool next to her. There was only one extra stool on this side of the bar—someone was going to have to bring a stool around from the other side.

"This is my friend Tracer Schmidt," he said, pointing to the giantess. "Tracer, Florence." Everything about her appeared large—she was probably close to six feet, neither pretty nor plain, with thin brown hair slicked back under a headband. Max had the shiny good looks—weak, spoiled—of a prep school boy: he had gone to Princeton and was working on a novel, in addition to writing for *Antiques and Collectibles* magazine.

"This is . . ." She had momentarily forgotten Darryl's name. It was embarrassing, but there it was, a blank spot in her head when she looked at him, just as if a portion of a recording had been erased. Fortunately, he turned to Tracer and, introducing himself, began to chat with her, off to one side.

"Ooh, where'd you get this one, Florence?" Max said.

"What do you mean?" Florence said defensively.

"He's really cute. Just my type."

"I don't think he's interested."

"You'd be surprised. Three-fourths of my boyfriends started out saying they were straight. Actually, I've never been attracted to straight men. It only leads to trouble. But for some reason, they take one look at me and decide to change."

"Max, do you know a guy named Raffaello di Castignolli?" Florence asked, changing the subject.

"Yeah," said Max. "I mean, I've met him. He's a count, or something. Or, as Chico Marx would say, he's no-a-count! His family owns a huge vineyard, in Tuscany. I used to hang out with him at the U.S. Open. Why?"

"No reason. I just met him."

"Where?" Max had an exaggeratedly coy way of asking questions, as if he were pretending to be a five-year-old.

"At Natalie de Jongh's."

"He's completely unreliable," Max said. "He screws a different girl every night. I think he's got a coke problem, or something." He looked her up and down. "I'd say you're too old for him. He likes them in their twenties. You're out of your league if you think he's going to settle down with you. You better make your selection fast, Florence, if it's going to happen at all. What's wrong with poor old Darryl?"

"That's just it," said Florence.

Max giggled. "The musical chairs are running out fast, Flossy!"

"Gosh you're vicious."

"Am I?" Max was delighted. "I think I'm just honest."

"Hi!" Tracer said nervously. She had been standing alongside them, shuffling back and forth. "Excuse me for just a minute?" She headed in the direction of the women's room.

"Where'd *you* get *that* one?" Florence said.

"Old Tracer?" said Max. "She's got millions. She's got *sooooo* much money! She just moved here. I knew her from college. I've offered to help her adjust, take her out, you know? She just bought an apartment in the San Remo. She wasn't planning to buy an apartment, but it was only four million and she said it was such a good buy she couldn't afford not to do it. I'm living with her for the time being. There's, like, fifteen bedrooms in the place."

"Tracer," she said. "What a fake name. I'm sure her name was originally Susan. Anybody who has one of those names—a man's name, you know, like girls who call themselves Douglas or Mitchell"—she knew one of each—"or women who call themselves Stockard or Sigourney—you know when they were born their parents didn't hold up a little blond baby and say, 'Oh, let's name her Stevens.' All those girls, their parents named them Susan. They always hated being a Susan, so when they went to college they either renamed themselves or took their middle name, their mother's maiden name, whatever. But no matter what they call themselves, all you have to do is look at them and you can see they're a Susan."

She realized she probably sounded quite nasty. There didn't seem to be any way around it. As soon as she said aloud what she thought, she came across as an unpleasant bitch. Women were supposed to spend their whole lives making themselves sound likable, trying to be liked. They could deny it, but the desire to be likable was so ingrained they no longer knew the truth. They were spending their lives as cunning supplicants. There were various categories: women who wanted to be liked by men and women, women who wanted to be liked only by men and were therefore nasty to women. Then there were the women in New York who considered themselves powerful: they were nasty to women and nasty to men—but only the sort of men who actually enjoyed this, hired lackeys, usually gay, who enjoyed the boot in the face. These men had taken on the role of women, trying to be likable. Being likable took a tremendous amount of energy. Every day consisted of multiple failures. Now, almost certainly, Max would see to it she paid for her words.

Max leaned over and began to whisper to Darryl. Wait until he finds out he's an advocate for the homeless, Florence thought, although she wasn't entirely certain whether this would bother Max or not. When Tracer came back from the women's room, she took the stool next to Florence and looked at her eagerly. "So what do you do?" Florence asked.

"I'm trying to start up a magazine," Tracer said. "On the World Wide Web."

"On what subject?" she muttered.

"It's going to be a sports program," Tracer said. "I've hired Max to help me."

"Great," Florence said. Darryl caught her eye. He was desperate. He had gotten separated from her by two barstools. Max had stopped talking to him. Suddenly she no longer wanted him either. What could she have been thinking of? He wasn't even that good-looking. Maybe she could escape now by leaving him with Tracer. She wouldn't know any better; that would fix Max, too, by dumping him with a sincere midget. Not that Darryl was a midget, exactly, but he couldn't have been much taller than five six. Probably if

Max had appeared interested in him, she might have fought for him. Anyway, it didn't matter—Max wasn't interested, and now she couldn't be. Well, he had all those expensive clothes, at least that was some recompense for her jerking him around. She rose. "Darryl, I've got to go," she said. "It was great to see you. You met Tracer, didn't you? Tracer, it's okay if Darryl stays here with you and Max, isn't it?"

"We were going downtown to meet—" Max named a famous retired tennis player. "We're trying to get him to write for Tracer's magazine." He half whined in despair. Why did he care if he had to take Darryl along? He must know he would be doing her a favor. A sulky expression came over Max's face. "Tracer, Florence said you changed your name from Susan."

"I didn't say you changed your name, Susan," Florence said. "I mean, Tracer."

"Yes, you did." Max smirked.

"No, I said that a lot of women with boys' names changed their name from Susan."

Tracer had turned white. Her nose was even shinier than before. It seemed to Florence that a little powder or foundation wouldn't have hurt Tracer's appearance. She didn't want to think of herself as judgmental—she had always told herself that if some women didn't want to wear makeup, that was fine—but now she found herself doing a private remodeling job on the poor girl. The first thing she would have done if she were as wealthy as Tracer would be to fix that nose of hers. Tracer glared at her with hatred, as if she could hear what Florence was thinking. "We should get going," she said to Max.

"That's okay," Florence said. "Darryl can tag along, can't he?" She grabbed Tracer's forearm. "He's such a hunk. I'd take him home, but I promised some idiot I'd meet him later."

Tracer was baffled, torn between needing to win Max's approval and wanting to bring Darryl. He really was attractive, with a boyish magnetism. She was about to speak, but Darryl interrupted. He addressed Florence. "No, I must see you home."

"Oh, don't worry," Florence said. "You have a car, don't you? Why don't you give Tracer and Max a ride downtown?"

Tracer seemed to have made up her mind. "Yeah, give us a ride downtown, Darryl. At least come in with us for a drink."

Tracer could afford to take on a guy who's an unpaid lawyer for the homeless, Florence thought as she walked back to her building. She's so rich and plain, she'll have to settle for someone poor and good-looking.

And she saw herself, for a split second, living in a huge apartment in the San Remo that she owned, with huge, spacious rooms, beautifully furnished with antiques that were neither too formal and fussy nor too rustic and primitive; some good oriental rugs; a couch covered in rumpled dusty gray-green velvet; herself in a soft Chinese robe, entertaining and impressing a few select friends. The husband—perhaps a talented, successful artist, with a studio downtown—carrying out a tray of drinks. She would have a house in the Hamptons too!

She didn't know why she felt so sick. It wasn't her problem. Darryl's wounded, stricken expression, those intense blue eyes that looked at her so sorrowfully, as if he would go on loving her even though she had broken his heart—she hardly knew the guy! She didn't have what *she* wanted; why did it have to be her fault that he didn't have what *he* wanted.

The answering machine was broadcasting when she walked in the door, a man's voice blaring in the dark little hall, and she ran to pick up the receiver. "Ah, you are home." It was the Italian. "I am back a little earlier than I expected. I was saying, if you are free, to come for dinner. I'm in the restaurant now, with some friends."

She jumped into a taxi and was on her way downtown.

IO

East Prussia, the restaurant, was crowded with people who were stunningly good-looking by virtue of their clean, expensive, fashionable clothes and crisp haircuts—less than perfect facial features were turned to advantage by being subtly emphasized as aristocratic or endearing traits. If men needed glasses, they wore large rectangular frames in black, mocking or reviving the sixties (Peter Sellers, Yves Saint Laurent), or tiny tortoiseshell spectacles identical to those of their great-grandfathers. A woman with a huge nose wore her hair scalped back and held her head proudly, as if imitating Lady Ottoline Morrell or Diana Vreeland. A short, withered man who might have been put together with Krazy Glue acted as if his dissipation had been acquired deliberately and at much cost. Usually Florence took a quick survey of any room and judged herself the most attractive woman, but for the first time she thought she looked ordinary, and that she belonged in some Midwest beauty pageant whose entrants would only be sneered at here.

He was handsomer than she had remembered, but to her disappointment he was at a table with three women and two men. He rose to greet her, then introduced her—the women gave her cold, brittle smiles, their eyes dead with disappointment equal to hers. "This is my friend Michelle, visiting from Argentina," Raffaello said, "and my cousin Paola, from Italy, and her friend Letizia, also from Italy. And this is Tommaso, and Marco, so you are alone in being an American. Sit down. We have already ordered, I'm afraid. We were all starving. Are you very hungry?" He flicked his wrist and a waitress appeared with a menu. She was of Thai ancestry, or Vietnamese, dressed in a skimpy black outfit, in dark red lipstick, impossibly beautiful. Florence looked at her with jealousy. She could bet that Raffaello would get the waitress's phone number at some point in the evening. Already he was smiling at her. "And another champagne glass for the lady," he said. The most beautiful waitresses worked at the most fashionable restaurants. It was a position similar to working at an art gallery or auction house: advertising oneself as available for marriage. The difference was, the waitresses all claimed to be actresses, while those in the galleries were scheming or claiming to scheme to become consultants for private collectors.

The group were chattering among themselves in Italian, probably about the waitress. In New York the Italians gathered with the Italians, the French with the French, the English with the English, and so on; though they had left their countries and moved to New York, some temporarily and some permanently, they could not feel comfortable with Americans. The trick was to have as little to do with them as possible—the Americans, even the New Yorkers, were so provincial, so lacking in humor. It was no different from a group of ex-pat Americans associating only with one another in Paris or in London; after all, it was the Americans who, even at the end of the twentieth century, continued to be unsophisticated. The foreigners lived in the city but felt superior to it; unlike the Americans, they did not have to take any of it seriously, they knew this place did not really exist at all.

The Italian conversation escalated into what sounded like a heated argument. Florence didn't mind being left out; it gave her a chance to recoup. She looked down at the menu. As soon as she no longer appeared to be paying attention, Raffaello began talking to her. "They are discussing the Giacometti retrospective at the Museum of Modern Art," he murmured, leaning over toward her ear. His aftershave seemed to reach paralyzing tentacles up her nose. "You have seen this exhibition?"

"I think I'll have the baby artichoke, Gorgonzola and tomato salad," she said, closing the menu.

"Is that all?" He raised his eyebrows as if she had made some terrible social error, but she ignored this. "Come with me for a moment, I must make a telephone call."

"You can't call by yourself?"

His nostrils flared slightly. "I would prefer your company." She took a swallow of champagne and rose stiltedly. "Take your glass, please. Excuse us for one moment, please." He half bowed to the others at the table. "I must place a call to Monica."

"Who's Monica?" she said as she followed him down the pink marble stairs at the back of the restaurant.

"Monica is my wife. Are you jealous?"

"No," she said. "Just disgusted."

"Why?"

She couldn't think. She supposed she was disgusted with herself, to rush downtown to have dinner on what she thought was a date, only to find herself with a married man and a group of his friends. She could hardly say this, however, as it would imply she *had* thought this was a date. But he saw through her all too clearly in any event. "So where is your wife?" she said, trying to cover up. "How come she couldn't come to dinner? Don't you let her?"

"My wife is in Venice, where she lives. We are separated. She has just had a baby. I am calling to find how they are doing as to their health. I hope to wake her for my little revenge."

"Who's baby is it?"

"Mine." The telephones were in glass sarcophagi in the back, beyond the toilets, and before she knew quite what was happening, he had pushed her in the booth ahead of him and had the back of his fist, sprinkled with a line of powder, under her nose. "Breathe!" He gave her a jab. "Breathe!" She inhaled; it was cocaine, fairly smooth. "Good, no? I am afraid it is all I have left, but I thought you would like some. You seem very nervous." He grinned his wolfish grin, a smirk of satisfaction.

"I'm not nervous!" But she was even more disgusted with herself—how could she not have known exactly what was going on? Going to the telephones or the bathroom with a man meant only one thing, and she had always done her best to avoid it—it was only too clear that to begin an evening this way was never going to lead to any genuine relationship. At least in this instance she didn't have to worry; a married Italian with a new baby, even if separated from his wife, wasn't about to get a divorce and marry her. She hadn't meant to go out and start snorting coke on a Sunday night. If she was fortunate, that would be all the drugs he had.

Anyway, she couldn't feel entirely ungrateful. The air suddenly seemed brighter, rich in oxygen; it was as if she had been handed a pair of glasses without even knowing she needed them. She gave him a brisk smile.

"Good?" he said patronizingly. "That's all I have." He squeezed past her into the booth and sat on the stool, pulling her onto his lap while he dialed a colossal string of numbers, somehow managing to relight a fat cigar at the same time. He stroked her hair and the back of her neck while he jabbered away into the receiver in Italian. Her fingertips examined the faint, delineated stubble on his chin—he had obviously not shaved that day on purpose, a deliberate weekend look—but irritatedly he pushed her hand away. Such expensive clothing, a Sea Island cotton shirt, everything so crisp and heavily scented; she wondered what it would be like to grow up as a rich Italian boy. No doubt he had grown up in an average or ordinary apartment in Milan, on a family estate in Tuscany, whatever; experienced the same sort of daily activities—breakfast, soccer practice—as any growing boy. But what was so wrong or peculiar was the absence—in him, in them all—of what she thought of as emotion or affect.

He was shouting into the phone now. She would have thought he had forgotten all about her, except that he reached one hand up under her skirt and tried to pull her panties down as he half tilted her off his lap. She struggled to escape. For the longest time he held on to the elastic. It was hard to understand how she could feel flattered, aroused and annoyed all at the same time. One part of her—the nice girl—was indignant. The part with low self-esteem was pleased at the attention. And her body responded without any connection to her mind.

Just when it seemed he was determined to rip off her clothes right there in the public phone booth, she broke free. As she went back upstairs she turned to find him looking at her with an amused grin while he continued to argue, in Italian, into the phone.

II

When she returned everyone except Tommaso was smoking cigars. The women had skinny black ones that gave off a not-unpleasant odor. They stopped talking as she approached their table. The restaurant had been written up in the press as the first public smokers' club in the city; an updated incarnation of Josephine Baker prowled from table to table selling various forms of tobacco. Now she was sorry Raffaello didn't have any more coke. She had no idea what she was doing here, with this table of complete strangers. Tommaso was fat—at least pudgy—with the slinky, saturated, hooded-eye expression of a character in a Fellini film. He might have been forty-five. Marco was younger— perhaps younger than she—with longish hair and a sporty look, maybe the Italian equivalent of a surfer dude; he probably ran from the ski slopes of the Italian Alps to the windsurfing resorts of the Caribbean, or wherever these people windsurfed and raced cigarette boats.

She didn't even bother to inspect the women. She almost never did, actually. She could hardly think of a use for them. She had nothing in common with other women; if she began a conversation, it seemed invariably the other female curled her lip and turned away. She never got to the point with those of her gender where any real confidences were exchanged. Men could be drawn out, she could tease them; all in all, she felt more affinity with the opposite sex than her own. If a man told her something boring— the plot of a movie—it was a kind of wooing, a kind of intimacy. If a woman told her the plot of a movie, or details of her job, or plans for decorating a bedroom, what was in it for her?

The Italians, who had been staring at her, suddenly looked embarrassed and, *en masse,* began chattering again. Tommaso pulled out her chair and gestured for her to take her seat; she had left her champagne glass in the phone booth, but new glasses arrived and the waiter poured red wine. "I am afraid we were discussing your name. Do not take it personally, but for us, you understand, in Italy you would be called Firenze, you know, which is our city of Florence for you. So it is amusing to us; as Paola was saying, as if here a person was named Detroit."

Florence gave Paola a quick glance. It was impossible to guess if Paola was trying to be bitchy or if there was no hostility intended. In a way, every human interaction was a double effort: the first, to attempt to keep some conversation flowing; the second, to gauge the underlying intention of the words being used. The woman had to be forty-five. Often by that age women stopped being so hostile to other women; that she was a foreigner made her less easy to interpret. They were incredibly sophisticated, these Italian women. Paola's hair was casually polished, lopped off at the nape of her neck; she wore a pair of harlequin glasses in tortoiseshell, a gray mannish suit, beautifully, loosely tailored. Letizia was more glamorous, less arty. She wore a rope of huge moony pearls, crisp striped cotton dress, cashmere cardigan clipped fifties style, with a little chain at the neck. Michelle had on a black cocktail dress and looked as if she had stepped out of a Bunvel film.

Such spontaneously casual elegance; to look so perfect and so casual was a real accomplishment, elements of design intended purely to be noticed only by other women. It had to be that way: there were no men to notice. The gay men were too busy looking at other men; the straight men were looking only at the twenty-year-olds, or were already married and didn't dare.

Paola was still staring at her. She felt awkward. "I'm terribly sorry," said Paola. "I should have asked you sooner. Would you care for a cigar?"

"No, no thanks," Florence muttered.

"What did you say was your surname?" Tommaso said.

"Florence Collins."

"Oh!" He practically shrieked. "Collins, Collins! Do you know, I lived with Harry Collins for nearly four years?" He was trying to be friendly, but the wall of sound he produced succeeded only in blocking her out. Another European would have understood the code, jumped in to participate in the overly animated frenzy, like a flock of cockatoos descending on a field of grain.

"With who?"

"Harry Collins." This was pronounced "Hairy Coleens." "You do not know Harry? He looks so much like you, I thought you were perhaps related. Although you are more beautiful as a girl than Harry is as a man. Of course, he is a considerable amount older than you. He lives right here in New York. You are not related? He has the most beautiful apartment I have ever seen in this city. I decorated it for him. It is more than seventy thousand square feet."

"Seventy thousand?"

"Yes, believe it! He owns two entire floors of thirty-five thousand square feet in what was formerly and old bank on Wall Street. One floor, however, we devoted entirely to plants and birds. He loves birds, especially chickens."

"Chickens?"

"Oh!" Tommaso shrieked indignantly. "Chickens can be very beautiful! These are very fancy, rare chickens, with many plumes and colorful wattles. Wattles, you call them, yes? It was my idea, however, to raise orchids. Beautiful orchids, many of which are incredibly valuable."

"Orchids are beautiful. Chickens, I don't know."

"If you saw these chickens, you will change your mind. You must promise to come with me some day to view the chickens. I miss them terribly. Marco, weren't my chickens incredibly elegant and beautiful?" Marco shrugged and went on talking to the other women. "He knows nothing. He is interested only in mountain climbing. Do you like to mountain climb?"

"No. I mean, no."

"Good. Nor am I. So much work! To climb and climb, and then you are at the top of the mountain and must climb back down. I think it is silly, don't you agree?"

"Yes."

"So tell me, where do you know Raffaello? He is always meeting new people. What sort of business do you do?"

"I work at Quayle's—I'm in the jewelry department."

"Oh, I love jewelry! I have so much jewelry, which I have picked up on my travels over the years, and an extensive collection from the family—rubies, pearls and diamonds, that sort of thing—which I have been meaning to have appraised for the insurance. There is a marvelous diamond tiara which belonged to my great-grandmother I think you would like very much. Do you do that sort of thing?" His white clownish face represented some grinning terminus at the end of a line of Italian aristocracy. She seemed to recognize its origins in a Renaissance painting by Fra Angelico.

"We can—"

"And is that how you meet Raffaello? Did you see his new cuff links? Very lovely, I think, though not to my taste. I prefer something a bit more sparkly, with a bit of a flash. I am like a child in that respect, though many say my taste is not discreet. But I am doing all the talking. Were you with Raffaello in the Hamptons this weekend? I rarely go to the Hamptons. I am allergic to the countryside, I think. Everyone is talking of the big scandal."

"What big scandal?"

"It occurred at a woman's house, a woman who is the editor of a magazine, I believe. She had a house guest who attempted to drown her daughter, a little girl, and seduce her husband. Somehow, before she left, she managed to destroy the hostess's house. Burnt it down, I think."

"Burnt it down," Florence repeated blankly.

"It is like one of those movies, don't you think? Or perhaps there was already a movie of this sort, about a nanny who went crazy. It was a good film, very frightening."

Raffaello returned from the phone with a pleased expression. "Why do none of you offer my friend a cigar?" He pointed at Florence and she suddenly realized he probably had forgotten her name.

"They did offer," Florence said. "I don't—"

"You don't smoke a cigar?" He took a puff. "It's delicious. To me, there is nothing like a really good-quality cigar. It's such a shame that the Cuban cigars are not the quality they once were."

"Raffaello, you only started smoking cigars last month," said Paola.

"Yes, but when I take up a hobby, I do it only in the right way. So!" He smacked the table for emphasis. "I have decided. I am getting a divorce." He gave Florence a wink.

"Oh, Raffaello!" The women murmured condolences. "It is for the best," said one. "But so sad, with the little baby only three months old. Still, she is crazy."

"Completely *pazza*," Raffaello agreed. He addressed Florence. "Very beautiful, she was a ballet dancer, but she had to retire at only twenty-three years of age when she broke her legs in a skiing accident. Her career was finished. Of course, I do not believe she would ever have had much of a career—and I think she must have known this, too, or she wouldn't have gone skiing—"

"And with such a terrible drug problem," Letizia said. To Florence the story—their lives, their very existence—seemed completely unreal; it was impossible not to imagine that when she left the room they would disappear completely. To think that each of them felt themselves to be the center of the universe! Cardboard cutouts with a sense of self-importance. Yet if she were suddenly transported inside one of their heads, she supposed she would appear as unbelievable, as unreal, as they did to her.

"She doesn't want the baby," Raffaello said. "My mother will look after it."

"Not to want her own baby! Why don't you give it to me? I'll look after it."

The food arrived. By now she was somewhat drunk, though alertly so. The group resumed talking in Italian. "We will go as soon as we have finished our meal," Raffaello muttered out of the side of his mouth without looking at her. One of the restaurant's owners, a chubby-faced Londoner, came and sat down at their table, and gave their waiter some lengthy instructions: shortly the waiter reappeared with a bottle of grappa—produced, apparently, on Raffaello's estate in Tuscany—which was poured out in short glasses. The grappa, dense and viscous, tasted the way nail polish remover smelled; her mouth felt stripped of saliva. The women at the table—and Tommaso—merely sipped it, but everyone praised it highly and reached over to stroke Raffaello as if he, personally, had spent hours preparing an antifreeze cocktail just for them. She wondered if he had been in some kind of fight, or boxed as an amateur: glancing at him from the side, she saw his nose had been broken; it was part of what gave him that slightly sinister expression he had whenever he looked at her.

She had spent her whole adult life in New York preparing for this. The perfect clothes, the expensive grooming, the sleek pelt of hair, the job in an auction house. There were hundreds, perhaps thousands, of women like herself: they worked in art galleries, on magazines, for investment companies. They all had poise, little black cocktail dresses, black pumps with the latest heel. They went to screenings, to parties at the Museum of Modern Art, to fashion shows. They had manners, conversational skills, apartments furnished with flea-market finds, forties glass coffee tables; their clothes were dry-cleaned; they worked out at the gym. They skied in Colorado in winter and managed to get in a trip to St. Barts in the spring. Summers they weekended in the Hamptons. Hundreds of these women, aged twenty-five, twenty-seven, thirty-three, ageless, and if they showed signs of age, they knew the right plastic surgeon and were prepared to spend. But the men—their counterparts—Raffaello—were so few and far between! Now here she was, she had found one: tall, handsome, moneyed, Italian, he had stepped from the pages of a magazine and together they would exit through the door of the restaurant and into the future like a god and goddess, ready not to rule the world—who would want that?—but to bask on a silvery beach, to ride across the Pampas on some Paso Fino steed, to climb Mount Kilimanjaro and glimpse the rare snow leopard.

All at once she was nervous. There were a million others more qualified than she. She couldn't imagine what he wanted from her. Perhaps it was a joke. They would go outside and he would see another woman—richer, more beautiful, younger, a tawny princess who had everything going for her that she did not. "I am afraid this must be extremely dull for you." He gingerly stroked her blond hair as if she were a doll, and she felt herself melt. If she had been a cat, she would have wanted to rub against his legs. He seemed to sense this. "Come, we will go."

The others were ignoring them, chatting among themselves as Raffaello rose with Florence and said good-bye. "We are still discussing your name." Tommaso looked up at her with a mischievous smile. He was familiar, but perhaps only because he was a specific type whom she could not exactly place. "Letizia is thinking of what she will name her next child—we have decided it will be called Düsseldorf."

"No, no!" Letizia cried. "I am still preferring Detroit."

"Quito."

"Cleveland."

They left them arguing in loud voices that did not even make a dent in the dense wall of noise created by the French accordion music of the thirties blaring over the loudspeakers, the shouting of the other diners and the tiny rattle of forks and knives against the white china plates.

As the hot air from the street met the air-conditioned interior, the smell of grilling meat and perfume permeated her nostrils, thick as embalming fluid.

part two

I

In the taxi he insisted she stop by his place for a nightcap. It was on her way home, but still, she was uncertain. If she went back with him, he would expect to sleep with her. What else did she have going for her except that she hadn't yet slept with him? How fortunate the women of China were going to be in twenty years; and those in fifty, the luckiest of all. Already through selective abortion there were a third more boys born than girls. Soon nobody there would give birth to a girl at all. The occasional accidental female who did get born would be in such demand, outnumbered by men ninety to one, life would be complete paradise. Men would gather outside her window, sending up jewels, bouquets of lemony orchids, spewing forth love letters, like a crowd of male dogs in front of the home of a red-ribboned poodle in heat.

While she was brooding over this he asked her a question about some man who had been in the news recently—something to do with left-wing views, or right-wing views, but whether the man (who was actually in the news every day) was Speaker of the House, or Secretary of State, or of Defense, she had no idea. She tried to cover up, muttering something along the lines that the man was just another white American male. She was certain Raffaello saw through her. Had he questioned her as to what the man's official title or position was, she would have been caught out. She paid no attention to politics.

Her education had been minimal but standard. There had been some differences between Sarah Lawrence, to which she had transferred, and the local community college where she had spent her first two years—not so much in the quality of the courses but in the caliber and type of the students. At Sarah Lawrence they had seemed to her, at first, to be extremely sophisticated: some lived in Manhattan, they all came to classes dressed in black, with surly expressions and expensive, messy haircuts. The women saw the latest movies, attended concerts of modern music in small East Village basements, had lesbian affairs and took drugs. At the community college many of the students had been older people who worked all day at jobs in Wal-Mart or as house cleaners and who were going back to school hoping to get better jobs. But whether she was at the community college or the private college, Florence had still pieced her education together out of "Introduction to" courses.

She had had introductory philosophy, where various weeks were devoted to Plato, Hobbes, Kant, Hegel and Heidegger. Introduction to Anthropology: a standard textbook, and then a choice of monographs to read and write an essay on—kinship relations of the Pawnee, the Australian aborigine, the pygmy or the Yoruba.

Someone had once visited these people, studied them, extracted any juice, life, personality or warmth and written about the culture in as dry a manner as possible. In any event, as she knew full well, these were all people who (if they still existed) were sitting around watching TV or selling tchotchkes to tourists.

There were studio art classes (painting still lifes); pottery classes (lab and materials fees extra); the required science class (Geology for Poets); Basic Computer 1; freshman English (a week on Chaucer, a poem by Blake, a poem by Pope, a little Milton, then excerpts from Spenser, Hardy, James, D. H. Lawrence and James Joyce), with two-page essays each week and a final paper of ten to fifteen pages. Other English classes: theater history (Aristophanes' *The Frogs, Gammer Gurton's Needle,* a play by Sheridan, by Shakespeare, by Ibsen, by Chekov, by Clifford Odets, Harold Pinter and Edward Albee). One could take classes where the work of women was featured and discussed, but these were usually listed in separate categories under Gender Studies. None of it added up to a thing; all of history was chopped up, broken into little bits—the Pre-Raphaelites, Afro-American literature, Native Americans, gay and lesbian studies, French I and II—the academic attempt to make sense of the world left only a mess of crumbs on the kitchen floor.

Finally she settled on art as her major. There were art history surveys: surveys that began with Egypt and continued to the Middle Ages; surveys that covered cathedrals (Romanesque through High Gothic); twentieth-century art and sculpture. History of Photography, History of Cinema; and a few specialized classes—Braque and Picasso, Fellini, Japanese Architecture, Pop Art.

It was the sort of education a young woman might once have had simply in order to be able to make civilized conversation at dinner. In no way did it prepare her for life, for a job or even, really, to think for herself—the emphasis was on writing papers (very short in length, for the most part) that simply repeated either the statements of the teacher or those in the textbook. What was she being prepared for? Ninety percent of the women at Sarah

Lawrence were well-to-do—or so it appeared to her—and though no one would dare say or think it, the objective after graduation was to get married. Nevertheless, apart from those who had family business or other connections, eighty percent would go on to get degrees, which would prepare them only for entry-level jobs in all fields, where shortly it would be made clear that nothing much was going to happen to them in the working world.

As for her skill in carrying on a civilized conversation at a dinner party: it was less her education that had provided her with an encyclopedia of references than life in the city. Hoffman, Alvar Aalto and Bugatti: furniture designers. Falling Water: home designed by Frank Lloyd Wright. George Eliot: it was less important that she was author of *The Mill on the Floss* than that when she married at sixty, her husband was twenty years younger. Feng Shui: Chinese philosophy whose practical application involved moving bits of furniture around the room until bad vibrations or demons chose other locations to inhabit. Eighteenth-century figure of a Guanyin (valued at eight to ten thousand dollars), Yoruba twin figures, the Neapolitan mastiff, John Lobb shoes, the difference between pashmina and shatoosh. The Rudolf Steiner School, ancient Peruvian textiles, Adlerian psychiatry, Brandywine tomatoes, photographs by Tina Modotti, Russian icons, Celtic torques, the work of Otto Dix. She knew where to get a horsehair mattress custom-made and who was the most important florist—not that she could afford either. Simply trying to keep up was enough to drive a person out of her mind. And this factual information would be of use to her only so long as it was fashionable and current. Soon other, more obscure references would be in use. If only she had been a gay man, somehow, she thought, it all would have come naturally to her.

But she had never been to a dinner party where there really was any conversation. It was always either superficial discussion of the above (never any talk of aesthetics, only who had bought what, where and for how much) or else various monologues in which people bragged about how important, influential or successful they were. *The Red and the Black* was a reference needed only if the book had just come out as a movie and was a topic of discussion. The most useful part of her education had not even been her classes on motion picture history (which were the most popular, crowded lectures, apart from gay studies, women's studies and Afro-American studies) but having rented, night after night, various films at the video store. Knowing that Bette Davis had starred in *Mr. Skeffington* was the only piece of information she knew that had ever enlivened a conversation, begun a discussion or gotten her points of any kind in terms of appearing intelligent.

She supposed that without such an education she might have felt stupid, inferior. The problem was, she felt these things anyway. There were women younger than she who had published novels, who were heading PR companies; there were women older than she who were more muscular, who were married to the heads of movie production companies; there were always others who were more. New York—especially for women but for men as well—was in the convulsive, terminal stages of a lengthy disease, the disease of envy, whose side effects were despair and self-hatred. But as it was such a secret disease, never mentioned, as cancer had once been, Florence didn't know she wasn't alone in it.

She went back to Raffaello's apartment with him. "I can't stay long," she said. "I have to go to work in the morning."

He gave her a contemptuous grin. "You are nervous." He was handsome in a foreign way, his dark Italian eyes with a look in them American men never had—sexual, intense—American men always looked away, as if they were afraid of being raped. Still, he did make her nervous.

"No!" She tried to sound indignant.

"Look how you are sitting."

It was true she was hunched in one corner of the black-leather-and-chrome couch. He had a two-bedroom apartment in a modern building on a fancy block in midtown. It was furnished in deliberately shabby old things, or things designed to look old—overstuffed chair and sofa, piles of art books, walls painted Pompeiian shades of red, umber, grayish lemon. "I am hardly in New York," he explained. "My family keeps this apartment for when we are here, but now, I am thinking, I will stay in Manhattan for quite some time. I like it here." His mother's family was in the textile business—over dinner he had told her about the factory outside Turin, known for its production of fantastic, intricate silk brocades; an old warehouse that was filled with remnants and rolls of cloth dating back to the seventeenth century, when the company had sprung into existence. During the fifties the family had begun to manufacture exclusive items in addition to the textiles—scarves, a few simple shifts, men's ties. The products were incredibly expensive, and now he had been sent to New York to try to revamp the line, which in recent years had become dated.

She felt dizzy. Perhaps she had drunk too much at the dinner.

He got out a few bottles from a cupboard beneath one of the bookshelves. "Would you like some after-dinner drink? I have some very nice cognac. I am sorry I cannot offer you any more cocaine. I had only a little left that had been given to me on my birthday."

"I should get home; I've got all kinds of things to do at work tomorrow." She had made up her mind she wasn't going to sleep with him.

"Come with me for one moment. I have something I want to show you."

"Can't you show me in here?"

He rolled his eyes. "Do you think I will attack you?" Apparently he had never seen anyone so stupid in his entire life. She hated the way he kept staring at her so intently; she almost would have preferred it if he had been the other type, the kind who kept looking around the room, over her shoulder, in the hope either that he would find a better prospect or that someone would see them together. The intensity of his gaze was impolite; she had come up against it before. It wasn't infatuation, it was a challenge, a method of demanding if she could handle him, of letting her know that he was the alpha dog in the pack.

She followed him past the kitchen. There was a huge refrigerator, all glass, like those found in restaurants, and in the brief glimpse she got she could see there was virtually nothing inside; the other appliances were on an equally lavish scale. For some reason these details impressed her more than the obviously expensive apartment. He went into a bedroom and from a cabinet began to remove, one at a time, really exquisite netsuke; though she didn't know much about the little ivory carvings, as he placed them one at a time in the palm of her hand, she could see that they were not reproductions—a tiny monkey, a rat holding an acorn, a man with a grotesque face bent nearly into a ball. The carving was intensely detailed, and each one, as she felt it, seemed to have an aura, a resonance. "Oh, they're beautiful!"

"You like?" He was smiling. "I like them very much. I have been collecting them since I was fifteen. At one time, I could find them rather inexpensively. Now, the good ones are quite rare." He touched the back of her neck and it suddenly seemed silly not to go to bed with him—he was a grown man, at least in his late thirties; it wasn't as if she had never slept with anyone before. He sat on the edge of the bed, which was covered in a rich brocade. "I will show you what else I like." He took her head between his hands and pushed it down.

"You are a very understanding woman," he said when she was finished. He sat up, covering himself in the ornate purple bedspread across which zigzagged embroidered yellow crosses and shapes resembling mailboxes. "So beautiful." He sighed and offered her a cigar, then lit one for himself. "Would you like to meet me tomorrow for lunch?"

"Things may be a little hectic at work," she said. She didn't know if she would ever want to see him again.

"Shall I ring you in the morning?"

"Yes, sure." She rose from the armchair and collected her things. He didn't offer to take her home.

"Where do you work? Put the telephone number by the phone."

"I work at Quayle's," she said. "The auction house. It's in the book. My name's Florence Collins."

"Of course I knew that!" He roused himself slightly from his torpor. "I'm just joking with you. You are very serious."

"Talk tomorrow!" She made her way to the door.

"What department did you say you were in?"

"Estate jewelry."

The drowsy doorman had to unlock the front door. He, too, did not offer to find her a cab, and it never would have occurred to her to insist that he did, let alone inform Raffaello that it was his obligation to put her in one if he wasn't actually going to escort her home. There were women who demanded even less than she. Had Raffaello picked up the phone at that moment, there were half a dozen women who would have come over to his apartment, had sex with him and left when they were told, without ever expecting to be taken out for dinner, or notified earlier in the day. They would have managed to delude themselves that this was a compliment, that he liked them enough not to bother with preliminaries—or that it was an indication of just how sophisticated and bohemian they were.

She walked over to Fifty-seventh Street. It was well after midnight. The exaggeratedly yellow streetlamps cast a medicinal hue. The few trees, shrouded in thick summer dust, crouched in their two-foot parcels of soil, prisoners of the city. There was no traffic on the street; no taxis came by. Finally, after almost forty minutes, a bus arrived. She felt good. She told herself that she was in control, that now it was up to her whether or not she wanted to see Raffaello again, and not the other way around.

There were four messages on her machine when she walked in

the door, all from Max Coho. In two of them he begged her to give him a call, no matter how late she got in. She paid him no mind.

It took her almost a half hour to remove her makeup and wash her face with three different compounds (a routine that had cost her almost three hundred dollars in products and instructions at a small, exclusive skin clinic—in addition to seven hundred and fifty dollars for a series of eight facials). She brushed her teeth with a fancy red-and-white-striped Italian toothbrush and an English toothpowder that came in a tin. She hadn't had a chance to exercise at all in almost four days. And even the one line of cocaine had left her wound up. She drank a cup of chamomile tea and lay awake for at least forty minutes before she finally fell asleep.

2

Monday morning she was late for work. Quayle's employees were expected to arrive at nine; usually she walked to work or, if running late, caught the eight-thirty bus and got there a few minutes before the hour. She awoke to the phone ringing. Looking at the clock, she realized it was already after nine, she had slept through the alarm. She didn't have the energy to make a dash for the phone, and when the machine picked up, the caller left no message. Though she didn't remember having drunk a huge amount the night before, her head throbbed and she felt stiff from the air-conditioning. A sudden wave of anxiety swept over her as she tried to retrace her steps over the weekend.

The events of only a few short hours ago, which had made her feel powerful and in control, now seemed inconceivably depraved. A man she had met once had taken her home, she had decided to sleep with him, but when he didn't want to she hadn't protested, simply given him a blow job.

She had never hoped for love and probably wouldn't have recognized it had love stabbed an arrow in her. Still, though she had previously been indifferent whether or not she would hear from him again—though certain she would—now she was equally certain that not only would he never call, but she would die if she didn't get to see him.

She called the receptionist at Quayle's front desk. "Polly? Could you please tell Marge when she gets in that I had an appointment and I'm going to be a little late?"

"What time are you going to be in?"

"Probably ten o'clock."

She intended to go through the stack of mail—bills, bills, bills, payments and responses she had delayed for weeks—but she was too groggy and there really wasn't time. Maybe she would stay in this evening and try to figure out what was going on and where all the money in her checking account had gone.

She showered and washed her hair with a shampoo that had— at least according to her hair stylist—been formulated especially for her. When she needed to order more, she called the salon and gave them her ID number and an assistant mixed it before pouring it into an expensive hand-blown glass bottle. There were two kinds of conditioner, one used before shampooing and one afterward. Her towels, huge and thick, of unbleached Egyptian cotton, were brand-new; though the towels her grandmother had owned were quite expensive, Florence hadn't been able to bring herself to use them after her death. She had bought a whole new set, in shades of raspberry and vermilion, but then decided even after they were washed that the dye in the fabric irritated her skin—and that the bright colors made the antiquated bathroom look even more grim. So she had gotten rid of those and bought this new set. Each time she had spent well over five hundred dollars.

She put on a flared striped cotton skirt, in shades of forest green, mustard, dark brown and beige; a pair of dark green patent leather flats, hand-made in a French shop; a brown-and-beige sleeveless floral-print silk shirt with a Peter Pan collar. Around her neck she tied a thin cotton sweater in lime-green. She pulled her long blond hair back in a ponytail and, rummaging for her new sunglasses, put them on top of her now-sleek hair. She wore hardly any makeup; a little lipstick in a neutral tone, some powder. Though the other women at Quayle's would be wearing simple black linen shifts, tightly fitted, with jackets they removed once evening came, or suits, Florence's outfit was more expensive than any of theirs. The overall effect was a subtle fifties parody, a bit different than what anyone else had on but which on her somehow managed to seem like the latest style. Quite often it turned out that what she wore was what the others ended up wearing shortly thereafter.

It had cost more than fifteen hundred dollars to look fresh-faced, a simple country girl. But the truth was, she didn't even really care about her appearance or that she was beautiful. She wasn't vain. Her facade was her property. It was an item she possessed, which she groomed and dressed in order to achieve her goals.

She jumped in a cab and got out a block early to buy a large cappuccino to take with her. Her office was located up on the seventh floor—the top—in the very back; it was a tiny office, almost a closet, with one window that looked directly out onto a brick wall. Reference books and old catalogs were stacked to the ceiling. There had been no renovations at Quayle's—one of the lowest of the second string of auction houses, or perhaps the third—in more than fifty years. Mr. Gabe Quayle was over eighty, but still came in every day; it was expected that when he died the business would be run by his nephew, Barry Plotsky.

Whether or not Marge Crowninshield, her immediate boss, had already arrived, Florence didn't know. Polly was away from the front desk and there were no porters in sight; she had jumped on the back elevator and snuck into her office hoping that Marge hadn't already come to check on her. She began to go over the copy she had been working on last week for the November catalog: *"Pink Sapphire and Diamond 'Bee' Ring, Tiffany & Co. Schlumberger."* Her telephone rang.

"Quayle's Arcade Auction, Estate Jewelry, Florence Collins speaking."

"Don't you ever return your phone calls?"

"Max!"

"Did you see today's paper?"

"No."

"If you had returned my calls, I could have warned you. I just want you to know, I was the one who got Gus to turn it into a blind item. He wanted to run it with your name on it."

"What are you talking about?"

"Get the paper. You want me to fax it to you?"

"No!" She tried to sound as if she were completely indifferent, though she felt panicky.

"Believe me, I'm sure everyone's seen it in your office by now. Want me to read it to you?"

"No. I'll get it later."

"So why didn't you call me back? Didn't you go home last night?"

"First you insult me, and then you think I'm going to return your phone calls?"

"Insult you? How did I insult you?"

She honestly couldn't remember. "It doesn't matter."

"So, you want to have dinner tonight?"

"With who?"

"With me!"

"Oh."

"Remember, I did you a big favor. I spoke to Gus yesterday, and if it wasn't for me, that item in his column would have been a lot worse."

"Aren't you generous to do me a big favor. I never asked you to do anything for me, Max. I don't even know what you're talking about. Excuse me, I have to go now." She hung up the phone as coldly as possible. Then she walked down the hall to Sonia's office. Sonia, a researcher, weighed nearly three hundred pounds. She sat in an armchair as if it were part of her, sunken beneath her lap. A little typing table on wheels was pulled up close in front. "Hi, Sonia. Did you see if Marge came in yet?"

"I didn't see her. I saw the paper, though. That was you, wasn't it? It had to be you, I figured." She looked at Florence with gleaming hatred. "They're going to flip out around here! Did anybody say anything to you yet?"

"I don't know what you're talking about. If you see Marge, tell her I had to run across the street to the store for a minute. Do you want anything?"

"Are you going to the deli? I'd love one of those lo-fat cheese Danish."

She knew Sonia hated her and that it was inevitable, just as she couldn't help but hate Ibis, the movie starlet. Even if she hadn't weighed three hundred pounds, Sonia would have hated her. That was how the system was organized. Women judged and evaluated themselves—and one another. Only when they found they were roughly on the same rung of the ladder could they ever possibly be friends. And it was trickier still when it became clear that two women on approximately the same rung might decide they were in competition for the same thing. Then friendship was automatically ruled out. Still, in the face of Sonia's gleeful fury, she had to do something to protect herself. "You know, those lo-fat cheese Danish have, like, three hundred and fifty calories."

"Get me a plain bagel, then, with one of those little cups of whipped cream cheese on the side," Sonia snarled. "And a tea with lemon, no sugar."

Florence crossed the street to the deli. While she was waiting for the order, she surreptitiously opened the paper on the shelf below the counter to the gossip page.

. . . **WHICH** aging filly-about-town reeked havoc over her Hamptons weekend? In less than twenty-four hours the blond auction-house assistant director in estate jewelry managed to seduce her hostess's husband and nearly drown the couple's daughter. Her hostess—and former friend—is that infamous magazine editor, now said to be bent on revenge . . . **KEEP YOU POSTED!**

Her hands were covered in perspiration. It really wasn't so bad. Honestly, it could have been much worse, she supposed. At least Quayle's wasn't actually mentioned by name, so she didn't see how Marge could complain. After all, maybe people would think it was somebody at Sotheby's or Christie's. Nobody lost his or her job over so trivial a thing. And it wasn't the kind of item that would put anybody off going out with her. Men were willing to tolerate far worse. There was that porn star—or stripper—who had married that society billionaire. And there was the girl found on the boat with the politician. *His* political career had been ended, but she got married to a rich businessman and disappeared into a normal life with children. Only someone as silly as that Charlie Twigall might take such an item seriously. And he had made up his mind against her even before it came out.

"Hey! Blondie!"

"What?"

"I've been talking to you for five minutes. Here's your order. You want anything else? That was you today in the paper, wasn't it? I knew as soon as I saw it this morning."

Of course, Rasheed would know it was her; she came into the deli just about every morning, and he knew she worked across the street. Besides, that was what those gossip columns were for: to feed the workers—at least those who could speak English—with glimpses into a different world, like Cinderella not being allowed to attend the ball.

At the cash register she grabbed a handful of chocolate nuggets stuffed with hazelnuts and cherries, wrapped in gold foil, a dollar twenty-nine apiece. "We reading about you this morning!" Benny leered. She opened a candy and crammed it into her mouth. What difference did it make, they were always leering; some of the time she thought she would even miss it if they stopped. It was her daily reality check, or unreality check, to be leered at. She took some bills out of her dark green leather satchel and flung them onto the counter.

"You got a phone call. He didn't leave his name." She and Sonia answered each other's phones if they were there. Only people who knew her had her direct extension. If someone had been making a business call, it would have come through the switchboard. She handed the bagel and tea to Sonia and gave her the last chocolate, still wrapped in foil, slightly squished and sticky from her hand. "And Marge came through on a rampage. She had to go to a meeting. She wants to see you when she's out."

She went back down the hall to her office, realized she was practically scuttling along the wall and forced herself to stop and walk calmly. Surely there were appointments she could go on to take her out of the office for the rest of the day? A demented-sounding woman had called the previous week, saying she had a large collection of Russian jewelry that had belonged to the Romanovs, which she was interested in selling but didn't want to take out of her safe-deposit box. At the time, she figured the woman was just a nut case and had told her she'd get back to her. Or the other woman who kept phoning—an hour away out on Long Island—who had sent some snapshots of things that might be worth a bit; it was impossible to judge from the photos.

The phone was ringing. With any luck it would be Raffaello. It was almost lunchtime; she could coax him to come back to the office and tell Marge that he wanted her to appraise some of his family's stuff. He was so glamorous and aristocratic in appearance; Marge always swooned over that sort of man—at least it would delay her wrath for a day.

"Hello—this is Tracer Schmidt—we met last night? I was with Max Coho? I was wondering—maybe you wanted to come over tonight and have a drink? Or . . . we could meet someplace?"

Florence hesitated. "What is this in reference to?" she said after a pause. She hadn't meant to be bitchy; still, if this girl was going to try to pry something out of her, had read the gossip page, she wanted no part of it.

"Well . . ." Tracer was embarrassed. "Nothing, really. I mean, I just thought it would be nice to have a drink, and talk . . . and . . . actually . . . I wanted to ask you about your friend . . . Darryl?"

"I really don't know anything about him. But—" She hesitated. "Sure! I'll come by your place. About six?"

She had not had a close girlfriend since Allison. Even they had not been all that intimate. They shared an apartment (she had moved out of her grandmother's place for a while, until her grandmother became ill and she realized that in order to hang on to the apartment she was going to have to live there); they went out every night picking up men. They did things together, borrowed each other's clothes, but had very little to say, nothing in the way of confidences, though occasionally they would spend evenings at home of giggling and giddiness.

But anyway, meeting Tracer for a drink wasn't the same as becoming friends, and more than likely it would end there. She picked up the phone and called the woman out on Long Island who had been trying to get Florence to look at her jewelry for six months. Virginia Clary—Maspeth. Too ill to travel into the city. Florence didn't even know if it was possible to get to Maspeth by train. She would have to take a taxi—the car service charged a four-hour minimum to go outside the city—and see if she could hand in her expenses this month without too much bitching from Marge. She grabbed her things and went back down the hall. "Are you going to be around later on, Sonia? Can I call in to you for my messages?"

"If I'm here."

"Fine. I had an appointment to go and look at some jewelry which I can't get out of. Please tell Marge I'm sorry."

"Are you coming back today?" Sonia had a little sneer.

"I'm going to try. She's out on Long Island, though, and I don't know how easy it's going to be to get back. Tell Marge I'll call in this afternoon."

"I wish you'd tell her yourself."

"Yes—and she'd tell me to go. This poor woman's been trying to get me to look at her things for six months. I made this appointment with her ages ago."

She took the back stairs and went out the back entrance hoping to avoid Marge. John de Jongh was coming around the corner, carrying a small bouquet wrapped in yellow tissue and clear cellophane. When he saw her he flinched, looking sheepish, and thrust the flowers at her. "Florence!"

"Hi, John." She drifted into weariness at the sight of him.

"Are you okay?"

"Fine." The flowers were like puffs of velvet—chunky, expensive white tuberoses and yellow freesias, which, in combination, sent out a blast of fragrance so thick it was almost a drug.

"I was . . . I was just going to drop off these flowers for you. Our offices are just around the corner. I tried to call you earlier, but your secretary said you weren't in yet. I thought . . . if you were in, and free, you might want to get a bite to eat?"

"I'm supposed to be on my way to Maspeth."

"Um . . . so why don't I take you? My car's in the lot just around the corner—I'll just tell my secretary to clear my calendar. Maspeth—that's not far. We can stop for something to eat along the way and that'll give us a chance to talk. I've . . . I've got some exciting news . . . about the restaurant."

3

It was late afternoon when she woke. He was still asleep. He had claimed they were lost, taken her to lunch in the restaurant of a hotel near the airport, then begged her to come up to a room. He made her put the room on her credit card, telling her he would bring her the cash the following day. It was just that she had felt so sorry for him. He had the desperate hunger of a man addicted to crack cocaine, something devouring him from inside. She couldn't bear to see something, someone, so tormented, like an animal with fleas gnawing frantically at itself. Maybe it was simply a weakness on her part. Her body meant so little to her, except as a commodity that nobody seemed to want to buy or own; she might as well hand it over to him for a few hours at a reduced rate. No doubt she was partly responsible for his agony.

In books by Jane Austen and Edith Wharton there were always women wandering around suffering for love, determined to stick to a lifetime one-sided commitment to some guy they had seen only for a few days and never even kissed. She couldn't understand it. There were a billion or more people on the face of the planet, very nearly as interchangeable as one alligator with another. If John de Jongh was obsessed with her, it wasn't really anything to do with her personally; and if she felt herself drawn to him, it didn't mean that the following week, or day, or hour, she couldn't dismiss him and move on to someone else. He grabbed her around the waist as she slid over to the edge of the bed and sat up. "Where are you going?"

"Nowhere. To the bathroom."

"How are you feeling?"

"Okay."

"I feel fabulous! I feel like I just played a few games of squash and I was in such good shape I'm not even tired."

"I haven't been to the gym or exercised in ages."

"This was exercise, wasn't it?" He half sat up, leaning back against the headboard, pulling the sheet over him. "I wish I had a special name for you. For some reason I can't call you Florence. I don't know why. You just don't look like a Florence to me. It's too much like a friend of my grandmother's, I guess."

"But you named your daughter Claudia."

He looked momentarily blank, as if he had forgotten who Claudia was. "That's different. Anyway, it was Natalie who named her, not me."

"How is she?"

"Fine! Natalie's thinking of sending her away to school, which I'm opposed to. I said, 'Wait until she gets a little older.' I don't see what the problem is. I think Natalie feels she spends too much time on her own, since both of us are so busy. Natalie says at a boarding school she can get extra help with her learning disabilities."

"But . . . is she still in the hospital?"

"Oh no. She came home yesterday. No, no, that's all fine. You know, it wasn't your fault. It could have happened to anybody."

"I still feel so terrible."

His face darkened and he scowled slightly. "Well, don't! I was far more surprised that you weren't angry with me. But you kind of put me in a position, you know: you locked me in that bedroom for at least an hour. I had no way of getting out! Anyway, finally somebody came down the hall—I don't even know why they were up there—and I was shouting, 'Let me out!' " He laughed uproariously. "For some reason they couldn't get the door open from the other side either, and by the time they got hold of a screwdriver, it was too late, everybody at the party was saying how you locked me in. I couldn't get into the whole thing without making things sound worse. I'm afraid Natalie is quite angry with you."

She went to the shower and he followed. "Listen, I have some good news," he said. "I told Derek you wanted to invest in his new place—he agreed you could buy a half share. How much did you say you had? Forty thousand?"

"It's only twenty-five."

"Did you bring your checkbook?" She shook her head. "Okay, don't worry about it: you can put it in the mail when you get a chance, or I'll stop by later to pick it up. I'll cover it for you in the meantime. So how do you feel? You should be very excited about being part owner of a place that's going to be extremely popular. I didn't tell you before, but as part owner you can call and get a table whenever you like. Anyway, Derek knew who you were. He said to tell you, 'Welcome aboard.' And of course we'll have a party in the place before it's opened."

"Really? Derek knows who I am?" She smiled.

"He thinks you're really hot."

"He's never said two words to me."

"Because he knows his wife would kill him." John grabbed a bar of soap from the sink and tried to come into the bath with her.

"Want me to help?" Now that she was really able to see him for the first time, she saw what a peculiar body he had: oddly large, feminine hips and a narrow chest, like the Eighteenth Dynasty pharaoh Amenhotep.

"No, thanks."

He began to laugh again, as if she had just said something hilarious. "You know, Florence, you're really something. I'll just wait until you're finished then, shall I?"

She rinsed and grabbed a towel from a rack on the wall. He was pacing restlessly, a sheet around his waist. "I've really got to get going," she said.

"Yes, me too," he said. "I'm going to have to reschedule everything. Things are getting a little out of hand."

"I'd better call the client," she said.

"The client? Is that what you call them? I like that."

"I should have been there by now. How am I going to get to Maspeth from here?"

"I don't know. I'm afraid I should get back to work, I'm running so far behind. You don't mind, do you, if I don't take you to Maspeth? It's really going to slow me down. Why don't I put you in a taxi? I'll pay for it."

He gave her fifty dollars and said he would say good-bye to her in the room; he had to run.

She couldn't understand why she had done it. It was just that since she had already slept with him, albeit against her will, it no longer seemed such a big deal—there was no awkwardness in taking off her clothes and getting into bed with him. Besides, he had seemed so nervous, he had so obviously wanted her, she couldn't help but be flattered. Or maybe, in retrospect, it was because *she* was so nervous and mad at herself, waiting all morning for Raffaello to call. By the time she bumped into John, she had given up hope of hearing from him; it was her way of getting even.

Anyway, it hadn't been a mistake, not if he could double her money in a few months. She saw the twenty-five thousand becoming fifty. She could take out some and invest it in something else. If she could just not touch the income, in a few years she might really have something.

There was no problem in finding a cab to take her to Maspeth, but it took the driver quite some time to find Virginia Clary's address. The location was so bleak—burnt-out industrial warehouses, yards filled with ruined hulks of cars behind metal fences—that momentarily as the cab drove away she wondered if she had the right place, or was being lured to some kind of depraved stalker's home. The house was like an imitation of a house, ranch style, aluminum siding, tiny windows heavily barred, as if too much mascara had been applied to dirty eyes. On the sticky street she pressed the bell. A riotous clamoring rose up—the screaming yelps of what sounded like hundreds of dogs. A narrow, shifty face, missing a side tooth, nearly bald, pressed up against the bars on the front door before letting her in.

"How do you do?" said the woman in a surprisingly babyish, little-girl voice. "Do come in. Please excuse the mess. No one will bite you. Candy, get back!" Florence looked down. At her feet were what appeared to be a half-dozen rodentlike animals, tiny dogs emitting furious squawks.

"You must be Virginia Clary; I'm Florence, from Quayle's, Estate Jewelry." She tried to hide the dismay from her face, but it was already apparent to her there was no way this woman would have anything of value.

"I think maybe it's a little cooler in the kitchen, if you don't mind. I've put all my nicest bits of jewelry in a box on the table in there. I have such pretty, special things, I know you'll love them. I'd never let them go, but I have to pay my mortgage. That bank has been writing nasty letters, and if I have to leave, what will happen to my baby doggies?"

"Why don't we take a look at what you've got and see what we can do?"

"You just rest for a minute, it's so hot outside. My air-conditioning doesn't work very well. I have to keep the windows closed because of that plastic factory nearby; the dogs get asthma. You see, most of my dogs are rescue animals, they all have various handicaps—"

The voice reminded Florence of Shirley Temple's. It was hard to listen to what she was saying, that peculiar little voice was so mesmerizing. Virginia seemed determined to tell Florence every detail of the animals in the menagerie. "Little Bruno I found on the street. Can you believe it, they had fed him to pitbulls! And Betsy—where are you, Betsy?" While she spoke she went to the avocado-colored refrigerator and returned with item after item, one at a time—large bottles of grape soda and diet Pepsi and ginger ale, a bag of potato chips and a tin of rather uninteresting-looking Danish butter cookies. Apparently she was going to insist on a tea party, even though Florence looked nervously at the wall clock and muttered from time to time that she hoped to find a taxi someplace to take her into the city by five.

"I'm sure by now you've recognized me."

"Um . . ." Florence didn't know what to say. "You do look familiar."

"Oh, I know I haven't aged all that well. Back in the fifties I was on the cover of just about every fashion magazine—I think I counted them once, there were at least fifty—and of course, Richard never does mention my name, but it's a well-known fact that I *made* his career—"

"Richard?"

"Avedon, of course. Well, nowadays, of course, modeling is a whole different business. If I ever went back to it—I'm talking now as an *older* model, of course—I would be a supermodel, the way these girls are now. Oh, they earn fortunes! Whereas, in my day, we got paid very little, by the hour, and there was none of the glamour associated with it; of course, I was one of the first, a John Powers girl—"

So this crone had once been a model. It seemed impossible to believe. Perhaps inside her was a great beauty, the way it was always said that inside every fat person was a thin person scream-ing to get out. But looking at the lined face, the wrinkled lips barely concealing the missing tooth and mouthful of other, grimy teeth, the gaps in her blond ponytail revealing her bald head, it seemed impossible to believe.

"Of course, I did get to travel, and have a lot of fun, though it wasn't for me. And it did provide me with my two husbands. The first was a businessman, *very* wealthy, we used to drink *soo* much, but back in those days we smoked and drank like there was no tomorrow—but when he left, all I had from the marriage was my little poodles. I used to make Ralph buy me the cutest little French poodles, which was before I knew better than to go to a pet shop and buy a dog. Of course, I should have gotten a large settlement; Ralph always said that I *made* his career. And then there was my second husband, the true love of my life, and it turned out he had been in love with me for *years,* when he used to see me on the covers of magazines. He was a jazz musician—such a tragedy when he died in the car crash. They said I was lucky to be alive, though at the time I didn't care, I thought he was *lucky* to have died and not me. I should have been rich from his royalties, but his contracts were so lousy I never did see a dime. All I had from either of them was the jewelry; I used to make sure they both gave me lots of jewelry." She pointed to the box on the table. "Not that I'm materialistic, but now I'm happy I did it, because my little baby boys and girls need so much love and attention!"

Someone had urinated on the floor. The place was sweltering. Florence wondered if she was going to be sick. As her eyes adjusted to the gloom, she could see what appeared to be cockroaches scuttling busily up and down the walls, alongside and over what must have been a photograph of Virginia in her modeling days. She really was stunning—the long white neck, the swanlike limbs protruding from a black fifties Dior evening gown—it was impossible that that Virginia and this were one and the same.

Each time Florence moved toward the box, hoping to at least see the items Virginia Clary was talking about, Virginia put her hand out and held hers down. She had surprising strength for someone who looked so frail. "Oh, I've forgotten plates, and napkins!" She went to the yellow Formica counter and came back with paper plates decorated with sheep, and matching napkins. "Go ahead and eat—have some chips—and then I'll show you the things. And maybe you'll pour me a little grape soda? I have trouble lifting heavy objects. I always worry, you know, that I may drop something, and some of these little babies—Constancia and Nanette—are completely blind. We think they were owned by a family with little children who poked out their eyes! Can you imagine? Oh, how thoughtless of me! I know it's a little warm, but perhaps you'd like a cup of coffee."

"Yes, thank you." She felt anxious, panicky, trapped in this grim house, as if what might be catching was not collecting stray animals but old age. How could this woman have ended up out here with a hundred crapping yowlers and a bag of crummy jewelry skimmed off men? It all seemed so pathetic. "May I use your bathroom?"

"It's down the hall, through the living room on the right."

She walked past cages—it was too dark to see their shrieking occupants hurling themselves against the bars—and narrowly avoided a shelf of junk. (Were they Avon bottles?) Little kittens bobbed their heads. The curtains were pulled together, blocking out the hot sun but giving only an illusion of coolness. The living room housed a huge TV, built-in bookshelves that had never seen a book, a rocking chair with a rust-colored pillow; a square-shaped couch covered in glazed chintz, its pattern of cabbage roses in a truly bad shade of muddy mauve; a polyester braided rug in muddy pink and grayish-blue; a dying deffenbachia—or was it a corn plant—two spindly trunks topped with pathetic leaves; brown curtains with metal hooks on a rod over a picture window. The view was of another house exactly like this one. In the bathroom a crocheted clown sat on the toilet tank, obscenely housing a roll of toilet paper beneath the lavender skirt. The toilet, too, was dressed in a fuzzy puce snood. The tub was hidden behind a shower curtain with a pattern of flying umbrellas. Pink soap was in the shape of little shells in a dish by the sink. Every item in the room, in the house, represented a choice, a decision, an object pored over and debated at Wal-Mart or some discount department store. She imagined taking pictures of each room and sending them in to a magazine for a make-over. There was nothing that could be done with such a place.

While the woman's back was to her as she turned on the stove, Florence began to unzip the jewelry bags. A diamond pendant surrounded by small diamonds, late Victorian, looked quite nice, but when she examined it more closely through her jeweler's loop, something wasn't quite right about the stone. "Oh, I had that appraised—years ago—and I was told it was worth ten to fifteen thousand, so I know it's gone up in value!" Virginia handed her a mug of coffee and snatched the pendant from her. "It's a canary diamond, I believe, and it's a very old piece, an antique. I imagine it's doubled in value. If I sell just the necklace, I'll have enough to pay the vet bills and build roofs on the cages of the dogs who live outside."

"You have more dogs outside?" Florence asked politely.

"Fifteen at the moment. My big babies. I can't keep them all in the house, but I'm already in trouble with the Board of Health and that lousy ASPCA, who say I can't operate a kennel without a license. I told them, 'I'm not operating a kennel! These are my babies!' They wanted to take them away. You know what they do when they get them: they put them to sleep. I have one or two that might suit you—I don't let just anybody adopt them. Would you like to come out and see them?"

"I'd love to, but maybe another time." Florence sipped the coffee. Her mouth filled with a horrible taste of something burnt and chemical—it was instant coffee. The diamond pendant would be lucky to get an estimate of fifteen hundred dollars. "I wonder if I could just go through the things quickly before giving you my opinion," she said, setting down the mug. There was a large sapphire-and-diamond cocktail ring of platinum, from the fifties, with quite a nice large sapphire, though a bit dark in color, that might be worth two thousand. A pair of French enamel earrings, two hundred dollars at best; quite a sweet ruby-and-pearl bracelet from the twenties, with surprisingly good rubies, which might go for a couple of thousand. A handful of gold bangles; a gold pin studded with diamonds in the shape of a pickle ("My aunt worked for the Heinz company for fifty years and that's what they gave her when she retired"); a necklace of topazes that Virginia assured her were yellow diamonds; some cuff links; quite a few rings; a pearl necklace with white and black pearls; and finally, at the bottom of the box, a large gold brooch of a bird, enameled, with diamonds and an eye of ruby. "Just costume."

"No, it's not," Florence said. "I'm guessing this is the most valuable piece you have—it might bring six or seven thousand."

"But surely the diamond pendant is worth much more than that. It was appraised at—"

"Yes, I know. But diamonds really haven't gone up all that much; and I'll have to get someone to take a better look at it. I can't really see under these conditions. It looks like it has quite a large flaw—it's a shame, because it is a large diamond. My rough estimate would be if you sold everything you might get twenty thousand—after our commission."

"But . . ." Virginia was in shock. "These pearls—I know a pearl necklace like this is very valuable. These are black pearls."

"Cultured pearls—they were dyed black."

"Even so, I'm sure giant pearls like these have to be worth a fortune."

"I'm afraid if a pearl necklace isn't worn, the pearls have a tendency to deteriorate."

"And this ring? A ruby? It's a star ruby, isn't it? It must be worth twenty thousand alone."

"It is a ruby. But there are all kinds of rubies, some more valuable and some less so. You're welcome to bring your things in elsewhere, but I doubt you'll get a better figure."

"I don't know what to say. I'm in shock. I thought all this time I would be getting at least a hundred thousand. Now you're telling me twenty thousand at the most!"

"Bring it in to one of the other auction houses."

"I did write to Christie's and Sotheby's. But you were the only one who offered to come out and look at my things." She shoved the items furiously back in the velvet bags. "Here, you take them. Get whatever you can. There's some other stuff you didn't see, in a couple of other bags somewhere. But I've shown you the best things."

"Why don't you see what someone else says?" Florence wasn't even sure the stuff would bring in twenty thousand. The whole thing was going to be more trouble than it was worth.

"No, I trust you."

"I'll have to make out a receipt. It would be better if you could bring it in yourself, or have someone bring it in for you."

"I want you to take it and get it out of here."

"I'm sure I'll be fine, but I'll have to get you to sign a paper absolving me of responsibility—if I'm mugged, you understand, or there was, say, a train wreck."

"A train wreck?" The woman practically shrieked.

"You know. I mean, if there was an earthquake, or armed robbers boarded the train, or—I don't imagine anything will happen, but I want you to understand. You'd be better off to FedEx it to me tomorrow."

"Take it. I don't care." The woman was growing depressed and enraged. "I've made a list of the things, two copies, one for you and one for me."

"I can take your list, but I'm also going to do one of my own— I have a special way of recording it." She carefully wrote out an itemized description of each piece and had Virginia sign it.

4

Seven o'clock, midsummer evening. The anorexic army marched
across Manhattan, necks ribboned with sinew, dressed in the
skimpiest clothing imaginable, on their way to or from the gym.
Techno-pop music blared from second-story windows and women
could be seen pumping furiously on stationary bicycles, rows of
them facing the street; or female infantry brigades flailing their
arms as instructors shrieked aerobic commands. The smell of fried
sausage rose from corner carts.

It was too late to go home; she went straight to Tracer Schmidt's apartment still lugging the jewelry in an oversized plastic bag from Wal-Mart. The train had taken only an hour, but for her, sitting by the window as it rattled slowly through the gray wasteland of suburban Long Island, it felt much longer.

It was inconceivable that someone Tracer's age could be so rich, with wealth not acquired through marriage. Her apartment was huge, the penthouse floor of the Central Park West building. She gave Florence a tour, muttering embarrassed platitudes the whole time. There was a huge living room with views over the park, simple early American furniture and a massive blond sofa with winged arms and curled back ("But I don't think the couch goes with the rest of the furniture; it's some Biedermeier thing that Max said would look great in here"); a TV room/library ("And I had the sound system installed by these guys who Max recommended, and I still can't get the darn thing to work in half the rooms"); an exercise room with mirrored walls, stuffed with StairMaster, treadmill, weight training equipment; a huge kitchen with antique laboratory cabinets and restaurant stove; a double staircase, which led to four bedrooms upstairs, and beyond this another staircase, which led to a huge empty water tower, built to balance the genuine water tower on the other side of the building.

Inside the fake water tower was a circular room several stories high and at least fifty feet around, which Tracer had insisted on purchasing with the apartment. Though she had redone the interior, paneled the walls, installed windows, lighting and an additional, miniature kitchen complete with microwave and dishwasher, she still hadn't decided what the space would become. "Maybe my studio if I decide to do photography again—I majored in photography in college." Around the exterior of the water tower was a terrace with a view on all four sides, so that in the distance looking one way the Hudson River could be seen and in the other direction the park and the lights of midtown Manhattan.

"Great view." Admiring other people's possessions was always a bit awkward. If she was too enthusiastic, it would sound as if she were fawning; if she was too dry, it would be interpreted as coldness—or jealousy.

"Honestly, I know it's too big for one person, but I really couldn't not buy the place. I needed somewhere to live, and the owner had died, and the family was desperate to sell—of course, the reason it was so cheap is that the maintenance is so high—" Blathering nervously, she went back down to the kitchen, followed by Florence. She opened the refrigerator door and peered in as if she had never seen its contents before. "You want a beer? Or there's a bottle of champagne I could open—"

"A beer's fine." Tracer's nervousness was contagious. Florence couldn't remember why she had been invited. She didn't think she had been very nice to Tracer when they first met. There was always a jockeying for position between women, like dogs trying to establish themselves in a pack. An instant evaluation took place at introduction—which was younger, prettier, richer, had more social status, a better job, a better boyfriend, a husband. If even the slightest miscalculation occurred, the two women might well be enemies for life.

She couldn't see the importance of friendships with women. It didn't occur to her to confide in someone. Nor did she realize women friends might have introduced her to men. Women were objects with which to compete. But as long as Tracer acted admiringly, did a golden retriever friendly shuffle, she could tolerate the disparity in their economic situation. Ninety-nine percent of the time other women expected her to admire them; it was the equivalent of a paw placed firmly on her back, a warming gesture. But she could never bring herself to assume the lesser position. At least Tracer, who seemed to want something from her, was not expecting her to walk around praising her apartment; if anything, she seemed chagrined by the situation.

"So . . ." Tracer handed her a beer and sat at the wide French provincial table. "Um . . . what about this friend of yours?"

"You like him?" Florence wanted to know what was going on before she gave Tracer any information.

"He's . . . oh, gosh, he's so cute! We really hit it off last night. I don't know a thing about him and . . . are you going out with him? I mean, I didn't want to step in if he was your territory or . . ."

"Going out with him? Darryl?" Her eyes flickered; it would be a sign to the other woman that the thought had never crossed her mind, that Darryl wasn't even worth considering on the eligibility scale. If Tracer was like most women, Darryl would be devalued and perhaps discarded because of something so minute as this.

"I mean, I couldn't really get him to tell me much . . . he doesn't seem to want to talk about himself . . . but he's so clever and funny, it was like having a really great girlfriend to talk to, he's not like most guys. He's not . . . is he gay?"

"Darryl? Oh, gosh, no." It was true he was incredibly funny and bright; odd that she had never thought about this before. She looked at Tracer resentfully. "But, gosh, he's so short, and, well . . . wouldn't it be silly? I'm so tall! You are too. He's like a little . . . he reminds me of . . . I don't know, there's something sort of sickeningly good-looking . . . Montgomery Clift?" Her voice faded. She looked at Tracer, but none of the animation had left her expression. She was nodding, but with just as much eagerness as before.

"But I think a man is sexy if he, you know, looks at you in a certain way, or is funny, and interested in you and asks good questions."

"I don't know where I met him. I've known him since I moved to New York. Actually, I think he was the brother of somebody? No, I think . . . did I meet him at some junior thing at the Museum of Modern Art? Or maybe it was an opening. Anyway, we've only ever been friends. You can have him." Yet she felt slightly uneasy at these words.

"He's got a book coming out soon. We were talking about it last night."

"Oh." She was slightly embarrassed that he hadn't revealed that much to her. "I figured."

"It's nonfiction, following the lives of some of the people he's worked with."

"Yeah, I think he mentioned something like that."

"He's an incredibly brilliant lawyer, he could make a ton if he wanted." Her eyes were glittering with infatuation, her horse face young and sincere. "He graduated top of his class at Harvard—he didn't say that, but I had my uncle look him up in some book—he was a Marshall Scholar at Oxford, then he was working for that very fancy company, but he gave it up to do advocacy for the homeless. He said if I wanted I could come with him to the soup kitchen this week—you know, he goes on Thursdays and helps them with legal advice after the meal."

"Ugh." She pictured a room of foul-smelling drunks, lunatics, encrusted with grime, eating something boiled and white, drinking apple drink from paper cups. And Darryl—with his small, rounded shoulders, those little spectacles perched on the end of his nose which always appeared about to slide off, saved only by the fact that his nose was so boyishly upturned—hopping eagerly from one foot to the next, sincere, inquisitive, never patronizing. How the thought irritated her!

"I can't believe there's nothing between the two of you. I didn't want to start thinking about him if there was something . . ." She stared at Florence earnestly. "I knew I couldn't compete with you—he talked about you every two seconds."

"He's all yours, if you want him!" Tracer could afford to buy someone like Darryl—advocate for the homeless! Maybe if *she* had millions, and was plain, she wouldn't mind a poor and homely good-deed doer. She would have liked to think so. But she could not, for one second, imagine such an existence, just as she was certain that Tracer could not imagine having this hunger, this gnawing inside, to be rich, to be able to walk into a room and have people practically bend to the ground, kowtowing with respect and admiration at the sight of so much money. "So . . . where are you from?"

"I grew up mostly in Pennsylvania, I guess—I mean, we have

a big house in Bucks County, I call that home, but I lived all over the place—my father's a diplomat, he's retired now, but I lived in India, and London—my mother's French—"

"And your name—that's Schmidt as in Schmidt's Pharmaceuticals?"

"Mmm—that was my great-grandfather, he made a ton of money." She paused and her eyes glistened again. "I just thought he was so cute, in that black T-shirt and baggy brown linen pants—any guy who's dressed that way is usually gay. You're sure he's not gay?"

"I don't think so." She was torn between wanting to make up stories and wanting to help Tracer. Her farm face was kindly. It would have been too easy to spoil. "I really like your hair," she said suddenly.

"You do?" Tracer winced, as if Florence's compliment was a trick.

"Honestly? I don't think the cut suits you, but the color is fabulous."

Tracer raised her chin to look at Florence, exposing her throat as if she were telling Florence she had nothing to fear. "You don't think it's a good cut?" she said. "I just had it done."

"You should wear it longer. Wispier." Florence studied her critically. "But it doesn't matter, that color is so beautiful; it looks completely real. Who's your colorist?"

"It's my color," Tracer said.

"Seriously."

"I am serious. It's always been like this. When I was a kid it was white-blond. But what should I do, about the cut?" Absently she began pulling at some hairs in the center of her crown.

Florence didn't respond. She was wondering if Tracer was telling the truth. She couldn't imagine it could really be natural, mainly because she couldn't imagine anyone who didn't do something to alter their appearance. In her own case, there was nothing that was real—except, thank god, for her nose and her jaw, but that was a lucky accident of fate. In a few years, she had already planned, she would have her eyes done, and then after that her face, though she still had time. She might have it done when she was thirty-five.

"So do you think I should call him?"

"Who?" She was so busy thinking about her face-lift she had forgotten where she was.

"Darryl."

"You're not still thinking about Darryl, are you? I can't believe you'd actually have a crush on him. Sure, call him. Why not?"

"Yeah, but what am I going to say? I'm not real good about asking guys out. Maybe I should give a party or something. If I gave a party, would you come? You could invite your friends. Hey, what if you gave a party, but we could have it here, and I would buy all the booze and cook something."

"Oh, gosh," said Florence. "I don't know." It didn't appeal to her, to supply Tracer with a ready-made bunch of friends, all of whom would probably like Tracer immediately, and more than her; anyone who met Tracer, and saw how rich she was, and how gullible, probably would find all kinds of good uses for her. On the other hand, it might do something to restore her image, and anyone who came to her party wouldn't dare say mean things about her—at least not right away.

"Please say yes. He's your friend. You could call him up to invite him and it wouldn't seem like I was coming on to him."

"No, that's not weird. This is New York—people do stuff like that all the time. They're probably used to it."

"Why don't you think about it, though," Tracer said. "I love to cook. I'd love an excuse to cook. Call me later tonight, or tomorrow or something. You want to go get something to eat? I'll take you out to dinner. Or we could just order in. Are there any places in the neighborhood you like? I only know about two places near here."

"I should get going," Florence said. She grabbed the bag of jewelry. "I've got all this stuff I had to get out on Long Island, and it's making me nervous to carry it around. Thanks for the drink, though."

"It's Monday night in the middle of the summer, and there's

nothing to do!" Tracer paced agitatedly. "Please say you'll give a party with me or I'm just going to go out to Aspen for the rest of the summer—this city makes me so nervous."

"Fine, sure, I'll give a party with you." She turned to wave good-bye in the hall and, as she shut the door, caught one last glimpse of Tracer, a frightened dray-horse startled by slippery cobblestones after a rain.

She staggered in the door of her apartment, exhausted. At least Tracer had seemed to be genuinely friendly, one of the only women she had met in ages who didn't give her a blank, superior stare, a form of domination used in Manhattan by women upon other women; the look that managed to say, "I really have no idea what you're talking about and I'm afraid I can't be bothered with someone as peculiar as you." It was a look that inevitably managed to put down the one who was looked upon. She had used it herself on occasion. Now her spirits were lifted at having spent even a little time with someone who seemed to admire her. Maybe she really would have a friend, someone to talk to, someone who would understand her predicament and fix her up with some rich, cute, young guy. Maybe Tracer knew someone in Bucks County, or Aspen, who wouldn't think she had been around a bit too long and who would want her to come and share his life.

There were no messages on the machine. She was so tired she almost fell asleep in the bath, reading an article in a travel magazine about an exclusive island in the Bahamas where in the off-season rooms were available for six hundred dollars a night. She wondered if she should book now to get away for a few days at Christmas. Maybe Tracer would want to go with her? By then she would have had time to get Tracer made over: suggest a fluffier, softer haircut; motivate her to lose weight; go shopping with her for new clothes. Perhaps there was still some hope for the future. The main thing was not to let anyone know just how low she was feeling. She could look at her life as a half-empty glass: two years past thirty; a low-paying job that was going nowhere, and where she was disliked and in trouble; a seedy, rundown apartment that she couldn't afford to hang on to; no real boyfriend or relationship; thirty; having slept with too many men in what was basically a small town. Or she could take the same items and rewrite the script, packaging it into an acceptable treatment: barely in her thirties and never looked better; a classy job in an auction house; a charming apartment that was located in the best zip code in Manhattan; pursued by many men.

The perfumed bubbles frothed and hissed in the old-fashioned bath, releasing their fizzy tuberose perfume. She put the magazine on the floor and, pulling the plug, turned on the tap. The water gushed rustily while she held on to the sides of the tub as if it were a lifeboat going down.

5

Marge Crowninshield and Sonia were in her office. When she walked in they stopped speaking and stared at her. Sonia burst into uneasy laughter.

"Good morning," Florence said after a pause. "Marge, I'm sorry I wasn't here to see you yesterday. I had an appointment in Maspeth I couldn't get out of."

Marge looked at her skeptically. "Anything good?"

"A small lot, nothing really special, but the woman was desperate, and it may bring twenty or twenty-five thousand. I thought we could put it in the winter sale. A bunch of small things, but we did so well with the small things last year. People seemed to like the inexpensive stuff for Christmas presents—I don't know if it will be any different this year. There's one piece—" Suddenly she realized that the things were still in her apartment. She had meant to bring them to work that morning and get them into the vault. The security in her building was not that great. The doorman had the keys to all the apartments.

"I wonder if I could see you in my office after lunch." Marge, nearly six feet tall, with a ridiculous lemon-and-white chiffon scarf around her neck, swept out the door.

"Of course. Two o'clock?" Florence said, more to herself than Marge. She pushed past Sonia and sat down at her desk. There was no reason Marge couldn't have spoken to her now. She just wanted to make her sweat it out until afternoon. Sonia stood looking at her, an evil little grin on her thin-lipped face. Florence thought she was about to make some cutting remark, or give her a warning, but with the contented sigh of a hippopotamus about to stagger into its water hole, Sonia turned and shuffled down the hall.

She had gotten a good night's sleep, hadn't had anything to drink, but she still felt tired. It was as if a huge bird, perhaps a vulture, invisible to everyone, had landed on her head and nested up there happily, with heavy claws fastened onto her shoulders, determined not to budge.

Someone had raised the blinds; the office was dark except for an hour or two in the morning, when the light slanted in, collecting on top of the green metal filing cabinet in a dirty pool. She couldn't stay in this prison cell, though she had come in with the best of intentions, determined to put in a full day's work cataloging—she had a whole list of simple, easily identified pieces of jewelry on which the research had already been done. What excuse could she make up to get out of there? Maybe nobody would even notice that she was gone.

Raffaello still hadn't called; she would be damned if she was going to sit there all morning waiting and hoping. She could say she had to look up something in the library at the museum, or talk to someone over there (a piece actually had come in, some time ago, whose age she had been unable to determine, possibly Celtic in origin). Maybe nobody would ask. But there was Sonia, positioned at the end of the hall, door open, spying on her every coming and going.

She walked past Sonia's office; to her relief, Sonia looked up at her with a guilty expression—she was bent over a box of something like a carrion bird over roadkill.

It was another beautiful day, crisp and windy, all too rare for the end of July in New York. Pedestrians sailed by, summer garments stiffened in the breeze as if they were vestments or the starched linen uniforms of another era. Up on Madison the restaurants crowded the sidewalks with outdoor tables, the doors to the shops were open, and there was a circusy atmosphere of celebration in the air. She wanted to stop at one of the cafés and get an iced cappuccino, but there was the risk of being seen.

She passed a tiny store that sold Italian hats; the window, done up to resemble the stage of a children's puppet theater, pink and red and blue, was full of straw cloches and boaters dyed the color of bruised fruit. Each hat was covered with frothy tulle, yellow-and-pink netting, strewn with glossy brown strands that looked like molten sugar on cakes.

Before she knew it she had gone in and was trying them on. The woman who worked in the shop was also the designer, a diminutive woman who fluttered around plucking the hats from the stands and chirping as she put them on Florence's head. The hats were so amusing, and looked so good on her, she couldn't choose and bought two. They were four hundred and fifty dollars each. She wanted desperately to wear one out of the store, but if she returned to work in something different than what she had arrived in, probably Sonia would wait and comment on the new item when Marge appeared. "And I'll pick them up this evening," Florence said, signing the credit card slip.

"No? You don't want to wear? You should wear now. It looks so good on you, with that outfit!" Once a tiny milliner from Italy would have been among the poorest of the poor, working her fingers to the bone for rich ladies. Now a hat designer—with her own shop on Madison Avenue—was a rich girl, desperate to prove that she had talent, that she had a business, whether or not it ever made any money. There were no jobs for poor women as milliners now.

In Central Park the middle-aged men sailed their three-thousand-dollar handcrafted sailboats across the little lake. These guys, ruddy, glossy, in white shirts and khakis, were in their mid-forties and trying to squeeze out the last drops of boyhood. They were would-be actors, or stockbrokers playing hooky; they had ex-wives and kids; they had sexual problems that came from living in New York—or the problems were why they had come to New York in the first place. They were not real people, only imitations. All day long women and men cruised the pond, eyeing them, trying to pick them up.

She stopped and sat on a dry patch of the low wall that retained the water. A yellow retriever, illegally chasing a stick, jumped over the wall and plunged into the murky water, almost knocking down a child. She imagined, briefly, that this must be what places in Europe were like—Europe was somewhere she had never been. If things didn't work out for her here, she supposed she could always go there, but really she wouldn't have a clue: how to get a job, what kind of papers she would need, where she would live. It was awful to have worked so hard to acquire a veneer of New York sophistication but, due to circumstance, be basically provincial underneath. Her friends—her acquaintances—were widely traveled; Paris, London, Prague, all these places were nothing to them.

Anyway, it was twelve-thirty now. She was permitted to be seen having lunch; even Marge couldn't complain if someone spotted her. She walked back to Madison Avenue. The outdoor café tables at the various restaurants were already fully occupied. A bit higher up she entered a very expensive bakery/sandwich shop. A table for two in back was empty. She ordered a glass of dry white wine scented with a slight hint of woodruff, and the day's sandwich—tapenade, sun-dried tomatoes and smoked mozzarella, served on thickly sliced peasant bread.

She sat staring blankly at the wall, and when her sandwich arrived she chewed methodically, without tasting, like an animal at its feed. But whether that was because the food, though attractive in appearance, in fact had no flavor, or because she was distracted, she didn't know. She was oddly unsatisfied, as if she had just consumed an illusion. The sandwich came with a tiny salad—a spray of mung bean sprouts, three yellow pear-shaped miniature tomatoes, a leaf of endive. Nevertheless, she couldn't understand how she had spent almost twenty dollars for a lunch that was nothing more than a few bits of things that tasted like salt and rubber.

She had done her best to put Raffaello out of her head, but it was no use. It was as if a huge bubble were rising up from her stomach, a bubble with thick, viscous walls; the bubble was making her rummage in her pocketbook for change, for a pen and paper—the bubble wanted her to call him. For the past day she had done her best to fight the bubble, popping it with a pin, weighing it down, but the bubble would not be stopped: it grew back, its walls thicker, more determined than ever. She had to speak to him.

She settled her bill and found a phone in the front entryway. "Hi, this is Florence." She spoke to his answering machine. "Are you there? I thought we were going to get together for lunch. Give me a call when you get a chance." She tried to sound nonchalant, but her voice had the creaky squeak that came into it when she was uncertain.

As soon as she hung up she was sorry she had left a message. She should have waited until he was home and answering the phone. She had no one and she was nothing, she told herself. She was completely alone in the world. She was thirty-two years old and there was no hope for her future. Life was like a game of musical chairs. Ninety-nine percent of them were taken, and she couldn't see where the empty ones were positioned. Besides, if there were any empty chairs left, they were empty for a reason—broken legs, ugly styles, cheap imitations.

Outside, the morning air had fled. The day-turned-to-afternoon was no longer so pleasant. It was unnatural, the weather in New York, with each day or even half day unconnected to the rest, as if someone on top of a skyscraper had access to various temperature-control switches and dials. It was beginning to grow humid. A chemical cloud seemed to have blown in from New Jersey, and now that the breezes had died down, it languished overhead, gray and foul-smelling. There were still forty minutes until she had to meet Marge, not enough time to go to the gym, not really enough time to do anything. It occurred to her again she had left Virginia Clary's jewelry at home, though she had meant to bring it in to work. The thought weighed her down.

She waited on line at a row of corner pay phones. A drug-addict-type woman with a pimpled face, dressed in a purple nylon jogging outfit, swung at the end of the metal telephone cord, turning to face the sidewalk, then back to the phone again, chewing gum, yodeling and chortling, oblivious to the fact that others were waiting to use the phone; or perhaps she was fully aware and was reveling in her power. A messenger type, in a pair of tight nylon shorts, a T-shirt, and a long shawl over his head, huddled in the middle booth. The last phone was out of order, the receiver dangled limply between the legs of the booth.

There were several others ahead of her; the druggy woman still didn't get off the phone, but the messenger left and the next man departed without making his call. Another man—really a boy, he had to be ten years younger than she—came and stood behind her. "Are you waiting for a phone?" he said in a voice so low it was practically a mutter. He wore a blue-and-pink bow tie, a silly checked jacket and striped trousers. His hair was plastered down and he had on old-fashioned round horn-rimmed glasses—one of those types trying to appear as if he lived in an earlier era. She nodded. His eyes lit up with a zany love, he couldn't stop staring at her. At least someone found her attractive. When the man in front of her had finished, she dialed Raffaello's number. His machine answered and she hung up. She was about to leave when the boy in the bow tie blocked her way. "Is your name Kerry?" he said.

She shook her head and started to go around.

"No, wait!" he said. "I—I'm sure I—did you go to Bennington?"

"No, I didn't." She pushed past him and headed back toward work. She decided she might as well pick up the hats now. She was allowed to shop on her lunch hour; Marge couldn't control her free time, and there was no way she wanted to make this detour on her way home from work, even though she had originally planned to come back this way.

She was turning into the door of the hat shop when she realized the idiot had followed her. The poor moron had a cigar clamped between his teeth, which he removed like a horse freeing itself from the bit. "Excuse me!" he was calling. "Excuse me!" She rolled her eyes and stopped. "I'm sorry to bother you. I know . . . you're a woman, men probably bother you . . . it's just that . . . let me introduce myself: my name is Spencer Hubert Fairbrother the Third." He paused, as if she would either be impressed with this information or feel obliged to offer her name in return. "I'm sure . . . well, I'm fairly certain I did meet you, at a party, or at least I saw you. But now I'm thinking: do you occasionally go to Quayle's, the auction house?"

"I work there," she blurted, taken aback that he actually had seen her before.

"Oh!" He was pleased with himself and puffed on the cigar before remembering it was unlit. "I knew I knew you from someplace. It's your smile. You have such an unusual and kind smile, almost as if you didn't realize it when you were smiling. I know this is probably somewhat presumptuous on my part, but I was wondering if you wanted to join me—and a group of friends—later this evening."

"Probably not." He couldn't have been twenty-two; was he oblivious to her age? She could see herself with him and a bunch of his friends, all twenty years old, rich boys pretending to be Round Tablers at the Algonquin. It was too cute. On the other hand, did she have anything to lose? Maybe his father, divorced, or widowed, fabulously wealthy, the owner of the restaurant, whatever, would stop by.

Spencer Hubert Fairbrother the Third looked at her from behind his thick glasses. His eyes were huge, timid, the color of cement, yet at the same time his expression was superior and bemused. "Why don't I write down the information and you can give me a call if you change your mind?"

"Sure," she said. "Write it down. If I can't make it tonight, maybe I'll give you a call some other time. By the way, what's a good place to buy cigars?"

6

Because she stopped in a tobacco shop and bought a ridiculously expensive device to nip off the ends of cigars, she was late for her meeting with Marge. She couldn't navigate around pedestrians so quickly carrying the huge hatboxes. Then the elevator was stuck somewhere; she finally took the stairs and arrived in Marge's office out of breath. Marge was on the phone and nodded regally for Florence to take a seat. Then she continued with her phone conversation. Florence waited. Ten minutes passed. She gazed into space with the expression of someone thinking deep, inner thoughts. She knew this would drive Marge crazy, when she noticed; Marge wanted to torture her. It occurred to her she had learned this technique—of staring vaguely into space—from her mother, who could switch on or off seemingly at random.

Marge might have been punishing her for being late to the meeting. Or it might always have been part of the plan. "Then I'm going to meet Carlos for a week in Morea. He's got that place that belonged to his father. You know, his Alzheimer's seems to have stabilized." Marge had a high, imperious voice. On the telephone it cut into the ear of the poor listener like a metal probe. She wasn't even discussing business. Finally she put down the phone and looked at Florence as if hoping she was going to ask about her upcoming trip to Morea. Florence continued to gaze off into the distance, and at last, as if rousing herself from a more important event, she turned to Marge with a dismissive smile.

"I'm sorry I wasn't able to see you yesterday. I had an appointment out on Long Island I was unable to cancel."

"I know," Marge said. "Anyway, that isn't what I wanted to talk about. I'm afraid I've been meeting with Caspar Baumgarten"—he was the associate director of Quayle's—"and he's felt for some time it's necessary to make some cutbacks. He met with the board of directors last week and basically the conclusion was to reduce staff in several departments: Estate Jewelry, Musical Instruments, African and Oceanic Art were the first three areas. Unfortunately, Florence, he left it to me to let you know."

"I see." She deliberately kept her voice as calm and disengaged as possible. "And are you offering me any severance?"

"It's a difficult time. Even Sotheby's and Christie's are making cutbacks. It's this new taxation. Quayle's profit margin has always been much weaker than the larger concerns. However, I did speak to Caspar about this. He would like to offer you a week's pay for each year you've been with us. I think you've been here four years."

"Four and a half."

"Yes, well, I'll have to speak to him about those six months. Anyway, at least that's a month's pay; and of course you have a few vacation days—"

"Ten."

Marge, though in pain, appeared to be enjoying herself, as if she were scratching a mosquito bite or poison ivy rash. "And he wants you to know he's going to keep you on Quayle's health insurance program for ninety days."

"I'd like him—and you—to provide me with letters of recommendation." She was surprised at how cool her voice was.

"Yes, well—I'll certainly bring that up at our next meeting. Anyway, why don't we just round it out to two months' pay—and that, plus the three months' health insurance, should certainly see you through to your next job, Flo. And you really don't have to worry, do you? I mean, you're just working here for fun."

"Yes." She gave Marge a cold, superior smile. Now she was sorry she hadn't worn a suit to work that day: something sharp and crisp, more expensive and glamorous than anything gawky, awkward Marge had in her closet. Two months' pay! That would give her around thirty-two hundred dollars; remembering Quayle's payroll department, she knew her taxes and Social Security would automatically be taken out. It would scarcely cover a month's mortgage and maintenance. Quayle's offered no pension fund; although, as she recalled, they would have matched two thousand a year if she had started an IRA. That would have been sixteen thousand dollars, but she hadn't put any money away in a retirement fund. In the back of her mind she had always thought something—someone—would surely come along to rescue her before then. What good would it have done if, at age sixty-five, she had several hundred thousand dollars in a retirement plan? By then the money would be worth the equivalent of only several thousand dollars. She had always thought that she was better off spending the money on improving herself—making herself into a more marketable commodity. Well, at least she wouldn't have to go and buy any new outfits for her job hunt.

Her eyes prickled as she packed her things, though she was

determined not to cry. Within moments Sonia had appeared in the door, plugging the room with her smug presence. "So what are you going to do?" she whined.

"Actually, a friend has wanted me to go to work for him for a while," Florence said. "He has a private foundation—he's funding all kinds of enterprises in China." She was surprised at how quickly the fiction poured from her mouth.

"Oh!" Disappointed, half disbelieving, Sonia shuffled away. "Well, that's great! You should tell Marge. She's been very upset about this whole thing, you know. She really likes you."

"Mm." She didn't know if she should just trash the stuff in her desk, or actually go and start searching for a box to lug the things home. It was remarkable how much she had accumulated in her time at Quayle's. Expensive bottles of nail polish, stockings with runs, extra pairs of new stockings, a pair of dirty stockings, which she had taken off when she had arrived at work after staying the night at some guy's apartment. Toys she had bought during her lunch hour to cheer herself up: a tiny kaleidoscope, its exterior made of polished rosewood and brass; inside, the glass shards when shaken fell into patterns resembling elaborate molecular structures. She peered into it, holding the end containing the bits to the light. It made her think the universe had been tapped with a hammer and tossed into a garbage pail. Two plastic windup toys, one in the shape of a chicken, which waddled and clucked; the other, a minute hopping kangaroo. A bag of glistening, gemlike lollipops, some of which had fallen out and in the heat melted to the metal surface of the desk drawer. An empty tin of currant-flavored pastilles. A horoscope booklet, a year out of date, on her sign of Scorpio. A Mont Blanc pen with chipped enamel. A small, partially consumed bottle of vodka. Quayle's Christmas gift of last year—a bottle of wine, still in its silver foil wrapping. A Looney Tunes mouse pad for her computer, Tweety Pie sweating in her cage while Sylvester, red-nosed, in a frenzy of aggressive lust, panted just beyond the bars. A broken opal that must have fallen out of some jewelry setting, quite a nice one apart from the fact that one side was split, almost black with flecks of prancing colors. It wasn't hers—but whom to return it to? She swept it up with the other junk.

"Oh, but you can stay until the end of the week." Marge was in the door. "In fact, I'd like you to stay until the end of the month. I wasn't expecting you to go today! I'd like to go over everything you've been working on—your files, the cataloging—before you go. I don't want to lose all the material for the October sale."

In that case, you should have waited to fire me, she thought. Or made that a contingency of my severance. She turned and smiled sweetly at Marge. "I'm afraid that won't be possible. A friend wants me to start working for him right away, and I'd like to have a few days off in between." Somehow this didn't come out as credibly as when she had spoken to Sonia.

Marge suddenly looked flabby and watery, as if her face were a slice of zucchini boiled a bit too long. "You won't stay until the end of the week?"

Florence shrugged. All these years Marge had never given her a single extra day off, deducting time spent at the dentist, hovering over her every second and in between regaling her with stories about various eligible bachelors who had been at parties the night before—parties that Florence could have attended had Marge not snatched the invitations (a dinner at the Met, which had been sent to both of them; a lecture followed by dinner at Asia House) without telling Florence until the day after. Or had wined and dined the interesting and important clients or dealers and not let Florence join them. Which was the least she should have been included in, considering what Quayle's paid her. There had been a cruise in the Bahamas—Marge was to lecture for free passage. She couldn't go, but could have suggested Florence. And on and on. The woman was fifty-four years old; by her age, shouldn't she have acquired some generosity of spirit?

"I'm afraid in that case I'd like to see everything you're taking home with you. It's simply part of our new security program."

"Of course. Take a look." As if after all these years she had been so stupid as to snitch jewelry and keep it stored in her office. Marge no doubt thought this would be humiliating, but what did she care? She pointed to the piles of stuff. "I think I'm throwing out most of it. I can't lug it all across town." There was a small electric clock-radio in the pile. She could see Marge eyeing it acquisitively. She moved it over into the heap of things she was going to keep.

"What will you do with the things you don't want?"

"The stuff I don't want? I'll just put it in my wastebasket."

"Really I wish you wouldn't. The staff gets very upset. If there are things you don't want, could you donate them to charity if they're useful, or take them home to throw out with your own rubbish? Hardly any of the cleaning staff is left; they've spoken to me several times about the garbage and recycling situation." Marge was standing in front of a large mirror that Florence had hung on the wall years before. She could see herself just over Marge's shoulder. No wonder Marge hated her and wanted her out. Marge looked like a cartoon character flattened beneath the weight of a falling anvil. Next to her Florence was an exotic flower: slanted, luminous gray eyes, lips permanently fixed in a bemused smile. But that was simply the way her face appeared in repose. Didn't Marge know that the tawny hair and skin, the head perched on the long stem of a neck, were as arbitrary a fact of nature as Marge's own appearance? Inside her were bitter seeds. She was not beautiful on the inside; her exterior was pure luck, and she didn't see why Marge was so determined to punish her for that.

"I'll just take a few things out now, then," Florence said. She picked up as much as she could—her hatboxes, the oversized shopping bags full of stockings, tape cassettes, a few books, some letters—and headed down the stairs. She hailed a taxi and got in. Let Marge or Sonia figure out what to do with the rest of the stuff. As far as she was concerned she was never going to go back. Or . . . perhaps one day, when she had millions and millions of dollars and a famous, rich husband, perhaps then she would tell her driver to stop, sweep upstairs dressed in a baby-blue Chanel suit, looking not a day older, greet Sonia and Marge patronizingly as if she could scarcely remember who they were. She would point to a page in the catalog, a pair of emerald ear clips costing fifty, sixty thousand—the most expensive item probably ever to come Marge's way—and coolly tell Marge she might be interested. How Marge would scurry to get the item from the case, hover over her, offer her tea, coffee, a glass of wine, the little peppery cheese sticks (ten dollars a pound) that were presented only to the richest and best clients. Then she, Florence, would look at the jewelry, shrug, say, "Who's shooting your catalogs these days? They certainly looked much nicer in the picture." And making it clear that nowadays when buying jewelry she almost always went to Cartier, to Christie's, to Van Cleef's, she would smile, pick up her alligator handbag (the mildest, purest, beautifully glazed baby-blue to match the suit) and show herself out.

The perfectly crisp day had melted. The humidity was rising, the air growing sticky, as if it were a living organism that was aging and becoming irritable. Laden with possessions, crushed in the backseat of the sweaty cab, she stared out the open window at the dead buildings, stacked in the heat like some vast necropolis, while on the street pedestrians shrouded in wrinkled linen suits vanished as the cab passed in a cloud of hot air and exhaust.

7

She changed into a pair of tight knee-length exercise pants in gray cotton blend and a tight pink T-shirt. Her jogging shoes took her longer to find; she had kicked them under the sofa after her last run and forgotten where they were. She found her portable radio on the hall table; it was tuned to a black soul station, the music she always listened to while she jogged. She headed toward Central Park, stopping on the way from time to time to stretch. She put her foot at waist level on a lamppost and bent forward, feeling her tendons pull like taffy. For an hour she ran without stopping. It was the only time she didn't have to think, didn't want to think or need to. It must have been how racehorses felt, simply moving without worry or anguish or reliving events of the past. Every step she took brought her closer to something, though what it was she could not be certain. As if there were something behind her, coming up fast, and her only job was to stay ahead of it or be caught. Maybe she should get a dog, a beast who would love her unconditionally, who would be at the door thrilled to greet her, anxious to hop into bed at night and fall asleep in her arms. The problem was, while she liked the idea, she didn't particularly like dogs—shedding fur, drooling, permanently dirty in a doggy way.

She picked up her pace. The ring around the reservoir was crowded with desperadoes, thudding laboriously in the heat. The obese, the anorexic, the muscle-bound, the inhumanly perfect gay and the soggy straight, dashing headlong in a frenzy. Blind as the mass migration of wildebeest or eland, their heads tossed, lips flecked with custard, eyes rolling as they thunderously pawed the ground. Only Florence ran with such an animal grace—a young lioness or a cheetah—it was impossible not to notice the predator among the herbivores, but somehow lost, charging erratically through the stampede as if she had misplaced her prey.

At last she gave up. It was as if she had temporarily beat herself into submission. She trudged toward home, praying the chant would not begin once again to echo in her head: *What is to become of me? Who was going to want her now?* There was a man standing on the corner of her block and he came eagerly toward her. She didn't have a clue who he was, though he obviously knew her. Just as his face began to crumple with injury, she realized it was John de Jongh. She couldn't imagine what it must be like, to be so amphibious, transmutable in appearance that even women who had slept with you didn't recognize who you were. "Hi, John," she said warily.

"Hello dere! I tried to call, but I think something's wrong with your phone. I was in your neighborhood and just wanted to drop by. It's about that stock that you bought—" He looked around apprehensively. "Do you mind if I come up? With my luck, some-body I know will bump into us."

"I've just been for a run. I have to take a shower."

"I can see!" He was joking in a way that seemed lewd; it assumed intimacy. He looked her up and down with an assessing, hungry gaze. "I have a few minutes. I can wait. Or, I could join you!"

She could see he was determined to come in with her. Irritation swept over her. It was so rude to stop by without warning. She nearly always hated having people come into her apartment unless it was her own idea. She had no sense of being connected with this man in any way. He seemed to think something had passed between them; dressed in a business suit, navy-blue tropical wool, he slung his arm around her sweaty shoulders. It was all she could do not to kick him in the ankle or step on his instep, clad in its hideous little Gucci loafer of a rich brown color, capped with a snaffle bit. She ducked out from under the arm. "I'm all sweaty! You'll ruin your suit!"

"I don't mind."

The doorman gave her a sneering look. Since when had the doorman in her building begun to sneer? She ignored him as they got into the elevator. There was a message on the wall about a meeting that evening for co-op owners and tenants. "I never go to those dumb things."

John ignored this and slid his hand up under her shirt. "I've been thinking about you all day." He started to reach under her brassiere, but found it impossible—these exercise bras were stiff pieces of flexible rubber, Lycra really, and thank God he wasn't going to be able to get it off. She backed away. "I'm sorry, I can't help myself." He pulled a handkerchief out of his pocket and took off his glasses, wiping his ruddy face. "I think I'm going crazy. Nothing like this has ever happened to me before. Natalie has thrown me out of the house; I'm staying at the club. I'm like someone possessed. What have you done to me?"

"John, I—" The elevator stopped and she got out and started

down the hall. He really did seem to have gone crazy. She'd be damned if she slept with him now just to gratify his personal fiction. It had nothing to do with her. She was repulsed. "Listen, I'm really sorry—" she said as she began to unlock her door.

"I didn't want to tell you, I didn't feel you should be burdened with it," he said. He seemed to be waiting for some word of approval from her, or her insistence that he share everything with her, that she felt as he did.

"Well, I'm sorry you're having such a rough time of things now. You had to move into your club? Natalie's out in Bridgehampton full-time over the summer, isn't she? You couldn't just stay in the apartment in the city?"

"I don't want to talk about myself. Let's talk about you. You know that Derek has so many people wanting to invest in his new restaurant he's not letting anybody else in?"

"Really?"

"Mmm. See, I'm taking care of you. Write me out a check, though, will you, for me to give to him? I want to get it over to him quickly, or you'll get shut out."

He came up behind her and cupped his hands over her breasts. It was all she could do not to turn around and belt him in the face. She shut her eyes for a moment as a wave of pure nausea and hatred swept over her. It wasn't his fault; but she couldn't remember when she had felt so inanimate, as if she were a melon at a market or a silver Victorian cigarette case containing an obscene enamel picture under the lid, an object both coveted and sneered at. "Let me go get my checkbook." She scuttled from his fleshy grasp and grabbed her bag. Quickly she wrote out a check. "So if I wanted, I could sell my share in the restaurant and make a profit?"

"No, no, honestly—he's only doing me a favor because we're old friends. Anyway, you'll be holding on to it for a bit—you want to make some money."

"So who do I make it out to?"

"I guess you should just make it out to me, since I'm business partners with him on this."

"What's the restaurant going to be called anyway?"

"I don't know. I forgot to tell you—if you have a good idea, let me know. Derek's open to suggestions. Maybe we'll call it *Florence*!"

She scribbled on the check and began to back away. "I just want to see what came in the mail, John. Help yourself to something to drink!" she called to him from the hall. "I think there's some beer in the refrigerator—or I could make us some ice tea."

"Actually, I'd love a gin and tonic."

"Whatever you can find," she muttered. She hadn't opened her mail in months and she carried it to the coffee table in the living room. At least it would buy her some time—maybe he would get the hint and go away when he saw how much mail there was. He came in the living room and lingered by the door. "So, John, let's say I could come up with some other money—sell some jewelry or something." She separated the items into three piles as she spoke, an excuse not to look at him. "What would be another good thing to invest in?" She didn't really have any decent jewelry, but it was always nice to know in case she unexpectedly won the lottery or found a diamond ring on the street.

"You have some jewelry? You should definitely sell it and invest. There's a small family business I know of—I have it on reasonably good authority it's about to go public. If you can come up with the cash, I can buy some for you on the first day. It will probably triple almost immediately. Back in the mid eighties I bought Bermese Python at—I think I paid twelve hundred a share. It's worth thirty-five thousand a share today. But, you understand, I can afford to be a little more daring on these personal investments than I can at the office. Say, ah, where do you keep the gin?"

"Look in the cabinet just opposite the stove." She waved vaguely down the hall. Every envelope she opened seemed to have something from the management—threatening notes about her maintenance payments being overdue. But the maintenance was supposed to be paid automatically through the new program at the bank. Envelope after envelope—"Maintenance Due." "Overdue."

Penalties. Warnings. Letters from lawyers. It looked as if it hadn't been paid in six months—which was about the time she had kind of stopped bothering with the mail, and about the same time she had signed up to have her maintenance and mortgage bills paid electronically. Sickened, she put the mail on the floor. It wasn't her problem, was it? It was the bank's problem: she would go in there tomorrow and let them deal with the situation. She knew she had something left in her savings account, even after writing out the check—perhaps she had thirty. She did the math in her head, mostly by guessing, since she didn't bother to keep a record of checks she wrote out, let alone balance her account.

John came back into the living room holding up a bottle. "There doesn't seem to be a heck of a lot in that cabinet," he said. "A bottle of aquavit? Who drinks that stuff? Obviously nobody, since this and some kind of Peruvian firewater are the only two bottles with anything in them left. I think you had an eighth of an inch in the gin. You have to call up and get these things delivered; they don't just refill themselves!" He laughed uproariously. "Why don't I call up now and order some gin and—what would you like?—shall I tell them to send up a couple of bottles of champagne for you?"

"No." She put her feet up on the coffee table and immediately John circled around and lunged forward, his hand attaching itself between her legs like a suction cup on an octopus's tentacle.

"I could get a restaurant to send up a pitcher of frozen margaritas and some Mexican food," he said. "Would you like that?"

"No!" If there had been a knife handy, she would have picked it up and plunged it into his white button-down shirt. "Get your hands off me! Get out of my house, do you hear me? Get out!"

She sat for hours in her dark bedroom. Apparently she owed at least eight thousand on back maintenance. If the bank hadn't paid the mortgage, that was another seventeen she owed. Well, she supposed she could call John tomorrow and tell him not to deposit her check; perhaps she wouldn't lose so very much. Or she might not even bother to speak with him—she could just call the bank and order a stop payment. Maybe she had more cash left in the bank than she thought. There had to be options. She might get a roommate, charge fifteen hundred a month or even two grand. But even if she found a roommate willing to pay that much—and sleep in the living room!—her monthly expense totaled more than three thousand and she would never catch up with what she owed. Or she could sell the apartment and find a studio rental. But the problem was, in the present market she doubted she could find a buyer, let alone one who would pay as much as she owed the bank . . . Maybe that girl Tracer would let her live with her, free of charge? Tracer had more than enough room. She picked up the phone. "Hi, Tracer?"

"What time is it?"

"Oh, gosh, I don't know. Not late. Eleven? Did I wake you up?"

"Um . . ."

"Oh, I'm really sorry! I didn't think it was that late. What time is it?"

"After midnight." Actually it was closer to one A.M.

"It's just that . . . I was thinking about our party! And I had all these great ideas. But . . . I'm sorry I woke you up. I can call you tomorrow."

"That's okay. I'm awake now. The thing is . . . I kind of decided to get out of here for a while, and I don't know when I'll be back, so I think maybe we should put the party idea on hold."

"Why?" It was all she could do to control her anxiety. "I thought you wanted to have a party. Did something happen?"

"No, no. I just think I should . . . well, you know how New York can be. I had a rough day. Anyway, my dad wants me to spend some time with him . . . he's down in Mexico. He's got some people he's entertaining and needs some help."

"Oh, gee. That sounds fun."

Tracer didn't respond. "I saw some people you know tonight, for dinner."

"Oh really? Who?"

"Um . . . gosh, what was his name?"

"Oh, tell me!"

"John . . . John something-or-other."

8

She had lived with her mother in a large innocuous house built in the late fifties in Orange County. The houses in the area were all alike, facing busy four-lane streets, yards planted with squat palm trees, scratchy grass almost artificially green, spiky yucca. This district was not a fancy part of California, but over the years as the property values rose, it became progressively more upscale— the city arranged for flowers to be grown in hanging baskets above the traffic lights; an upscale shopping mall complete with Neiman-Marcus and Italian *cucina* was built several blocks away. It was perhaps fortunate that her father had died when she was little. There was not a single friend of hers whose parents had not split up—inevitably it was the fathers who ran off with the new, younger girlfriend or produced someone who had been mysteriously waiting in the wings. When the mothers found someone it was almost always temporary, a construction worker or eighty-year-old retiree. Her father had been an insurance salesman and of course had not bothered to take out a life insurance policy on himself; at the time of the accident it was believed he had suffered a slight stroke. There was no other explanation why he would have run a red light. Florence's memories of her father weren't particularly vivid—a grayish man who had rarely been home. Perhaps had he lived, her parents would have stayed married, but it was unlikely.

After his death their standard of living dropped considerably; her mother eventually returned to teaching fifth grade, which she had done before Florence's birth—but her salary scarcely paid for local property taxes. The area above the garage was converted into an apartment and rented out. One afternoon every other weekend was spent visiting her retarded sister in a state hospital almost an hour and a half away. Bethany, two years younger, suffered from cerebral palsy in addition to severe retardation; it was doubtful whether she even knew who her mother and Florence were, though her mother swore she recognized them.

Apart from these few minor quirks her childhood had been perfectly normal. She was popular, the prettiest in her group of friends; all of them had played with troll dolls or Barbies; then participated in tennis lessons, horseback riding, ice skating, gymnastics; and as they got older, found after-school and summer jobs at Disneyland.

She attended a nearby branch of the University of Southern California and lived at home for the last two years it took her mother to die of breast cancer. When it was over she sold the house and was surprised to get almost half a million dollars for the poorly constructed place in which she had grown up. With the money she moved to New York and got her degree from Sarah

Lawrence, though she was never quite certain what had motivated her to go East. She had fit in, in California; it was kind of nice to be blond in a world where everyone was brunette, and she felt powerful and certain she was destined for great things.

When she had graduated she bought a small one-bedroom apartment in a building that had been converted from a convent. The apartment, like the home where she had grown up, was dark and low-ceilinged; it was in the back, facing other buildings that were almost within touch. One entered a dark and narrow hall, passing through a kitchenette—so small there was room only for a miniature refrigerator—to get to the living room, which, aside from furniture and filing cabinets, was filled from floor to ceiling with boxes of knickknacks, all the things she had picked up in her years in New York that reflected her rapidly changing tastes, none of which went together but with which she was unable to part. The bedroom was equally cramped, the two closets nearly exploding with clothes—voluminous satin skirts like parachutes, vintage jackets, hats, riding boots, ski clothes. Beyond the bedroom, the crumbling bathroom, with its steam pipes hissing rust and rage. At night the tiled floor, beneath her bare feet, would get so hot she would actually hop about in surprise, soles nearly scorched.

Despite the chaos and profusion of objects, she insisted on everything being kept clean, if not organized. The sight of one infant cockroach was enough to get the exterminator—moronic, excited, carrying a heavy tank—to douse the place with the greasy, yellowish ejaculate that smelled of death. Because the place had formerly been a convent, the hallways were of a peculiar configuration, and her two rooms lay at the end of a private corridor next to the stairs, where the garbage was deposited. A faint whiff of decay sometimes blew under the door. On Mondays the doorman gave the keys to a cleaning woman, Ivana from Russia ("my housekeeper" was how Florence referred to her), who, for one hundred dollars, spent a half day dusting the two rooms, scrubbing the decaying bathroom, taking laundry to the machines in the basement and ironing each garment on an ironing board set up in the only empty space anywhere, at the foot of Florence's bed. An endless heap of clothes went to and from the dry cleaners—the most expensive cleaners, who charged an exorbitant rate and delivered each item back to the building stuffed with beautiful puffy pink tissue.

The important thing: the building was in one of the best locations, in the eighties between Madison and Park; it seemed to her that if she was going to live in the city, she should live only in the most exclusive area. She had been so certain she would be rich very soon that she made only the minimum down payment and took out a balloon mortgage; the first five years her payments were very low (though the maintenance at such a fancy address had always been very high, over a thousand a month) but then suddenly escalated to more than two thousand a month—at the very moment the whole market for one-bedroom apartments collapsed.

And the money she had inherited, which had seemed so limitless initially, had—apart from the twenty-five thousand—completely vanished. Yes, a chunk had gone on tuition and living expenses during those two years at Sarah Lawrence, perhaps a hundred grand. And she had some equity in the apartment, but not much. Another piece had been paid in taxes. A trust had already been established for her sister in the institution. She had lived in the apartment for six years, with mortgage and maintenance forty-plus thousand a year—her salary from Quayle's was so nominal it could hardly be factored in. Gone, and she was no closer to having any real life than if she had been living at home in that damp house built on ground which had once been a stream, or a swamp, and which had long since been filled in but still squished underfoot, reluctant to abandon its origins entirely.

In the morning she was up and dressed before she realized she no longer had to go to work. It was still only eight o'clock; she headed downstairs and up the block to get a cappuccino and a sweet roll at an Italian restaurant and bakery that served its coffee Italian-style at a little standing bar. The sun on the street was so strong it hurt her eyes. The curtains in the bakery window were pulled down halfway; otherwise, the cakes placed in the display cabinets would have melted. Such lavish, garish marzipan confections, colored and painted to resemble beach scenes, zoo animals, other inedible concoctions for those whose fantasy it was to devour the undevourable. The cakes cost fifty dollars, sixty, eighty, even more depending on their size—she was almost tempted to purchase a smallish one, which looked like it might have been chocolate, crowned with an underwater scene of chunky-armed mermaids and orange-and-blue fish. But she knew in her present state she would have gone home, gotten between the sheets and eaten the whole thing, turning the bed into a sea of crumbs.

Instead, she selected a huge cinnamon roll studded with pecans and raisins and took it over to the bar; the coffee was bitter and hot, and between mouthfuls she ate the roll, unwinding the yeasty dough and tearing off pieces. She had only a hellish day to contemplate. Her first move would be to call John and get him to return her check, or at least let her sell the stock he had bought for her; if he had said something nasty about her to Tracer, or to anybody else, she would get that out of him too.

The bar grew crowded with businessmen and -women grabbing coffees. *They* were all on their way to work. There was a particularly cute guy wearing what looked like a custom-made pinstripe; any other day she might have been tempted to try to pick him up. But today she pushed her way through. On her way out she stopped again at the bakery and got a pound of assorted cookies, dappled with orange marmalade and almond slices, dipped in chocolate. The smell of butter and sugar was overwhelming and she knew, as she opened the box walking down the street, nibbling at the cookies' edges, that if she got home without having devoured them all, she would spend the morning in an unconscious frenzy eating the rest. When she got back to her building, she handed the box to the doorman. "Thank you!" He was a young guy, in his late twenties—Russian or Greek; she had never really chatted with him—who hadn't been on the job very long, with a big, sorry face and a droopy expression, as if his balalaika had just been taken away. The cookies cost eighteen dollars a pound. He looked more frightened than pleased at her gift, an open box of crumbs.

She spent the morning trying to find John. He had said he was staying at his club, but she didn't have a clue what club he belonged to. She tried the University Club, the Cornell Club and the Yale Club in rapid succession, to no avail. She didn't even know what firm he worked for—if it was his own company, it wasn't called anything like his last name. There was no way she could call Natalie, who would only hang up on her, or worse. She wanted to tell Natalie her husband's lunacy had nothing to do with her, but she knew Natalie would never believe her.

She called Raffaello, but as usual only his machine answered. She spent an hour opening boxes stuffed with papers, trying to find her old resume so that she could begin to update it, but turned up nothing. She would have to start over from scratch, an unbelievable nightmare. Then something occurred to her. There must be another listing for di Castignolli—Raffaello's last name. After all, there was a shop on Fifty-seventh Street—he had said he was working on modernizing and updating the store and merchandising.

"Di Castignolli." The voice that answered the phone was Italian.

Her voice cracked with nervousness. "Ah—I'm looking for Mr. di Castignolli—Raffaello."

"Who is calling, please?"

"Florence Collins."

"And what is this in reference to?"

She couldn't help but feel the question had prurient overtones. "Um . . . he'll know."

"One moment, please."

"How did you find me?" He sounded amused.

She was so taken aback that he was actually on the phone she couldn't remember what she was going to say. Why had she wanted to humiliate herself in this fashion? Until he actually was on the other end, it had seemed not a humiliating thing to do but something forceful, taking charge of her own life. Now she saw she had been deluding herself. "What about our lunch?" she blurted.

"Oh, yes, would you like to have lunch?"

"Maybe . . . I have a little present for you."

"What is it?"

"You'll have to see it in person!"

He laughed. "Shall we say Egezio's? Two o'clock."

It was after eleven. She got the paper and skimmed the Help Wanted ads while she had her nails done around the corner. There were no positions that seemed even remotely possible—in any event, ninety-nine percent of them were alleged offers through agencies, and she suspected the jobs weren't real, merely scams to get women into these offices, from which they would be sent on interviews for receptionist placement.

But it seemed to her that any job she might obtain would only be a position in which to be humiliated. If she found a job at another auction house—and there weren't that many auction houses in Manhattan, let alone positions in jewelry, the only area in which she had training—there would always be someone above her, with more and better connections, experience, background, money. Even if they left, she would not be the one to be promoted: someone new would be brought in from the outside. Or if by some quirk of fate she was made department head, what real status was there in that? The money wasn't great; one wasn't put on the cover of a magazine for heading a jewelry department at an auction house. And how much pleasure did the work provide, when she could never afford to own what she spent the day handling? Any other job—working on a magazine, booking models at an agency, working in a shop or an art gallery—only led down the same dead-end street.

If she had been born fantastically wealthy . . . but even there, the two rich women she knew were always slightly sneered at; somehow, there was always a faint smirk when their names were mentioned, because they weren't married. And the women she knew or read about in the press who did have jobs of some power—running a magazine, heading a literary agency—were also sneered at, or loathed.

No one wanted to admit it, but even now the highest status for women in New York was to be married to a rich man. Marriage was still the great achievement, and single women, no matter how powerful, were still considered suspect, desperate or damaged. It was best to be married to a successful artist; otherwise, any rich man would suffice. Wasn't her view the only realistic one? It might not be such a great thought, but if that was the way things were, why deny it? No one questioned or pitied a married woman (until she was dumped for a younger woman). Having a man and a family was still the best protection a woman could avail herself of. Without a man, a woman was nothing.

"Pedicure too?" She nodded and pulled some pale gold polish—the latest color—from her bag. The Korean manicurist looked at it lustfully. "Very nice," she said, and mentioned the name of the shop where Florence had purchased it, the only shop where this polish was available. Even the manicurists, eking out an existence in tips, knew about such things, and spent hours studying the latest magazines (which were already six months out of date by the time they were published) out of some fear they would be left behind as the great tidal wave of fashion swept past.

Her feet were small and neat, the nails like little jingle shells. She looked at them admiringly while they were scrubbed and cosseted. Manicure and pedicure passed an hour and a half. She trudged home carrying her shoes, wearing paper slippers provided by the salon, the bits of cotton wool still protruding from between her toes. It took her another forty minutes to dress—half the items in her closet were strewn over her bed before she settled on a slightly peculiar skirt, made of gray and pink chiffon petals, and a gray T-shirt. There was a jacket that matched the outfit, but she decided it was too dressy and instead grabbed a thin gray cotton sweater and tied it around her neck. The little cigar pruner was wrapped in fancy dull paper, thick and expensive.

She jumped in a taxi and was at the restaurant by two. He was nowhere in sight, nor was there any reservation under his name.

She sat at the bar, drinking a glass of white wine. The restaurant was full; perhaps when he showed up and there was no reservation, they would have to go elsewhere.

Only the waiters looked at her admiringly. There was a table of four men—three were older, gray-haired; she recognized one as a publishing magnate—but if they noticed her, they were so cautious and subtle in their glances she didn't pick up anything. Next to them two women sat in front of huge salads—only mineral water on the table—nibbling so disdainfully on a single leaf at a time she knew they were vying to see who could eat less. They were so dowdy in their drab suits and pale makeup she didn't see what difference it would make if they were thinner. The whole place was like a funeral gathering, the only color in the room that of the pale pink tablecloths. The men wore gray, the women wore black. Egezio's was a well-known publishing world hangout, but all of New York was like this.

A rather attractive Asian man, slim, with clear, cold eyes like those of some martial arts expert, was seated next to her at the bar, attacking a plate of huge grilled mushroom caps, black and glistening, with knife and fork. For a moment he looked over at her as if he were about to say something, and she saw he was wearing a really good suit; he looked like Hong Kong money. She was about to smile at him encouragingly when someone tapped on her back. She turned to find Raffaello.

"I'm sorry to be so late," he said. "I got stuck at the office." She looked at her watch. It was after two-thirty. She smiled wanly, not knowing if she was supposed to act irritated or understanding. For a moment she could see him as a boy, in his family's huge house, or apartment, whatever it was, behind some ancient gates or wall and courtyard, pampered by the family maid, the fat cook—how they giggled and fussed, giving him bowls of the sweetest cherries on ice, the most garlicky, juiciest olives, the tenderest cutlets—as spoiled as a maharajah or prince. His face was dissolute, but attractively so, with a petulant charm; his nose must have been broken at one time—which was probably a help; he looked like a streetwise Apollo instead of a too pretty one.

"They didn't seem to have a reservation."

"What?" He exchanged a few words with the hostess, the same one who had treated her so rudely forty minutes before, and immediately they were led to one of the better tables, to the side of the room under a skylight. A waiter arrived with a basket of crusty rolls and a dish of butter molded into miniature, individual shells. Thirty-two years old, and she was still nervous about having lunch with an attractive man! But perhaps it wasn't nerves, exactly—perhaps it was closer to the excitement a tiger must feel when in hot pursuit of healthy prey. She pulled the napkin off the bread basket, exposing the firm tan mounds, and offered it to him; he grabbed a roll from the top and put some of the butter on his plate. Of course, she could not eat butter: was there any woman in the room who would touch the stuff? Lumps of fat, pure calories—oh, the horror—yet she longed for the creamy smoothness. So she took a roll and broke it open, nibbling at the hard surface, in order to have something to do. "Will you drink white wine?" he asked. Only foreigners in New York drank at lunch; though she usually had a glass of wine, this was not the norm. "Ah!" He was perusing the wine list. "Good, good, they have something here I think you will like to try."

"What is it?"

"A surprise."

"Oh, good. And here's my surprise for you." She handed him the box. "It's only sterling. I saw it and I thought, Well, if you already have one, I'll take it back and use it to curl my eyelashes or something."

He unwrapped it and, looking at it quickly, nodded and slipped it into his pocket. "Thank you. It's from Leaf's, no? That's a very nice shop."

She ordered grilled artichokes heaped with slivered Asiago cheese to start, followed by pasta in squid ink. The wine, when it arrived, turned out to be from the di Castignolli estate—very few bottles were made, let alone exported, but the owner of the restaurant, a friend of Raffaello's, had specially requested it and kept a cache of the best bottles hidden for him.

It was now a game of hunter and hunted. She used every trick at her disposal: she gazed at him admiringly while he spoke and asked him all the questions she could think of to draw him out. He had done some racing in cigarette boats—this was the most fascinating thing she had ever heard, and she wondered at the danger of it all, and that he wasn't scared. Travel—his trips to Alaska and Iceland for the fly-fishing. The latest movies he had seen. The personalities of his parents. His three brothers. By the time she asked if he was seriously pursuing a divorce, it was the question of one good friend to another, not the question of a woman prowling for a mate. Wasn't it almost impossible for Italians to divorce? Oh, the marriage hadn't taken place in Italy—that was clever. A second bottle of wine was ordered and brought to the table. "So delicious!" she said. Though he had snatched at the bread, it remained untouched. He ate almost nothing; the piles of delectable morsels lay heaped before him glistening with expensive oil.

The afternoon light came through the glass over their heads. The other diners had long since gone. The wine was very cold and crisp, and when the waiter did not replenish their glasses, Raffaello did so, tenderly, debonairly, himself. But it was no use.

"I must be getting back to the office," he said abruptly, drinking a slug of water. It was four-thirty. Not a single sparkle had crystallized in his eyes. She couldn't figure it out; she had done her best, as gracefully insinuating as a tapeworm, but there were not even the remotest signs of infatuation emanating from him. He was just as cool and distant as he had been a few nights back when they began chatting on line at the buffet—his eyes had roamed the room then as if hoping for a more succulent morsel, and they did so now. He was just as much the hunter as she.

To her surprise he suggested that she go back with him to his office; if she would give him a few minutes, he would see if he could finish up early, and they could then go to a movie, or perhaps a museum. He took her arm as they walked down Fifty-fourth Street.

9

She wandered around the shop while he went upstairs to the offices. The items were phenomenally expensive and did not seem to be related to one another. There was a large overstuffed chair covered in a shimmery orange, red and gold fabric, almost Persian in its lush ornateness. This did not have a price tag, but a fabric book cover and a tapestry weekend-bag were marked five hundred and fifteen hundred dollars, respectively. There were a few items of clothing—a dressing gown, a pair of purple-and-cream trousers—

and a fabric lampshade. There was nobody in the shop apart from the two salesgirls, who ignored her, and while she looked around no one else came in. It was impossible to imagine how such a place stayed open, or made enough in sales to even pay the rent. All over the city there were equally peculiar operations, empty stores filled with expensive products, art galleries of ten thousand square feet with a pair of metal-and-rubber sculptures for sale. Unless they were fronts for some other kind of enterprise, such endeavors seemed to be of no use whatsoever. She had waited for almost forty minutes, and was about to ask one of the salesgirls to tell him she was about to leave, when he came down the stairs looking flushed and jittery. "Oh, you are still here!" he said. "I did not know if you would wait this long. I am afraid I am having something of an emergency and cannot get away. Will you take a raincheck?"

The salesgirls, ruby-lipped, brunette, twittered like grackles in their black garb at the back of the store. "You have nice things here!" she said, a bit too loudly. "I've got to get going anyway—I'll give you a call." He stepped forward and performed a little dance that entailed holding her by the shoulders and pecking the air on either side of her cheeks.

It was after five, the streets full of pedestrians leaving work. The atmosphere had that overworked, overused quality which comes before a storm in summer, when too many people have sampled and recycled the same breath of air over and over, until only a scant quantity of oxygen is left. She walked up Madison feeling like an idiot for having drunk so much at lunch, for having hung around so long in the shop when it was obvious he wasn't going to emerge from his office. Her head hurt. At least she hadn't offered to pay for her half of the meal! She realized she was walking more and more slowly. She didn't want to go home. She couldn't face her dark, overcrowded apartment, the moaning air conditioner in the bedroom sending out an erratic, narrow blast of damp, mildewed air that only occasionally accomplished anything. There had to be someone she could call, someone who would meet her and do something with her. When she got in she would go through her address book. Or perhaps there was something written in her diary, a party or event she had forgotten about.

She went into a bookstore, a narrow, cool little shop with the latest novels beautifully arranged on a piece of blue velvet in the front window. These were not trashy beach books or those rated on the bestseller lists: they were all evocative gems, with titles like *Stars Drifting Through Granite*, *A Milky Dance with Jolson's Nose* and *Fossils of Whales and Birds*. The shop represented calm sophistication, an atmosphere charged with the notion that there was a higher order of existence and intelligence. It was a place that tried to suggest the old New York of culture could still be found. But it was an illusion, a movie set designed to soothe, a shop stocked with placebos.

She picked up three or four books that she had heard people mentioning—or had she seen them mentioned in magazines?—and though leafing through them she could see they were pretentious and unreadable, she felt this must be her fault and ended up charging a hundred and twenty dollars for four—three novels and a biography of a Jewish lesbian poet who had never been published before her death in 1940. She almost purchased a fancy art book about netsuke. The book cost a hundred and seventy-five dollars; a gift for Raffaello. It was all she could do to stop herself, but in her heart, a place she did not want to contemplate, she knew that even giving him the sterling-silver cigar cutter had been a mistake.

At least if she were able to calm down and stay home, she would have something to read; and if she went out, she could say she had just bought thus-and-such. She longed to think of herself as the sort of person who might easily spend a quiet night at home, thoughtfully reading, answering letters. She wasn't hungry, but in case she might be later, she stopped at a gourmet delicatessen and bought a container of cold gazpacho, for seven dollars, and a half pound of tomato, basil and mozzarella salad in virgin olive oil.

But when she got inside she knew at once she was going to be unable to stay put. Please let there be an invitation to go out, she thought when she saw that the message light on the answering machine was flashing.

"I was going to try and pick you up." It was Darryl Lever. "But I'm running late, I'm barely going to have time to run home and change—could you just meet me at Avery Fisher at a few minutes before eight? The tickets are in my name."

It came back to her—she had agreed on Sunday to go with him to some concert at Lincoln Center. How she wished she hadn't agreed! She must have been more drunk than she remembered. She had forgotten about it completely. If not for his message she could have taken a cool bath, put on her white cotton pajamas, gotten into bed between her Egyptian cotton sheets . . . Now she had no desire to go out whatsoever. There had to be some way to reach him and tell him she wasn't well. She called his office. The receptionist had left for the day; there was no way to leave a message, the machine merely stating his hours. At first it had seemed there would be nothing worse than having to stay home— now she saw that to sit at some concert while Darryl held her hand would be far worse. "God damn it!" She could just blow him off, not show up, wait until he called and say she was sick, but that just seemed too vicious. It wouldn't even have been so bad if he could just accept that there was nothing between them but friendship; she always had the feeling, however, that he thought if he waited long enough, there would be more.

She opened her Filofax and was about to leave a message for him at home when she saw she had written a couple of things down for today: an inaugural cocktail reception for an exhibition of works by a nineteenth-century French artist, at a fancy gallery off Madison Avenue in the sixties, six to eight (a girl she knew who worked there had added in ink, "Hope you can come!"); and another party nearby at around the same time. She had received the first invitation in the mail; the second, by telephone a few days before—the hostess was throwing this cocktail party for a jewelry designer visiting from Egypt.

If she was going to sit through some dreary concert of classical music, she might as well dash over to the two cocktail parties first—at least that way by the time she met Darryl she wouldn't feel like staying in; she might even be a bit oblivious.

She peeled off her petal skirt and jumped in the shower. Her hair felt lank and droopy. She washed it and ran a comb through it and was about to put on a black sleeveless silk cocktail dress when she decided against it and instead put on a red-and-white-checked cotton dress, fitted at the top, with a flared skirt—it was cooler, less dressy, and she knew that all the other girls, at the first two events anyway, would be dressed in tight black cocktail dresses—why look exactly the same as they? She had a pair of strappy bright red patent leather sandals, very expensive, slightly slutty, and she wore these with bare legs.

The art gallery was in a former mansion some blocks away; the gallery was family-run and specialized primarily in old masters, French academy and so forth; the front doors were glass-covered, with ornate iron bars. An armed security guard examined her suspiciously before pointing across the marble-floored lobby to a reception desk where names were being checked off on a list. Fortunately, the woman who had invited her, Marisa Nagy, was standing nearby, waved hello and ushered her in past the check-in line.

Marisa, tall and black-haired, was dressed in a black cocktail sheath. "Oh, it's so good to see you! How've you been?" Florence couldn't understand why Marisa had invited her, but she must have—her card had been included in the invitation; she had never been invited to an opening at this gallery before. Marisa worked there, in the research department, they had some mutual friend in common, both had gone to Sarah Lawrence—but Marisa was four or five years younger than she. "I want you to meet my boyfriend." Marisa pointed to a putty-faced man in his late thirties who was holding a glass of champagne. "John Henry Pugh, my friend Florence Collins."

She shook the man's hand. He had on a gray suit almost the same shade as his skin. He looked well-to-do but not fabulously rich, and a bit more human than Marisa, who was too perfect. Her cocktail dress was tight-fitting and of some matte fabric, perhaps crepe de chine, with a wide band of black satin around the hips; there was a little matching jacket flung over one arm, and even in this heat she wore sheer black stockings. The pumps were black satin and, Florence noted, just a tiny bit too big in the heel. Her legs were not as good as Florence's either. But her body was nearly perfect, and her face, with thickly lashed huge brown eyes and tiny nose, had on hardly a speck of makeup and was superior to any fashion model's. A fashion model had to appear drab and understated or she would be announcing that she was wrapped up in her own beauty. A nonmodel, on the other hand, could afford to advertise herself a bit, and most of the time the nonmodels wandering around were more beautiful than the models to begin with. Marisa's costume was that of the woman advertising herself for sale as wife to a wealthy man.

Florence took a glass of champagne from a waiter; another waiter came around bearing a tray containing triangles of smoked salmon and crème fraîche on pumpernickel toast points.

"How've you been?"

"I might come in to see you, Marisa. You want to have lunch this week? How do you like working at Saskeleone's?"

"Yes, let's have lunch. I love working here! It's been such a learning experience! You know, I've been in the research department, but I've just started to do a bit of dealing, which has been great."

She realized Marisa hated working there. Still, if she had lunch with her, Marisa might know who had just left work or been fired elsewhere, and Florence could apply. She turned to John Henry. "And are you in the art business?"

"No, no," he simpered, and from a platter took a miniature pastry tart stuffed with what appeared to be tiny cubes of buttered mushrooms. "It's a subject I know very little about." Perhaps he was richer than he appeared. Or had Marisa simply grown desperate and, seeing that the prospects were slim, settled on him while hoping something better came along?

"Oh? What field are you in—"

"John Henry, I want you to come and meet my boss." Marisa took his arm. "Excuse us, Florence, I have to go and check things downstairs. We'll see you in a bit."

She was left alone observing the crowd. She knew no one else in the room; this was the environment of the genuinely rich— elderly women with gray bouffant hairstyles in ancient black beaded evening gowns and amethyst-colored suits, teamed with gray-haired men who walked with shuffling steps. There were scarcely any young people here, but the room was powdery and decayed, perfumed with money.

Cocktails were not permitted in the viewing galleries. Black security guards gleefully restricted guests from entering until they had put their glasses down on trays. The floors were covered in plush gray carpet, like pads of soft fat. The paintings themselves were bland, pleasant scenes—sailboats, the French Riviera in 1880, fishermen, "The Grape Harvesters," a mountain village— banded in heavy gold frames, intended to be hung in the homes of the affluent and never noticed again; it was hardly more subtle than hanging thousand-dollar bills in diamond-studded frames. But there was something soothing about the taupe-and-custard- colored scenes, the artful spotlights casting satin hues, the paired- off wealthy couples who were the last vestiges of their kind in Manhattan. They would go off to dine in dim French restaurants that no one young and fashionable had ever entered, or in dining rooms in apartments facing Fifth Avenue. She would willingly have accepted one of the shuffling old men if it brought with it acceptance and needlepoint cushions. But none of these rich men would bring acceptance with him. The men who were part of this world, if seeking to remarry, would choose someone from their own group. They gave her a wide berth, though she saw, from time to time, one or another glance at her, slightly leeringly, and quickly pretend to be studying whatever painting she was positioned by.

She made her way downstairs, halfheartedly searching for Marisa on the way; she should thank her, mention again about getting together for lunch—she should say "I want to take you to lunch" to let her know she was paying—and make a concrete stab at establishing a friendship. There was no sign of Marisa, however, and she was slightly relieved not to have to express public gratitude for having been invited. It was too similar to a ritual of dogs; she would have to display her submissiveness, and she already felt too lowly to do the dance that would enable Marisa to demonstrate her grandeur.

Almost no one was out on Madison Avenue; the East Side always seemed shut down at night, except for the rare entity darting into one of the scattered restaurants or the occasional building. It was as if the rich grew naturally furtive or wary at night. For their own protection they scuttled as if they were mice while owls huddled behind the gargoyles overhead. The other cocktail party was only fifteen blocks away. She could have walked, but she still didn't know whether or not she would bother to meet Darryl at the concert—if she was going to meet him, she wouldn't have much time at the next event, so she jumped into a taxi.

Lisa Harrison was divorced. Her apartment was smaller than the one she had lived in with her husband, but was still at a good address; Florence hadn't been here before. Lisa must have had help from a decorator. Everything was chintz, porcelain monkeys, gold mirrors, windows heavy with balloons of pink-and-white-striped taffeta topped with contrasting plaids and paisleys. A waiter at the door asked if she wanted white wine or Perrier. It seemed rather sad that Lisa couldn't or wouldn't provide more than that. The minimal space between overstuffed furniture was occupied by men and women in their thirties—the men in suits, the women in the ubiquitous black cocktail dress.

As she stood there Lisa tottered down the stairs—the apartment was a duplex—followed by three wheezing pug-dogs. There was a blank, startled expression on her face, as if she hadn't a clue to where she was. She took Florence's arm. She was wearing a gray satin dress, badly fitted, her blond hair in an elaborate bouffant atop her head. "I only just came down," she said. "I was hiding in my bedroom. I just got my period. Actually—in all confidentiality"—she raised her voice—"I'm in the middle of having a miscarriage! It's the second time this has happened to me; the last time was much worse, I was much further along, and it was in the middle of a reception at MOMA. I suddenly realized my shoe was all wet, and I looked down and I realized it was absolutely full of blood, and my stockings were drenched! So I went down to the ladies' room, leaving, of course, a trail of blood everywhere—" She turned as another guest came into the room. "Oh, hello, Maura, I'm in the middle of telling Florence about my last miscarriage, I'll be with you in a minute. I can't believe I agreed to do this—it's so tacky, a party for some jewelry designer! I can't understand why I decided to do this. I met him in Cairo, I bought some of his jewelry, and I said, 'Give me a call when you come to New York and I'll organize something.' But I never thought he'd actually turn up! This is awful."

She was already drunk. She had a reputation for drinking too much and taking pills, but at least she had a marriage in her past, to a wealthy Chinese restaurateur; it somehow put her in a better position than if she had never been married. Lisa tottered off—she wore immensely tall high heels—and Florence crossed the crowded floor to the dining room, grabbing a stalk of asparagus from a waiter. She was starving. She felt she couldn't go on another minute without gorging herself with food. But whenever she saw a waiter he had a tray of flaky pastry made of butter and stuffed with cheese, or something equally fattening.

The party looked as if it had potential. Lisa knew only rich people—she made sure she knew only rich people. Probably she would want something from Florence in the near future. It seemed hard to believe she had forgotten Florence wasn't rich. Then she remembered it was a party to buy jewelry. Anyway, Lisa didn't know how poor she was—she assumed Florence could afford to buy the things. The jewelry designer, as round as a punching bag, wore a fez decorated with cutout felt bunnies and was standing beside the dining room table, which had been covered with purple velvet. The jewelry was scattered on the surface, huge gaudy chains made of commercial-grade emeralds and rubies that looked like glass nuggets, plastic baubles. She picked up a choker. "Let me fasten that," the designer said. "It looks fabulous."

Florence shrugged. "How much is it?"

"This one?" He opened a little notebook. "Three thousand. It's all made by hand, you know." He studied her with greed disguised as friendliness. "It looks beautiful on you! Are you a model? If you buy it, I hope you will allow me to photograph you for my brochure. Look, look!" He snatched up a similar choker of blue stones, this one with a dangling thing in the middle, and held it up to his neck. "You may wear it like this, or this way—each piece is designed to be multipurpose. You know the work of the designer ———?" He named a well-known fashion designer. "She is using my necklaces for her spring collection. I will only be selling them at a few select shops. This one is of blue topaz. Why don't you put it on? I think it would look very nice with your blue eyes."

"Very pretty." She studied herself in the mirror. It did look nice on her. She wondered if she should buy it. It was a lot of money, but perhaps she could pay him over a year or two. Silly not to get something if it really made her look fantastic—it was an investment in her future. She bowed her head so he could undo the clasp. "Let me try on a few other things."

"I think you're the most interesting-looking person in this room." A dark woman, rather plain, in a bright red suit with terrible puffed shoulders was standing next to her. "Are you buying anything?" The woman had a nasal voice, like someone trying to sound as if she had gone to boarding school. It didn't quite work. "I'm thinking of getting the amethyst bracelet. This is my friend Thor."

"What a nice compliment! I'm Florence Collins."

"You see, Thor? I told him, that's the most interesting-looking woman in this room. And you're nice too!" The woman scurried off, but the hapless Thor stood miserably nearby. He was very cute, but probably in his mid-twenties.

Florence took his arm. "I have to think about whether or not I'm going to buy something," she told him. "I'm going to sit down while I think."

He didn't seem to know whether or not she was inviting him to join her. "My name's Thor Thorson."

"Sit down with me for a minute. The jewelry's pretty, isn't it?"

He clumped dutifully alongside her to two of the black-and-white-striped dining room chairs that had been pushed back against the walls to make room for people to look at the jewelry. "Lisa's apartment's pretty, isn't it?"

"I think it's very daring, how she's done the dining room walls in off-black. Almost a charcoal black, wouldn't you say? It's nice."

"Yeah, it's nice."

He wore a pinstripe suit and Gucci loafers, with socks that were also pinstripe. She liked his eyes, baffled behind thick glasses. "Nice socks, Thor!" she said. "You rarely see a man who has pinstripe socks."

"Oh, do you like them? Sometimes I go a little wild, with my socks. My favorite pair has little turkeys on them. I like these too. This might be the first time I'm wearing them."

"Nice. Of course, the problem with socks is that if you have a pair you really like, you always lose one."

"I have a friend who wears garters to hold up his socks."

"That must cut off his circulation. It can't be very good for you."

"Are you a nurse?" Thor asked.

"No, I'm not a nurse." She tried to think of what to say to keep some semblance of conversation going. "Why? Are you a doctor?"

"Yes."

"Oh, that's . . . I'm really interested. What kind of doctor?"

"Actually I don't practice medicine." He looked on closer

examination to be no more than twenty-four, but perhaps he just appeared youthful. "I invest in companies."

"But you were a doctor?"

"Yes. I used to be a doctor."

"What kind?"

"I never really practiced after medical school. I decided to go into investing in new medical technologies."

"Wonderful."

"You know that new procedure they have to correct vision. That's going to be the wave of the future. I've got a lot in that."

"That frightens me."

"It's perfectly safe."

"If you had gone on to practice medicine, what kind would you have done?"

He shrugged. "Dermatology."

"I wish I had been a doctor. Not that I could have been. But I always wished I had become a doctor, and I would go on those junkets to Third World countries where doctors go on a ship and set up a floating hospital, or a jungle hospital, and they operate on children and change people's lives." For a moment she could really see herself surrounded by a bevy of grateful brown-faced children and their mothers, sobbing with gratitude, bearing armloads of watermelons and bunches of bananas. She smiled, more to herself than Thor, who had suddenly turned very white, as if she had slapped him. He rose to his feet.

"I'm doing good in the world by investing in new medical technologies. That will probably end up being of more benefit!" Without excusing himself he walked quickly over to his friend, who had attempted to push them together in the first place.

Maybe she was losing her touch. She had no idea he would be so bruised by her chitchat. Did he think she was accusing him? Anyway, there was something creepy about him—he hadn't seemed interested in her, it had been his female friend who liked her and thought she would be appropriate. He was probably just some minor con artist, hoping to find a rich girlfriend, and had assessed she had no more money than he. Or maybe he could see she was almost ten years older. Perhaps he was very wealthy, but what he really wanted was some famous fashion model—they all did, didn't they?

It was twenty to eight. There was barely time to get across town, but she decided to meet Darryl Lever at the concert after all. She was about to ask the jewelry designer how long he was going to be in town, and see if she could leave him a deposit, when Lisa burst across the room pursuing a boy, perhaps in his early twenties, with long greasy black hair and a goatee, wearing a striped suit in green and blue—the outfit she recognized as being by a French designer known for his wacky and eccentric menswear. "Lisa wants to tell you something," the boy shouted shrilly to the jewelry designer. His voice did not seem to belong to his appearance, which was an attempt to resemble a guerrilla/pimp/music industry executive from Latin America.

"Charles says you should be giving me a necklace, or at least a choker, in return for my having this wretched cocktail party for you!" Lisa said. "It's so tacky, having a party like this! I might as well be having a Tupperware party!"

The goateed boy laughed uproariously. "I wouldn't announce that, Lisa."

"But it was your suggestion to have a party!" The jewelry designer looked as if he had been sent from Central Casting to represent a character in a forties spy film—seedy, mildly ominous, now reduced almost to tears by the wife of an SS officer or the Dragon Lady. "I haven't sold a thing!"

IO

She got to Lincoln Center only minutes before the concert was scheduled to begin. She wasn't even sure if Darryl would still be waiting for her, but he was standing in the lobby looking uncomfortably nervous; his face softened with relief as she crossed the floor. "Sorry."

"Hurry! Come on!" He grabbed her arm and hustled her upstairs; they were among the last to enter the auditorium. The woman usher at the door held an armload of programs and Florence reached over to take one. "Do you have a program?" the usher said, retracting the pile from her grasp. Florence shook her head and again attempted to take one. "Do you have a program?" the usher repeated, this time with a surly curl of her lip.

"No, we don't have programs," Darryl said. The usher was about to hand him two, but Florence reached over trying to take the top one. The usher snatched both away.

"Do you have a program?"

"Do you *see* me with a program?" Florence said. She could feel a whistling hostility beginning to bubble up. The woman glared. "No, I don't have a program."

"Would you *like* a program?" The woman waited for Florence to respond. She couldn't bring herself to answer. The usher handed a program to Darryl—only one.

All right, perhaps the woman was crazy. She glanced down at the ticket stubs in Darryl's hand and took them from him to try to see where they were seated. "Do you need assistance finding your seats?"

"Yes, that would be good." Darryl was doing his best to soothe the usher—somehow, Florence felt, he thought she had done something rude to provoke the usher.

"I'll be happy to help you find your seats if you would let me see your tickets!" This was addressed to Florence; the woman was now directing unreserved hatred at her, and she couldn't help but feel hatred in return. She realized she was still blankly staring at the ticket stubs, and the woman seemed to think this was an act of deliberate malice on her part. Almost against her will she handed them over. The woman glanced at them briefly. "You're sitting down there," she said, pointing.

"Thank you so much!" Darryl was always exaggeratedly polite, particularly to anybody who seemed—in Florence's opinion—particularly rude, but it was a politeness without irony or hostility. Nobody ever interpreted it as sarcasm, as they no doubt did hers. Everyone was soothed by him. He led them down to their seats. She looked back briefly to see the usher staring at her scornfully. She simply couldn't fathom what had occurred. The woman had just seemed to take an immediate dislike to her and go out of her

way to act as if Florence was churlish. She wished she could learn
to dismiss this type of incident or at least not take it personally.
There was no use even asking Darryl if he thought something odd
had happened. He was oblivious to such things. Or if he had
noticed, he would have said that it was her own doing, that she
often acted imperious. Perhaps she did act a bit arrogant. But
unless she acted important, no one would treat her that way. How
could Darryl understand this? He was a man—men, white men,
were always treated as if they were important. He had been to
Harvard. It was his own choice to work with the poor. Men who
were at the top of the ladder could afford to be magnanimous to
those positioned on the lower rungs.

He helped her into her seat in an almost motherly fashion and,
when she was trapped in her chair, looked over at her with satisfaction. "I was almost going to tell you not to bother coming, after
what you did to me the other night," he said defiantly. The orchestra filed onto the stage. They were badly dressed, in shabby black,
apart from the women, who wore hideous bright tops in purple and
green, as if the conductor had told them to "wear something bright
and cheerful for a change." A panicky expression crossed Darryl's
face—having been chastised, she might suddenly get up and
storm out of the theater. "Just kidding," he said, taking her arm.

Some women, she was sure, might have found him charming,
even sexy. Every nerve ending in her body twitched against him.
He was so clean, like a little cat—not that she had anything
against cleanliness, it was just that chemically her body rebelled
against him. He wore his black hair curled at the back in an oddly
old-fashioned little flip; his tiny steel-rimmed glasses were
perched at the end of his rather aristocratically turned nose. Even
his slight chinlessness contributed to his refined demeanor. He
was vain—he had to be, with his small hands, white and plump,
the nails buffed, and smooth, baby-soft skin—but what gave him
the right to be? Didn't he see how silly he looked in his frumpy
old-man's dark blue suit, probably bought at some thrift store?

She liked big blond men, California types, with a sexy stupid-
ity to their faces, or those like Raffaello, with their tanned Euro-

pean ski-slope thuggishness. Thinking of Raffaello, she felt herself sink into depression. Was it that, since she had given him a blow job, he felt he had conquered her and no longer had any use for someone whose pursuit he had already accomplished? But she hadn't slept with him, and after all, Europeans didn't take such things seriously; they weren't the same as American men. If she had given Darryl a blow job, he would have been even more in love with her than he already was and would have accepted it as a sign they were engaged, or getting serious. If it was the other type of American male, the surfer dude, he might have fled out of fear. But surely Raffaello didn't fall into either of those two plebeian categories.

The soloist, a famous flautist, came onto the stage; the audience applauded and the music, a Mozart concerto, began. She couldn't seem to settle down. She looked around at the crowd. From the back the audience appeared almost entirely gray-haired. The woman next to her was wearing a really hideous long floral skirt, and from what she could see of the others, they were invariably dressed in crummy out-of-style tops, flowered, puff-sleeved, or with drab shawls over their shoulders, protection against the mostly imaginary air-conditioning. What was she doing here in the middle of this group, who resembled a bunch of old professors and grannies who knew nothing of fashion, of decent restaurants, of winter trips to St. Barts and summers in the Hamptons?

Darryl was in a kind of blissed-out state. No doubt he was so happy to have captured her for the evening and squashed her into a seat like a butterfly in a killing bottle. There was no way she could abandon him and flitter off with some other man. How could he just sit there, acting so absorbed in some out-of-date music? She knew that classical music was something she was supposed to enjoy and appreciate. It wasn't that she didn't like it; there was probably a place for it. Maybe as a sound track for one of those period films when the heroine attends a dance. But it was dead, it should have been locked in a box, it had no bearing on the world at the end of the twentieth century. There couldn't be any real pleasure in digging up an old corpse reduced to dust and withered tendons.

Between movements Darryl turned to look at her, eyes shining in private ecstasy, as if expecting that during these lulls they would be united in a place she had never been. After the first movement she had caught on and during the next smiled at him, albeit weakly—it seemed to be enough. After each movement the audience broke out in a frenzy of coughing. The next piece was by Bach, the soloist a tiny Vietnamese violinist; this time after the second movement there was a hushed silence, following which the audience suddenly burst into a spontaneous sigh of rapture. "That was the finest . . . I have ever heard it . . ." a man behind her muttered. Darryl was almost swooning alongside her. What was wrong with these people—or with her? Were they all simply pretending to be suffused with emotion, or was there something stopping her from feeling? All she could think about was intermission, and getting a drink.

"Fantastic, wasn't it?" he said, and then, more shyly, "Are you enjoying it?"

"Mmmm." It was irritating that he so longed for her corroboration. He had bought her a plastic glass of really terrible champagne and a Coke for himself, which he carried over to her position on a padded bench by the escalator. The people looked even worse now that she was getting to observe them close up. There was a woman she recognized from the papers as a moderately well-known writer—probably in her late thirties, with frizzy hair, schlumpy, wearing a long plaid skirt and red sweater, completely out of style. Why didn't she do something to fix herself up? It seemed ridiculous to live in Manhattan and not be attuned to the right thing to wear and how to look. No wonder she hadn't had a successful novel in at least ten years. She looked like some old hippie, frumping away; at least she could get a decent haircut and not go traipsing around in an old plaid granny skirt. Of course, that was basically the way all the women in the audience looked: one woman had on a black dress and brown sandals, with a white jacket on top; another had on a blue floral polyester dress and white fake-leather pumps suitable for Mormon country.

Maybe they were all tourists, or mentally ill. She didn't know why it enraged her so, to see such hordes of shabby misfits. Even the theater was badly designed and tacky, like an airport. At one time, attending such an event would have been a subject fit for an Edith Wharton novel, and the music would have been the least of it: everyone in society would have been there, the young people eyeing one another and the grown-ups arranging marriages and business deals. Now it was a house of losers who had scraped and saved to buy tickets for their pathetic night out.

". . . so tomorrow they want to redo the tests, and if it comes out positive again, I'll get X rays."

"What?"

"You weren't listening to any of it, were you?"

"Just say the last part again."

"I said, my doctor gave me a TB test when I went in for my checkup, and it looked somewhat positive. But it was one of those results that they couldn't be a hundred percent certain of, so they're going to do it again."

"How could they not tell if it was positive or not?"

"They give you an injection: if it swells up and turns red, it's positive. In my case it turned red, and swelled up a little bit, so they can't tell if I have TB or it's a false positive."

"Oh! That's horrible! I mean, that's awful. What would happen if you have TB?"

"They have medicine now. It's no big deal. I mean, you know, TB is on the rise in the city, especially with the homeless, and that's who I'm dealing with all day. You know, from their sleeping on the street and not getting the right food, and taking drugs, a lot of their immune systems are down—you wouldn't believe the diseases that some of them have. I got kind of friendly with this one fellow and I noticed that every week his right leg was bigger and bigger. After a while he could barely walk. I ended up taking him to Bellevue. It turned out he had some kind of tropical disease the doctors just couldn't believe somebody in Manhattan had. 'Have you recently been in Africa?' they kept asking him—but he hadn't. You know, Bellevue's the best place in the city for tropical diseases; the guys there are really experts in tropical diseases and gunshot wounds, from having to work with the homeless and people that can't pay for treatment. And now with all these cutbacks, there's not going to be anyplace for them to go."

"It's disgusting."

Intermission over, she quickly drank the last drops of her champagne and followed Darryl back to their seats. It was ten after nine. Surely the concert would end by ten o'clock. She sat down prepared for an interminable fifty minutes. There was a work by Vivaldi, and by some Baroque German whose name she had never come across before. She hoped she would not have to sit for almost an hour worrying about what was going to become of her, or obsessing about Raffaello. When she was nervous she would pick up one problem, one issue, one idea, and go over it and over it like a scratched groove on an old-fashioned LP. To her surprise, however, it seemed that only a minute had gone by and the audience was applauding wildly. "What happened?" she asked Darryl, perplexed.

"What do you mean?"

"The second half of the performance—it was so short!" She looked down at her watch. It was ten o'clock; fifty minutes had gone by. Where had she been? It was very peculiar. Was that the point of a concert, to make you disappear out of your body like a zombie? If so, she still couldn't see the point. She followed Darryl out of the auditorium feeling baffled and somehow tricked. It was as if she had been abducted by aliens and couldn't account for the passage of time.

She let herself be led across the street to a noisy restaurant. The waiters skated through the crowds from one table to the next. She had a momentary pang of guilt—Darryl had no money, his advocacy group was funded entirely through donations, and he took almost nothing in the way of salary—but she was starving. Of course, this restaurant, full of abrasively loud pseudo-fashionable people, served only the most primitive items. The menu listed calamari, fried; hamburgers; several salads, which, judging from a large bowl located on a nearby table, would be primarily iceberg lettuce, romaine, croutons and dressing. Finally she settled on a plate of linguini with shrimps and seafood in marinara sauce.

With adoration he stared at her across the table. "So did you have fun the other night?" she said. It was almost a slap in the face, since she had completely ignored him and gone off with Raffaello, not even bothering to take him aside to say good-bye, but she could think of no other way to cut through the stickiness. "What did you think of that girl, Tracer? She really likes you! She actually invited me over—when was it? A couple of nights ago, I guess—to try and pump me for information. You wouldn't believe how rich she is! That girl's loaded." She supposed she could promote Tracer, since she knew Darryl would never fall for her. It was perhaps disloyal to Tracer, letting Darryl know she was trying to find out about him, but why did she have to remain loyal to Tracer? Whatever John de Jongh had said to Tracer about her, Tracer must have believed it—she had gone out of her way to be cold and unfriendly on the phone.

"She's nice. A nice girl." Darryl waved his hand dismissively. "Usually that type of girl, with so much money, is like a paper cutout—they've been sealed under Plexiglas. But she's very down-to-earth. You could use a friend like that, Florence."

"Mmm. Excuse me, I'm going to the restroom."

She made her way around the speeding waiters on their rattling skates. There was a phone by the toilets and she dialed her own number, then the code, to retrieve messages from her machine. She realized it was demented to think Raffaello might have called. Yet she was unable to help herself. She felt as if something in her head had cracked, as if the neurons were struggling to leap from synapse to synapse, never quite crossing the abyss. The beeps signaled she had three messages. She waited impatiently. The first was from John de Jongh; the second from Darryl, in the lobby of the concert hall, saying it was ten to eight and wondering if she was going to show up; and the third . . . but it was only John de Jongh again. She had thrown him out last night; he must have gone straight out to dinner with Tracer and the others, bad-mouthed her for revenge, and was back on the phone the next day as if nothing had occurred.

There was a somewhat cute guy waiting to use the phone—baseball cap, khaki pants, polo shirt, tanned—the kind who had gone from some vaguely toney East Coast boarding school to a middle-rated private college with a lot of frat houses and nearby ski slopes; and from college straight into his father's business. This was whom she should be having dinner with, not weird Darryl, staring at her too intently. "What's up?" he said as she put down the receiver.

"Same old same old."

"Yeah? I'm over at the bar—you wanna come have a drink?"

"I . . . yeah . . . No, I'm having dinner with a friend. Maybe if I can ditch him!" They both laughed.

"I'm Bill Smiley. My friends call me Smiley."

"I'm Florence."

"Florence! That's a kind of . . . different name. So come on, get rid of your friend."

"Maybe."

"Come on. Here's my card." He handed her his business card, printed with his name and the words GRINNING FLICK PRODUCTIONS above phone and fax numbers.

"What's Grinning Flick Productions?" she said.

"Movie biz. You an actress?" He used the question as an excuse to look her up and down in a near parody of sexual interest that somehow managed to denote the opposite. She shook her head. "So, I'm over at the bar for a little while—I'm just finishing my meeting—catch you later!"

She was dismissed; he hadn't even told her to give him a call. All the cards were in his hand—it was a sign of interest that he had dealt her even the one. He had everything on his side, very nearly—good-looking, obviously with plenty of money, in his early thirties, in the movie business—there were probably half a dozen women throwing themselves at him as soon as he got back to the bar. At least she wasn't losing her touch, her looks, entirely— chatting her up by the telephones was probably as much work as he had had to do in years. The women in New York were so aggressive; anyone else would have, on seeing him standing there, immediately begged him for a quarter, or a cigarette, or the time, anything to start a flirtation.

She went back to her table. The food had already arrived, but Darryl was waiting patiently for her. "That was quick!" she said. "You should have started!"

He looked distracted. Maybe he hadn't even noticed the food was there. "Florence," he began. "Can I talk to you?"

She noticed, across the room, Bill Smiley had returned from making his phone call and was back at the bar. He lifted his glass in her direction. There were two women at the bar, obviously trying to engage his attention. Involuntarily she smiled, flattered.

"I don't want this to sound like it's coming out of left field. But you've known for a long time how I've felt about you. I think we should get married."

II

"Oh, Darryl—" Was he nuts? Or simply pathetic? He must see they were incompatible. She had made it clear what she was looking for. She wasn't interested in him. She had never been interested in him.

"No, no, before you say anything, just listen to me. You might think I'm poor, but I—I don't have to be. I could give up what I'm doing, if you wanted."

"That doesn't have anything to do with it." What a liar she was, she thought to herself. It was true, she was out of his

league—he was in a better one. He was noble, pure, a good-deed
doer on a planet where good deeds were greeted with contempt
and a slap in the face or worse. He looked at her with adoration
across the table. Okay, she had slept with him a few times. But
that had been ages ago. She had only done it before he had left the
fancy Wall Street firm where he worked—one of the oldest and
grandest—to head off to do his saintly acts.

He didn't seem to believe that now, after their nights out, she
refused to go back to sleeping with him because she wasn't interested in him. If anything, he accepted her actions respectfully, as
if there were some curious modern rule in which a couple might
sample each other once or twice and then withdraw until after
marriage. "Look, Darryl," she said abruptly. "Don't you see that
you're . . . you're good and kind and I . . . I don't have any
ethics or values whatsoever?"

He took her hand and stroked it absently. "No, no, don't say
that. Of course you do. You're a very ethical person. You have a lot
of values."

"Get real, Darryl. At least let me be honest with you. I don't
have any values, except that I want money. Money and status. Do
you consider that a value? Sure, sometimes I feel bad that I'm
shallow and superficial, but most of the time I just think, This is
the way I am, everybody else around here is the same way, why
should I be any different? I want what I want, that's all."

"You're not shallow and superficial! I know you!" He was
upset. He refused to take her at her word. Obviously no one who
was shallow or superficial would admit it. But why shouldn't she
admit it? Manhattan was a shabby world, inhabited by cardboard
cutouts, and she walked among them. If a bee in an endless hive
of millions of other bees could talk, would it say that it was a
unique bee, looking for something other than the pollen for which
all the rest searched? Money and status were her pollen. Only by
ridding herself of any vestige of humanity could she acquire them,
and that did not seem such a big price to pay. The amount of
pleasure she had known was minute in comparison to the pain and
anguish she endured on a daily basis.

"Listen to me, Darryl. I know you don't want to think of me as shallow and superficial. I'm not a bad person. But I'm not a good one either. I don't even believe in goodness. I think it's wonderful, what you're doing. I mean, I think it's wonderful that you think you're doing good. Me, I don't see it quite that way. So you help get some law passed that lets homeless derelicts return a million soda cans to some supermarket that wouldn't let them before. Or fight a law that says they can't beg on the subway. Then they go back out on the street, smoke their crack and die. Or some soup kitchen, where you give somebody advice on how to get Social Security disability. What if this one guy manages to figure it out, actually takes your advice, gets on the payroll, finds some dingy, miserable apartment, and then—now that he's back in the subhuman mainstream of existence—he . . . I don't know, molests some child. Or beats up his girlfriend. I mean I just . . . I just can't believe in the possibility of improving the world. Anyway, it takes too much of my strength just to look after myself."

"I'll take care of you." He hadn't even been listening to what she was saying. It was the first time she had allowed herself to reveal how deep her cynicism and bitterness went, and he still looked at her and smiled, his brown eyes peering over the edge of those antiquated little glasses. He loved her. If only that were satisfying in and of itself. Probably it would have been for most women; it would have been for her mother—but then, women were grateful for crumbs!

"You have nice eyes," she muttered. They were as thickly fringed as a Jersey calf's—what a waste on a man. He almost blushed with embarrassment and pleasure at her compliment. Suddenly she put her head in her hands and began to cry. "Oh, God, Darryl, what's to become of me? I need money. I need money. I need a job. I'm in debt up to my neck and I'm going to lose my apartment. I need a husband." He got up and pulled his chair around to her side of the table.

"Don't cry, Florence. Look, I'm here. I'll look after you." He got a handkerchief from his pocket and held it awkwardly under her nose; she grabbed it from him and blew into it, feeling furious with herself. He put his arms around her shoulders and tried to hug her, but she pushed him away. "I said I'd marry you."

"Leave me alone," she said. "Don't do me any favors." Half of her knew his words had not come out exactly as he had intended. Darryl didn't pity her, he loved her. The poor man, he had stepped in quicksand.

"I'm just trying to help." He was hurt.

"If you really want to help, just leave me alone." Then an idea came to her. "Look, I have a bunch of jewelry. It's not . . . it's not mine. If I give it to you, would you hang on to it? I can say my place was broken into. Burglarized. The woman will get the insurance money, and . . ."

He pulled his chair back to his side of the table and began to shovel the now-cold food into his mouth. "You're kidding, right?"

"No."

"You're crazy."

"I don't want you to do anything. Just keep the jewelry in your place until I ask for it back."

"Florence, you're kidding, right?"

"Who's this going to hurt? I'm desperate. I don't have any family. Would you be happy if I lost my goddamn apartment? Then I could be one of your poor homeless clients! You'd really have to take care of me!"

He was looking feverish. He had devoured his entire plate of congealed food and stared at hers hungrily. She began to pick, absently, under the gaze of his animal stare. "There's nothing I can say," he said at last.

"So do you despise me?" She felt almost cheerful.

"No, no. I'm worried about you. I know you're not serious. But I've known you almost ten years now and I've never seen you so . . . desperate. That's not like you."

"So what do you want to marry me for, Darryl? Someone so desperate, thirty-two years old, who has what you would consider inferior ethics."

"Nonexistent ethics!" he blurted. Then he glanced away, ashamed. "I don't know what to say. I kept thinking I'd get over you, meet someone else, we could be friends. But I remember our time together, and what it was like, and wishing I could go back to it. I have a feeling about you, Florence. I know you're the one for me."

Perhaps she wasn't as crazy as she thought. He had to be nuts! Their time together? She had gone out with him—or at least screwed him, intermittently—for six months, at most a year, and that was eight or ten years ago. It had never been a relationship; it had been two people meeting to go to the movies or Rollerblading, having occasional sex. Hadn't that been during her cocaine phase anyway, when along with two or three girlfriends—Allison had a trust fund—they would get high, go out to bars, pick up guys? Which was normal behavior, quite typical for recent graduates, what they later referred to, jokingly, as their "postgrad degree." "All I'm asking is for you to just keep a bunch of stuff for me. You don't even have to know what it is."

"I . . . Florence . . ." He took out a handkerchief and honked his nose. "God, you're mean to me. Here I am, telling you I have TB and I'm in love with you, and instead of seeing how romantic this is, you want me to harbor stolen goods for you."

"Yeah, yeah." Despite herself she had to laugh. "You should be used to me by now. If you really want to marry me, don't harbor any illusions."

"Believe me, I don't."

12

At home that night she went through the bag of jewelry belonging to Virginia Clary. Tomorrow she would take the stuff over to Quayle's and leave it with Marge. She had never had any intention of getting Darryl to hold the stuff while she declared it stolen. She had only been saying that to test him—and maybe to test herself. She would never do anything immoral or illegal, however innocuous, mostly because she was afraid of getting caught. She had a guilty expression; it was part of her charm for men. It was part of the reason why women didn't like her: the cat who ate the butter.

In the bottom of one of the little velvet sacks was another sack of yellow Chinese silk, swaddled beneath tissue paper, which she hadn't even noticed before. More junk, she supposed. It felt like a bag of rings. They would probably be costume, or zircons, or more low-grade diamonds and sapphires in garish settings that at the most would bring five hundred or a thousand apiece. The whole country was full of women weaseling gems from husbands or lovers, women who spent too much on garbage, shopping at jewelry stores in suburban malls so that they might glitter in front of other women. What man would appreciate a fat, puffy hand, fingers strangled with too tight bands? Dimpled hands, lacquered nails sharpened and glistening red. Women might as well have been in purdah for all the attention they got from men after, say, age twenty or twenty-five. Even before that, the men paying attention were mostly old greasy guys in their sixties, riding motorcycles, or pimpled employees of Hardee's and McDonald's. In Saudi Arabia the rich women bought couture outfits and—if they went out at all—had to hide under dark shrouds.

But to her amazement the jewelry in the bag was actually valuable. She couldn't be certain, yet as she peered at the stuff with her jeweler's loop, the quality of these stones looked very fine indeed. A huge ruby surrounded with pearls; an oddly shaped cabochon sapphire; an elaborate pink-diamond-studded flamingo not dissimilar to the one designed by that pathetic, sad little duke for the Duchess of Windsor. What should have been the romantic love story of all time had been turned into a farce. But this flamingo—it was definitely real. And then—there it was—an opal ring, the opal of truly great quality, intense, huge, a deep blue-black shot with explosive veins of candy-red fire.

She was up for hours, unable to go to sleep, wired, agitated. The same thoughts played over and over in her head. She had been

joking when she suggested to Darryl that he hold on to the jewelry
so that she could report it stolen; now it was beginning to seem
like a reasonable solution. After all, some of it hadn't even been
listed; was Virginia Clary unaware of its existence? Perhaps
she had forgotten all about it, in which case she would never
miss it. Florence didn't even need to involve Darryl—she could
just bring the other stuff to Quayle's and leave out the one valuable sack.

Against one wall of the living room was an old-fashioned
wooden filing cabinet. She had never gotten around to actually
filing anything—any papers she thought she needed to keep she
merely flung inside—and now she emptied the contents onto the
floor, hoping that among the scraps she would find some solution
to her present predicament. Perhaps a letter rejecting her for a job
but suggesting she apply again in a few years, or an overlooked
bank account belonging to her mother that would now save
her.

She remembered so little of her past. A manila envelope revealed a stack of photos from a ski trip taken eight years before;
the man—boy, really—who had invited her, and paid for her to
accompany him, had long since disappeared from her life. Who
had he been? A lawyer, or perhaps an architect, now married to
someone else, living in San Francisco. His ruddy-complected face
was topped with a sheared crest of reddish hair. She didn't even
remember his name. Why hadn't she married him? In retrospect,
he was a nice enough guy. How dull he had seemed to her then.
She was twenty-four and still thought that a famous artist, a rock
and roll star, a billionaire, would come her way, that she would be
attached to the kind of man to make other women jealous when
she walked into the room. The architect (Brandon—his name
came back to her) was boyish and ordinary, designing office buildings and weekend homes. Eventually, after marrying, he had gone
off to start his own company with several boyish partners, all
similar to himself.

Here was a picture of herself at Allison's baby shower—for
the first baby—sitting on a couch between a girl named Daisy

and another named Clare. Or maybe it was Clare-Alice. Daisy was holding up a green terrycloth towel with a hood designed to resemble a dragon's head. The towel had a little spine of orange cloth as well. The child would be able to dry itself on the beach or after a bath by climbing into the dragon costume. Daisy had married a fantastically wealthy boy from Dallas, reputedly very stupid; Daisy was known for her terrible temper, which she had managed to keep hidden from her fiancé, though not from Florence. They had had a falling out shortly before Daisy's wedding, which took place in Bermuda. Daisy, she now remembered—the picture emphasized this—looked just like an ostrich, the same protruding eyes set too widely apart, the receding chin, an expression of gormless astonishment. She was nowhere near as attractive as Florence, yet she was the one who managed to end up with the rich boy. And Clare-Alice, holding up her gift, a stuffed-and-diapered ape almost four feet tall, the F. A. O. Schwartz box on her lap. It had probably cost someone three hundred or more dollars. True, the man she had married had two children by an earlier marriage, who resided with them, but the year before he had been cowinner of a Nobel Prize in . . . chemistry, or physics. At the time of Clare-Alice's marriage she had thought how dreary it would be to marry an academic, a research scientist.

Everything was strewn in heaps on the floor. Old business cards acquired at cocktail parties, scraps of paper, corners of napkins and matchbooks with scribbled phone numbers belonging to first names that meant nothing to her. Postcards, Christmas cards, receipts, bank statements, credit-card bills. Photos, stamps of extinct denominations, restaurant reviews torn from the *Times* of now-closed restaurants. A valentine to her mother she had hand-made at age eight. A fake Chanel wristwatch she had bought on the street for ten dollars that no longer worked. Perhaps it needed only a new battery, but whenever she had worn it her wrist had turned green. Little bottles of perfume, given as gifts following various parties, along with five baseball caps: one from the opening of a new gym, another from a party given by a

French clothing company for an event in a giant warehouse on a pier. It was her entire life, her history of existence in New York, and all of it added up to exactly nothing. The negative results of a Pap smear, a keyring with a tiny attached flashlight in the shape of a fish. A mushy note from Darryl, inviting her to a black-tie dinner at the Waldorf, at which someone he worked for was going to be given an award. The note was ten years old; it dated back to when he was working for the prestigious old New York firm. Amazing to think that he had been in love with her— or at least had a crush on her—even back then. A letter from Carlos, after the abortion. He was wealthy. For a while she had been in love with him. There was even talk of getting married. But neither of them was ready for a baby. It had been their mutual decision. Shortly afterward he had gone back to Chile. She hadn't heard from him again. And a snapshot of her with James on the beach. He said he had outgrown it, but the fact that he had been gay—okay, it was at boarding school and the year after, in England—made her uneasy, that and his femininity; he was all too clearly looking for someone to be strong for him. How could she have known that within eighteen months after she broke it off he would come into a title and a huge estate in Scotland—or was it Wales?

There had been a million opportunities open to her—she saw now—and she had slammed the door on every one. She found a piece of stationery and wrote a note: "Dear Tracer. How's it going? Hope I didn't do anything to offend you, and that your idea of throwing a party is still on when you get back. Have a great trip— you're not missing anything here in NYC in August! Call me! Yours, Florence. P.S. Saw Darryl tonight and we talked about you!"

A tiny hand, waving a white handkerchief, emerged at a great distance from the middle of a wave far out in the ocean. She woke from her dream in a dead sweat. The air was completely still. It was so quiet it took her a moment to realize the sobbing air conditioner must have broken down. Its usual groans of torment and despair were gone, no musty and damp gusts flapped through the room. Only the bedside clock struggled glumly, counting off its morose seconds with bludgeoning ticks.

part three

I

Despite the expense of her monthly maintenance bills—almost fifteen hundred dollars for a one-bedroom—and the supposedly grand address, her apartment—and the building—was a complete mess, with antiquated wiring and a tendency for the fuses to blow if more than one electrical item was turned on at the same time. When she tried to turn on the light, half the time nothing happened. Everything in the place was a disaster. The windows were old-fashioned, with little panes; cold air blew in during the winter, and in summer they could never be opened fully. Probably the upstairs neighbor, who was on her same circuitry, had arrived from Australia and tried to turn on his air conditioner at the same time. She was fortunate he lived in Australia and kept the place only as a rarely used Manhattan pied-à-terre.

It was late August, more than three weeks since Darryl had proposed, and she hadn't seen or spoken to him since. It was just as well: if he was so easily offended by her, shocked or disgusted by her suggestion that he hold the jewelry so that she could report it stolen, she really wanted nothing further to do with him. Didn't he see that his ethics and morality were just as tenuous as hers, if he was the kind to drop someone just because he didn't agree with his or her views?

In an odd way she felt vindicated. What kind of man proposed to a woman and then, on finding she was in trouble, broke and desperate, decided to forget the whole thing? He had made up a story in his head about who she was and what she was like, and when she refused to conform to it, he had executed her—only in his own mind, it was true—as quickly as possible.

The whole point had been to get rid of him. But now that he was gone she was surprised to find she missed him. It seemed to her that he had been her only friend. She hadn't really intended to declare the jewelry stolen, but it was beginning to seem like the only solution.

Raffaello had gone back to Italy for August—anyway, she wouldn't have asked him for help; she was still too infatuated—and there wasn't one person she could think of who could help or whom she could trust. If only she had worked harder at making some real friends! August, and the phone rarely rang now, everyone had gone away; and as if they could sense or smell her despair, nobody wanted to include her in their weekend plans or midweek nights in the city. That was how things worked here: when things were going well everyone wanted you around; when things were going badly nobody wanted to catch your disease.

Almost a month later, and she was in an even worse state than she had been before. The bank had begun foreclosure proceedings, egged on by the co-op board, furious at not having received maintenance for more than six months. Maybe it wasn't that the electricity had blown up, maybe it had been turned off, as they tried to drive her out. She had been unable to track down John de Jongh to get her twenty-five thousand back, and by the time she contacted the bank to cancel payment, the funds had been deducted. Though she realized her job search had been only half-hearted, nothing even remotely interesting or possible had come her way.

She envisioned herself as the months went by, still jobless, unable to pay the maintenance, unable to catch up with the mortgage, evicted, with not even enough money to put her things in storage. Where would she go, what would she do? She was unable to go back to sleep, the same thought repeating itself over and over as if something had gotten stuck. The phone was ringing. She looked at a clock, luminous hands creaking arthritically in the dark. Three-twelve A.M. "Hello?" Her voice emerged in a croak.

"It's me." She was silent. "Please, may I come over?"

". . . Raffaello?"

"Please, please, let me come to your place. I don't want to be alone."

"Where are you? I didn't even know you were back! I haven't heard from you in so long—"

"I just arrived today. You are the first I have called. Listen, I am at a club, it's on—" He put the phone down for a moment and she could hear him talking to someone else. "It's on Fourteenth Street, near the highway. It's about to close. I can't go home."

"Why not?"

"I will explain when I see you. Please, give me your address."

She gave him her address.

"*Ciao, bella.* See you in a few minutes." His voice sounded blurry.

She put down the phone and jumped in the shower. In her bottom drawer she found her cutest pajamas, striped cotton, and a matching robe. She looked in the mirror. This was good. She wanted to look cute and adorable but not seductive, or it would seem unnatural. Her nose needed some powder. She put on some lipstick and wiped it off, so that her lips were tinted red but didn't look made up. She wondered if she should change the sheets but decided against it. She quickly tried to straighten up the room, make the bed more inviting, plumped up the pillows. It was three-thirty in the morning. She was angry for letting him come over, but at the same time nervous, restless, excited. She fiddled with the air conditioner controls, trying to make it work. Finally it came back on, emitting a harsh, complaining whine.

She paced back and forth, despising herself for allowing him to come over so late, to show so little respect. On the other hand, she had long since gotten over her crush. She didn't care if he respected her or not. It was nice to have another body in bed; and if her infatuation was gone, she could at least take advantage of her physical attraction. It would be using him, in a sense, to have him come over, enjoy herself and send him away in the morning. It was the way she had always been treated, only now the tables were turned. Besides, they did things differently in Italy. The sort of world he inhabited was based on this kind of activity, seemingly so casual on the surface, but in fact reflecting true camaraderie and acceptance.

She had nearly given up and gone back to bed by the time the doorman buzzed her intercom and sleepily announced she had a visitor. "Tell him to come up." She tried to sound imperious, as if it were perfectly natural for a woman living in the building to have strange men arrive in the dead of night. It wasn't the doorman's business anyway. He was supposed to be discreet. But she knew when he left, at six, he would tell the day doorman the events of the night before; the day doorman would tell the janitor, and there would be smirks, and for a while she would be inspected more closely to make sure she hadn't abruptly begun a career in prostitution.

She heard the roll of the elevator as it opened and he was at her door. She had forgotten how handsome he was, how woozy she felt under the influence of his odor of aftershave and foreign cigarettes. His hair was mussed, his Armani suit wrinkled, his hooded eyes half closed. He swayed on his feet as he reached out to embrace her; one hand slid over her backside. *"Bella, bella,"* he muttered in Italian as he kissed the side of her neck, her hair, her ear. He also reeked of gin and sweat. "I missed you so much."

She had no intention of letting him have the upper hand. She had planned for things to progress slowly, berating him in a teasing voice for a while, offering him a cup of tea. But now she found she couldn't be bothered—she was dizzy with the sheer physicality of his presence. She let him untie her robe and unbutton her pajamas; then he picked her up and carried her into the hall closet. "Your bedroom," he said as piles of clothes cascaded onto their heads. "It is awfully crowded and small, no?"

"Um, actually this is the closet. The bedroom's down the hall. It would probably be more comfortable."

"Whatever you wish." With a fake-leopard fur jacket hanging over his head, still carrying her, he stumbled down the hall, crashing into the wall and the door frame before depositing her on the bed.

"Leave me alone. I want to go to sleep."

"Oh, how selfish. You have had your fun, now you want to sleep, and you will just leave me here like this?" He pointed to his erection, then got up and paced around the room.

"I'm not trying to be selfish, but I'm sore. What time is it anyway?"

"Six in the morning. Okay, so I know I am not going to be able to get any sleep feeling like this. Let's do something. Let's go out."

"It's six A.M.!" She had never seen anything like it; he was as agitated as a trapped tiger. "There's nowhere to go. You must be jet-lagged. Can't you just lie next to me quietly, and after I've gotten a few hours' sleep, I'll be in the mood to try it again."

"No, no, I know myself when I get like this. It's no good. It will only make me more anxious, to lie still, then I will start thinking once more. I thought you would help me, to stop thinking.

Come on, I know an after-hours place—it will definitely be open by now. I am a member. It will be lots of fun. It just opened this week; everyone will be going there, in the fall."

"I'm exhausted! Maybe you don't need to sleep, but I do. I don't have the strength to get up, get dressed and go out to a club."

"You don't need to dress up. Just wear some jeans and a T-shirt. Come on, just for a little while."

"But I'm so tired!"

"Quit complaining."

"I'm not . . . I wasn't complaining." She was as shocked as if she had been slapped. She never wanted anyone, especially a man, to think of her as the kind of woman who complained.

"Come on, this is one time. You can take the day off tomorrow."

"I'm in between jobs at the moment."

"So, you see? And soon you will have another job and have to get up in the morning. It's August in Manhattan, you are young, we are having fun together, maybe even falling in love, you don't need to act like such an old lady. Come and have some fun. This is the sort of place like you will never see without me. I know you are tired."

"I must look awful."

"No, no—just sexier than ever. Here, come on—smoke this." From the pocket of his jacket, flung over the end of the bed, he took a glass pipe and a tiny vial with a red top.

"That's crack." Alarmed, she propped herself up in bed.

"So? There's only a little bit. We share. Come on, don't be difficult—that way we can be together." He opened the vial with his teeth and tilted the crumbly white contents into the bowl, then placed the nib of the pipe in her mouth.

2

She hadn't known or understood how powerful a chemical could be. It was as if a wedding had taken place, her marriage to something inhuman. A substance on the planet had been there all along, ready and waiting, wanting to marry her. She had walked into another universe, one that was icy-cold, a shifting facade constructed of geometric molecules, an ancient civilization of alchemy. They were on the floor, going at it like reptiles, two coldly slithering, hissing bodies. Or perhaps what her body was experiencing was the way a particularly malevolent virus felt as it reproduced, eating up some brain in the last stages of AIDS or cancer, alien, prodding its host toward death. Nothing was left of her. Whatever it was that had been Florence, a human entity, had fled. But in this icy vacuum, this void, she was unafraid; she had no feelings left.

The two bodies churned and flopped mechanically for some time before abruptly, in unison, they detached from each other and stood. Some sight returned to her and she realized she had been—temporarily—completely blind, but for how long she didn't know.

"Come on, let's go." Whatever was standing across from her was not human either. Its eyes were red, its skin covered with a waxy film of yellow grease. It pulled on an outer skin that she realized must be its clothes. The smell—that odd, weird smell— reminded her of oranges, not real ones, but those made by Martians to tantalize a human kept in a cage; it was worse than artificial air-freshener, but she inhaled deeply, she couldn't get enough of it.

"Now I know what Pandora felt like when she opened the box." It was her body speaking, the husk that had once been she.

"Are you just going to stand there? Put some clothes on."

"I feel like my blood's been replaced with formaldehyde." Her teeth were gnashing, gnashing. Even though the air conditioner had groaned to a halt somewhere along the line, she was freezing cold.

"Here, I'll help you get dressed." The entity in the room—who or what it was she was still uncertain—went to the chest of drawers and removed some items. "Put your arms over your head," it said. "You're not helping at all. Come on, pick up your legs, one at a time." She tried to lift her right leg, but it was like a frozen haunch of lamb, unrelated to her, and she fell over onto the bed. "Look, you just lie there and I'll do it myself." Whatever the entity was doing hurt her skin very much.

"What are you doing? What are you doing?" Her arms flailed and she practically screamed.

"Ssshh, ssshh, keep your voice down! I'm putting your legs into your trouser legs, what is the problem?"

"Oh." She lay clutching herself and shivering.

"Are you all right?"

"I don't know. I think I'm going to puke. How much did you give me?"

"We scarcely smoked anything at all—perhaps one puff each. You must have a very low tolerance for such things."

"I'm going to die, aren't I."

"No, no, come on, you'll be fine. We'll go out and get some fresh air and have a drink and you'll feel better."

The streets were still dark, but she had no way of knowing whether that was because it was still night or she had gone blind once more or her eyesight had been permanently diminished. They were in a taxi. The driver seemed to be a friend of the entity's. Something was happening anyway: Raffaello had gotten out of the car and she didn't want to be left alone; she kept trying to follow him and the driver kept saying, "He's coming back in a minute, just wait for him."

But she got out anyway, and walking down a narrow flight of steps that stank of urine, she opened a door. The ceiling was so low she banged her head but felt nothing except some stickiness, and curiously, when she reached up to touch her forehead, her hand came away wet with an odd red goo. She was wandering through a narrow corridor, half crouching; the ceiling was even lower here, and there were all kinds of objects in the way—pipes, things whose meaning she didn't understand—it was almost pitch-black, so narrow her hands could touch both walls.

She opened a door. It seemed like an amusing adventure. After the darkness of the hall the room was very bright; a bare lightbulb swung on a cord. There was a mattress on the floor, a broken chair. Standing in the room were five or six men, who looked startled and jumpy. "Oh, hi!" she said gaily. "I'm looking for Raffaello."

One of the men detached himself from the group and she realized it was Raffaello. She was embarrassed. At least she hoped he *was* Raffaello—in fact, she wasn't entirely certain. "What are you doing here?" he said angrily. "I told you to wait in the car."

"I didn't know if you were coming back."

"I told you I'd be back in a minute."

"This is really wild! What are we doing anyway?" She held on to him like dripping wax. The group of men grinned. One of them slipped something to Raffaello, who passed back a bunch of money.

"What happened to your head?" He looked horrified.

"My brains are coming out, I guess. Look at my hands!" They were thick with a layer of soot. She held them up to the men.

"Come on, come on, we have to go. Thanks, Fafaa, I appreciate it." He pushed her ahead of him back down the hall, practically making her run. The taxi was still outside. "What is wrong with you?" He took out a handkerchief and started to wipe her forehead until she yelped in pain; then he tried to wipe her hands, but the stuff would not come off. "I told you to wait in the taxi! Don't you know what kind of danger you could have been in?"

The taxi ricocheted in the dark. She didn't know how long they had been driving. "Where were we just now?"

Raffaello laughed and leaned to the partition, muttering something to the driver. There was definitely some kind of conspiracy going on. Something was happening, or had happened, to which she was not privy. When the cab stopped at a red light, a man on the street approached the car on the passenger side of the front seat. From beneath a coat he took a rifle and stuck it through the open window, pointing it at the driver. "You want to buy this?" he said.

"Ah . . . no thanks, man," the driver said. With the end of the rifle still pointing into the cab, he stepped on the gas and drove through the intersection, with the light still against them. "Whew!" he said at last. "That was kind of heavy."

"That was unbelievable."

"What happened?" Florence said. "Was he trying to rob us?"

Nobody answered. Raffaello took out his little pipe and a tiny vial with a blue cap. Then he lit up, inhaled and tapped on the Plexiglas divider between front and back. The driver pulled over and Raffaello handed him the pipe. Then the man in front passed it back to Raffaello, who handed it to her.

"Here you go," he said, flicking his cigarette lighter.

"Hey, where'd this come from?" she said. "Oh, is that what you were doing in that basement, buying the drugs? Boy, I must have been really out of it!" She put the pipe between her lips and closed her eyes while Raffaello held the lighter over the end. The icy wind that swept down her throat was like an old friend. Now she knew what it meant to go to Kelvin's absolute zero—it was an actual place. If there had been one of those pressurized containers holding vials of stored, frozen semen, a solution of nitrogen and dry ice, she could have entered it quite happily, or gone through an air lock into outer space and enjoyed feeling her body break into chunks, brittle and dry as diamonds.

She was giving him a blow job in the backseat when the car came to a halt. One piece of time was unconnected to the next, as if bits of film were connected to one another with black leader, so that the plot was lost and she had to concentrate to remember: she was in a taxi, the man whose lap her head was in was some Italian guy, they were going to a club.

The taxi driver was somehow now part of the group; he put the cab into a parking lot and got out with her. "Are you coming with us?" she called gleefully, wiping her lips. She turned around as Raffaello, still fumbling with his fly, closed the door on her side.

"Yes, he's coming with us. You've asked him that a million times."

"Yeah, I'm just about off duty. I've been here before." The cab driver was actually quite cute—she was surprised not to have noticed it before—tall, with long blond shaggy hair and a muscular build.

"Where did you say you were from, Gideon?" For some reason

she seemed to know his name. She put her arm through his while Raffaello took her arm on the other side, as if she needed assistance in standing up. "I'm okay!"

"I'm from Utah, Florence. Look at her." Gideon spoke around her, addressing Raffaello. "She's very cute. She's got a great smile. You should hang on to this one."

"I plan to," Raffaello said grimly.

"And I'm going to hang on to him. He's my Italian movie star. Whoops!" She stumbled and they hoisted her to her feet. "So, Utah! What were you doing in Utah? Tell me everything about yourself."

"Well, my parents were Mormons—"

"Mormons! And did your father have more than one wife?"

"Naw."

"And did you go on one of those things?"

"A mission? Yeah. That's how I ended up here."

"But you're not a Mormon anymore, are you?"

"No, I—" He would have said more, but it was obvious she wasn't listening.

"Look at this! Here I am, out with a Mormon and an Italian—probably the only two categories of men in the world who wear sacred undergarments."

The two men smiled complacently, bonded in their comparatively sober state. As they walked the sky changed from a murky color—blackness illuminated by the yellow light of the city—to navy, then to periwinkle blue shot with pink. The sight—a lost and wasted night turning into day—sickened her; self-disgust crept up from her toes. "Come on, it's down here." Raffaello pulled her around the corner and they descended a short flight of stairs.

3

"*What's this?*" She was sitting on a barstool. It was incredibly difficult to keep her balance; she kept slipping off, first to one side and then the other.

"That's your drink."

"What kind of drink is it?"

"It's a Southern Comfort on the rocks."

"I don't drink Southern Comfort! Ugh."

"That's what you've been drinking."

"Really? I asked for it?"

"That's what you said you wanted—you seemed to enjoy the last three."

"Where's what's-his-name?"

"Who?"

"Um . . . you know."

"The Italian guy? Raffaello? Why, do you miss him?"

"I—"

"He got sick and went home. You don't remember?"

She shook her head and took a sip of the drink. "I can't drink this."

"What do you want? You've probably had enough."

"I want a drink! I want . . . a vodka."

"You don't need a vodka, not on top of all that Southern Comfort."

"You don't want to buy me a drink?" She puffed out pouty lips. "Maybe somebody else will." She looked around the room. It was like a miniature Roman bath: everything was tiled—the walls and floor and even the ceiling—in a gold-and-dirty-white mosaic. The ceilings were low, held up by Ionic columns, and in the center of the room was a small pool, perhaps a fountain, which explained why the room reeked of chlorine and mildew. On closer inspection there seemed to be mildew sprouting everywhere, furry and gray, but whether it was a real growth or bits of old tufted carpeting, she didn't know. The lighting was subdued—here and there various broken floor lamps had been positioned—and around the walls were overstuffed sofas upholstered in velvet on which people were seated.

There were maybe ten or twenty people in the room all together, she couldn't tell; perhaps more were hidden behind the pillars or in another room, if there was one. They seemed to be primarily men, faces a grayish hue, in black T-shirts, jeans, tattooed, with greasy hair and little goatees, all apparently waiting for something, as if the place were a brothel of satyrs-for-hire. Though in one corner a group of five—three men and two women—must have been students from an Ivy League somewhere, smug and slumming, looking like their parents had given them money for drugs. And at another sofa two women were entwined, kissing passionately. When they took a breather Florence could see that they were young, pretty, with defiant expressions, though it was perfectly obvious that they were accepted in here, that there was nobody to defy.

The cab driver was talking to her, but the pulsating music was so loud she couldn't make out what he was saying, and it took all of her energy to stop him from splitting into two people; she had to remember to squeeze her left eye shut or she didn't know which one of him to look at. "I said, 'Why don't you have a beer?' " he shouted.

"A beer? I hate beer."

He gestured to the bartender, a boy in his twenties with short hair and wearing a pink-and-white polka-dotted-and-flounced dress. "So what do you want?"

"What about . . . you don't think I should have a vodka?" His name was Gideon, she suddenly remembered.

"You want a glass of wine?"

"Yes! I'd like a large glass of white wine, with a lot of ice and some soda." She leaned forward and spoke to the bartender intimately. "He's a Mormon named Gideon whose father had seven wives."

"My father didn't have seven wives!"

"Oh yeah?" The bartender wasn't interested; he wiggled his hips in time to the music.

"Yes. Gideon's going to deny it, but he's here on a mission. Don't let him try and convert you!"

"Cool. White wine spritzer and—"

"I'll have a Heineken," Gideon said. "That's a nice dress."

"Thanks!" the bartender said. "I designed it myself."

"You designed it yourself?" Florence said. "You're *very* talented."

They were standing on the sidewalk. The streets were crowded with people and cars, and the light was so bright it hurt her eyes.

The scurrying pedestrians, freshly dressed, carrying briefcases and take-out cups of coffee, seemed to belong to a different species entirely. "What time is it anyway?"

"I don't know," Gideon said. "I don't have a watch. Nine o'clock? Ten?" He shrugged. "Maybe later. What do you want to do? You want to go someplace else? You want to go have some breakfast?"

"I want to go home."

"Fine. I'll take you home. I just have to remember where I left the taxi."

They stumbled around for ages, trying to find the cab. She couldn't even figure out what part of town they were in. The city seemed to have changed overnight, as if she had accidentally fallen out of her own universe into one that was only slightly different. The streets were labeled with names she didn't remember ever having seen before—Mata Hari Avenue, Ketchup Street—but she didn't want to say anything in case Gideon looked at her as if she were nuts. Perhaps the streets had always been named in this fashion, or else whatever she had been smoking all night had left her brain damaged in some peculiar way.

The car didn't seem to be where Gideon remembered having left it, but when he was about to give up, he spotted it in the parking lot. "Are you sure it's the same cab?" Florence said as he waved to the attendant and they both got in the front seat.

"This is all my stuff," he said, puzzled. At that moment he looked exactly like a little kid, or a perplexed golden retriever puppy, wildly attractive, and she leaned over and stroked his blond hair. "Oh, look!" he announced. "She's petting me!"

"You're so cute!" she said. "So cute and sweet! Like a baby bird." They began to kiss, and did not stop until he had started the car and backed out of the space. They started again while waiting for the attendant to come over to be paid and open the front gate; they continued to kiss at every red light or when traffic didn't move.

"Hang on just a second!" He stopped the cab and jumped out, leaving it double-parked.

Someone got into one of the cars at the curb and began to honk. The person unrolled the passenger window and yelled over to Florence, "Hey, you're blocking me! Move your goddamn cab!" She tried to ignore the man, staring straight ahead. The man got out of his car and, shouting a string of curses, began to come through the traffic around to Florence's side of the car. "What's the matter with you? Are you deaf? Move the goddamn car out of the way!"

Gideon came back carrying a large brown paper bag. He seemed to determine immediately what was happening; he went around to the trunk of the taxi, opened it, put the bag in and took out a large wooden baseball bat, which he held up in the man's direction. "I was only double-parked for two minutes," he said calmly.

He found a space just in front of her building. "You're really lucky with finding parking places!" she said. "Unless, when you come out and try to find your car, you have to find where it's hidden itself! Does that happen to you a lot?"

"Naw. That was weird, I have to admit. So what are you going to do? You going to ask me up to your apartment?" His eyes were shiny, like a doll's eyes, bright blue. He took the paper bag from the trunk of the car and followed her into the building.

"Make yourself at home." She pulled the blinds shut in the living room; though the light was not bright—her living room was in the back of the building, with any view or sun blocked by another building standing directly behind—but even the idea that it was daytime made her head throb. "You want a cup of tea?"

"No—I have something better." Gideon removed the contents of the bag with a flourish. "A six-pack of beer for me . . . and for mademoiselle, a bottle of chilled champagne. Veuve-Cliquot. I hope that's okay."

"Divine." It wasn't the best champagne, but it was certainly drinkable—and had probably set him back fifty dollars. She went to the hall cabinets and removed a box containing her crystal champagne flutes. The glass was so thin it was scarcely thicker than a piece of paper—ridiculously expensive, and already she had broken a couple. Several years ago she had begun buying fine china and crystal, as if shortly she would commence a married life of entertaining for which such things would be essential. This might have been inspired by attending someone else's bridal shower; she no longer remembered. Brandy snifters, martini glasses, a Tom and Jerry punch bowl with matching mugs in orange and blue, from the fifties—everything neatly bubble-wrapped and boxed for an existence that must have belonged to someone else.

She found a mug for his beer, and he popped the cork on the champagne bottle and filled her glass. Foam bubbled over the top and spilled onto the floor. "Cheers," he said as he cracked his can of beer.

"So what do you really do?"

"What do you mean?"

"You drive a cab—but I bet there's something else that you do, your real work."

"Yeah, sure. I, uh, I'm a writer. I haven't published anything yet, though."

"But you will. I bet your writing is really good."

"I must be the luckiest guy in New York, to have met you. I just think you're the best thing I've ever seen." He sat next to her on the couch and put his arm around her shoulder.

"I hope you're not going to be disappointed," she said. "I'm not usually this wild." She drank the champagne and he attentively refilled her glass.

"No, me neither," he said. "But what the hell, everybody's entitled to go crazy once in a while. I like you, being wild. I bet I like you just as much when you're not."

She slid out from under his arm. "Maybe I'll go to sleep now and see you another time."

"Hang on," he said. "Don't quit on me now. Look what Raffaello gave me." He took out the pipe and a nearly full vial. "It's so beautiful out. Aren't you having fun? We can go to Coney

Island, or whatever. Let's finish it off and you'll get your second wind."

"I don't know if I want to go on like this."

He lifted her hand to his mouth. "Look at your hands. You have the most beautiful dirty hands I've ever seen. I can't stand it. They're like swans—dying swans or something."

"I'm starting to feel kind of sick."

"You're not going to feel any worse, and you'll probably feel better. Then tonight you can sleep, and by tomorrow you'll be back to normal." He poured her more champagne, then he prepared the little pipe.

Somehow he had removed half her clothes. She was naked from the waist down, his fingers were inside her, and then he had unzipped his fly; his pants were halfway down and he was pushing his way in. "Hold on." She tried to scramble out from under him. "I'm not sure . . . I don't even know you, can't we just . . ." It was impossible, she couldn't escape. "Just quit it! Get off me!"

But even while the top half of her protested, her lower torso rose up to meet him as if their bottom parts were organisms on the seafloor—blind, brainless—starfish or squid or sea cucumbers. "You want it? You want it? You want it?" He grunted. "Come on, tell me you want it!"

She heard something that sounded like a cat mewling and realized she was making the noise. "A condom." She managed to blurt out the words at last. "What . . . about . . . a . . . condom?"

"Don't worry about it." His fat thumbs dug into the tender area between her ribs so ferociously she thought she heard something crack, galvanized nails splitting a chunk of wood.

4

She slept. When she woke it was after five in the afternoon. Early evening, really, though at first she thought it was five in the morning. The date on the digital readout clock indicated it was almost forty-eight hours later. The ice cream truck jangled its demented tune on the street below. She remembered little of what had taken place. Most of the day, from the time she had arrived back in her apartment until the taxi driver had left, was a complete blank.

She was weak and had a splitting headache. There was nothing to eat in the kitchenette except for a packet of instant miso soup. She boiled water and poured the mix into a mug. She was a little stronger after drinking it—she hadn't eaten in what must have been days; the salty taste was delicious—but she still felt awful, as if all that was left of her were the shell of some insect that had been sucked dry by a spider. Her skin had become a lampshade; her bones, powder inside the dead membrane. Her eyes beneath the paper lids were as dry as a carcass on a tarry roadside in the desert. A rattlesnake crushed by a car, still twitching. A brown paper bag. A handful of teeth.

But the worst part was that every cell in her body was alive and screaming for more crack. Her cells had never called out in individual despair before. But now each one felt like an octagon or mathematical shape in which one side had been removed. The cells hated having a hole, a gap; the only thing that could glue them together once more was to be filled or conjoined with cocaine.

She had not known until now what it really felt like to want to die. A part of her, something vital, had been sold for a mess of pottage and was gone forever. Her body screamed its hunger. Images of her animal behavior—worse than an animal—flashed jeeringly, mockingly, in front of her eyes, flickery as an old black-and-white TV set with poor reception.

Maybe there was some chocolate somewhere in the house. There had to be—half a bag of old Raisinets; half of a raspberry creme from that Godiva ballotin someone had given her ages ago (though maybe she had bought it herself) which she had stashed away to nibble at secretly during one particularly bad bout with PMS; a Callard & Bowser chocolate toffee. She opened every handbag she had, dumping out old dust and pennies on the bottom, hoping to find something. Finally the interior of the kitchen cabinets—way in the back—revealed an elderly chocolate Easter egg wrapped in shimmery foil, side dented in. She peeled off the silver. The chocolate was so old it had turned to whitish powder, but she stuffed it in her mouth.

No good. She still wished she had some coke. She turned on the water to take a shower and studied herself in the mirror. She looked tired, but that was the only obvious change—perhaps no one would be able to tell the difference. The water was as hot as she could tolerate, but the cells calling for more cocaine were scarcely distracted. It occurred to her that she had Katherine Monckton's baby shower this evening—seven-thirty onward; it was written down in her diary. She had even picked out something a few weeks before, a silver rattle from Tiffany's, as useless a present as one might ever find, but the sort of thing that would be expected of her. It had cost a hundred and seventy dollars. But if she wasn't stronger, there was no way she was going to attend.

She turned down the hot water and turned up the cold. That was better. At least now her cells were jolted into insensibility, temporarily too shocked to continue their screaming demands, as if they were monstrous baby birds in a nest, pterodactyls ready to peck the mother bird to death.

She probably should stay at home. But she was so miserable and full of self-hatred, the thought of being alone with herself was repugnant. With shaking hands she spent an hour and a half shaving her legs, applying makeup, trying on and discarding one outfit after the next. Finally she decided on a mushroom-brown satin silk slip dress, over which went a sheer silk chiffon full-length coat in varying shades of brown and dull chartreuse. Her legs were bare beneath the dress; her shoes—hand-made in France—were pearly mushroom-kid sandals with a court heel. The outfit was simple, yet beautiful.

Still, no matter what she wore, no matter how expensive or nice, she always had the feeling that the dress or suit was a mere watered-down imitation of what elegance was supposed to be. A hundred years ago money could really buy clothing; things made back then had hand-rolled hems weighted with lead, delicately embroidered buttonholes, better-quality materials. Even the most expensive couture gown nowadays didn't have beadwork of real pearls. And then, too, she always had the feeling that whatever she wore was not quite up to date. If she bought it in a showroom—not on sale, but next year's things—by the time the weather was right for wearing it, other, similar items were in the stores. And by the next season anybody who really knew about fashion had moved on to something new.

She tried to put up her hair in an elaborate nest, but after the shower it refused to obey, as wild as a bag of electric eels; finally she remembered her straw hats with tulle and she squashed one on her head. She was perhaps a little overdressed for a baby shower, but the address where the party was being held—a fancy one—was nearby. And at nine o'clock, the invitation said, the gentlemen were welcome. Perhaps she would be invited out to dinner afterward.

Anyway, the whole point was to never fit in *exactly:* ninety percent of the time it was better to wear tight black jeans and a black T-shirt to a somewhat fancy affair, making all the other women in little suits feel overdressed, or to wear a beautiful skirt or gown to something more casual, making the other women feel like slobs. It all had to be done within reason, of course. If the dress was too fancy—a strapless evening gown, say—then it was merely foolish, one couldn't relax, the other women would sneer. It had to be something beautiful yet simple and easy to wear.

At least, having spent so much time over herself, she felt better; it was a successful disguise. She studied herself in the full-length mirror behind the bedroom door, then decided some jewelry was in order to complete the costume. She pored through her jewelry chest. It was all junk, some things too trendy, the others out of date. All at once she remembered the bag of stuff that belonged to Virginia Clary. There were a few good things—there was no reason why she shouldn't borrow them to wear out for the evening; it was silly to have them just sitting by the door until she had time to bring them over to Quayle's.

She had to search for a while to find the Wal-Mart plastic bag. She must have moved it—or the housekeeper. Twenty minutes went by before she found it thrown behind a chair under some other things near a stack of boxes in the living room. She was running late by now, and poured the contents onto the sofa. She was uncertain, but it appeared that half the things were missing— at least the rings and the one valuable pin that had been in the imperial-yellow Chinese purse were gone. Surely they were in the apartment. Perhaps she had tucked them away somewhere for safekeeping.

It was almost eight o'clock. She began to yank things from drawers, tossing them onto the floor and chairs at random; grabbing heaps of files, old folders, photographs, a box of Barbie dolls; opening the lid of a ceramic elephant that served as a coffee table and snatching a handful of matchbooks, an electric curling iron, rolls of Scotch tape, a tape measure, a screwdriver, a single lacquer chopstick, two miniature airline bottles of vodka, a broken traveling alarm clock, four cassette tapes of outdated pop music, an emery board, pens leaking ink, a silver turtle pillbox, triple-A-sized batteries that were probably no good, a large agate marble, safety pins, a dark red lipstick worn down to a stump—but the jewelry was nowhere to be found.

These things, these things—if her entire apartment had burned, there was nothing in it she would miss or even remember. There were people who lived lives of Zen simplicity. Their drawers were empty. There were no zippered cases stuffed with too many scarves and shawls under the bed. They did not open their medicine cabinets to have seven lipsticks, empty bottles of hand lotion and random Q-Tips topple out. But it seemed to her only the truly wealthy could afford to live without things. The more one had, the less one needed.

She gave up the search for the jewelry. The room looked as if it had been ransacked. She should never have started hunting while wearing such a fancy dress. Some kind of ointment or grease had made a spot—in front, just above the knee. She felt like ripping off the whole outfit and throwing it away. She grabbed the two vodka miniatures. There was one ice cube left in the top tray of the freezer, and the bottom one was completely empty. Only a slob would put an empty ice-cube tray back in the freezer. The remaining cube had a tired smell, but she put it in a glass—there were just glasses in the cabinet; somewhere along the line she must have broken or lost the others—and emptied the vodka into it.

At least she did not feel quite so shaky after the drink; she grabbed a washcloth and scrubbed at the spot with soap and water. A big wrinkled wet area formed a circle, but the darker center remained unchanged. There was no way she could wear this outfit. Probably the cleaners would be unable to do anything—grease on satin—and she would have to throw it out. The chiffon overcoat was one of those items that would never go with anything else. It would end up hanging in her closet, years would go by, and every time she remembered the coat and tried it on, she would be reminded of the dress, which had cost nearly nine hundred dollars at a sample sale in a designer's showroom.

She wanted to scream. She tried to pull the dress over her head but somehow got entangled in its various layers. She grabbed a steak knife from a kitchen drawer and slashed the dress down the middle, attacking it as violently as if it personally had done something to her. She stepped out of it, leaving a puddle of silky brown on the floor. She stuffed the whole thing into a trash bag under the sink, the trash smelled like spoiled milk and rotten cantaloupe—she should have tossed it out a week ago.

She was late. She had nothing to wear. She didn't want to go at all. In her underpants and bra she opened the bedroom closet, yanking winter and summer clothes alike off their hangers, throwing everything onto the floor until she found a full-striped cotton skirt, still in its dry cleaning bag, in shades of ochre, lemon and brown. It was tight around the waist. How could she have gained weight? She wanted to die. She hadn't been to the gym in ages, she hadn't gone running. At least the skirt wasn't fitted but ballooned out.

From a drawer she grabbed a tight mock-turtleneck with short sleeves, patterned with daisies in colors that matched the stripes of the skirt. Then she had to find different shoes—she would have worn flat white patent leather thongs, but she hadn't had a pedicure and her toenail polish was old and the wrong color; at least with the mushroom-colored sandals, the front bit covered her toes. She pulled out shoe after shoe from the closet, but there wasn't a single one that had its mate anywhere nearby.

Practically in tears she finally found a pair of dark-blue Belgian shoe-slippers she had never had properly soled, the bottom was only thin leather, not really intended for street wear. But she stuck them on her feet, grabbed a dark blue satin bag with gold-chain straps and—flinging in her keys, money, credit card, lipstick, compact and the robin's-egg-blue box from Tiffany's, tied with white ribbon and containing the silver baby-rattle—headed out the door.

5

The shower was being held in the apartment of Victoria Ford, who lived in a Fifth Avenue building only a few blocks away. She didn't know Victoria well; and she hadn't even seen Katherine Monckton, who was having the baby, in almost a year. But in the days when she had been roommates with Allison, the three of them had spent a lot of time together. It started to rain on the way over, soft, plopping gray drops that increased in intensity; by the time she arrived her shoes were wrecked.

The doorman ushered her in with a wave of his hand—apparently he knew Victoria was expecting quite a number of guests—and directed her to the elevator on the left side of the foyer, where an elevator operator closed the old-fashioned metal gate, polished brass, by hand. There was only one door in the outside hall on the fifth floor, where a coatrack and umbrella stand had been set up. A man in uniform stood by the rack, looking at her disdainfully while she dripped and squished down the hall.

She came into the party as miserable as a sparrow huddled on a branch in the driving rain. A bar, complete with bartender, had been set up in the foyer, which had been decorated to resemble a miniature library. The shelves were filled from top to bottom with what, on closer inspection, turned out to be a variety of coffee-table-type books: *America's Country Kitchens, Indian Moghul Palaces, Swimming Pools, The History of Buttons, Collecting Hats, Honky-Tonk Highway, Birds of the Serengeti*—all of them glossy, oversized, fifty-dollar books, hundred-dollar books, probably unreadable, unopened, reeking of fresh ink.

She took a glass from a tray in front of the bartender, something pale-green and repulsive in appearance, but which turned out to be delicious, limeade and vodka. There were various appetizers on the table—a huge wheel of Maytag blue cheese and water crackers, smoked salmon and cream cheese on toast points—and she grabbed a couple of these before a waitress passed, carrying a platter of grilled chicken on skewers, with some sort of dipping sauce in a bowl in the center.

She slid the chicken into her mouth and poked the skewer back into a porcupine-shaped stand. The chicken was cold and dry, but she was so hungry she could have eaten the whole platter. She followed the waitress through the living room doorway.

The party was in full swing. Twenty-five or so women had gathered in a circle, seated on chairs and sofas, around Katherine, who was unwrapping the presents. Florence put her somewhat bedraggled Tiffany box on top of the pile heaped to one side. She recognized Tracer in the group, and Allison, and a woman she had actually known and grown up with in California, who had moved to New York at about the same time as she.

Then she saw Lisa Harrison, whom she hadn't seen since Lisa's party for the Egyptian jewelry designer. She had never called to thank her. Maybe Lisa wouldn't remember. She was dressed in a baby-pink suit trimmed with what appeared to be upholstery fringe—expensive, maybe Chanel?—her hair upswept in a casually elaborate coif. On her lap was her dog—a slavering, gargoyle-faced, fawn-colored thing, with a protruding tongue that could have been mistaken for a draped strip of raw bacon. It wore a pink patent leather collar that matched Lisa's suit. She looked incredibly expensive, but at the same time wasted. For a moment Florence was relieved: here was someone even worse off, psychically, than she, until she remembered how bedraggled she must look.

She couldn't be certain, but she suspected the woman whose back was to her was Natalie de Jongh. She took a step to one side, making sure that even if the woman turned around she wouldn't see her; she wasn't certain yet what she should do. Katherine was holding up a baby's silver mug while the women surrounding her made little encouraging noises. What could a baby possibly do with a silver mug, except dent it or break its own teeth? Next came a mobile—apparently intended to be hung over the infant's bed— from which dangled large black-and-white pigs with gilded wings.

There was a minute pair of black cowboy boots; a tiny black-leather motorcycle jacket; a stuffed koala bear; a large hideous yellow plastic windup music box in the shape of a smiling crescent moon that played "Twinkle, Twinkle, Little Star." Each item was crooned over with sounds of hushed excitement, as if fireworks were going off. A baby's antique hairbrush of vegetable-ivory; a marquetry picture-frame. A porridge bowl decorated with Peter Rabbit was accompanied by a set of the works of Beatrix Potter. "Oh, how cute!" She tried to join in the general enthusiasm. The entire ritual seemed as odd as some ceremony performed by a Nubian village tribe or remote mountain people in Myanmar.

The formalities were over. All the presents had been unwrapped. Katherine's friends stooped to gather the shimmery piles of tissue, the pink clouds and yellow sunbursts of wrapping that littered the floor. The mother-to-be sat on her throne, legs spread beneath her stomach, smug and regal, with the air of a princess or potentate.

Some of the women got up to inspect the presents; others headed back to the bar. The men—friends of Katherine's, husbands or boyfriends of the women—began to enter. With their advent the atmosphere began to liven up. They were all boyish stockbroker types, with sickened expressions; a cocktail party was one thing, but a baby shower was only a reminder of their imprisonment, past or future. The women were all extremely elegant. Victoria Ford, the hostess, stopped to say hello to Florence on her way to the kitchen. "How are you!"

"Fine! I can't believe the summer is practically over!"

"Oh, I know," said Victoria. "I can't believe it either!"

"Aren't you wonderful to do all this for Katherine. It's so exciting that she's having a baby! This is so nice."

"Do you like it?" Victoria seemed to think she was talking about the apartment. "We just bought the apartment next door and we're going to combine them. I've decided I really want to start having children, right away, and we'll need a lot more space."

"This place looks quite big, though."

"Does it? But it just looks that way. It's three bedrooms, but I need a study and Hank needs a study, and then we'll need a room for the baby and a room for the nanny. Excuse me a second." Florence wondered what Victoria would be doing in her study— reading the coffee-table books? She bit the inside of her cheek, trying to retrain herself not to have this sort of thought.

"Tracer!" She reached out and grabbed her by the arm. Tracer was rich, but with her big horsy face, she looked kind; she looked like someone who in the end would be her true friend. "Tracer! I didn't know you were back yet. Did you get my note?"

"Yes, thank you." Tracer swept nastily past. For a moment Florence wondered if she had actually been physically attacked. The sensation was as if she had been stabbed, liver and intestines spilling onto the floor for everyone to see. Her hands went to her stomach.

If she had done something to Tracer, couldn't she at least tell her? She tried to reshape her humiliation into fury. Perhaps she had hurt Tracer's feelings, betrayed her in some way—but she just couldn't guess what it was. People had an obligation to tell others if they were hurt or wounded. Then she could apologize. Under such circumstances, it seemed to her, *she* was the one who had the right to be angry, not Tracer.

A tall woman in a mannish gray-brown Italian suit slouched along the wall next to Florence. "Oh, God," the woman said. "I don't know whether coming to these things makes me anxious to have a baby, or anxious not to have one. All I know is, it makes me anxious."

"Mmm," said Florence noncommittally.

"I'm Anne Barrett, by the way. I think we met a few years ago, at something of Katherine's."

"Oh, yeah, yeah, right. Vaguely, vaguely. I'm Florence Collins."

"So do you have any children, Florence?"

"No. Though I'd like some. I think. You?"

"Well, my husband has custody of his kids, from his first marriage, so they live with us. We get along very well!"

"Oh? How old are they?"

"Cary is fourteen and Louise is twelve." Anne was boyishly attractive, slim; her face had good bones. Her hair was tied back, she wore very little makeup. Florence dimly remembered Anne had been in television—broadcasting, some kind of entertainment show.

"A boy and a girl?"

"No, two girls. They like me better now than their own mother. Jeremy wouldn't mind if we didn't have kids of our own. The house is so huge, in Bedford Hills, I stopped working after I got married, and I'm thinking that I'm getting to the point where I wouldn't mind either. Of course, then I'm sure I'd spend the rest of my life being even more anxious. Did you hear about Natalie and John's little girl?"

"Who?"

"Natalie and John de Jongh—you know them, don't you? Natalie's here, somewhere. I can't believe she actually came to the party. I guess she's at the point where she can't bear to stay home."

"What happened?"

"The little girl—I guess she was about eight or nine—she just died."

"Claudia? She *died*? I can't believe it! What happened?"

"You know, I'm not really sure. I just heard. She had been sick for a while, though, I think."

"Oh, God. How awful." Without excusing herself she staggered back to the bar. The bartender replenished her sticky green drink. Allison, her former roommate, came up alongside.

"Florence! Hi! How are you! I can't believe I made it back in time for this from my trip. It was unbelievable! Florence, you have got to do it—it was just so fabulous. Honestly, I'm not making this up. To spend three weeks on a canal boat through the French countryside—it was just like a dream. I feel like I've been away for ten years in a Zen monastery. Honestly, I'm just so collected now—it gave me time to think, to meditate, to really evaluate my life—and the kids loved it, of course, although thank God we had the nanny with us full-time, or I truly—"

Florence interrupted. "Allison," she said. "What happened to Claudia?"

"To who?"

"To Claudia. Natalie and John's kid?"

"Oh, my God, it's just awful, isn't it? Can you believe it?"

"What happened?"

"I don't know, exactly. Apparently it was some type of pneumonia."

She sank with disbelief. It must have been a joke, it just couldn't have been real. Children didn't die that way; they didn't die of pneumonia, except perhaps in Victorian novels. She was sickened by her own behavior. It would have been so easy to send the little girl a get-well card or a horse book. An image came to her of Claudia hauled out of the water, her fragile, pale skin almost translucently blue, a dab of cherry jam trickling from her mouth. Even then Claudia was determined—with the determination of a far older person—to punish her mother. "Pneumonia! But people don't die nowadays from pneumonia! They have all kinds of antibiotics—"

"Well, apparently, earlier in the summer she practically drowned. They didn't realize it at the time, but some water must have gotten into her lungs. Anyway, you know how they ended up closing the beaches? The bacteria count, some kind of sewage thing? I'm not sure of all the details, but whatever she had, if it was pneumonia or whatever, didn't respond to the antibiotics. It might have been the same kind of thing that old people get, and AIDS patients, cyto- . . . cyto-something-or-other."

"I can't believe it."

"Let me tell you, I was just so relieved that we *didn't* spend the summer in the Hamptons. There was no way I would have been able to keep the kids out of the water—"

Allison was still chattering aimlessly when out of the corner of her eye Florence noticed that Natalie had spotted her. She crossed the room with a look of such pure hatred on her face Florence could feel herself shriveling, her tender flesh seared as if she were being dipped in a bucket of salt and alum.

6

"*I want to let* you know that what you have done to me—to my family—has been indescribably cruel."

"I just found out about Claudia, Natalie. I am so sorry." She was crying.

"Of course you are." Natalie's voice was calm, but she was shaking. "Because now I'm going to make sure that your life is as much of a living hell as you've made mine."

"But what did I do?" She was genuinely baffled even while the hot tears continued.

"I'd like to hear your thoughts on what you think you've done."

The other guests at the party had stopped talking to eavesdrop. It wasn't difficult; Natalie's voice was brutally shrill.

"I don't think I've done anything."

"Excuse me, but in order for you to say that, you would either have to be incredibly stupid—which I don't believe you are—or a complete sociopath."

Someone came in from the outside hall. Florence's back was to the door, but she could hear a man's blustery voice as he entered the room. "Hi, Katherine! How are you? Wait until you see what I've brought you. You're going to hate this present more than anything!" Out of the corner of her eye Florence watched the man display a plush white stuffed rat with red eyes and a pink tail. "Now, listen to this. This will really get you."

Abruptly the man realized that something was going on—it was unnatural for a group at a party to be so quiet—and he fell silent. But he had already pressed a button in the rodent's ear. A mechanical voice blared out across the room. "I'm Ratty Rat! I'm Ratty Rat! I love you! Do you love me?" The rat's babyish speech was a parody of artificial sugariness: "wuv" instead of "love." Or else the quality of its internal organs—the tape player—simply wasn't very good.

Still holding the gibbering toy—there seemed to be no way to turn off its voice—the man scuttled into the other room. "I'm very sorry about Claudia, Natalie, but you can't possibly blame me."

"Don't put on that act with me. You've played that routine from the beginning."

"I realize Claudia wasn't supposed to go to the beach that day, but it could have happened just as easily in the pool at your house." The interruption by the man with the talking rodent had given her a chance to collect herself, and she was surprised at how calm she sounded even while she couldn't seem to stop her mouth from trembling and the endless stinging drops from pouring from her eyes.

"Tell yourself whatever you like, but the truth is that you are directly responsible for my daughter's death. You come to my house for a weekend, murder my daughter, seduce my husband, completely destroy the place after I told you not to use that toilet, and for what reason? Jealousy? Spite? Because you've slept your way through New York and didn't make it?"

"Excuse me, Natalie. I realize that you're upset over Claudia and need someone to blame. But since you've brought it up, I think you should know: I never seduced your husband. He's not my type, believe me. He came up to my room and virtually raped me. I had the feeling that you invited single women all the time to your house to provide for your husband's sexual gratification—so you didn't have to." She felt, somehow, that she had won the argument, the battle, whatever had just taken place, and that, having made her summary statement, she should leave the premises.

"My husband tells quite a different story." Natalie tried to get in the last word as Florence began to walk away. "And I had to have the ceilings redone on two floors! Do you have any idea what it cost, the damage you did?"

As she walked out the door Florence could still hear the cloying chirp of the rat: "I'm Ratty Rat! I wuv you! Do you wuv me?"

It wasn't until she was in the front lobby of the building, staring out at the rain, that she realized the gravity of what had occurred, that Claudia was dead, that her tears were connected to an emotion. In some way she was really responsible for Claudia's death, even if in some way she wasn't. Claudia had died from a lack of love. That poor child was so pathetic, so wizened, why had she been born into this world at all? Florence would have gladly traded places with her, if anyone had asked.

But now that she was gone the others would gather around Natalie, commiserating, trying to find out all the lurid details— and Natalie could make up anything she wanted. Tactically Florence had made a bad move. Who would ever believe John de Jongh, bland as mashed potatoes, would rape anyone, let alone steal her money? She never even had a chance to mention the twenty-five thousand dollars he had gotten her to hand over for some supposed investment.

"No umbrella?" The doorman was speaking to her.

"What's that?"

"You don't got no raincoat? No umbrella? You need a taxi?"

"A taxi." The mention of the word brought back all the memories of the night before and she cringed. "No, I don't think so." She headed out into the pouring rain.

A few blocks away she found herself in front of a pay phone, rummaging for a quarter, dialing Raffaello's number. Once, public phones had been contained in phone booths, complete with seats, protection from the weather, even phone books. Now she had to stand, getting wetter, in front of a stainless-steel stand that not only provided no soundproofing but resembled and smelled like a urinal that provided privacy only to the top half of the user.

His machine answered the phone. "Hello, Raffaello? Are you home? If you're screening your calls, pick up, please." There was no response. "It's me, Florence. I'm wondering—I don't want to bug you—but could you help me get some more of what we had last night? I'm not planning to do it often, but I'd like to have some around, just in case, and I don't know—" There was a beep and she realized she had been cut off.

She went into a nearby coffee shop. The place was deserted except for an old man eating fish and a bag lady sitting at the counter, talking to herself and picking at a corn muffin. There were only a few coffee shops in this neighborhood; in fact, there were scarcely any restaurants at all. The coffee shop might have been busy at lunchtime, or during the day on weekends, but at night only the few poverty-stricken denizens of the area came into the place. The fluorescent lights flickered erratically, casting a hard, cold light on the lime-green vinyl seating and Formica tables. She squished down the aisle and flung herself down in a booth for two. "Good eve-a-ning." The waiter appeared out of nowhere. He was Greek, tiny, in a white shirt, a black tie and jacket. "One person?"

"Yes."

He whisked away the other setting opposite her—paper napkin, cheap knife, fork and spoon. The menu was huge. It seemed impossible that one place felt capable of offering roast turkey dinner, eggplant moussaka, tuna fish sandwiches, Southern fried chicken, pancakes, steak and fries, along with a thousand other things. "You like something to drink?"

"Um . . . do you serve alcohol?" He pointed to the back of the menu. There had to be something on it that would cheer her up, something different from what she usually drank, maybe an amusing combination.

"How about this? The Frozen Strawberry–Pineapple Rum–and–Curaçao Supreme?"

"Which one?"

She showed him the picture of something pink and artificial.

"Gimme a Frozen Supreme!" he shouted over her head. "What else?"

"Maybe a cup of tomato soup. That's it."

"Just the Frozen Supreme and a cup of soup? You look kind of wet, you should eat a dinner, you don't get sick. We got a nice fish tonight, maybe you have some spaghetti—"

"Thanks. I'll see how I'm doing after the soup." The man behind the counter had removed a carton from the refrigerator and was pouring it into a blender—probably her fancy, prepackaged, manufactured drink.

It tasted like chemical fruit mixed with a solvent. Suddenly she was haunted by the memory of the crack. If she could taste it, smell it, just once more! It wasn't even the effect that she craved as much as the smell. Her cells twitched miserably, begging her to stuff them with the smoky salve. She got up and went to the pay phone. Maybe it was dumb, but she wasn't calling him to see him—she just wanted the address of the place to go, or some contact number to call. She had slept with him, what, little more than two days before; now she'd be damned if she sat around waiting for him to call.

No answer except the machine.

She went back to her booth. The soup tasted lousy, the drink tasted lousy—maybe some Jell-O? But when it arrived, topped with a big mound of canned whipped cream she had to scrape off to one side, it was like mouthfuls of slightly hardened rubber.

"No good? You no like?"

"No, it's fine. It's just that—I don't know what I'm in the mood for. Maybe . . . what about a plate of spinach? And . . . could I have a double shot of vodka, whatever's your best brand, on the rocks with just a little splash of fresh-squeezed orange juice?"

The waiter didn't even flinch. Obviously he was familiar with any and all eccentricities. The derelict woman at the counter had finished her tea and was carefully wrapping her used tea bag in a bit of aluminum foil provided by the counterman.

The area around the base of her stool was littered with five or six shopping bags, some paper, some plastic, stuffed and overflowing. The freckled brown sleeve of an old sweater protruded from the top of one. Actually, the woman's outfit must once have been quite fashionable, of good quality. Her shoes were completely worn down at the heels, stuffed with newspaper against the rain, but they, too, looked as if they had once been very good shoes. She had on heavy pinkish-nude orthopedic stockings that ended just below the knees. On her head was a little hat—the sort of velvet evening hat worn back in the fifties—twisted around the wrong way, so that the black veil came down over her right ear.

There was money in Florence's pocketbook and she threw a handful of it onto the table without waiting for the other things. It was still raining, a milder drizzle now. She began to walk, heading toward her block, but when she got there she kept walking. The rain had collected in deep puddles, in places almost a foot deep and no way to avoid them. After another six or seven blocks her shoes were completely ruined, melted into paste. They would never be salvageable and they made walking even more difficult. She took them off and tossed them in a trash container.

The sidewalk felt good beneath her bare feet, though the water in the puddles at the corner was warm, with a slimy texture that made her uneasy. It was probably a combination of rain mixed with Manhattan's black, greasy soot and the vast quantities of sputum that covered the sidewalk. It seemed to be a pleasant pastime for three-quarters of the men in the city to spit huge gobs wherever they walked. Probably if a nuclear bomb fell, destroying all human beings, it would be from the water in New York puddles that life would spring anew.

There was a telephone on the side of a building. Broken. A few blocks later, a bank of three telephones. All broken. A few blocks more, two telephones, back to back. One was in use, so she picked up the receiver on the other and put in a quarter. The money spat back out at her. She tried again. Okay, it wasn't working. She would wait for the other. The man using it was oblivious to her presence. He talked and talked, in what language she could not determine. She paced back and forth nearby, trying to let him know she was waiting. Then it became obvious he knew she was there; but he still had no intention of finishing his call. He talked endlessly. Whoever was on the other end had equally lengthy answers. She couldn't understand what anyone would have to say that would take so long, particularly at night, standing in the rain. He turned his back so that he wouldn't have to see her.

At least twenty minutes went by. She stood restlessly, thinking the phone would be hers at any minute. Finally the man looked over and saw she was still there. "I'm going to be a while," he said in a furious, heavily accented voice.

She was near enough to Raffaello's building; perhaps he was already home, or she could wait for him to return. Anyway, she had nothing else to do. She entered the marble lobby dripping and raggedy as a used paper towel. Her hair was soaked, flattened against her head. Beads of water slid into her eyes. The doorman sniffed suspiciously. "Can I help you?"

She tried to shake off some drops. "Um, I'm here to see Raffaello di Castignolli?"

The doorman looked at her—and the mess on the floor—disapprovingly. "Just a minute, please." He dialed Raffaello's intercom number on the house phone. "There's no answer. He's not home . . . was he expecting you?"

She ignored the question. "He's not back yet? Do you think you could let me into his place, to wait? Then I can dry off."

He stared at her with a mixture of embarrassment and contempt. "No, I'm afraid not."

"I'm a friend of his."

"I'm sure you are. But I can't let you in."

"Why not? You must have the keys."

"You can wait in the lobby, if you like, but I can't let you into a tenant's apartment."

If she hadn't been so bedraggled, he wouldn't have treated her like this. She would show him. She sat on a fake Le Corbusier couch between the doorman's position and the elevator bank. Very few people went in or out—a man with two West Highland terriers, a deliveryman with take-out food, an older couple returning from dinner—but every time she saw someone she made a big production of shivering and looking even more pathetic than she was. She really was freezing; it was no fun being so wet, and barefoot, but by now she was determined to see this through. An awfully long time passed in this fashion. The doorman tried not to notice her. Finally he must have grown desperate, or bored. He walked over to where she was sitting. "Are you sure he was expecting you?"

She looked up, wiping her nose with the back of her hand. "Oh yes. He's always late. He said if he was late I should wait inside his place. I got so wet on the way, but I figured you'd let me in to dry off. He's going to be upset if I catch a cold."

"I'm sorry." The doorman was uneasy. "It's just that . . . if he had left me a message, verbal, or written . . . Do you happen to know where he is now? You could give him a call and put me on, just to see if that's all right."

"I didn't bring the number with me. I never thought he'd be this late." She knew she should go—that it was the most pathetic thing she had ever done—but somehow she could not. Determination had glued her to the seat. It was the same kind of compulsion that made fourteen-year-old girls harass some boy by calling him over and over.

At that moment she saw him coming in and she creakily rose to her feet. "Here he is." Relief crossed the doorman's face. They both realized at once that there was a girl with him. Still, that wasn't her problem. "Raffaello!" she called. She tried to sound as if he were of course expecting her.

"What—what are you doing here?"

She averted her gaze from the doorman's baffled expression. "I tried to call, but I think there's something wrong with your phone, and I . . . had to get something from you . . . something important. Didn't you tell me to drop by tonight?"

He didn't respond. She looked up and down at the elegant blonde he was with. The girl was a bit like her, only ten years younger, not overdressed, nor bedraggled and wet, but casually elegant. Still, the girl wasn't anywhere near as interesting-looking as she; she was completely bland, a manufactured android.

"I don't understand," he hissed at last. "What are you doing here, you have no business—"

"I thought . . . after last night . . . Goodness, Raffaello, you told me to come by! I would have been here much earlier, but I had plans I couldn't get out of . . ." She stared patronizingly at the other woman and smiled coyly. "I'm Florence Collins." She put out her hand. The other woman took it disdainfully, flaring her nostrils, and muttered something that might have been her name in return.

"I never told you to come here! You can't just come here, unannounced, and sit for me in wait!"

"You don't have to get so angry! There must have been a misunderstanding, that's all . . . Anyway, I can see you're . . . busy as usual, but I wondered, could I just have a quick word with you? I have to ask you something important."

"Not right now, I'm afraid." She could see he was almost having a nervous breakdown, acting as if she had come after him with a knife. It served him right. "If you like, you can call me—at my office—tomorrow. Now, if you'll excuse us." Raffaello took the woman's arm and they swept past her and into the elevator. The woman had a triumphant look on her face; how sad and pathetic Florence appeared to her.

"Didn't work out like you expected, huh?" said the doorman in an overly familiar tone.

7

Labor Day weekend passed neither slowly nor quickly. She could
have gone somewhere, she wasn't exactly sure where, but no doubt
something would have turned up if she had pursued it—but she
didn't want to. She kept thinking about Claudia, wondering if she
could have saved her. Can anyone be saved? she wondered. Darryl
wanted to save her, but his love felt fabricated, a dream he made
up and invested himself in. It had nothing to do with her, she told
herself. But the thought failed to comfort her as she contemplated
how to fill the long hours of a holiday weekend, stuck in the city.

She rented some videos, ordered in Chinese food, ran in the park and went to the gym. Her membership was due for renewal. She put the fifteen-hundred-dollar fee on her credit card.

New York could be this way sometimes. It was usually on the weekends, but there were times when she might have been living alone on top of a mountain: no one called, there was nothing to do; complete isolation. Then things would get busy again. By now she had learned to ride out the quiet times and not to panic when things suddenly became overwhelming. There was never just one guy she might be interested in: there were three or four, or else none.

On Tuesday morning the phone began ringing. She reached for the receiver. "Hello?" Her voice came out cracked—she hadn't even had a cup of coffee. But she felt vindicated; obviously things were going to begin happening for her now.

"Florence? It's Marge Crowninshield. Are you all right? What's wrong with your voice?"

"Nothing. It just comes out that way sometimes."

"Are you still asleep? Did I wake you?"

"Oh, no, no." She looked at the clock. It was after nine.

"Good. I have to say, I'm afraid I'm extremely upset with you, Florence. I'm going to send a messenger over for the jewelry. He should be there shortly, and I wanted to tell you so you didn't go out. Will you be there?"

"For a little while."

"I've been out of town—I was in Morea for most of August—"

So what? she wanted to say. Even now Marge couldn't resist trying to brag, Florence thought. It was an ingrained habit. Was she supposed to be impressed? And say "wow" or "golly." She was surprised Marge didn't feel it necessary to add that she was going to have lunch at the Four Seasons, or whatever . . . "Well, I should be around for a while. If I have to go out before the messenger comes, I'll leave the stuff with the doorman."

"Please don't leave it with the doorman! Have you always been this irresponsible, or are you just feeling angry with me for having had to let you go? I'm certainly willing to write you a recommendation, if you like. You must realize there were plenty of reasons why Quayle's couldn't keep you. I did try to give you ample warning to shape up. And now, this! I can't believe you didn't send the jewelry over before now. That poor woman has been calling and calling."

"Well . . . I've been out of town too. The next estate jewelry sale doesn't come up until late October. I assumed if it was needed you would have sent someone to collect it by now." She hung up, none too gently. It wasn't until after she had gone into the kitchenette to make a cup of tea that she remembered some of the jewelry was missing. Maybe no one would notice, after all. The things weren't on her list; she could always say she had never seen them. She didn't know what else to do. The few valuable brooches and rings certainly weren't in the apartment. Anybody could have walked out with them: the cleaning woman, Raffaello, Gideon, the doorman leaving a package.

She felt no guilt—after all, she hadn't done anything, had she?—only fear that it would be discovered, she would be caught, blamed, humiliated and punished. Perhaps there was something wrong with her for not feeling guilty. It wasn't as if she had stolen the stuff, or lost it deliberately. In this instance Marge was the one who should be feeling guilty. If Marge hadn't fired her, she would have brought the jewelry in to work long ago.

She cleared a stack of mail off the table, throwing it on the floor in a pile. Bills, bills—she really had to do something about them, or the next thing she knew her gas and electricity would be cut off. She sipped her mug of tea and honey, trying to shake loose from her headache. She should probably make an appointment with the dentist—maybe she was grinding her teeth in her sleep.

For an hour she searched once more for the missing pieces of jewelry, turning everything upside down in the apartment—although everything already was upside down; she had been through everything a hundred times. It was awful, she was aware of that, stealing from a handicapped widow. It was probably breaking one of the Ten Commandments. On the other hand, it wasn't her fault. The pendulum of panic swung back and forth.

Finally the doorman buzzed to tell her the messenger had arrived; she had him come up and at the front door handed him the bag. He was a young kid, dressed in baggy jeans and some kind of dumb cap, who peered—it seemed to her—too inquisitively past her for a glimpse of the apartment. If Marge was so concerned, she should have come to collect the things herself, or Sonia.

She was shutting the door when the telephone rang again. It seemed to ring so rarely now, she was startled. "Hello?" Her voice was still a creak.

"Good morning! It's Max Coho calling!"

". . . Hi, Max." She wished she hadn't picked up the phone.

". . . So how are you?" It wasn't just a polite question—he was probing.

"Fine."

"That's good. What's been happening?" It was too early in the morning to hear his sing-song voice, boyish and bubbly. She was almost positive he had heard about the scene with Natalie last night and wanted the details.

"Not much." She'd be damned if she'd confide in him out of the blue.

His disbelief was practically audible. "Actually, I was calling to invite you to be my date tonight at a little dinner for Mike Grunlop—you know Mike, don't you? The painter, and his wife, Peony? It's at their loft. I could pick you up at, say, seven, seven-fifteen. We can go to the opening and go on from there."

"Okay." She didn't want to sound too excited. "How many people are going to be at the dinner?"

"I don't know. Thirty or forty, I should think. The gallery's having it catered. It's for his show. He's got a huge loft. If it doesn't rain, he'll probably have it up on the roof. It's really a fabulous space. See you later!"

How nice of him, that he was going to pick her up and take

her out—it sounded like a pretty good event. Finally somebody was coming through for her. Maybe there would be a single, straight male artist at the party; if he was successful, that was practically the best status symbol a woman in this city could have.

She knew she should have spent the day working on her resume, making phone calls, getting the word out that she was looking for a job. She should have started doing all that long ago. But it was still only the day after Labor Day; nothing would have been happening, no one would be hiring until now. Some people were still getting back from the country. There was no real rush. Anyway, it was all too depressing. If she was really going to have to go out and search for a job, it would help to look her best—for tonight too.

Fortunately, she was able to get an appointment with Enrique. The receptionist of course kept saying he was completely booked, but she insisted she put him on the phone and he agreed to squeeze her in.

The unfortunate part was that although he said he could take her, he had also said the same thing to everyone else. She arrived at the salon at eleven, but by the time she got her color and conditioner and cut, it was almost five. It was unbelievable. This wasn't the first time it had happened, either. Still, they always brought around good sandwiches for lunch, and she was charged only half price—a hundred fifty dollars for the color, the same for the cut—which would have come out to six hundred, not three, so she really couldn't complain. Then she raced home to change.

In one of the bedroom closets she found a short, tight black skirt, crumpled up at the back, and she put this on along with a tight black top that looked more like an exercise bra than a shirt. Then she decided it was too trashy, and panicked until she remembered a really cute dress she hadn't worn in years, sleeveless, a cotton print of black curlicues on white. It was vaguely fifties in style, but tight enough so that it was sexy in a demure way. Nice and girlie, she thought, admiring herself in the mirror. At seven o'clock the phone rang. "Would you mind terribly if you just met me at the gallery?"

She looked around the room for Max. The gallery was a huge fourth-story space on Fifty-seventh Street off Fifth Avenue, with shiny bleached-white floors, a bartender pouring sweet white wine into plastic cups in front of a crowd of shabby thirty-year-olds dressed mostly in thrift-store finds. The real collectors had seen the work earlier; they didn't come to the opening but would probably be at the dinner. She spotted the little enclave—three demented men in their sixties, known as Mo, Curly and Larry. They were dressed in cheap suits, shoulders covered with dander. Not a single art exhibit in New York took place that they did not attend. They somehow knew about every opening; they were a ubiquitous presence. But whether they came to drink the cheap wine or to continue their endless, futile pursuit of trying to pick up women, no one could be certain.

Curly—the one with the bald head ringed with a frizzy bush of hair at least eight inches long that stuck straight out—spotted her first and headed in her direction like a steer who sees the farmer with a bag of molasses-sweetened grain. She quickly sped past him and into the main room.

There was Alonso Butts—her heart sank and she slunk into a corner to avoid having to speak to him. There had been a going-away party for him when he went to Bali, and another when he came back. That was five years ago. He had conned his way into getting free airfare and the fanciest hotels by claiming he was writing a book. It was doubtful the book had ever been written. Even if it had been, he didn't have a publisher. Now he went every year. If she said hi to him now, he would tell her that he had just gotten back, or was just going. He would once again tell her how beautiful his house was—he rented or had bought a place there—and his vegetarian diet. No animal products: this included sea-life, eggs and dairy. He was particularly suited to a vegetarian diet. He had become purer, calmer. People who consumed milk and cheese stank of butterfat. In Indonesia, it was easy to be a strict vegan. There was coconut milk, rice and noodles, the diet of the people. Of course, he couldn't tolerate any spices, his stomach was too sensitive, and in Bali that could be a problem, but he was able to afford his own Balinese cook. Bali, Bali, Bali.

It was painfully boring, particularly so, as his self-involved monologue had no point or interesting anecdotes. One was required to stand attentively while his spittle spumed toward his audience. He always launched into long sagas. He no longer knew who all the movie stars were, for example, because in the Indonesian countryside he lived without the latest films and no TV. She—everyone—was supposed to be impressed, she supposed.

And there on the other side of the room was that actor, the one who had had one hit movie ten years ago. She had slept with him, once—but who hadn't, before and during his marriage to a much older heiress? How come there hadn't been any mention in the press of his mini face-lift and chin implant! Nor of the fact that he had been going to Harlem for years to buy his heroin. Whenever she saw him all he could talk about was his forthcoming movies, which somehow never materialized, and that all of his suits were tailor-made in London. She could only pray these were not the same people who had been invited to dinner.

"Florence! Florence, how are you?" It was Hypatia Bradstreet, built like a canister, barreling her way toward her.

"Hypatia! Hi! How've you been?"

"Oh, I'm great! I'm just going to India—I've been invited to stay in a palace in Kerala and make some prints. Do you know I have four shows coming up as soon as I get back? One in San Francisco, one—"

She continued her monologue even as they were joined by Fritz Czykwicz. "Hi, Florence, hi, Hypatia. How are you? You going to the dinner later? I don't know if I should go or not—I'm on deadline to finish my script. It's going into production in January. We've just lined up someone incredibly famous to play the lead. I can't say who it is yet."

The three were joined by Ned Halstead-Heath. "I have the

worst jet lag!" he said. "I just got back from Peru. I was in Lima, on assignment to write about the lesbian countess who murdered her Indian lover. First-class trip, all the way! You wouldn't believe how people live down there. I was staying with some friends—an incredible place—it was unbelievable. I was shot at on two separate occasions—"

She was going to scream. There wasn't a single person who could talk about anything besides themselves. Each one had to show how important he or she was. Why? Would that make her like them any better? Their need for attention was desperate, consuming, it was a disease. It wasn't considered rude to approach anyone in the room and begin to launch into a speech about one's present or future success. Nor was it considered rude for the other person to launch into his or her monologue in response. But it was a sickness of some sort, a late-twentieth-century cancer.

Then she saw Derek Richardson. "Oh, I have to go speak to Derek." He had bright red hair, such an Irish, pixie face, at once dissipated and dissolute. Avoiding Alonso Butts and the movie actor, she ran over to him. "Derek! How are you?" He hesitated. "Florence Collins," she reminded him.

"Of course, don't be ridiculous." He nuzzled the air by her ear. "You're looking gorgeous, as usual. Did you lose weight?"

"Oh, I wish! So, Derek, when's the new restaurant opening? I thought of some names for it—"

He caressed her back, sliding his hand to her rear end. She was flattered and purred next to him. "What new restaurant?" he said.

"Don't tease me like that! The one opening in the fall. The one you let me buy one-third of a share in."

"I don't know what you're talking about."

"You're kidding me, right?"

"I don't understand. Who did you buy a share from?"

"It was a third of a share. John de Jongh set it up."

"Oh." There was a pause. "I'll just have a chat with him, then, shall I, and see if there's just something I've forgotten."

"I . . . I gave him the last of my money, Derek," she said

plaintively. "I was so thrilled, you see, when he said I could get involved."

"Don't worry about it. I'll speak with him, and give you a call later on. I'm sure it'll work out." He began to back away rapidly.

"Wait, don't you want my number? I'm not listed."

"No, that's okay, I've got it, I'm sure, or I can get it." Two big white hands with nails painted grape-black suddenly covered his eyes, and he turned. "Oh, here you are! Have you met . . ." Derek looked at Florence blankly.

"Florence."

"Florence, this is my fiancée—"

She could have sworn he said the girl's name was Derma. She appeared to be no more than thirteen, maybe sixteen at the most, at least six feet tall, with albino hair; absolutely stunning, no doubt a model, chewing pink gum, young enough to be Derek's daughter. He slapped Derma's fanny, swathed in tight, iridescent turquoise pants, and they departed.

A certain grayness swept over her. She supposed she had hoped or thought, unconsciously, that flirting with Derek—whom once she would have thought beneath her, a restaurateur—might lead somewhere.

Max was standing at her shoulder. "Sorry I'm so late," he said, not looking sorry at all. He was sparkling. He gave the appearance—though perhaps it was merely an aura or illusion—of having just stepped out of the shower, on a day in which he had taken at least three or four showers. His face was scrubbed, his khaki pants were crisp and pressed, even his cotton polo shirt, dark blue, seemed as if it had—improbably—been ironed. The city was inhabited by a million of his cloned replicates, every one of them five feet nine inches tall, smelling faintly of aftershave and talc, not a hair out of place, with earnest, boyish expressions and eyes that cruised the room.

"I don't understand any of this," she said.

"The paintings? I like them." She looked quickly at the paintings for the first time. They seemed . . . so badly painted, so amateurish, such soulless imitations of Chinese brushstroke calligraphy, densely black lines, almost oily in appearance, on matte chalkboard-colored backgrounds. They were assumed to be the height of elegant sophistication. Maybe they were. If she ever got rich, really rich, she would put one over her living room couch. "No, I'm not talking about the paintings. I just saw Derek Richardson. I had invested in his latest restaurant—he was supposed to open one this fall? And now he just said he doesn't know anything about it."

"Kiss that money good-bye, sweetheart. Where have you been? Everybody who invested in his last place lost everything. People put in seventy-five thousand, the restaurant was a huge success, nobody got a dime out of it, not even their original investment."

"But . . . but how?"

"Creative bookkeeping. Come on, let's go. If I have to talk to Alonso Butts and hear about his inner spiritual life in Bali, I'll scream."

8

As they left the building a woman—a street person, a derelict, whatever, dressed in layer after layer of filthy rags—approached them nervously, looking over her shoulder like a hunted mink or weasel. " 'Scuse me! 'Scuse me!" She spoke aggressively for someone who looked so jittery and frightened. "I wonder if you could help me out. Do you have five dollars?"

"It's just like the decline of the Roman Empire," Max said delightedly, ignoring the request as he stepped into the street to find them a taxi. Suddenly an odd memory came back to her. As a child she had been sent out into the garden to kill snails and slugs that were eating the plants. At first it had disgusted her, pouring grains of salt onto the flabby bodies and watching them writhe and curl in death. But then after a while she had gotten used to it, and even stopped using the salt in order to make their deaths more personal by stabbing them with the tip of a knife. No matter how many she slaughtered, after the infrequent rains they came out of hiding by the millions. Once in the middle of the night she had awakened to find one on her face: it must have gotten stuck or crawled onto her earlier in the day and gradually made its climb toward her moist mouth and eyes, leaving behind a trail of slime.

The woman was blocking her path, pleading with her. "Please, miss."

She was about to step past when she saw something in the woman's eyes—what it was she wasn't certain. Fumbling in her bag, she averted her gaze. She was going to give the homeless woman a dollar, but paused. Fifty cents was enough. "Here." She handed the woman the coins.

"Fifty cents!" the woman said. "What's that gonna do me? You got your *Vogue* magazine, that's five dollars; your cup of cappuccino, that's a buck seventy-five—"

Florence could hear Max giggling from the street as a taxi came to a halt.

"Okay, okay," said the woman, "Got a cigarette?" Florence shook her head. "How about a match?" There was a hole in the woman, a hole that could never be filled, no different from her own empty space. She threw the woman a bill without checking the denomination.

"Hurry up, would you?" Max was holding open the door to the cab. "What were you doing all that time? She was awful. You shouldn't give those people anything. They'll only spend it on drugs." He leaned forward to speak to the driver. "Leonard Street, please." He gave Florence a nudge, gesturing toward the front; the driver seemed to be wearing full Indian wedding regalia, an elaborate pink turban and a bejeweled jacket.

"Believe me, if I was on the street, the first thing I'd do is buy drugs or a bottle of vodka." She was surprised to hear herself sounding so defensive. "He who asks shall receive. I think anybody who is so low they have to beg should be given money."

"Oh, so it's St. Florence, now. Florence Nightingale. Is somebody feeling a little guilty? You can tell your Maxi. I can keep a secret."

"I'm very nervous . . . I'll tell you what I really want, Max. I want to smoke some crack." There, she had said it.

"Are you kidding?"

"No. Do you have any?"

"No . . . but I know where I can get us some, if you really want."

"Oh—so you've smoked it too."

"It's not that big of a deal. I can't say I've ever actually gone out of my way to acquire any before. I usually just smoked it if I was out in a club or something, and somebody gave me a pipe. My recreational drug of choice is actually heroin—not to shoot it, of course, just to snort it."

She nodded gratefully. So perhaps it wasn't all that big a deal. Max had a good job, he traveled; drugs in Manhattan were just another form of entertainment like going to a good restaurant. It was only the ones who couldn't handle it, the weak ones, who ended up in Alcoholics Anonymous or NA.

"No wonder you gave that woman a quarter. You didn't want to bump into her buying crack at the same time as you."

"I only smoked it once, Max."

"That's what they all say. Driver," he called, "Ninth Avenue and Eighteenth Street, please." They continued in silence. "Just here!" he said, and began to get out. He addressed the driver. "Hang on. Keep the meter running. I just have to run in and get something; it'll only take a minute."

She sat staring at the dirty-red door he had entered. In the front seat the driver squirmed impatiently. He had a radio or intercom of some sort, from which, from time to time, a harsh static spilled and the sounds of a man screaming in what must have been Urdu.

A few minutes later Max returned. "Here you go." He handed her a vial. "Now just remember, you owe Max one."

"You—you got it so quickly. That was amazing!" She threw her arms around him.

"It's only a twenty-dollar vial, for God's sake. Where's your dignity, girl?"

She untangled herself. "Where did you go to get it anyway?"

"That's my little secret. See how I can keep a secret? Now, spill the beans."

"Maybe."

"Maybe after you've smoked? Driver, could you take us to Eleventh Avenue?"

"What are we doing there?"

"We can smoke."

"I don't have a pipe."

"I got you one. Don't say I don't look after you, even though it seems to me a certain someone was on the phone screaming at me earlier in the summer."

On Eleventh Avenue they got out and began to walk, hoping to find an empty alley or side street. Costumed prostitutes—trashy vinyl miniskirts, low-cut gold-spangled tops, fishnet stockings—tried to flag down trucks and passing cars; one approached them and suggested she could entertain Max. "Sorry, honey, I don't go that way."

"Don't worry about it," the prostitute said. "It's no problem. Underneath all this, I'm a real boy. My name's Pinnochia. Every time I get a compliment, my dick gets bigger." He laughed shrilly. His sad eyes were encased in clouds of mascara. "Wait a minute!"

Pinnochia was prettier than any picture in a magazine. He probably would have resembled a top model if he hadn't been so overdressed and heavily made up. Once, the garb of a prostitute had been separate from that of other women. Florence tried to explain this to Max. "I remember, one Halloween, I was invited to a party, and I had just broken up with some guy, so I was hell-bent on revenge. I wanted to look my sexiest—I put on a really short skirt, and heels—and I met this man. I wasn't really interested in him, but we were talking. A few weeks later I saw him at something else—he came over to me and said, 'I remember you, you were the one dressed up as a prostitute on Halloween!' But I hadn't been dressed up as a prostitute—I was just trying to look attractive."

She glanced over at Max to see his response. He wasn't listening. He had cultivated the New York skill of tuning out completely the moment anyone began a story longer than two sentences, unless each sentence was about him.

A pair of beautiful naked legs protruded from the open door of the driver's side of a parked car. The legs were so long they extended to the sidewalk, the feet in purple patent leather with heels so high their wearer must have been as uncomfortable as if he or she had bound feet, pre-Republic Chinese style. "It's either a prostitute who's been decapitated from the waist up," said Max, "or he's busy giving someone a blow job. Come on, this is a good place." He pointed to a sheltered alcove behind some Dumpsters. The area reeked of stale urine, a male ammonia smell worse than the stench of a bunch of cats.

She waited. Max filled the pipe; he waved it under her nose, trying to tantalize, then lit it and hogged it all to himself. "Oh, Max, come on!" she pleaded. "You don't even like that stuff."

"Maybe you should ask me more nicely."

"Come on, please." She got on her knees, trying to be sarcastic and funny, but somehow, she realized too late, it didn't come across that way.

He glared at her with contempt and glazed eyes before refilling the pipe and handing it to her. "God, Florence, how pathetic. You're disgusting."

She didn't care. At least maybe she would have some relief from her screaming cells, whining insensibly like hungry babies. She took his lighter and eagerly touched the flame to the rocks in the bowl. This time the crack was a big disappointment. Nothing really seemed to happen. The babies stopped crying, but remained disgruntled, as if they suspected their bottle of milk had been watered down. It was like looking forward to a beautiful piece of chocolate cake from the bakery, a slice that looked rich and dark, only to find it tasted like cardboard.

There were no cabs on Eleventh Avenue and they had to walk for ages, heading east, and then south, before any came along. By the time they got to TriBeCa, they were late.

A servant had been hired to open the front door. The Grunlops apparently owned the entire building. She was about to enter a door on the right when the servant stopped her. "The party's on the fourth floor," he said. "Take the elevator."

"That's Mike's studio," Max said, referring to the door she had attempted to go through. "The basement is the pottery workshop and kiln; Peony's studio and darkroom are on the second floor; I forget what's on the third floor—kitchen and kids' rooms, I think. Fourth floor, living room; fifth floor, bedroom; then the roof garden." They got in the elevator, industrial-sized, which opened onto a huge loft space, at least three thousand square feet. If every floor was the same size, that meant they had more than fifteen thousand feet of living space. Her apartment was around seven hundred and fifty square feet.

The space was meant to be simple—Zen-like in its austerity—but standing just outside the fourth-floor elevator door, she could see it was one of those places where every carefully selected item might as well have carried a price tag. There was a chandelier of steel-and-glass tubes that she knew sold for around twenty thousand dollars. A huge Japanese chest along the wall, of some extraordinarily richly hued wood—seventeenth century?—might have cost the same.

Over by the window was the prow of a canoe, New Guinea, possibly Asmat. She wouldn't have been surprised if it was worth a hundred thousand dollars, though she didn't know all that much about Oceanic and tribal art. There were brilliant pre-Columbian textiles on the walls, the colors and patterns as simple and modern as Mondrian's, used to wrap corpses and perfectly preserved by the moisture-free desert sand. A hundred years ago the home of a successful artist would have been stuffed to overflowing with heavy Victorian furniture and Oriental-style velvet drapes. A hundred years from now, no doubt, this loft would be as laughable, as clichéd, as the home of Rodin or some Hudson River School painter. "Come on," said Max irritatedly, tugging her arm.

She stiffened as they entered the room. "Max, what's that music?"

He paused for only a moment. "Callas . . . *Gianni Schicci.*"

She misunderstood. "Oh, from the Gianni Versace ad?"

"Very funny. Puccini."

She cringed with embarrassment. She could only pray Max had really thought she was trying to be amusing or he would never let her forget her dumbness. Now she wished she had taken a couple of music history courses in college; just to have some background. She had never really liked music all that much, except whatever was current, to keep her in the mood of the times or the day. The more factual information a person acquired—being able to identify names, really, was all that was needed—the less likelihood there would be of making an error. The biggest mistake of all in this city was displaying ignorance. She remembered the time someone had referred to a Gillows table, discovered in an antiques store in Alexandria and purchased for very little money. This had happened ages ago—she was far less sophisticated then—and had asked aloud what a Gillows table was. She never forgot the look of disbelief on the other person's face. She realized immediately how her worth had been diminished.

The space was crowded, too crowded to really have a look around and see how it had been decorated. Obviously this was no small sit-down dinner for forty—they had invited hundreds.

"Where's the bar?" Max said.

"I don't know. This place is so crowded! I thought you said—"

"I know! He told me it was going to be a small dinner. I never would have bothered coming if I thought it was going to be a mob scene."

"Who invited you anyway?"

"Mike's assistant."

So it wasn't even an exclusive event, then, if the artist's assistant had been permitted to invite his own friends. They pushed their way through to the bar. Mike was standing in the center of a group who were all telling him it was his best show ever. "Hi, Mike," said Max. "Congratulations." She hated the way he got so coy and girly whenever he addressed someone rich or famous. "Where's Peony?" Mike gestured across the room. A Chinese woman in a purple brocade robe was surrounded by a crowd of her own. She wore her hair in pigtails, but her face was as crumpled and cold as that of the Dowager Empress.

"Everybody knows the only reason Peony has a career as a photographer is because she's married to a famous painter," Max said. Florence didn't think they were even out of earshot of Mike, but Max was oblivious. "Her pictures—have you ever actually seen them?—are the worst. Technicolor pictures of dying animals and mangy dogs. Anybody who hires her for a job just happens to receive a little sketch or drawing from Mike, as a gift. Some gift! They can turn around and sell it for twenty or thirty grand. Still, I suppose her work is no worse than old what's-his-name, who takes pictures of his dachshunds dressed up in little outfits."

"Yeah, well, it must be nice to be married to such a rich, famous artist and have a career, even if it's for the wrong reasons."

"I know, but Mike's had one girlfriend after the next and Peony is pathologically jealous. I think the only reason he doesn't divorce her is because he's afraid of her. Look at her! Can you imagine her in bed, with those fingernails? How can she even take photographs?"

She asked the bartender for a vodka and cranberry juice, and Max got a bottle of beer, in keeping with his boyish appearance. She looked over her shoulder. There had to be somebody cute in the room, or at least recognizable as a heterosexual. "Ursula, this is Florence. Florence, this is Ingo Crandall, Ursula and Ingo Crandall." She turned back to shake hands. This couple was very attractive. They resembled two tall, skinny twins, not so much androgynous as neuter. They had huge alien eyes and the exact same haircut, chopped off and boyish—her figure was as slim and boyish as his. "Are you guys back from Albania already?" Max said. "How was it?"

"Marvelous," said Ursula. "We're thinking of taking a place there next summer."

"We stayed in Victor's castle," said Ingo. "You know Victor, don't you, Max? He's heir to the throne? Remarkably, the government made full restitution of his property, although of course the castle is basically a ruined shell."

"I didn't know Albania still had a throne," Florence said. "I thought . . . isn't it Communist?" Ingo and Ursula stared at her with the calculated expressions of praying mantises examining possible prey before—with dismissive nod—they disappeared into the crowd.

"He's quite a bad cabaret singer," Max explained. "But he travels around the world playing in fancy places like the Carlyle because of his snotty, fake Noël Coward act."

"But they're married?"

"Yeah. He has his boyfriends and she has her girlfriends—but they only sleep with people who have a title. Right now she's going out with Princess Magda of Yugoslavia and he's been with Baron Leonid of Prussia for two years."

"You know everything about everybody."

Max pointed to a glum woman who might have been attractive except for her morose expression. "That one went to Tibet—Nepal—someplace like that, for two years on some kind of Peace Corps teaching thing, and she got *worms.*" He suddenly raised his voice to a bellow and shouted at an equally surly-looking man halfway across the room. "Henry, what kind of worms did Missy get when she was in Nepal?"

"Tibet!" Henry corrected him, shouting back. "Tapeworms!"

"Tapeworms, thank you. So Henry went over on a visit to see her, and they were about to have sex, but then he looked down—you know, down *there*—and he saw a little white thing sticking out. So he bent down for a closer look—it was the head of a worm that had popped out and was staring at him."

"It had eyes?" Florence said.

"I don't know if it had eyes or what—you want me to ask him?"

"That's okay."

"But I distinctly remember him telling me that it had a little mouth, and, well, naturally he couldn't help but scream. So Missy goes, 'What's the problem?' And she looked down, saw the head of the tapeworm and started to pull it out. Apparently it happened all the time."

"But didn't it break?"

"What?" Max asked.

"The tapeworm. Aren't they about six feet long or something?"

"I don't know." Max yelled across the crowd again. "Henry, when Missy pulled the tapeworm out of her vagina, did it break, or what?" He turned to Florence. "Do you think that was very wrong of me?"

"What?"

"To say the word 'vagina' so loud? Was I awful?"

9

They waited on line for food—risotto with cremini mushrooms, peas, and prosciutto, scented with rosemary. Bowls of Parmesan cheese, slices of Italian bread and a large green salad were help-yourself. There weren't enough seats for so many people; though a few tables covered in white cloths had been set up around the room, they were already occupied. There had to be at least a hundred people, if not more. It wasn't so simple to balance a plate, tableware and a drink while standing up. They ended up deciding to go and sit on the floor in the stairwell. Almost immediately another couple, also searching for somewhere to sit, joined them on the nearest step. "Hi, Clifford," Max said coyly. Florence concluded that Clifford was either rich, famous or a prospective love interest for Max.

"Hi, Max. This is my girlfriend, Rosemary."

Rosemary was English. Florence had had enough experiences with English women to not even attempt to chat with her. Usually the English men were nice; but the women could or would only be friends with other English women; they somehow managed to behave as if Americans—at least women—didn't smell very nice.

Clifford was American, though he lived in England. "What do you do, Clifford?" Florence said.

"I'm a novelist."

"You must have heard of Clifford, Florence!" Max said, interrupting his conversation with Rosemary.

"How could she have heard of me? My first novel hasn't even come out in this country yet."

"What's it about?"

He sighed wearily, as if he had already had to answer this question a million times. She was sorry she'd asked. "It's about being made to work as a child-porn star by my parents when I was seven."

"It's—it's a novel?"

He shrugged, obviously thinking of something else. "I've pretty much decided, no interviews. I think a real writer shouldn't be out there doing self-promotion."

"What's the name of your book?"

"It's called *The Voyeur of Nothing.*"

"And when will it be out? I'll look for it."

He hedged. "My agent is deciding which offer to accept, in this country. In England it was published six years ago. It was just sold to television. Pretty big budget too: a BBC production. I'm working on the sequel, about how I rescued an Aleut child-prostitute. It was very dangerous—I was practically harpooned, twice. And paralleling this story is a multigenerational history of New Jersey, dating back to the Ice Age and continuing through to the time I was sent to boarding school. I'm already up to page eleven hundred."

"Oh. So how do you know Mike and Peony?"

"Through Rosemary. Rosemary's a photographer's rep. She's Peony's agent in England. You know the problem with English women?"

"What?"

"None of them know how to give good blow-jobs. I finally figured it out: it's because English men are so bad in bed."

"Come on, Florence," Max said. "Let's go up on the roof." He rose, leaving his plate, napkin and glass on the floor. Dwarf trees in pots and gravel had been arranged to resemble a Japanese garden, complete with stone lanterns and a pool filled with koi. The view was splendid, buildings cutting like cubes into the sky-line, though every surface on the roof she looked at closely was covered with a fine film of grayish black dirt.

Two cherubically plump English boys, resembling Humpty-Dumpty and Tweedledee, were standing by the railing, chattering excitedly, apparently having just discovered each other. For some reason they gave the illusion of wearing invisible straw boaters; perhaps it was the effect of their striped, too tight suits, as if they were an old-fashioned vaudeville routine. "And then of course there was the dreaded *cold spoon* treatment," one was saying.

"Oh, the *cold spoon* treatment! Wasn't that wretched!"

"What's the *cold spoon* treatment?" Max asked. Florence knew he was doing his dumb-American-boy routine, which so many seemed to find appealing.

"The *cold spoon* treatment," said Tweedledee, "was back in public school—"

"What you call private school over here," said Humpty-Dumpty.

"And if you were ill and had to go to the nurse, she had to examine you—"

"The *cold spoon* was if you had an"—Tweedledee glanced at Florence with an expression of coy embarrassment and raised his voice—"erection, which of course naturally sometimes one couldn't help—it was an involuntary *response*—but then, you know, Nurse would just briskly give one's penis a quick tap with the *cold spoon*—"

"In order to make it go away!" Humpty-Dumpty said gleefully. "It was *unbelievably* painful!"

These were examples of the simpering idiots who were taking over New York. More than two hundred years ago there had been a Revolution; the Americans threw the Brits out. Now they were welcomed back, ushered back, swooned over—the descendents of the same fops who sneered and looked down on the colonists. And whose descendents were sneered at today, only now maybe rightly so. What had been the point of any of it, the death, the gangrene, lives dedicated to a cause? The only difference was that now a corrupt American government levied a tax on tea bags.

Max joined a group who were standing in a circle smoking a joint. Florence decided to go back inside. She hated smoking marijuana. There weren't many women she knew who actually did like doing it. For some reason it seemed to be a man's drug. All she could ever remember happening to her when she smoked was that she felt incredibly nervous. Anything she said, even an innocuous comment about the weather, resonated in her head and she would spend the next hour wondering how she could have said something so stupid.

A man was pontificating on the stairwell about his new-found obsession with the works of Madame Blavatsky. He was talking to two other men—they all looked heterosexual, or at least they didn't look as attractive, well groomed and dressed as those she knew to be gay. One of them interrupted to talk about his Gurdjieff classes. She thought of hanging around this enclave and listening with rapt attention, but she didn't have the strength. Not another Gurdjieff proselytizer! She had had to listen to too many Elmer Gantrys during her years in New York: the Buddhist chanters, the followers of Guru Mai, the fund-raising acolytes of the Dalai Lama, the worshipers of some new diet that rejected bread and rice.

To join meant to feel superior—at least for a year or two, until the trend or fashion passed in a heap of accusations, pointing fingers and discouragement that the reaping of rewards was not likely to be immediate. She had had to sit through an entire meal at which a wealthy dermatologist lectured the assembled about her conversion to Islam and her trip to Mecca. Since that time her practice had tripled.

If only she had a religion! But she couldn't get any of it to mean anything to her. Honestly, was she so much worse than everybody else? She could scarcely believe that she had less spirituality than these others, who seemed like competing lemmings, trying to be the first to jump into the sea . . . She wandered around the loft, studying the art Mike and Peony had bought or obtained by trading works of their own.

The most expensive contemporary works constituted their collection: a derivative, pseudo-childlike painting, black chicken scratches on a gray background; miniature green-faced clowns cavorting in mud; heavy dull-gray sculptures nine feet high that resembled petrified turds. And the mingling artists themselves— there was Chip Moony, flabby and porcine; there was Dorp Whitman, neurasthenically thin, as if this somehow balanced his huge houses in Telluride and East Hampton, wearing a hooded djellabah, a fake display of holiness—men all.

Okay, so she had no values. Who here did? That lawyer, Neil Pirsig, who had skimmed millions off deceased artists' estates and then went to court to get more? He smiled at her across the room, but she ignored him. Surely he must know just how low she thought he was. As if he could hear what she was thinking, he winced and slunk off like a pariah dog. That artist's wife, nostrils flared, brunette hair flowing, superior, snobbish?

So she had no morals. Who did? Only a Red Guard, beating an old professor in the name of Mao Tse-tung.

She hadn't killed anybody after all, despite what Natalie

claimed—Natalie herself had done that, through lack of love, but that lack was in itself something Natalie couldn't help. Florence hadn't stolen money. Everything that had happened had an explanation. Even if her thoughts weren't so pure, was that a crime? It was just that . . . the child, Claudia, had seemed so pathetic, a child who on the surface had had everything and yet, when the surface was examined closely, had less than the poorest urchin in the barrios of Rio. And somehow . . . Claudia's death was worse than if she had drowned herself.

It was impossible, there were no men at this party. Two women, one of whom she knew vaguely, were standing alongside a telephone and she stepped toward them. "Florence, you're not going to use the phone, are you?"

She couldn't remember the girl's name. "No, I—"

"I'm expecting a call." The girl flashed a coy smile. "From a man, naturally; I told him to call me here and I'd let him know if I could meet him later. I'm trying to play a little hard to get. He's fantastically wealthy."

"He's absolutely gorgeous too," the other woman said. "Fiona always lucks out."

"Of course, the way he made his money wasn't exactly so great!" Fiona and the other woman laughed uproariously.

"Why?" said Florence. "How did he make his money?"

"He had this Thai girlfriend—and she had a kid, a little girl about eight or nine years old, and she and Jason would get the dope from Thailand into this country . . ." Fiona's voice faded.

"They would stick the heroin up the kid's ass!" the other woman said. "Nobody would ever think to search a little girl. Isn't that gross?"

"That was ages ago anyway, and Jason's retired from that business. He's completely legitimate now. What am I going to do if he doesn't call me, though? I thought I was coming awfully close to getting him to propose."

IO

She was about to go home when Max came over. "Let's get out of here. This sucks."

"And go where?"

"Home."

She was disappointed. "You don't want to go out someplace."

"No." He looked spoiled and petulant.

"That's fine by me," she said, though the thought of returning, alone, to her empty apartment sent her into a panic. "Where's the host and hostess? Shouldn't we say good-bye?"

"I already did. They're upstairs in their bedroom, pretending to be John and Yoko. I'm not going back up there—I'm sick of paying homage to people. I'm leaving. Stay if you want to."

"No, no. I'll come." The dinner had been cleared from the buffet table and displayed now were plates of strawberries—each as large as a fist, pointed ends dipped in chocolate—all kinds of ornate butter cookies and tiny tartlets of various kinds. Only the chocolate interested her. Three little girls—one about ten, the other two perhaps thirteen or fourteen—were wolfing down the sweets. All three were quite plain; or if not plain, then completely uninteresting-looking. She recognized two of them as Mike and Peony's girls, the other as the daughter of an even richer and more famous artist. The two older ones, she thought, might have been called Babcock and Gudrun. She hoped she didn't wake up in the middle of the night still trying to remember what they were called. "Hi!" she said, thinking they might reintroduce themselves.

The girls looked at her balefully, somehow already conscious that their social status was superior to hers. Dressed in baggy jeans, hair in dreadlocks and braids; no doubt from the earliest age they had been sent to the fanciest private schools, spent their winter break in Greece or India. They seemed completely, hermetically sealed off from the world, as if continual exposure to what their parents considered to be culture had been wasted on three marshmallows. She wrapped two of the strawberries in a dinner napkin and followed Max.

They shared a cab uptown. "Thank God I didn't see Colin there with his new boyfriend," Max said. "I still think he was the one who stole those photographs from me. That Tina Modotti that I found in the Paris flea market! And my grandmother's silver. It just kills me. I keep thinking, it had to be Colin. I mean—"

She couldn't bear to hear this saga again. "Yeah, and thank God I didn't see Natalie," she said, hoping to distract him. She took one of the strawberries out of the napkin. It was so perfect it appeared unreal, tiny green seeds flecking its red hide, stem intact, dipped in sleek brown.

"Yeah?" Max said. Her tactic had worked. He snatched the

other strawberry from the open napkin. "I heard she started screaming at you at some cocktail thing the other night."

"Who told you?" The berry had no flavor. It was only a soft, tasteless pulp, an alien's hydroponically grown interpretation of an earthling's fruit. Even the chocolate part was flavorless. Nevertheless, she popped the rest into her mouth.

"Oh, I have my sources."

"I didn't realize the whole family was nuts. I had no idea Claudia had died—the poor kid, I remember how she loved horses, and Natalie was constantly putting her down and making fun of her that she wasn't any good at things—and I had no idea that Natalie would blame me. It was just an accident that she picked up that virus, or bacteria, whatever it was—wasn't it? It doesn't seem real. And meanwhile, you know John? She blamed me, but he came into my room at their house and basically raped me. And I had the feeling it was all a setup, that she put single women up there and looked the other way so that she didn't have to sleep with him. But to make matters worse, John was going to help me, and he took my money—to invest in a new restaurant of Derek Richardson's?—and I saw Derek tonight, and he doesn't know anything about it—"

Max didn't appear to be listening. He was looking out the window, checking out some boys on Rollerblades who were weaving in and out of the cars, grabbing on to the back bumpers of taxis when they slowed at the light. "Oh, that is the best-looking kid I've ever seen," he said. "I wonder if he comes here every night. I could use a new assistant. Do you think he's over eighteen? He looks like he's younger."

Her stop was first. She rummaged in her pocketbook for some money to give Max toward the fare. "Don't worry about it," he said. "I've got it."

"Are you sure? Thanks." They pecked and she slid out of the cab. Too late, it wasn't until she was walking in her door that she remembered she hadn't intended to tell him anything at all.

————

In the morning she felt strangely energized, as if, despite her regrets at confiding in Max, the sense of having been unjustly accused had been lightened. She still had her headache, a permanent condition, but it was now only a physical irritation. She showered, dressed, shaved her legs, put on makeup—things that in the previous weeks she had been unable to accomplish until well into the afternoon.

Her old resume had appeared and she hand-wrote the updated information: her position at Quayle's, job duties, goal-objectives. Then she took it over to the printer's to have it retyped and photocopied. She got a copy of the *Times* on the way back, though there were far fewer Help Wanted listings during the week than on a Sunday. Besides, she wasn't all that certain if the ads in the paper were legitimate. The real jobs were all obtained through word of mouth. But there was certainly no harm in looking.

On the way into her building she was stopped by Milton, one of the doormen. He was an older man with a huge, carefully waxed handlebar mustache, who usually worked only on weekends. "Miss Florence!" He had a booming voice and old-fashioned manners. "How are you! I didn't expect to see you. What a nice surprise. Taking the day off work?"

"Hi, Milton. Actually I'm involved in a job search."

"You outgrew your old position."

"Kind of."

"Let me see. You're involved in the antique auction business, am I correct?"

"That's right."

"You were working at Sotheby's, I believe?"

"Quayle's. I'm hoping to go to Sotheby's or Christie's next."

"I see. And your current situation—has that been your predicament for some time?"

"Yeah. You might put it that way."

"I see. Perhaps it is not my place to tell you—" Milton looked over his shoulder as the elevator door opened. "Mrs. Arthur! Good day. I have a package for you which just arrived. Would you like me to have it sent up to your apartment?"

"No, thank you, Milton," said Mrs. Arthur. "I'll pick it up when I return."

"Very good. Have a nice day, Mrs. Arthur." He held open the front door.

"What were you about to tell me, Milton?" Florence said.

"I don't want you to be offended, but I think you should be informed."

"So, shoot."

"I believe the co-op board is scheduling a meeting to discuss your eviction. Were you aware of that?"

"No . . . on what grounds?"

"It may very well be that you have neglected to pay your maintenance. No doubt you have forgotten. I simply thought it was my duty to keep you informed so that you were not caught off guard, so to speak. In addition, several residents have been registering complaints about late-night activity."

". . . Thanks. I appreciate it." She was unable to think of anything to say and stepped through the open elevator door.

There were no openings at Sotheby's, though she was welcome to drop off her resume in the personnel department. She knew a woman at Christie's who said she didn't think there were any positions but offered to ask around and mention that Florence was looking for a job.

A guy she knew who worked at Doyle's turned out to have left six months before. No job openings at the present time—they were not even taking resumes on file.

Suddenly she remembered Marisa Nagy, who worked at that fancy art gallery. As far as Marisa knew, the only job openings were as front-desk receptionist, for which Florence was overqualified, and she certainly wouldn't want a job with such a low salary and no future; as secretary to the eighty-year-old Mr. Berryfox, the founder's grandson, but Florence was no secretary, with her limited typing skills and so forth, and this was an executive secretarial position (though secretly, Marisa confided, it also entailed having to play nurse); and as Marisa's own assistant. "I've just been promoted to department head!"

"Congratulations!" Her mouth had become dry, her tongue a snail stranded on blistering rock.

"I'd love you to come to work for me."

"It's something I'd have to consider. Let me get back to you."

There was no way she would go to work as an assistant. How degrading that Marisa, who was younger than she, would think even for a second that she would demean herself to do such a thing.

In the Help Wanted ads there was nothing. She decided to take a nap and got back into bed.

II

The phone was ringing. Every morning seemed to begin with this jangle from sleep. "Good morning! Did I wake you?"

"Um . . ." It took her a moment to realize it was Max. "No, no. I was awake."

"So, darling, you've made the papers again today. Another blind item, but I think it's kind of exciting." He was playing dumb, as if he hadn't planted it.

"Max!" She was awake all at once. "You put something in the paper about me?"

"Never!"

"Was it something terrible?"

"Oh, I don't know about that. I can't say it was very nice. But you know what Andy always used to say, dear: it's the inches that count." Who did he think he was? It was like an imitation of some long-deceased society queen of the 1940s, or perhaps Max had modeled himself on an old movie actress *portraying* a New York dowager of the 1890s. She tried to think of whom he sounded like. Perhaps Margaret Dumont in those old Marx Brothers films. She badly needed a cup of coffee. "I've got to go," Max said. "I'm at the airport and just wanted to check in before I left! I'm off to Copenhagen to cover the royal family's garage sale."

"Wait a minute, Max—what did the item say?"

"Oh, a little of this, a little of that—mostly the same as what you were telling me the other night in the cab."

"Max, you fed the item to the paper, didn't you? How could you?"

"I was only trying to help clarify the story. It was for your sake. You shouldn't complain—I stopped Jimmy from writing that you smoke crack. You're the one who owes *me* a favor."

She was momentarily perplexed. ". . . But you were the only one who knew I smoked it."

"Oh, I heard it before that night. Believe me, word gets around. Everyone knows what everyone else is doing. Got to run, they're announcing my flight! I'll call you when I get back."

At least she was important enough to warrant a mention in the gossip column. She pulled her hair back in a ponytail, threw on a white sweatshirt and a pair of black leggings and her jogging shoes. She hated leggings, so out of style, but they were convenient. She didn't need anything, but she stuck fifty dollars—all her cash—into a tiny pocketbook and went out. In this neighborhood the nearest place to buy a paper was two blocks away. The cover story was about body parts found in the trunk of a pop star's limousine. Florence opened to the gossip page even before she had thrown her change into the dish. She stood out on the sidewalk trying to see which item was supposed to be about her. At first she didn't think there was anything. An aging movie star and her daughter had both had breast implants at the same time. A fantastically wealthy businessman was in an institution for an obsessive-compulsive disorder. Diners at a chic restaurant had all gotten food-poisoning.

"August is a slow month in the gossip world," the item began. "So we bring the following dregs from society with our apologies . . . *WHICH* blond home-wrecker has of late . . ."

It was so hateful, so horrible and ugly, so strongly directed against her, that her eyes filled with tears. She couldn't even finish reading it. She threw the paper in a trash container, looking over her shoulder as if someone might be observing her.

She bought the *Times* and went into the coffee shop. No job offerings listed at auction houses, though there were ads for forthcoming sales at Tepper and at Dixon, both of which she had forgotten to call. There were listings for upcoming auctions being held by someone named Quince Rector Co. & ASM Auctions Inc. This company seemed to specialize in everything—a sale in Brooklyn of a wholesale clothing distributor; a sale of sixty bank-repossessed cars in Amityville, Long Island, including a Hyundai Elantra, a Dodge Neon, a Pontiac Grand Am, a Chevy Lumina, a Honda Civic and a Mercury Cougar; the auctioning of the contents of a large number of unpaid storage units at a facility in New Jersey; and an estate sale listing "Mahogany Hepplewhite Dining Set w/6 Chairs, oil paintings, chests, writing desk, jewelry, quantity bric/brac, figurines, silverplate, antique violins, *Many New Items Still In Boxes.*" That one was happening this afternoon down on lower Broadway. So many different kinds of stuff, all being auctioned by the same company: it had to be a complete load of junk, worse even than what was offered by the lowest Manhattan-based auction house.

There was a position at an art gallery, but the specialty requested was an Art Nouveau background. Besides, at age thirty-two—almost thirty-three—she didn't want to start all over again as a front-desk art gallery girl. Plenty of jobs for graphic designers. Realtors. Salespeople for plumbing companies. Assistant editors in publishing. She finished her coffee and left the paper on the table.

Maybe a good walk would clear her head. She didn't feel like jogging—she was already jarred enough—but she knew she would feel worse if she didn't get some exercise. She set off, passing the fancy shops on Madison Avenue—the handmade-cowboy-boot store, with each pair in ostrich or alligator; the children's clothing shop in which each little outfit, every little dress, cost more than an entire week's salary for the child's nanny; the store selling antique pens—she saw none of this. It seemed that if she walked quickly enough, blindly enough, she might not have to think: she could outpace the miserable jumble inside her head.

The pedestrians wove in and out of one another, in a delicate unspoken kind of ballet where each city resident had been trained to come as close to someone else as possible without ever touching. They scuttled across the street after the light had changed, like crabs dancing between the cars.

But she did not observe the streets' delicate dance. Before she knew it, three or four hours had passed. She had worked up a nice sweat and was pleased that so much time had gone by without thinking, without seeing. Somehow she had ended up on Broadway, though she must have zigzagged back and forth, and was well below Canal Street.

It was right near where that auction was being held by Quince Somebody-or-other, and she decided to stop in. Maybe all this had been fated by God, her blind, blank walk leading her straight to the site of a fantastic job. Quince Whatever could turn out to be very distinguished, from a wealthy background, but a bit vague. He might fall in love with her, hire her, be unable to live without her. She would remake the company, turning it into something even classier than Christie's or Spink's.

The storefront in which the sale was being held turned out to be full of more junk than she could ever have imagined. There were school desks stacked in heaps, bent metal filing cabinets, open cartons containing hundreds of bottles of nail polish and perfume samples. Shelves stacked with Asian export ware—a few Ming blue-and-white ginger jars with mismatched lids, modern Imari, Satsuma, incense burners, umbrella stands. A jadeite horse, four feet high, crudely constructed and attempting to reproduce an antique. Stacks of rugs, wool but with garish colors. Three Indian motorcycles, possibly dating from the forties. A carousel horse with a broken leg. The mounted head of a tiger, made of plastic and fake fur. An opium bed. Stacks of dirty plates, mismatched, some from restaurants, and some rather fine Belleek tea sets. Nothing in the room made sense. The stuff was the detritus of a society without culture or values; everything was covered with soot and dust, a kind of *horror vacui* substituting for quality. Boxes of black-and-white photos of long-forgotten movie stars, cartons of rubber chickens. Framed paintings on velvet—flowers, ill-conceived landscapes—lined the walls. Nearly everything an imitation of something of great beauty. And the few authentic bits were broken and chipped.

She wandered around the room. Two rather sinister-looking Asian men were loading things—or unloading them, she didn't quite know which—but they ignored her. A pair of eyes blinked at her from behind a peeling shoji screen and she let out a startled yelp. Whatever was perched there resembled a giant toad, massive and thick-lipped, tongue collecting crumbs from a pink-frosted cupcake. "Are you—" she said. "Excuse me, do you work here?"

"Can I help you?" The toad seemed amused. "The auction begins at three. The preview doesn't officially start until one. But you're welcome to look around now."

She glanced at her watch. "It's nearly one o'clock now. Actually, I was wondering—I wanted to apply for a job. Are you—Mr. Quince?"

"Mr. Quince! I like that." The remains of the cupcake, furry with coconut, were stuffed into the toad's maw like a particularly plump, tasty fly. "I'm Quince Rector, yes. And you are—"

"I'm Florence Collins. I used to be at Quayle's, in Estate Jewelry, but over the summer there were cutbacks—"

"What is it that you were looking for with me?"

"Well, I'm not sure exactly. I thought, since I was in the neighborhood—"

"I see. Hmmm. Let me think." There was a pause. "No, I really don't need anybody."

"Could I—I don't have it with me today—but I could drop off my resume. Even something temporary, just to—"

"Wait a minute. I do have something. It probably has nothing to do with what you're looking for, however."

"Anything, really, would be great, just to tide me—"

"I had a young woman working for me until recently. Of course, you realize I get a great many dealers, coming to the various sales, and since I can never be quite certain how many dealers and individuals turn up for any auction, I need someone here just to . . . keep the bids above minimum value. In other words, by law I have to have at least two bids to make a sale. Now, if Joe Schmoe, say, bids my minimum bid and no one else bids, I can't sell it to him. Let's say I open the bid at a hundred dollars, Joe bids, but no one else increases it. Your job would be to bid—a hundred fifty, say, or whatever I've announced the increments to be—and we hope that will get Joe to bid two hundred."

She had never heard of this in the auction world. It seemed completely fictitious. "But if he doesn't . . . I've just bought something I don't want?"

"No, no. In that case, there's no sale. I can't afford to let this stuff go for under wholesale. I keep this place as a wholesale shop, open to the trade, so if I don't sell it at an auction, I either sell it wholesale or put it up at auction again."

She was puzzled. "And don't people—if they come back— catch on when they see the same merchandise being auctioned again?"

"If anyone asks, I simply say I had more than one to begin with and I had the other taken out of the warehouse. If you want to try it out, this afternoon, I'm guessing the auction usually lasts about two, two and a half hours, and I can give you fifty dollars. We'll see how it goes."

"How will I know when to stop raising the bids?"

"Sit in the front so they can see you bidding. You'll have to use your judgment, and I'll try to look at you to stop. You'll get the hang of it."

Around five minutes to three the Asian men set up twenty or thirty folding metal chairs in the center of the room. It was the strangest group she had ever seen attending an auction. There was a Tibetan monk; three very large argumentative Russians, who she assumed were mother, father and grown daughter; seven black women looking as though they were attending church; four rather surly Long Island– or Brooklyn–type boys; several Soho/art world types; a couple from Belgium or the Netherlands; a man with a long ponytail and greasy appearance who might have been a dealer, and so forth. In all, there couldn't have been more than twenty-five people.

For two hours she concentrated on trying to inch the bids up to the price Quince seemed to want. The black church ladies bought quantities of embroidered Chinese pillowcases for eight dollars each, exactly the same price they sold for in shops in Chinatown. The Russians got into a fight when the daughter bid on a hideous carved Indian trinket box—the girl had offered forty dollars, competing with Florence, and Quince was about to say "Sold" when the father shouted he would pay fifty. Though the daughter began to scream at the father in Russian, it was obvious she was calling him a stupid idiot for not realizing she was the one who had made the previous bid of forty.

The Belgian couple began a three-way battle with the ponytailed man and herself over a large rug hanging on the wall. "Hand-knotted silk, more than a thousand knots per inch,"

Quince said. "This rug would sell for twenty thousand at AKZ Carpets. Can I get a starting bid of ten thousand?" Finally he had to begin the bid at a thousand dollars. In the end the Belgian couple, looking worried, got it for almost five grand. Florence was puzzled. Maybe it was really worth something; she didn't know about rugs. The things that earlier in the afternoon had looked junky were beginning to seem like possible finds.

She had tried to pretend to take notes on the items she had bid for and won. At the end of the afternoon, had she really been bidding, she would have come away with a three-foot-high carved-wood water buffalo; a pair of gold Satsuma vases turned into lamps; an ivory alligator; and a rosewood armoire. It simply made no sense.

He gave her fifty dollars after everyone had left. The other girl was coming back, he said, but if she gave him her number, he would certainly keep her in mind as a backup. "Thanks," she said. "But I think I really need to find something full-time."

Fifty dollars! She bought some subway tokens and headed uptown. Fifty dollars, what good would that do her? She had had to hang around for hours, and the work was exhausting, though not mentally stimulating or challenging. Fifty dollars wouldn't even buy her a decent dinner; it would scarcely cover the cost of a manicure and pedicure, not including tip. Normally she would have taken a cab home, but having taken so long to earn fifty, she didn't want to blow ten or twelve of it just on getting home.

It was rush hour. The subway car was so packed that there were no seats and she was squeezed on all sides by the other standees. The train rattled on uneven tracks, everyone was tossed from side to side, someone wearing one of those hateful backpacks knocked her in the side with it. Someone stank of McDonald's French fries, an immediately identifiable odor of tallow and grease. Someone was slurping on a drink. Another was clipping his fingernails; yet another was combing her hair.

A whole carful of a species scarcely less evolved, just as ill-mannered, as chimpanzees. The eyes of the commuters were glazed, faces sullen. Her eyes shut in disgust. She couldn't imagine having to do this every day, or twice a day: animals shipped to slaughter. The place was airless, and roasting hot, and abruptly the train—midway between stations—came to a grinding halt.

No one moved or spoke. It was as if they were organisms the opposite of amoebae; instead of being designed to replicate by self-dividing, the passengers were being forced to meld, to merge with one another against their will or die.

Ages seemed to pass. The subway motor, or whatever it was that made the loud noise, was shut off, then the lights in the car flickered off and everything was dark and quiet. "Ladies and gentlemen"—the announcement came over loudspeakers that were so inferior it was difficult to make out the words beneath the shrill crackle and hiss—"due to a fire at the Fifty-ninth Street station, we are experiencing delays. We will be moving as soon as possible."

The announcement was repeated four or five times before, almost half an hour later, the motor came back on and the train began moving again.

The doorman—Mario was on duty now—said nothing to her as she came in the lobby and collected her mail from her box in the alcove beside the elevators. It was just as well; she was too tired to chat, though she always tried to be friendly. She was rummaging through the stack—her box had been overflowing—when she arrived at her front door.

Her key did not fit in the lock. She tried to force it a few times before it dawned on her that something was different: a sign plastered like a billboard stated EVICTION NOTICE/APARTMENT SEALED BY ORDER OF CITY MARSHAL/ON BEHALF OF LIBERTY POINT BANK AND CO-OP BOARD.

12

He was looking toward the elevator but averted his eyes when he saw it was she getting out. "You might have at least said something, Mario, instead of letting me get all the way upstairs before finding out!"

"I'm sorry." He shrugged. "I didn't know what to say."

"Well, could you at least let me back into my apartment for the night? Where am I supposed to go?"

"I can't let you in. I don't have the key."

"They changed the locks?"

"I'm sorry."

"But you must have a copy of the key?"

He shook his head.

"But what about my credit card? My clothes? Those are my things in there. I have to be able to get them."

"You got to go to court."

"Who's responsible for this? June?" June was the head of the co-op board, well known for her delight in making trouble.

"You got the bank here, too, that said you didn't pay."

"But surely I should have been given some notice! Some warning! This is the first I'm hearing about it." She looked down at the marble-tiled floor, the worn black-and-white check. Maybe she had heard something about it before. There were heaps of bills stamped externally with ominous things in red she hadn't even bothered to open. "Well, what am I supposed to do? Where am I supposed to go?"

"You got a friend you can stay with? I'm sure you'll get this straightened out, in a day or so."

"No, I don't have a friend! I want to go to my own house!" In her panic she lashed out; she could have killed him. Easy for the doorman to say she should stay with a friend.

"You got a lawyer?" He was trying to be helpful, she saw that.

"A lawyer. I don't have a lawyer. I never needed a lawyer. My mother had lawyers, but that was back in California. Okay, maybe I can just call a lawyer."

Mario handed her the front desk phone. "But if Mrs. Koblenz comes in, you gotta hang up fast."

"Why? What's that lousy June Koblenz going to do, kick me out?"

"I don't want to get in trouble." He muttered this quietly, ashamed to think of himself in such circumstances.

"A lawyer, a lawyer. Who do I know who's a lawyer?" Suddenly she remembered Neil Pirsig. She knew he was sleazy, but he had always had a crush on her and would probably be glad to help, even if she had just snubbed him.

His office had closed for the day, but fortunately his home number was listed in directory assistance. "I just can't believe I'm having to go through this!" she complained to Mario while the phone rang at Neil's. "Not even to let me go in to get my credit cards and address book. A change of underwear! I'm sure this can't be legal . . . Neil? Hi, how are you? It's Florence Collins."

"Who?"

"Florence?" She hated the way her voice automatically turned it into a question.

"I don't . . ."

"You know me! I have long blond hair. We just saw each other at—"

"Oh, yes, yes, Florence. How are you?"

She didn't know if he really hadn't known who she was. Probably—he sounded embarrassed. "Actually, Neil, I'm in sort of a predicament. I've been evicted from—"

"This is about a case? Do you think I could call you from the office tomorrow, Florence? Because I just walked in the door and—"

"The thing is, I'm standing in the lobby of my building because they changed the lock on my door and I—"

"There's really not going to be anything much we can get done tonight. Also, it doesn't sound like the sort of case I'd take on— it's not my specialty. I'm not even taking on new cases at the moment, and I don't know if you're aware of this, but I charge five hundred dollars an hour. I tell you what: maybe I can come up with a few names for you. I'll give you a call."

"You don't understand, Neil! I don't have a phone—I can't get in!"

"So listen, check into a hotel and leave a message on my machine where you're at."

"I don't even have a credit—"

It was too late. He had already hung up. Mario was pacing

back and forth toward the front door, probably hoping no one came in and saw him letting her use the phone for personal purposes. What was he so worried about? There were plenty of jobs as doormen. There had to be someone to get her out of this mess.

Darryl. She should have called him ages ago, to find out how he was doing with . . . whatever disease it was he said he had. He loved her. She could make up with him, accept his marriage proposal. At least he had an apartment, a place for her to stay. Thank God his number came back to her almost at once. It must have been permanently branded somewhere in her head. She dialed. A harsh tone, almost a scream, came through the receiver so loudly she recoiled: "The number you have reached has been disconnected." The recording—whoever had made this message at the telephone company—was fat with poison. It was almost as if the telephone representative was imagining just such a situation as hers. She kept thinking that the voice would tell her what the new number was, but there must not have been one. Yet if he had moved, he surely would have left a forwarding number.

Outside the front door three overweight golden retrievers on plaid leashes squatted simultaneously to pee, right in the path of anyone coming in or out. She dialed again. "Allison, you've got to help me. I have nowhere to stay."

"Are you redecorating or something? Believe me, I sympathize. It was supposed to take three months to get our place redone and it ended up taking almost two and a half years."

"No, it's not that. I—"

"Oh, God, Florence. I wish I could offer to put you up, but there's not a single inch of extra space in the apartment. Thomasina and May were fighting so much we had to turn the guest bedroom into a room for May. And Georgie and the nanny are in one room until we get the playroom redone. Even my mother has to stay in a hotel when she comes into the city! I feel awful. I've got to run, sweetie, or Archie's going to kill me. But if you ever need me, I'm right here. You can always call. You know that, don't you? I'll try and call you when I get home, if it's not too late and if the kids don't wake up, for once. You don't know what it's like, three kids and just the one nanny—"

She put down the phone. It was as if every cell in her body had a hole drilled in it and was crying out to be plugged.

She tried to think of all her acquaintances, but she was beginning to doubt that any of them would help. Was it because she was—momentarily—an outcast over the de Jongh business? But more likely it was because none of these people were her friends in the first place. If someone had called her up and said what she was saying now, she would have told them to get lost too.

She called Lisa Harrison. She didn't know why she thought of Lisa. Whenever she remembered Lisa it was past the right time to make a thank-you call or to return an invitation. Lisa, with her overdone apartment, her parties for jewelry designers and the losers of the world—maybe Lisa had more money than she, but Lisa was perhaps the one person who was worse off: she was more desperate.

Lisa said, "Darling, unfortunately I'm leaving for Europe tomorrow, and I'd say you were welcome to stay here while I'm away, only I've . . . I've sublet the apartment. But you're welcome to come overnight if it's of any use."

The look of relief on Mario's face was overwhelming. On her way out she stepped in the puddle of dog urine.

"Make yourself at home, Florence!" Lisa called from the upstairs of her duplex.

It was so good to sit down. She hadn't even realized until then that she had been on her feet practically all day. The back of her calves ached. "Lisa, do you mind if I use your phone?"

"Go right ahead. There's some white wine open in the fridge, or you can see if there's a bottle of red. I'm just trying to pull myself together. I had rather a late one last night, and I haven't packed a thing, and I'm only just now getting out of bed. I'm doing one of those face masks—that's why I sound funny. It's like a plaster cast."

She found the Yellow Pages underneath in the cabinet and began to look up taxi companies. "Do you have someone who works for you named Gideon?"

"Wha?"

"His name's Gideon—he's tall and—"

"What's his last name?"

"I don't know, but he drives the nightshift and . . . if he works for you, I know you'd recognize him, he used to be a Mormon and—"

"Lady, you know how many drivers we got here? They work a week, a day, I don't know who's here. You got to know his last name or his number. You got his number? If you want the Lost and Found, you don't need to speak to a driver. Nothing's been turned in."

She called three or four other companies before realizing it was futile. "Are you going to be much longer? I just have to make one quick call," Lisa said.

"Sorry, sorry. Go right ahead. You don't happen to have a number for Darryl Lever, do you?"

"Who?"

"This guy—"

"Who did you say? Tell me?" Lisa suddenly sounded eager. She emerged from the bedroom and leaned over the balcony; her face had been completely covered in a cracked lavender goo.

"He's an old friend of mine, a lawyer for the homeless, which, in my present circumstance, is perfect for me."

"Did you say Darryl Lever?"

"Yeah. Do you have his number?"

"No! Do you know him? He's gorgeous. I've had a mad crush on him for years. *Everyone's* in love with him."

"Darryl?" Florence said.

"Yeah!"

"I don't have his number anymore."

"Oh." Disappointed, Lisa retreated.

She paced while Lisa was on the phone. Her call took nearly an hour. She inspected the apartment once again. Up close the ruffles and flounces had a soiled appearance. The windowsills were greasy with soot. That was the city: no matter how rich anybody was, there was no way anything could remain clean for long. And even though Lisa hadn't left for Europe yet, there was a quality of emptiness, as if no one really lived here. It was a place constructed for display; without anybody there to view it, apart from her, it was like a theater set without a play.

"Phone's all yours, darling! I'm terribly sorry to have taken so long."

She called Tracer Schmidt. "This is Florence Collins." Tracer said nothing. "Listen, I realize for whatever reason, you don't like me. But I was wondering, I'm trying to find Darryl Lever, only his number's been disconnected, I thought you might know—"

"He's right here. I'll see if he wants to talk to you."

"You do that."

"Hi, Florence." He was on the phone. She was astonishingly relieved to hear his voice; it was like a comforting blanket. "How are you?"

"Oh, Darryl. I'm fine, I guess. Not really. I've missed you! What are you doing with *her*? I tried to call you at home—there was just one of those recordings—"

"She's looking after me. I haven't been so good. The TB isn't responding to treatment."

"So that must be useful to you, having a private nurse." She didn't mean to sound so sarcastic, but that was how it came out.

"We're engaged, actually."

It took a moment before she could speak. "Oh. Congratulations. When's the wedding?"

"Not sure yet. Not for a while. We think we'll have it at my parents' house. My father and stepmother, actually. That'll be nice, don't you think?"

"I don't know . . . how should I know? Where is it?" Florence could barely believe she was having this conversation.

"You've been there." He began to cough. "In Bridgehampton."

"No."

"Anyway, you've seen it."

"When?"

"That night . . . remember when we went to the Russian nightclub? When I drove you back to the city? I had to stop at my folks' and I ran in. You waited in the car, I think."

"But that . . . that was a mansion! That was your parents' place?" Florence was having trouble catching her breath. "Look, I have a serious, complicated legal problem and I need your help."

"You know, it's just that . . . we were on our way out the door. We're going to Switzerland—there's a doctor I think who can help—and then we're traveling around Russia and the Baltic states. Listen, I hope you're not mad at me."

"For what, Darryl? If you mean I took you seriously when you proposed—"

"Oh, not about that. It's just that . . . morally, I felt obligated to repeat what you had said."

"About what?"

"About the jewelry, declaring it missing so you could sell it and the owner could get the insurance."

"I don't understand. I never said anything about taking jewelry—I mean, not seriously."

"You were drunk, but yeah, that's what you were saying. I guess I just felt that . . . well . . . if you were in trouble, and someone pointed out what was happening to you—the direction you were headed in"—he lowered his voice; probably Tracer was listening—"you might turn to me for help."

"But if only I had known that—" She didn't finish the sentence. How could she say that if only she had known he was rich, things would have been different. "So you told someone where I work? Who did you tell?"

"I really can't say . . . I just made sure it got passed on . . . anonymously. Did they . . . prosecute?"

"Oh, no. No. Of course not. They knew I would never . . . Look, don't worry about it. I, I have to go. Have a good trip!" She hung up before he could say anything else.

13

Sun was coming through the window. The sheets were clean and white, the blanket soft white cotton. She had slept strangely well, so solidly that for a moment on waking she didn't have a clue where she was. At last she got up and went downstairs, dressed in a white terrycloth robe Lisa had lent her.

She looked in the refrigerator. There was no milk, no coffee, nothing to eat. She hated to put on the same dirty things she had worn yesterday—maybe she could borrow a few things—but she put them on anyway and went to the fancy emporium on the corner, spending a fortune on takeout cappuccinos, coffee cakes, muffins, fresh-squeezed OJ. If only Lisa would let her stay. It was like buying an offering for Lakshmi—she might have been better off buying flowers and incense.

It was almost noon before Lisa emerged, pushing her Vuitton trunk down the stairs. "Whew! Thank God the pugs went to the kennel yesterday or they'd be screaming in hysteria when they saw the suitcase. Did the doorman call up to say if my limo has arrived?"

"No, not yet."

"So . . . I guess you'll be heading out too."

"Um . . . yes. Do you think I could borrow something to wear? I'll have it cleaned and sent back over just as soon as I can."

"Oh, my." Lisa looked her up and down. "We're probably not the same size. I don't know what I have that would fit you. I have some old jeans—but they're a size twenty-six. Would that fit you?"

"A twenty-six! . . ." Florence paused. "That would probably fit me in the waist . . . but how long are they? I'm a lot taller than you. How tall are you?"

"I'm five five."

There was no way Lisa was more than five three. "Gosh, I'm five nine. They'll be masses too short." At least now Lisa didn't have to find out a twenty-six would never fit her. Not that she even believed Lisa was a twenty-six—nobody could have such tiny hips.

"Anyway . . ." Lisa went to the window and looked out. "I can see that must be my car, waiting in front. Florence, could you buzz the doorman to come and collect my trunk?"

It wasn't a speech impediment, it was that Lisa had a fake French accent, Florence thought. All this time she had assumed it was some minor, slightly charming defect. Now she realized it was intentional, pretentious. "Sure! Oh, I almost forgot! Look, I got you a cappuccino, and a whole lot of different cakes, and some OJ." She looked at Lisa pleadingly. If Lisa was going to offer to let her stay, now was the moment.

"I'll take the coffee with me in the car. I can't eat a thing in the morning. Well, sweetie, I'm off. Two weeks in London; a whole month on a yacht in the Aegean. If I can stand it. Stanislaus hates the heat, but October shouldn't be too bad, don't you think? Then I'll probably go to Rome for a while. Come on, I have to lock up. Let's go, shall we?" Her face softened. "Are you going to be okay? I really wish I could let you stay here. It's just that . . . I've had some rather unfortunate experiences, letting friends stay, in the past. The building . . . has regulations, about guests staying when the occupant is away. Isn't that awful? And they threatened me with eviction if I ever did it again. You understand."

"I'll be fine. Have a great time." She didn't wait to see her off but went out the door.

She began to walk west through the park, her thoughts repeating in her head like a broken record. The mansion was his father's. He had only pretended to be poor. His father's mansion. Darryl was rich.

The leaves had begun to change, orange and yellow and dark red lightening to pink. Squirrels sat scratching themselves on the bright green lawn. She perched on the edge of a bench, crying. She didn't even have a tissue; she was about to get her period. When the sun went behind the clouds, it was cold.

"What's wrong?" A kind of humming, beelike, excited, came from someone standing nearby.

She looked up. It was only that filthy old Birdman. He had been around for years, feeding the pigeons. "Nothing. I've been evicted for not paying my maintenance. The bank's foreclosing on my apartment."

"That's terrible. The same thing is about to happen to me."

She looked at him skeptically. He looked a bit like a bird—Samuel Beckett's beaky nose, darting hawk eyes, shirt crusted with dried paste or worse. "The bank's foreclosing on your apartment?"

"Yes. It's not an apartment. It's a townhouse. *Mmm mmm mm.*" He hummed constantly.

"Where?"

"Between Fifth and Madison. Just a block away. Do you want to see? I'm almost done with my feeding." He held up a paper sack. "Fifty pounds of cracked corn today! This was full when I began. *Hmmm mmm mm.* Normally I don't allow anyone in my home, except for Marcia, who helps me with the birds. But in your case I'll make an exception. You look like someone who loves birds."

She hated birds, she thought, especially pigeons, with red beaks, fishy eyes, leaving white-green plops everywhere. The way a male chased some hapless female—the male so puffed up, as proud as Charlie Twigall displaying his nude photo, and the female scuttling to get away. The male was not interested in the female—he only wanted her to admire him.

Nevertheless, she got up and followed the Birdman. When he wasn't humming he talked nonstop. "I see so many people who are mean to the birds, letting their children chase them and so forth, and I can't understand such cruelty. *Mmmm hmmmm hmm.* Did you know birds are the direct descendents of dinosaurs? And yet a person who is fascinated by dinosaurs thinks nothing of kicking a pigeon."

He really did live in a townhouse, from the outside a nice lime-stone building on what had to be one of the best blocks. He unlocked the front door. A stench of birds, of old bird droppings, steamed out at her like guano from a bat cave or the underside of a highway bridge. "I have to keep the windows shut. You understand. My little birds—the birds I rescue—they're unwell and they need the warmth."

It must have once been quite a grand residence. A huge Vene-tian chandelier—glittering candy-colored pink and blue roses, drooping green ferns, entirely of glass—hung in the center of the huge room; on closer inspection she saw it was riddled with perching pigeons. They were everywhere—on the Empire sofas and chairs, in wire aviaries—and their soft, muffled cooing sounded exactly like the humming made by the Birdman himself.

"I reserve the main floor for my sickest birds," he said. "On the second floor I have birds that are ready to be returned to the wild; on the third floor, seagulls, crows and other species who don't get along with the pigeons; and on the top floor, the birds who have been restored to health but who will never survive on their own again—if, say, a wing had to be amputated, or a leg is missing."

He opened a cardboard box located on top of what must once have been a very fine Korean table, now etched and scarred with limy droppings. Reaching into the box, he removed a pigeon, completely featherless but fully grown, eyes that were empty sockets. The bird defecated on the carpet. It must once have been a very good Aubusson, but now it was rimmed with furry mold. She averted her gaze. Now that her eyes had fully adjusted to the gloom, she saw that the ceiling had leaked so badly that huge chunks of the rococo plaster were crumbling; a rusty stain, of blood or from a broken pipe, had come through one of the walls; the parquet flooring was bulging like the hulk of a rotting ship. "Poor little thing," he said, kissing the pigeon on its pink blind head.

She was good at walking. She still had that left to her. She walked. Hours passed. It was one of those days when the whole city smelled of fish and fishy water, a primordial fragrance churned from the limnetic source. This was how it must have smelled a million years ago on earth, the odor of something straining to become something else. Once again she thought of killing slugs in the garden. She had read somewhere that slugs had sex lives more passionate than humans'. Once, on stabbing a particularly large banana-slug with black speckles, she was horrified to realize that what had spilled onto the brick pavement was its liver and intestines—the same as a person's, in miniature. Was that, in the end, what she had been sent to hell for? Age seven, killing snails in the garden? Giving too little to a homeless person on the street? Perhaps it was not sending a note to a child in the hospital—or taking sex without love, out of her own fears and insecurities. And if there was no such thing as hell and there really was reincarnation, she would be destined to make—not the same mistakes, but similar ones, like a grade repeated in school, for though she wanted to, she could not understand the point of the lesson.

It was the end of the twentieth century, which was to say anyone robbing widows and orphans could find some justification for their actions. Maybe things had never been any different. Yet one would have expected more signs of evolution in the human race by now. *She* was an orphan, after all—an orphan who had never truly honored her mother and father. But that was not her fault either. Her parents had never existed. They had as little reality as she herself. They were simply a compendium of what was expected, a cocktail composed of what they were supposed to want. Had she really and truly committed a crime other than that of taking a child to the beach when her mother had told her not to go? But to come to such a conclusion was a Pyrrhic victory.

Still she walked, exhausted, on the empty streets. It dawned on her that Darryl was probably the one person she could have asked for money, but the realization had come too late; by now they would have left. In any event, his loyalty, his friendship, had proved more destructive than had he been her enemy.

A woman wearing what appeared to be a fluffy pink bunny suit—more suitable for a two-year-old on Halloween than a forty-year-old woman—was smiling a few feet away. Perhaps she recognized someone behind her; but when Florence turned around she saw the block was empty. Puzzled, Florence studied her more closely. She had a pixie cut of artificially red hair, black tights and pink high-heeled boots. She always wondered what people like that must have seen when they looked at themselves in the mirror. "How are you?" At first Florence didn't have a clue who she was. "Aren't you freezing, honey?" the woman said. "Where's your coat?"

"Excuse me. Do I know you?" It was coming back to her—the woman she had met at Natalie's, who charged two hundred dollars an hour to wave lavender scent in front of rich ladies' noses. But she kept the blank look on her face, as if she didn't remember.

"I'm the aromatherapist. Honey, are you all right? Can I buy you a cup of coffee? Is there something I can do for you? You look so sad . . ."

Natalie's aromatherapist! Had it come to this? Even now she could not reach toward the proferred hand. No better than hanging out with a waitress, or needing an exercise trainer for a friend, or accepting a construction worker as a boyfriend—like some desperate, aging pop star. She opened her handbag and brushed past the woman without speaking, pretending she didn't hear because she was preoccupied with looking for something in her purse.

There was half an old Hershey bar with almonds in the bottom, along with lint and scraps of paper. She tossed the detritus to the ground. A little brush, bristles entwined with blond hairs. A wrapped mint-flavored toothpick. An empty glass vial with green top that once contained crack. A business card from someone she couldn't remember meeting, in film production. In the side pocket she felt a lump. She unzipped it to find a yellow silk bag, Chinese, stuffed with tissue paper. Inside were the woman's valuable jewels, a brooch, a handful of rings, a glittering stone come loose from its mooring.

Peeling the silver foil from the chocolate, she gnawed at the cindery edges as she began to walk into the darkening gloom, toward the mouth of the Hudson and the Statue of Liberty.

Rite

She has been pursuing that accelerating demon,
    that overgrown T-shirt stenciled ILLUSION,
        that toothpick whirling on a lost horizon.

He's endowed—brutality,
    slim heels—if he entered he'd win,
        but they won't let him in.

Even on board he sprints around deck
    so swiftly the captain
        can't take hold and quits,

sobbing, stalled. Oh we're all after him—
    men, women, any age—all
        we want is a coupling, to feel

something inalienable—an eyelash, not much.
    Anyhow it's her turn to drop out
        and she hasn't caught up. "Hurry," he says, then

with glottal stop: "It's dime, it's dime." "Oh shut up,"
    she'd reply, if she could, to that bee-thrum
        drilled into her ears and brain, her crumbling

constitution: "It's dime, it's dime."
    Oh dear tour group it's time to say
        good-bye to the isle of weeping

beech and dangling moon, firefly with zoom
    lens, shingled cottage, the frail, illuminated
        room we have visited for so brief a lovely time.

—Phyllis Janowitz